A Time To Return

Tricia Linden

Kingsburg Press
San Francisco, California

Kingsburg Press
P.O. Box 475146
San Francisco, California, 94147
www.KingsburgPress.com

A Time To Return is a work of fiction. Names, characters, places, and incidents are a product of the author's imagination. Locales and public names are sometimes used for atmospheric purposes. Any resemblance to actual people, living or dead, or to businesses, companies, events, institutions, or locales is completely coincidental.

Editor: Barbara Millman-Cole
Cover Design: Killion Group
A Time To Return / Tricia Linden – 2nd ed.
previously published as Return In Time

ISBN- 13:978-1-946177-02-5
ISBN- 10: 1-946177-02-4
eBook ISBN: 978-1-946177-03-2

Other Works by Tricia Linden

The MacNicol Clan Through Time

A Time To Begin – Book 1
A Time To Return – Book 2

A Time To Belong – Book 3

A Time To Forgive – Book 4

.

.

.

Dreaming In Moonlight

.

.

.

Jules Vanderzeit novels

set in the Gilded Age of New York

Until We Meet Again

Until Their Hearts Desire

.

Coming Soon: Until You Love Me

Dedication
First and foremost, to Alex and Kelsey
Thank you for teaching me unconditional love.
To the moon and stars and back again.

PROLOGUE

Scorrybreac Castle, Isle of Skye, 1292

Souyer, the Master Druid of Scorrybreac, slowly climbed the long, winding stairs of his tower to reach the highest point of the castle mere moments before the first rays of the rising sun broke over the land. No sane soul should be forced to leave his bed so early in the morn, and yet, here he was, dressed in his finest ceremonial robes, ready to make his annual plea to the guardian spirits of the Isle of Skye, the ones who watched over and protected the lands of the MacNicol clan. Dawn would soon break, heralding the longest day of sunlight, and the druid was preparing to perform his sacred ritual in service to his clan. Much like generations of druids before him, Souyer believed on this one special day, the spirits of Skye would honor his request. If some of the glory were ascribed to him, so much the better. A circle of protection had already been cast, and he had personally blessed the space.

The druid looked out over the rugged beauty of the land and watched as darkness prepared to give way to the first rays of sunlight; his timing was perfect. Thank goodness he hadn't been late, or he would have had to wait another year to give this thing a try. He stood on the tallest tower of the fortress and faced the rising sun. To his right, he could see the island's craggy green hills formed centuries ago by the upheaval of the earth. To his left spread the vast expanse of the ocean that reached farther than his old eyes

1

could see, which was not nearly as far as they used to. If all went well, in this sacred time and place, the veil of separation would split for one brief moment, and Souyer would have a chance to present his request.

He knew the ritual well. First, thoughts, then words, then deeds were needed to create the manifestation. With his arms raised to the sky and his robes flapping in the wind, Souyer gave voice to his request. "Oh, great and good faeries, guardian spirits of earth and Skye, in the tradition of our holy and sacred bonds, present to me, here and now, knowledge from the future for the greater good of the MacNicol clan."

It was a fairly formal request, but he figured the fae would appreciate his show of respect. Hopefully it would do the trick. He had clearly stated his request once, and only once, as he had been trained, allowing the words to linger in the new summer air.

The wizard stood there awhile longer, watching the sun rise higher in the sky. For days, there had been a thick blanket of fog hiding the rays of the sun, which was typical for the northern Scottish island, but today the summer solstice sun rose into a bright, cloudless blue sky. He hoped it was a good omen.

Satisfied he had done all that was needed, he retraced his steps down the long winding staircase and returned to the comfort of his bedchamber. He placed another small log on the low-burning fire then climbed back into the comfort of his bed to rest, and perhaps to dream.

~*~

Lady Lydia, matriarch of the MacNicol clan, fiddled with the needlework piece she held in her hands. She was growing impatient, waiting to hear news from her younger cousin.

"Finally," she murmured, looking up as Moezell appeared in the room. "'Tis about time."

"I believe I have found the perfect fit for your needs, a woman who has all your requirements and more," Moezell said as she greeted her cousin with a self-satisfied grin.

"Wonderful. Where can we find her?" Lydia set down her needlework and focused her gaze on Moezell. She smiled serenely at the faerie standing before her, trying to mask her resentment that she was only part fae, and therefore forced to rely on her cousin's assistance.

"It is more like *when*," Moezell said, still smiling. "She resides several hundred years in the future, in a faraway land called California. However, on a day yet to come, she will be on the Isle of Skye, during the summer solstice."

"Perfect. We'll use the power of the solstice to bring her here." Ideas whirled in Lady Lydia's head. If all went well, she would soon see her eldest son married to Janet MacDonald, just as she planned. After three years of waiting, an alliance between the MacNicols and the MacDonalds would finally be sealed and all would be set to right.

"Did you not hear me? I said she's from the future." Moezell's smile took on a mischievous glint, brightening her faerie glow.

"Hah! Who cares *when* she lives, as if that were a problem?" Lady Lydia scoffed. "What matters is she will be on our isle and, thus, within our reach."

CHAPTER 1

Present Day

Teressa clung to the fleeting image of her sensual dream as it dissolved into the recesses of her awakening mind. Overlooking land and sea, she reached for the fierce Scottish warrior with broad shoulders, windswept hair, and smiling face, but he was fading away. *Wait, wait . . . don't go,* she called to the fleeting vision, but it was no use. He was gone.

Darn, she hated how her dreams always ended before she got to the good part. Unfortunately, her mounting arousal didn't fade nearly as fast as the dream, giving her a hefty dose of frustration. It was one of her typical flirting-with-a-hunky-man-and-just-about-to-score scenarios. Lately, it seemed the unfulfilling endings were becoming all too common. She lingered a moment longer, trying to think up a happy ending to the fragmentary dream. Nothing came to mind, so she set aside the fantasy and decided to focus on the reality of her surroundings.

With great reluctance and a good amount of effort, she kicked back the covers and forced herself to shrug off the cozy comfort provided by the warm sheets. Stretching, she felt like a cat uncoiling from a long, lazy nap. And rightfully so, she figured, glancing at the digital clock sitting on the bedside table. Teressa had just spent nearly ten hours comatose to the world, recovering from a major case of travel overload. She was near the end of her vacation and had traveled a great distance to arrive at the Scorrybreac

Village Inn in the small historic town of Portree on the Isle of Skye. After giving herself a few more minutes to contemplate her journey and savor the pleasure of having finally arrived, she rolled out of bed.

Still stretching as she walked, she went over to the window and drew back the heavy curtains to let the morning sun brighten the room. The Zen-like atmosphere of the sage-green room was perfect, even better than she had expected. Contemporary Scandinavian furnishings complemented the ancient inn, creating an interesting contrast between the old and the new. It appealed to her far more than the frilly or historical décors used by other village inns hoping to attract the tourist dollars. The Scorrybreac Village Inn was designed to be a relaxing, calming experience for the intrepid traveler who chose to go off the beaten path. It fit her perfectly.

Anxious to capture a few thoughts on paper, Teressa rummaged through her backpack and pulled out her travel journal. On the first page, she had written "Scotland, My Whimsical Summer Vacation." Several of the pages that followed were already filled with entries documenting her travels. She flipped to the next available blank page and began writing.

> *I arrived at the Scorrybreac Village Inn on Skye late last night. Lord knows the place isn't easy to get to, but it's worth the effort. I've traveled by planes, trains, and automobiles, not to mention the ferry that brought me to Portree, a picture-perfect seaside village on the Isle of Skye known for its magical legends. It's also a perfect setting for my get-away-from-it-all retreat. Now that I've arrived, I can get down to some serious rest and relaxation, and perhaps, if fate is so inclined, a bit of adventure. A handsome Scottish prince would do nicely, thank you very much. (Is this my dream talking or just wishful thinking?)*

As she clicked her pen against her chin, she thought of her mother and brother, Daniel, back home on the ranch. She turned the page and wrote a few more lines.

I hope I can entice Daniel to come here someday. It's too bad Mom couldn't come. I worry about her a lot more now, since Dad's passed away. I think Daniel would love this place. For some reason, it reminds me of him. Probably because it's kind of rough around the edges and rather old fashioned.

She closed the journal and placed it in the top drawer of the bedside table where she could easily find it when she was ready to make her next installment.

Teressa undressed as she padded over to the small but functional bathroom to take her shower. While she shampooed her long blond hair, her wandering mind dredged up thoughts of Jeffery, her ex-boyfriend. He certainly wasn't the hunky man of her dreams. Too bad for Jeffery. If he hadn't behaved so badly at her father's funeral by abandoning her when she needed his support, he might have accompanied her on this vacation; but nope, that's not how it worked out. Grateful she had seen his true colors before she made a massive mistake, she let out a sigh. Love me, love my family was her motto. While the bracing spray of the shower rinsed all traces of suds from her hair, she reaffirmed dumping Jeffery had been the right thing to do. Resolute, she shut off the water with a decisive flick of her wrist then dressed quickly.

With a final look in the bathroom mirror, she took stock of her *au naturel* youthful appearance, which often had people believing her to be younger than her true age. She looked good to go, dressed in comfortable, well-fitting blue jeans and a light green T-shirt, and felt ready to take on whatever the Isle of Skye had to offer. After lacing up her hiking boots, she grabbed her full-length gray leather coat; she liked the way the long coat swung about her legs as she walked, giving her a feeling of rugged yet classic style. The twenty-first of June might be considered the first day of summer, but here in the Highlands of Scotland, there was a chill in the air. As the sun began its ascent across the sky, she saw the prospects for a bright day breaking through the early morning clouds.

In the lobby of the Village Inn, she stopped to grab some of the tourist maps and brochures of the local area. She was considering which sights she wanted to explore when she spied a purple-and-green plaid wool scarf hanging in the gift shop window.

She loved scarves and had a basketful of them back home. Besides being one of her favorite accessories, she figured a Scottish plaid scarf would make a great souvenir without taking up a lot of room in her suitcase. Giving in to her shopping impulse, she strolled into the gift shop and was even more delighted when she encountered a familiar face.

"Good morning, Lilly. It's so good to see you." She flashed a bright smile at the young salesclerk. Lilly had been one of her clients at San Francisco State University, where she worked as a relationship coach. She had helped the foreign exchange student maneuver her way through the world of San Francisco metro males. Lilly claimed they were quite different from the traditional men she had known on Skye, and she had needed help learning how to deal with the big city breed of men.

For Teressa, being only twenty-eight years old and the youngest member of the college counseling center was both a blessing and a burden. The way she saw it, she was close enough in age to her clients to relate to them at their level, while still being experienced enough to present viable solutions for the younger undergraduates maneuvering their way through what was often the emotional rollercoaster of college relationships. Her work brought her deep satisfaction; she was confident she had found her calling in life.

"Morning, Ms. Ellers. I'm glad to see you took me up on my offer," Lilly said.

"You know me. I couldn't pass on a friends-and-family discount." Teressa laughed lightly.

"Will you be staying with us for long?" Lilly asked.

"I'm near the end of my journey, but I'll be here for a couple of more days before I head back home. You know, Skye isn't easy to get to. I've traveled by planes, trains, and a ferry to get here," Teressa said, ticking off the various forms of transportation on her fingers.

Lilly followed Teressa through the small gift shop as she browsed through the collection of items for sale.

"It's too bad your time is so short. You'll be wanting to see the castle ruins before you go. I know everyone goes to Dunvegan," Lilly said, referring to a well-known castle on Skye, "but I've always felt the real magic is here at Scorrybreac."

"It's the first thing on my agenda. Right after I get a cup of coffee," Teressa said as she perused the display of postcards near the front counter. Again, she noticed the scarf in the front window display. "By the way, do you have any more scarves like the one hanging in the window?"

Lilly looked over at the window display and frowned. "No, not that I know of. It must have just come in." She stepped over to the full-length shop window. "Must be one of a kind," Lilly said as she read the label. "Hand-made by Anne M. She's an artisan here on the island." She handed the scarf to Teressa.

Teressa ran her fingers along the soft-woven wool and then held it to her cheek. It felt so good, too good to pass up. "I'll take it," she said.

Lilly rang up the sale. "Do you need a bag?"

"No thanks, I'm going to wear it," Teressa informed her.

Lilly cut off the price tag for her then handed Teressa the scarf. "Zoey works in the coffee shop. Tell her I sent you, and she'll pour you a cup from a fresh pot."

"Sounds great. A fresh, hot cup of coffee. Yum." Teressa waved her farewell. "See ya later," she said, looping the scarf around her neck.

After introducing herself to Zoey, Teressa stood near the front of the coffee shop counter, admiring her new scarf while she waited for the waitress to brew a fresh pot of coffee. She was running her fingers through the colorful fringe when she heard a group of men enter the shop. From the looks of them in their rubberized boots and heavy all-weather work jackets, she guessed them to be local fishermen. When they got closer, their collective odor confirmed it. She waved her hand in front of her nose.

One of the fishermen, the tallest of the bunch, was busy trying to get the counter girl's attention, calling to her by name. "Hey, Zoey, make 'em hot and black, like always," he shouted.

Not wanting to lose her place at the front of the line, Teressa took a step toward the serving counter. Apparently, the fisherman wanted to defy the laws of physics and attempted to occupy the same space as her, causing them to collide as they each stepped forward.

Teressa stared up at the man, who was easily over six feet tall. "Excuse me!" she said.

The large brute stared back at her, as if she were an apparition.

"Excuse me, I was in line here," she tried again, moving to step around him. Unlike the others, he smelled of salt water and ocean breezes.

"What?" he asked, blinking.

"Where I come from, people are polite enough to say 'excuse me' when they're rude enough to cut in line." She stood her ground even though she had to tilt her head a bit to look him in the eye.

"Excuse me, miss. I didn't see you standing there." Spreading his arms wide, he bowed and stepped aside. He was still staring at her, but now he had a grin spreading from ear to ear.

"I'm glad you think this is funny." Teressa was trying not to crack a smile, but his grin was devilishly infectious. She dropped her arms to her side, relaxing her stance. He continued to hold her gaze with his dark green eyes. They were kind, and he had a ready smile. Maybe she had judged him too harshly.

"I see ye've picked up a wee bit of our local color," he said with a deep Scottish brogue.

It was her turn to stare blankly.

He reached out, touching the fringe of her newly purchased scarf. "A right fine choice."

"Here, Robert. Take your coffee and move out of the way." Zoey set a tall steaming cup of coffee on the counter.

"We've got a table over here," one of his buddies called out to him.

He picked up his coffee and raised the cup to her in a parting salute. "Have a nice day, lass." Still grinning, he turned away to join his friends.

"Sorry, miss, they think they own the place. Now, what can I get for you?" Zoey asked, drawing Teressa's attention.

"Large coffee with cream, no sugar," Teressa said, pulling her gaze away from the table of men. "Did I say make it a large?"

Zoey nodded, already busy pouring the coffee. "Would you like some breakfast to go with your coffee? Farm fresh eggs, and the cook makes a mean veggie scramble."

"You know, that sounds good. I think I will." Teressa took the last empty seat at the breakfast counter next to two young girls who looked to be sisters and an older woman she guessed to be their grandmother. She leaned over the counter and spoke to Zoey in a hushed tone.

"What's his story? How did he know about my scarf?"

"His aunt is the weaver. It's one of hers. Robert's the captain of our local fishing fleet. He usually brings his crew in here to warm up and get fresh coffee after a long night at sea. The younger one in the yellow jacket . . . he's my brother." Zoey set Teressa's coffee on the counter.

A Time To Return

"Sounds like you know everyone," Teressa remarked, somewhat impressed.

"We're all family here in Scorrybreac," Zoey replied.

Teressa pulled out her brochure for Scorrybreac Castle and began to look it over. From the first moment she had heard about the castle, she had felt a strong desire to see it up close and personal; she was looking forward to her sightseeing adventure. While she was reading over the brief history of the castle, she became distracted by the little girl sitting next to her. The young girl, who looked to be no more than six or seven, went from tapping her spoon on her half-empty plate, to swiveling on her stool while trying to kick the legs of the older girl sitting next to her. Not surprisingly, the older girl was doing her best to ignore her younger sister, giving all of her attention to her grandmother. Teressa took one look at the little girl and immediately sensed her problem. Setting down her brochure, she turned to the younger girl, leaned down, and whispered, "It doesn't feel good to be ignored, does it?"

The girl's innocent blue eyes darted a shy look at Teressa. "No." She shook her head with pouty defiance and then looked down at the uneaten food on her plate. A glance over at her sister and grandmother told Teressa they had finished eating some time ago, and now the younger child was bored.

"Is that your sister?" Teressa asked, still speaking softly.

"Yeah, and Grandmamma. My name's Moe. We're going to visit the castle today," Moe said, also speaking softly.

Teressa gave Moe a friendly smile. "I'm going to the castle too. It should be fun."

Moe nodded but remained quiet, looking down at her hands. Her shyness was understandable; she had probably been told not to talk to strangers.

"You must be very special," Teressa remarked, trying to cheer her up. She took a sip of her coffee.

"Why do you say that?" Moe asked, still whispering.

"Because I see you're wearing purple. Purple boots, purple coat, even your bows are purple."

Moe reached up to touch the bows in her hair.

"Did you know that faeries and elves have a special fondness for the color purple?"

"They do?" Moe's eyes opened wide, and a merry twinkle accompanied her happy smile. "You mean, like the color of your scarf?"

Teressa glanced down at the purple-and-green plaid. "Yes, like the color of my scarf."

The grandmother and the older sister rose from their stools, preparing to leave. Abruptly, the elderly woman acknowledged Teressa's interaction with her granddaughter. "Moe, stop bothering the nice lady and come with me."

Teressa looked up as Moe hopped down from her stool. "She wasn't bothering me. Your granddaughter is delightfully charming."

"Delightfully charming?" Moe repeated in awe, all bright eyed and smiling.

Teressa nodded. "Delightfully charming," she reaffirmed.

Moe skipped merrily away, following her grandmother and her sister. When she reached the door, she turned to give Teressa a wave goodbye.

Teressa turned back to the counter just as Zoey was setting down her breakfast.

"That was nice of you . . . talking to the little girl, I mean. Here's your breakfast. Enjoy," Zoey said.

"Thanks. She looked like she could use a friend."

"I know the family. The grandmother can be a wee gruff, but Moe's a regular pixie. Can I get you anything else?"

"Nope, I'm fine. It all looks good," Teressa said, lifting her fork.

She was nearly through with her breakfast when Robert, the sea captain, sidled up to the empty stool beside her.

"Can I get a refill?" he asked across the counter to Zoey.

The waitress was ready on the spot and refilled his cup with the hot brew.

Robert turned to Teressa. "I hope I've been forgiven."

Teressa turned to give him a once over. He was easy on the eyes. "Yeah, you're forgiven."

He held out his hand. "I'm Robert."

She wiped her hand on her napkin before taking his. "Teressa."

"Lovely name. Have we met before?" He looked deep into her eyes.

"You mean like earlier when you almost ran over me?" Or had he already forgotten? She raised her eyebrows and smirked.

"No, I mean like *before*. I know I don't know you, and yet I feel as if I do. And yes, I know this isn't making any sense."

Teressa gave him a puzzled look. It was perhaps the strangest, if not the most blatant, pickup line she had ever heard, but she decided to let it ride. The poor man obviously had no finesse.

"I don't think so. I've never been to Skye before. Have you ever been to San Francisco?"

"I've never left Skye . . . grew up here." He picked up the brochure for Scorrybreac Castle. "I've been here dozens of times," he said, waving the brochure. "The first time, I think I was only seven years old, with my parents. It was strange, but it was like I could remember how the place looked before, years and years ago, when it was still new. I could picture the original castle, the training grounds, even the stables. It was like I remembered living there."

Her first reaction was he must have had a rather vivid imagination. Then she wondered if this were a case of bartender's syndrome, where a person would sit down and start telling a perfect stranger their life story. Being a relationship coach, she tried to listen without judgment. "Sounds interesting," she said.

"No, it sounds crazy, but what can I say. Every time I go up to the place, I have the same feeling. I've learned to ignore it, but it doesn't go away. Are you planning to go see it?" He was starting to look uncomfortable, as if he had painted himself into a corner and were looking for a way out.

"Yeah, as soon as I finish here." She took a final bite of toast before pushing the plate away.

He glanced down at his work clothes. "I'd offer to act as your tour guide, but I've got an oil leak that needs fixing. I own a fishing fleet, and I've got four boats I need to keep running."

Looking over her shoulder, she noticed his crewmen waiting at the corner table, watching them as Robert flirted with her. They were probably betting on whether he would score. She would bet against it.

"Tomorrow I'm giving myself the day off. What are you doing then?" he asked, looking hopeful.

Teressa sat back on her stool, considering his suggestion. "I don't know. I'm thinking maybe I'll check out Dunvegan Castle." She bit her lip, forcing back a grin as she silently recalled her dream of a Scottish prince.

"Okay," he nodded. "Then maybe I'll see you around." He took another drink of his coffee, draining the cup, and rose from the stool.

"Yeah, maybe." She shrugged then watched him walk away to rejoin his friends before her grin made its escape. He looked good from the backside too.

Teressa paid her bill and was preparing to leave when laughter from the corner table drew her attention. The one whose mirthful voice stood out was Robert, the sea captain. His robust laughter sailed across the room. It was the sound of unrestrained joy, one she didn't hear often enough. Though she had not intended to look his way, when she did, their eyes met, and she had a sudden unsettling feeling they *had* met before. She looked away, but as she headed for the door, she knew he was watching her.

Leaving the warmth of the Village Inn, Teressa headed out on the path leading down to the bay. Farther down the shoreline, behind the Village Inn, was the marina. She could see the fishing boats tied to the docks, bobbing with the tide. The scene reminded her of the Berkeley Marina, a place she had often visited with her brother, Daniel. They both shared a love of the sea. The morning air was brisk, and she decided a walk along the seashore would be an invigorating way to start to her day.

She had read about the ancient castle of Scorrybreac sitting on the bluffs high above Portree and planned to do some exploring. The tourist brochure claimed the origins of the local fortress dated back to the thirteenth century. Many changes had been made to the original castle over the centuries, but according to the marketing brochure, the original foundation could still be found within the ruin. The history of the place appealed to her, and she decided to make it her first destination.

Already, the clouds were clearing to reveal patches of bright blue sky. A cool breeze coming off the ocean whipped loose strands of hair around her face. She enjoyed the crunch of the hard packed sand under her boots accompanied by the repetitive sound of the waves crashing along the wide sandy beach. The stretch of beach eventually gave way to harsh, jutting cliffs rising straight from the surging sea. Massive granite outcroppings of earth buffeted the crescent shoreline from the full strength of the wind coming in off the ocean. High above, at the edge of the sheer cliff, sat the ruins of Scorrybreac Castle. The fortress stood proud, as if birthed by the very ground it sat upon. One needed to look closely to see where the stony ground ended and the man-made structure began. Suffering from years of abandonment and the harsh weather, the fortress looked as though it had been there forever, a well-established fixture in its natural surroundings.

Teressa was beginning to feel the warmth of the sun shining through a break in the early morning clouds when the mild breeze suddenly turned violent. She pulled the hood of her coat up over her head for protection and leaned into the wind, wondering if maybe this wasn't such a good idea. Maybe she should turn back and retrace her steps to the inn.

Before she could take another step, a hot, fierce wind sprang up around her, engulfing her with tornado-like force. It whipped her long coat about her body, kicking up loose sand and debris. Teressa raised her arms to shield her face from the stinging specks of sand as another blast of the hot wind sucked the air from her lungs. She had to fight to catch her breath and began to panic. *What the hell is this*, she wondered, *some freakish tornado?* The combined force of the wind and the shifting of the ground beneath her threw her off-balance, and she began to twirl swiftly through a long black tunnel, surrounded by darkness, as her body was swept up in the swirling mass. A moment later, she felt herself falling, being hurled back to earth. *Dang, this is going to hurt.* As she dropped to the ground, she felt a tingling, prickly sensation flood through her body, and her vision blurred before everything went black.

CHAPTER 2

Isle of Skye, 1292

Duncan MacNicol was returning home from his early morning ride after rising before dawn to observe what proved to be a glorious sunrise for the first day of summer. He had just turned onto the road that ran along the bluffs overlooking the sea when he felt a sudden blast of hot wind rising from the crescent beach below. Turning away, Duncan quickly raised his arms to shield his face from the fierce gust while his horse pranced nervously, refusing to go on. Then, as swiftly as it had arrived, the storm abated.

That was damnably odd. He was about to continue on his way when he noticed a body lying on the sandy beach below. Duncan directed his horse to the seaside path and made his way down to the shore. Dismounting a few feet away, he rushed to see if the person were injured, or even still alive. As he knelt to examine the hooded figure, he realized it was a woman, and an attractive one at that. Stray strands of long pale blond hair fluttered in the breeze when he pulled back the hood of her long gray overcoat. Interestingly, she appeared to be dressed as a man, wearing strange breeches and boots. When he pushed back the overcoat to check for injuries, he couldn't help but notice how the body-hugging shirt revealed the curvaceous shape of a well-formed woman.

He looked around for signs of where she had come from. She was lying on the sand, well above the high tidemark, and yet the only footsteps anywhere near her body were his. It seemed illogical she had been able to walk along a sandy beach without leaving any footprints. Even if she had washed in from sea, there would have been marks on the sand, and yet there was no sign of where she had come from. It almost looked as though she had been dropped from the sky, but such an idea was ridiculous.

An unusual pack on the ground next to her caught his eye; most likely it belonged to the unconscious woman. He picked it up and slung it over his shoulder then gathered her in his arms. As he did so, he sensed there was something special about this woman, something he needed to know, as if she carried a message meant only for him. He hefted her over his shoulder like a sack of grain, and then mounted up on his large brown warhorse before settling her more comfortably on his lap. Holding her safe in his arms, he directed his horse back up the path towards the fortress perched high on the cliffs above the ocean.

Duncan crossed the bailey of the seaside fortress and, gently cradling the lass with one arm about her waist, dismounted in front of the stables. He handed his horse off to one of the stable boys standing at the ready then lifted the woman more securely in his arms. His brothers, Michael and Rory, had been training in the lists across the way but stopped what they were doing to take note of his arrival, as did nearly everyone else in the fortress courtyard. His youngest brother, Rory, seemed particularly curious, craning his neck as he took a step forward. Duncan gave him a halting glare and shook his head. Thankfully, Rory followed his unspoken order, and stood his ground. Duncan knew there would be questions. That was to be expected; he had questions of his own for this woman who had appeared from nowhere. Without stopping to speak to his brothers, he made his way into the keep and headed for the chamber that served as his study.

Taking care not to hurt her, Duncan laid the woman on the upholstered bench then dropped her pack on the floor next her.

Never taking his eyes off her face, he watched her as she regained consciousness, awakening from her daze.

~~~

Teressa awoke slowly, disoriented, as if waking from a dream without knowing exactly where she was. She scanned her surroundings to get her bearings. As her mind gradually worked through the receding daze, she realized she wasn't in her room at the Village Inn where she had slept the night before. She also realized she had no idea where she was; she was quite certain she had never seen this place before; and she certainly didn't know the large man standing before her. Mentally, she tried to retrace her steps. The last thing she could clearly remember was seeing Lilly at the gift shop and buying her scarf. She looked down to see it still wrapped around her neck. She wasn't sure what happened after that. Something was missing. Her memory was fragmented. She vaguely remembered leaving the Village Inn and walking along the beach, but she had no idea where she was or how she had gotten here.

As she moved to sit up on the padded bench, Teressa kept her eyes on the large and rather fierce man watching over her. He didn't seem very happy or welcoming. His dark auburn hair was long and pulled back with a leather cord to trail down his broad back, and his skin was deeply tanned. He wore strange, coarse woolen pants, or maybe they were leggings, that hugged his thighs, with an oversized white linen shirt belted at the waist, and damned if there wasn't an authentic sword hanging from his belt. His pants were tucked into leather boots laced up to his calves. She figured he must be wearing some kind of old-fashioned Scottish costume, and on him, it looked good. And he looked suitably intimidating.

He stood there, silently, as if waiting for her to speak. Still in a bit of a daze, she abruptly asked, "Where am I? Who are you?"

19

"I'm Duncan MacNicol, and this is my home." His tone was a bit gruff, but he sounded kinder than she had expected, with a thick Scottish brogue.

"Can you tell me how I got here?"

"I found ye on the beach below the cliffs. Ye fainted," he informed her.

"I fainted? On the beach?" This surprised her. She didn't consider herself a woman subject to fainting spells, and couldn't remember ever fainting before in her life. She may have passed out from pure exhaustion after a long day of work, or a few too many drinks, but as far as she knew, she had never fainted.

Trying to keep a grip on reality, Teressa began to recall the hot wind that had overtaken her on the beach. She wasn't sure what had happened, but she figured the force of being drop-kicked to the beach must have knocked her out. It would sure explain her nagging headache and achingly bruised body.

"Ye were unconscious. I brought ye here to recover." He was as big as a tree, but it didn't appear as though he intended to harm her, at least she hoped not.

As much as she was enjoying the appearance of this fine man, she felt uncomfortable being alone with him. She didn't want to come across as rude, but she had a strong feeling she needed to get back to the Scorrybreac Village Inn as soon as possible. Vaguely, she recalled her intentions to explore the castle ruins she had seen earlier from the beach, just before she lost consciousness.

"Umm, how very kind of you, but now that I'm feeling better, perhaps I should make arrangements to return to the Village Inn," she said. She didn't want to impose on his hospitality; however, since she didn't know how she had gotten to Duncan's home, she wasn't sure how she would arrange to return to the inn. Maybe she could walk; though, the very thought of it increased the ache in her head, and she raised her hands to brace her forehead against the pounding pain.

"Perhaps you should give yerself some time to recover. Allow me to offer ye something to drink," Duncan responded. He showed no intention of allowing her to run off quite so soon.

"Well, yes, thank you. I'd appreciate a drink of water, if it's not too much to ask. I'm sorry to impose on you," she said, grateful for his kindness.

"I insist," Duncan assured her with polite authority.

It occurred to her she wasn't making a good first impression. She focused on taking a few deep breaths to calm herself, as she was disoriented, in pain, and reacting poorly. Like it or not, she needed to pull herself together and deal with her unexpected situation.

Duncan walked over to the door and called out to someone named Bonnie. A moment later, Teressa could hear him instruct the woman to bring drinks to the room. She used the opportunity to stand up, or at least she tried. The dizzy buzzing in her head forced her to lean against the wall for support; still, she attempted to take stock of her surroundings.

She guessed the room to be an office of sorts. Tapestries hung on the walls of the hard stone structure depicted a hunting scene woven with vivid greens and blues, but the red, she noticed, seemed dull by comparison. The furnishings looked fairly new, but positively medieval. The sparse collection of furniture was limited to the padded bench where she had been sitting, a desk with a chair, and another pair of armchairs near the oversized fireplace. A large chest and cupboard lined one wall. The pieces were heavily carved and appeared to be handmade, fit for hard use. Apparently, his eccentric style wasn't limited to his clothing, judging by his selection of ancient décor. She wondered if his home were a reproduction of a historical manor, perhaps some type of tourist attraction for visitors to the island. If that were the case, it looked as though he had done an excellent job of recreating a medieval setting.

"For the moment, ye are my guest, however, I do have questions. Let's start with who you are and where you come from?"

"I'm Teressa Ellers. I live in Diablo Valley, near San Francisco. I came to the Isle of Skye for a vacation." She offered her hand in greeting.

Instead of receiving a handshake as she expected, Duncan took her hand to lead her to the armchairs near the hearth where a fire burned low in the large stone fireplace occupying one wall of the chamber. When she faltered slightly in her first hesitant step away from the bench, Duncan reached out to assist her.

"Ye must still be lightheaded from yer fall," he offered. His eyes held hers; he watched her, as if he expected her to do something crazy, or perhaps faint again. She hoped that wasn't going to happen.

"Yes, more than I realized," she said. Her head still throbbed as she moved to take the seat Duncan offered. Teressa blinked several times, trying to clear the daze invading her brain. She breathed deeply while reminding herself to remain calm and was finally able to reclaim control of her senses. Though she didn't usually have problems dealing with strangers, she had a feeling this man was far different from anyone she had met before.

"You say ye come from San Francisco?" Duncan asked as he sat down in the chair opposite of hers.

Teressa nodded.

"Is that in Spain?"

"No, San Francisco, California," she answered. Surely he could tell she was American by her accent?

"I've never heard of it."

"You're kidding, right?" There was no excuse for not knowing about one of the major cities of the world, even if he did live on the remote Isle of Skye.

Before Duncan could answer, there was a knock at the door. He went to the door and came back with a tray holding a ceramic jug and two pewter goblets. After setting the tray on a side table, he poured them each a drink then handed one of the goblets to Teressa.

She took a long, cool drink and nearly gagged. It tasted like bad beer.

"You don't like it?" he asked.

"Umm, no, it just seems a little early to start drinking," she said. There was no place nearby to set the cup, so she continued to hold it in her hand.

Duncan took a long drink before continuing with his questions. He seemed to like the stuff. "Ye still haven't told me what brings ye to the Isle of Skye, and," he added with emphasis, "it appears ye are all alone?"

Teressa recoiled, unexpectedly shocked by the sting of his observation. "You're right, I am traveling alone. This past year has been rather stressful, and I felt I needed some time alone, far from home. A kind of personal retreat." She wasn't sure why she felt such a need to defend herself.

"What could be so stressful that it required ye to travel so far by yerself?" he asked with skepticism in his voice.

"Earlier this year, my dad died. It was unexpected. He was barely seventy years old."

"I'm sorry to hear of yer loss, though it seems yer da lived a good, long life," Duncan offered.

"Anyway, after he died, I kind of poured myself into my work, putting in extra, long hours. It got to be too much, and I needed to give myself a break." Teressa deliberately chose not to mention Jeffery and their breakup. Her love life, or the lack thereof, was a tad too personal to be shared with a stranger. Needing to change the subject, she asked, "Now it's your turn. Tell me something about you. Why are you dressed up like some medieval warrior?" Although this day was not turning out at all as she had planned, she reminded herself, that when traveling, one must be ready to go with the flow and accept the unexpected.

Duncan sat back and crossed his arms over his formidable chest. He looked straight into Teressa's eyes and stated with complete confidence, "I'm Duncan MacNicol, Chief of the Clan MacNicol and Laird of Scorrybreac Keep. Ye are under my protection."

Holy crap! Chief of the Clan MacNicol, Laird of Scorrybreac Keep! Teressa's thoughts moved quickly from confusion to pure disbelief. She wondered what kind of kook she was dealing with, and how quickly she could leave. Though she had only seen the ruins of the Scorrybreac fortress from a distance, she could tell it was nearly impossible for the interior rooms to be this well preserved, and it was certainly in no condition to be housing a room such as this. He was either crazy or engaged in some kind of joke at her expense, taking his historical acting role way too far. Either way, she realized it was time for her to make her way back to the Village Inn—now. Trying hard not to display her concern over his startling announcement, she began to consider how to make a polite getaway.

"Umm, okay, so maybe I should leave now." She looked around for a place to set her goblet. He'd given her a goblet for Christ's sake, and with warm beer no less.

"My formal title seems to disturb ye," Duncan said, motioning for her to stay seated.

"Well, excuse me, but it's not every day I meet the laird of a castle, especially one that's known to be in ruins."

"I can assure ye, my keep is not in ruins," he answered sternly. "Ye appear on my beach, telling me ye've traveled *by yerself* from San Francisco of California, a place I've never heard of, and ye expect me to believe you?" He was kind of starting to bellow and it scared her.

His claim he'd never heard of San Francisco was another indication of his unstable mind. "You know, you've been very kind, and I really do appreciate all you've done, but I think it's time for me to go." Teressa rose from her chair. "I'd like to return to the Village Inn now. Is it close enough for me to walk, or do I need to call for a ride?"

"Ye will not be leaving, not yet," Duncan informed her as he stood to face her. "The village inn is no place for a woman traveling alone. And regardless of what ye think, I am the chief of this keep, and ye are under my protection."

"Oh, really? I'm under your protection?" she mocked, unable to hold in her indignation. "You act as if this is the thirteenth century and you have the right to tell me what to do."

"Aye, that is correct," Duncan stated.

Teressa's jaw dropped. She searched his face for signs that he was crazy, or maybe a little off his rocker. Instead, he presented an expression of firm conviction. His eyes shone clear with unwavering self-assurance.

Beginning to fear his grip on reality, she softly asked, "Can you tell me what time this is?"

"We are approaching midmorning, an hour or two before noon, I would say."

"No, I'm thinking more like what year?"

He looked at her queerly, but answered, "'Tis the year twelve hundred and ninety-two, the twenty-first day in the month of June."

"You've got to be kidding."

"Nay, lass, I don't jest."

She stared at him in shock and disbelief. *One of us must be crazy. The year twelve ninety-two? How could that be?* Unfortunately, he didn't seem crazy or feebleminded, it would be so much easier if he did. In her line of work, she had encountered her fair share of liars, men who would say anything to get what they wanted, but

Duncan's behavior didn't fit theirs. Even more noticeable, he seemed perfectly at ease with his surroundings. She was the one who felt out of place. An unpleasant awareness of something wrong began to seep through her mind. Her eyes quickly scanned the room before she turned to look at the narrow window sitting high on the wall behind her. The bottom of the window was too high for her to look out and see the ground below, so she pushed the chair in which she had been sitting to below the window and stepped up.

Staring into the courtyard, she saw a lively, bustling castle straight out of the Middle Ages and in the prime of its life. Washwomen, stable hands, butchers, and guards, all dressed in medieval clothing, were going about their daily business of tending to animals and working within the courtyard surrounding the castle. The harsh smells of human sweat, farm animals, and food preparation affronted her senses.

Teressa tried to convince herself it was only a working replica of an ancient castle and not the real deal, but the closer she looked, the more real it became. There were no signs of modern civilization, no telephone or electrical lines, no false facades, storefronts, or posted signage, and not one motorized vehicle anywhere in sight. She watched the activity below for some time, hoping to find something to confirm she was still in the twenty-first century. There was nothing. Filled with a mixture of horror and bewilderment, she grew more and more amazed by the richness of the history unfolding before her very eyes.

At the far end of the courtyard, men were training for battle with swords and shields. One of the men stood out from the others. From her vantage point, he looked like a younger version of Duncan. She glanced over her shoulder to assure herself he was still in the room.

When she looked back at the courtyard, her gaze returned to the men in training, honing in on Duncan's twin. How could she not? With arms straight out of Conan the Barbarian, he looked damn good waving around that big-ass sword.

Then, as though he knew he were being watched, the warrior stopped fighting and looked up to the window where she stood. Teressa's first impulse was to hide, as if she could conceal her spying, but she was caught, locked in his sights. Slowly, very slowly, a wickedly sexy smile spread across his hard chiseled face. For a long moment, they remained locked in a visual embrace, until Teressa could stand it no longer. Her frayed nerves failed her. She turned away from the window and slumped into the chair.

Looking back at the room, she made a closer inspection of her surroundings. For all appearances, it was truly a room from an ancient time. She sat there, taking it all in, the large wooden bench with its stuffed cushions, the sturdy handmade furniture, the candles on the desk, and the tapestries hanging on the stone walls to keep out the cold. There wasn't a phone or a clock or an electrical wire anywhere to be seen.

Time travel, to the past! This isn't possible. How can this be? Tears stung her eyes as fear raced through her body. Adrenaline pumped through her veins, causing her to break out in a nervous sweat. It was too much to bear and impossible to believe.

She looked over to Duncan, staring blankly. He'd been watching her as she made her inspections.

"Tell me, what day do ye think 'tis?" he asked.

Still fighting back her tears, she looked up at him. "This morning, when I woke up, it was June twenty-first, all right, but in the twenty-first century. Now you're telling me I passed out on a beach and woke up in twelve ninety-two. Excuse me while I try to get my head around this." She sat in stunned silence.

"Can ye show me any proof of who ye say ye are?" he demanded.

Her eyes jerked to his in amazement. "You don't believe me?"

"Do ye think I should simply take yer word on something this crazy? Yer ramblings have not led me to believe ye are well grounded in reality. Ye want me to believe a woman would be allowed to travel alone after the passing of her father because she spent long hours working? What manner of nonsense do ye speak? And now ye tell me ye come from seven hundred years in the future! Woman, ye ask too much." Just shy of yelling, his tone was a mixture of anger and disbelief.

"But I am from the future, and I can prove it." She hurried to retrieve her backpack from the floor near the bench. "Look at this material. Even the zipper on this pack; it's not like anything you've ever seen before, am I right?"

He reached out to examine the material, rubbing the strong futuristic fabric between his fingers, running the zipper open and close several times to test the novel device.

"Yer pack is unusual, I will admit. But it does very little to prove yer story."

She opened the front pocket of the pack and pulled out the tourist guide maps and brochures, documents from her time. "Here, look at these. I'm sure you've never seen such printing or paper. These things don't exist in your time." She spread the maps and brochures out over the top of the table.

Duncan examined the maps and colorful brochures, one by one. Finally, dragging his gaze from the pages, he stared up at her. "How did ye come by these things?"

"From a local gift store in the twenty-first century. They're common items from my time."

Duncan appeared to be deep in thought, but he didn't look convinced.

"Here, look at these pictures," she insisted, pointing out the brilliant color photos in the brochures. "These aren't done by an artist. They're photographs, created by a technology that doesn't exist yet." She was somewhat leery of showing him too much from the future, but if necessary, she would pull out her digital camera and snap his picture to convince him she was being truthful. She wasn't crazy and wouldn't allow him to think she was. "You must believe me. If this truly is the thirteenth century, as you say . . ."

"Aye, lass, of that ye can be sure," he reconfirmed.

". . . then I'm the one who must struggle to believe you, for I am truly misplaced and don't know what to do." She slumped into the nearest chair and let her tears run down her cheeks. Sad disappointment seeped through her body as she sat, quietly crying, her mind in disarray, not knowing what to think, or say, or do.

"Look at me," Duncan spoke sternly. "I understand ye are scared and confused, but if ye can trust me to return and promise to stay here in my chambers, I will go and seek the answers ye need."

Teressa blinked several times and nodded. What else could she do but trust this stranger who offered his protection? There was no place for her to go, no Village Inn to return to, at least not the Village Inn she had left this morning.

It took all her effort to regain her composure. She rubbed her hands across her face, wiping the tears from her eyes. "How can there be answers to this?" she asked, struggling with her confusion.

"Trust me to return, and I'll tell ye everything I know."

Teressa nodded, still unsure. What choice did she have?

He led her back to the chair near the hearth. "Will ye be all right?" he asked again.

"Yes." She managed a thin watery grin, even though she wasn't sure she'd ever be all right again.

"I will return as soon as I am able." He turned to leave.

"But where are you going?" she asked, suddenly afraid to be left alone. "Who knows what will happen next?"

"I am going to see a wizard," he said as he stomped out the door.

CHAPTER 3

Duncan had listened to Teressa's outlandish story, thinking she must be either addlebrained or touched in her head; neither was a pleasant thought. He wasn't in a mood to deal with a crazy woman, but as leader of his clan, he also couldn't send her off to fend on her own. Lord only knew what might happen to her.

He certainly wasn't prepared to believe her, at least not yet. It was hard enough to accept that she may have traveled a great distance on her own; the idea that she could be from a future time and place was unheard of. She was a strange one, of that he had no doubt, but the idea of her being from a future time he found difficult—nay, impossible to believe.

But then she had produced those strange documents.

One of the maps in particular had caught his attention. Even though he couldn't understand all the markings, he could easily see it was a detailed drawing of the Isle of Skye, showing every path and roadway, including many he had never seen before. He knew the island better than most, and the details presented in that image were far beyond any chart work he had ever seen.

The images on the fine quality paper appeared too lifelike to be drawings. They were realistic images of people and places such as he had never seen before. Either they were produced by magic, or they really were from the future, as she claimed.

He began to wonder if it truly were possible she came from another time and place. While her accent was rather odd, the manner in which she spoke indicated she was a woman of intelligence. Her earnest forthrightness also indicated she was speaking *her* truth.

As amazing as it seemed, the idea of her being brought here by magic did much to explain her strange and sudden appearance from nowhere, her unusual way of speaking, the strange style of her clothes, and so much more. It wasn't an easy thought to deal with, but then, nothing about this woman was.

Duncan realized, no matter how amazing he found her story to be, if it were true, she must find it to be even more disturbing. It seemed her appearance on the beach actually was an unnatural event, as he first suspected. He recalled the story of his great-grandmother appearing to his great-grandfather out of a morning mist, a tale he had always dismissed as a romantic legend rather than a real, supernatural event, but now he was no longer so sure.

When he had found her on the beach, it appeared she were trying to disguise herself as a man with her sturdy boots, strange blue breeches, and long gray coat, but if such were the case, her attempt was sorely lacking. The fit of her breeches and tight shirt beneath the coat allowed for no mistake in her gender. Her garments looked expensive and well made, but they certainly weren't in keeping with local attire for men or women. The only exception was the piece of Scorrybreac plaid she wore draped around her neck—another piece of the mystery. He knew this woman wasn't of his clan, and yet she wore the MacNicol clan's plaid.

She appeared highborn, clean and well fed . . . an attractive woman, he had to admit. Her long blond hair hung loose around her pretty oval face, and her skin was youthful, smooth as a bairn's bottom. Even more enchanting, he noted, were her smoky grey eyes. They were open windows to her feelings.

The more he thought about it, the more he knew his instincts were right. There was something magical about her appearance on the beach. He needed to know more about this woman and who or what had brought her here. Much as Duncan dreaded dealing with this unwanted intrusion into his life, he knew what he had to do.

He had reached the wizard's chamber and pounded on the door, releasing his frustrations upon the innocent wood. Souyer had barely lifted the latch when Duncan burst into the chamber.

"I have questions for ye, druid," Duncan announced as he stormed into the darkened chamber. "What on earth have ye done?"

"I don't know what ye mean," Souyer sputtered. He pulled on a gray wool robe to cover his nightshirt before he pushed back the heavy drapes covering the windows. The sun, now rising high in the morning sky, spilled through the narrow opening, filling the room with much-needed light.

"What spells have ye been casting, or should I say, miscasting?" Duncan glared at him. He had never trusted the supernatural rituals of the druids and cared even less for Souyer; he tolerated the old wizard to please his mother. The druid was an unwelcomed inheritance from his father, nothing more. But Souyer had lived at Scorrybreac for too long and was too old for Duncan to get rid of now.

"What has happened to make ye burst in here and ask such a question?" Souyer asked, indignant.

"A woman has appeared on my beach," Duncan began.

Souyer's eyes grew wide. "'Tis as I dreamed. Is she tall and beautiful with long blond hair?"

"What do ye mean 'as you dreamed'? Tell me what ye have done."

"I made a request of the spirit guardians for visions of the future. They granted me with a dream of a beautiful woman asleep on the beach." The old druid seemed quite pleased with himself.

"Ye made a request for visions, and it results in a woman appearing on my beach?" Duncan questioned the druid's nonsense, his voice rising along with his anger.

"Aye," Souyer nodded. "This morning, at the dawn of the summer solstice, I made my request to the faeries and spirits of Skye. 'Tis a time-honored tradition that the faeries and spirits will grant my request."

Duncan tried to follow the druid's wayward mind, but it only gave him the shivers. "Tell me exactly what ye requested," he demanded through clenched teeth.

Souyer cleared his throat and began, his voice inflated with pride. "Oh, great and good faeries, guardian spirits of earth and Skye, in the tradition of our holy and sacred bonds, present to me, here and now, knowledge from the future for the greater good of the MacNicol clan."

"Ye old fool," Duncan stormed, pointing his finger at the druid's chest. "I don't know much about magic, but it appears yer meddlesome faeries have conspired to provide something far different than ye intended." *Knowledge from the future, my arse.* The old wizard had summoned a God blessed woman, and now it was his chore to deal with her.

"Ye question my request? I asked for knowledge of yer future. Coming from yer master druid, such information should prove very helpful to ye."

"Ye may have been granted access to knowledge from the future, but I highly doubt this is what you envisioned. I happen to have a woman from the future sitting in my chambers with no idea how she got here, and we—nay, *ye* must do something about this."

"A woman from the future? How do ye know she's from the future?" Souyer questioned with disbelief.

"Because she told me, and now, thanks to you, I have reason to believe her." Like it or not, Duncan was beginning to accept the truth of her origins. After learning of Souyer's solstice request, he was more convinced than ever that supernatural forces were at work.

Souyer stared at Duncan in dumbfounded amazement. "A woman from the future," he repeated, as if saying it again made it more real. "What do we do now?"

"Ye mean ye don't know how to send her back?" Duncan was incredulous.

"Umm, I expect it will take some time to discover a way to send her back. First, I must be certain of how I got her here," Souyer sputtered out his answer.

"Hell," Duncan cursed. "Ye better figure it out, and soon. But before ye lift a finger or make another blasted request, ye will consult with me on yer intentions. Do I make myself clear?"

Souyer nodded.

"We will talk more on this later," Duncan informed him as he headed out the door. Being in the small bedchamber with the druid was unsettling, and he had no desire to linger in Souyer's presence longer than necessary. He was anxious to return to his chamber to assure himself Teressa was still there.

His interest in learning more about this woman who had suddenly been brought into his world by the whim of the faeries and a cantankerous old wizard was growing. He began to wonder how long she would be his guest. Much depended on whether Souyer could find a way to fix his spell. One could never be sure with faeries. It was possible she could disappear at any moment, or she could be stuck in this time forever. How would she react, he wondered, if it turned out to be the latter?

~*~

After Duncan left the room, Teressa sat and stared at the fire in the hearth, only vaguely aware of the flames. The daze from her earlier blackout was nothing compared to the fog settling over her brain as she sat in mind-numbing silence. Truly bewildered, she was unable to form coherent thoughts, or even begin to understand her unnatural situation. The questions *how* and *why* kept repeating within her brain.

Suddenly, she felt as though someone were watching her. She looked at the door, but it was closed. When she turned to look back at the fire, she was startled to see a lovely young woman standing nearby.

Teressa drew back and blinked. "Excuse me, I didn't hear you come in," she said.

"There really was no sound to announce my coming; I only needed your awareness of my presence," the woman said softly. She had long white-blond hair and wore a long iridescent silver-blue gown that draped softly over her body. A white glow surrounded the woman, adding brightness to the room.

"Are you the person Duncan is looking for?" Teressa asked hopefully, disregarding the woman's strange greeting.

"It is you who brings me here, just as we have brought you here. I am here for your assistance, as you are here for ours."

Talk about doublespeak, Teressa thought with a shake of her head. How could someone say something without saying anything? "Can you tell me why I'm here and how I got here?" she asked, hoping this strange woman could provide some sense to her extraordinary situation.

"You are here to be who you are. You were brought here in answer to a request from Souyer, our druid friend; although, we are certain you are not what he expected." The young woman's voice was laced with a hint of laughter.

"What the hell are you talking about?" The woman was making no sense, and Teressa was too distraught to be polite. She needed answers, and she wanted them now.

Instead of being offended, the woman smiled. "I am Moezell. We have brought you here to fulfill Souyer's request for knowledge from the future. I am aware this all seems very strange to you now, but all will be revealed in its rightful time."

At least she was starting to sound encouraging. Gaining hope that the young woman could provide some meaningful information, Teressa continued with her questions. "Who is Souyer, and am I really in the thirteenth century?"

"Souyer is a druid who believes he is a master; however, he still has much to learn. He performed the ritual of the summer solstice request, which, by tradition, we are honor bound to fulfill; although, perhaps not as he would have expected. We have chosen you to be the knowledge from the future he has requested. And yes, you are a twenty-first-century woman in thirteenth-century Scotland."

Moezell was finally beginning to provide some useful information, even though her situation still didn't make sense. "Who is this 'we' you keep referring to?" Teressa asked.

"*We* are the faeries and spirit guides of the Isle of Skye." She smiled and tipped her head in a gesture of greeting.

"Oh. My. Goodness. Not only have I traveled through time, but now I'm talking to a freaking faerie. Can any of this be real?" Teressa wondered if she were having a hallucination brought on by the blow to her head. Given a choice, she preferred a hallucination over going crazy.

"I can tell you this is real, given your understanding of reality. Rather than seek to understand, seek to accept and believe," Moezell offered.

"But why me? I know very little about thirteenth-century Scotland. I didn't even know they spoke English. I would have guessed they spoke Gaelic, or Scottish, or something like that," Teressa moaned with a heavy sigh. She realized she was whining and tried to get a grip, but it wasn't working as well as she would have liked.

"It is not your knowledge of history we find useful, it is your understanding of people and their relationships. But you are right.

Many people of this time and place do not speak English," Moezell replied.

"Guess I'm just lucky that Duncan knows English." Teressa was relieved to think something was working in her favor.

"Duncan speaks English much better than you speak Gaelic. However, we have arranged for you to understand these people and for them to understand you. It is a simple enchantment," the faerie explained.

"So he thinks I'm speaking his language?" Teressa asked, amazed.

"Correct, and to your ears, everyone you meet will speak English." Moezell appeared quite pleased with her enchantment.

"But how can that be?" Teressa questioned.

"All speech is simply sounds and symbols to convey messages. The enchantment is able to translate those sounds into a message you understand when it reaches your ears, much like creating the perfect pitch on a tuning fork. Simple," Moezell explained.

"Yeah, right, simple. And his strong Scottish accent?"

"It is his voice you hear, and his words; they are simply converted for your understanding."

Teressa was impressed by Moezell's explanation, but she realized anybody who could transport a person over seven hundred years back in time would have no problem with a simple matter of language translation. Since her situation was far too amazing for Teressa to fully comprehend, she resigned herself to following Moezell's advice and tried for simple acceptance.

Then the faerie said something completely unexpected. "When confronted with a distressing experience, it is beneficial to give yourself twenty-four hours to process the experience. This will give you time to evaluate the situation before you take action. It is important not to overreact in the heat of the moment. Such actions usually cause more problems than they solve."

Teressa stared at the faerie, speechless.

Moezell smiled and smoothed the folds of her gown, looking extremely pleased.

The words had hit their mark. They were right out of Teressa's master's thesis, "Critical MASS, the Benefits of Mutual Acceptance & Support Systems." That thesis, along with her master's degree in family counseling, had snagged her the job as a relationship coach at the university counseling center.

She felt the half smile make its way to her lips as she realized the irony of the situation. The very words she had written in her thesis were being used as advice for her wellbeing. Instead of following her own advice, she had been trying to make sense of a nonsensical experience. It was time to let go of her desire to control her situation, much less understand it, and just go with the flow.

Teressa wondered if she were up to the challenge. She was too overwhelmed and intimidated by the whole experience to be sure. Then she recalled another line from her thesis. *"Our understanding of any given situation has a way of revealing itself in time, usually as a benefit of hindsight."*

"Remember to enjoy the moment of now, for if you enjoy now, you will enjoy always," Moezell said, breaking the silence.

"You're telling me I'm going to be all right, aren't you?" Teressa asked, seeking reassurance.

Moezell nodded. "However, I must warn you. If you wish to return home, to your own time, you cannot tell anyone where you came from. This is most important." The faerie began to move toward the door.

"Wait! But Duncan already knows."

"Of this, I am aware. *You* must tell no one else."

"So you're telling me I'm going to return to my own time?" Teressa desperately hoped the faerie would answer this one question in a way that made sense.

A soft knowing smile brightened Moezell's face, and her eyes twinkled with mirth. "All will be well. It will be as you wish;

however, it may not be what you expect." And with her final cryptic answer, she simply faded from the room.

Now I know how Dorothy felt when she landed in Oz, thought Teressa. *Or maybe Alice when she fell down that rabbit hole.*

But as she often told her clients, acceptance of a situation is far more practical than denial. For her own peace of mind, it would be much better if she tried to accept her extraordinary circumstance rather than continue to fight against it. Besides, the mental struggle had given her a headache, whereas acceptance simply felt better.

She looked down at her watch on her right arm. It had stopped working and still showed 9:45 a.m., which would have been about the time of the windstorm when she blacked out on the beach. After she took off her watch and put it in her backpack, she continued to examine its contents, well aware she needed to hide the futuristic items. To think ordinary women were accused of witchcraft for much less than traveling through time, brought chills to her spine. Many innocent women had lost their lives for no other reason than they seemed different from the members of their community. These differences could have been anything from their appearance, to their unusual habits, or strange lifestyles. Heaven only knew what they would do to her if they saw her modern technology. Gathering up the tourist brochures and maps she had shown to Duncan, she realized the real danger they posed for her. In a rush, she stuffed the glossy papers back into the front pocket of the backpack and closed the zippered pouch.

The sunglasses and the camera would appear strange and would be difficult, if not impossible, to explain. She stashed them, along with her nonworking watch, in the inside zippered compartment.

Next, she took out the plastic water bottle and wondered how she was going to get rid of the futuristic material. She knew burning plastic was toxic and not a good thing to do, but at the moment, it seemed to be the most efficient means of disposal. First, she drank the water then tossed the empty bottle into the fire. The moment it touched the low burning fire, it burst into flames, quickly turning into harmless ash, as if by magic. She figured the faeries must approve of her actions and continued to inventory her belongings.

Finding the two travel-size packs of facial tissues, she clutched them to her chest. They were more precious than toilet paper on a camping trip. Chuckling at the thought, she stuffed them into the pockets of her jeans.

Teressa reached up to touch the plaid scarf she had purchased earlier that day—a day somewhere in the future. Pulling the scarf from around her neck, she brought the soft woolen fabric to her cheek and felt warmed by its touch. Somehow, it comforted her and calmed her soul. Drawing on its comfort, she lingered a moment longer with the fabric pressed against her cheek before she neatly folded the scarf and placed it in the pack. Hopefully, it would be safe there.

Looking around the room, she spied a large wooden storage trunk. She opened the lid and stashed the backpack inside, stuffing it to the bottom of the chest. Pleased with her efforts, she felt better, knowing she was doing what she could to take control of her situation. Feeling she had addressed her most pressing concerns, she returned the chair from under the window to its place by the hearth then sat down and waited for Duncan to return.

Sitting in silent meditation, she tried to come to terms with her bizarre situation, reassuring herself over and over everything would be all right. She was fairly certain Moezell had said as much, in her own peculiar way.

CHAPTER 4

As soon as Duncan returned, she began peppering him with questions. "Where did you go? Who did you see? Did you find out anything?" She wanted to know what he had learned before she told him about her visit from Moezell. In fact, it might be better not to say anything about meeting a faerie until she heard what he had to say. Her situation was already unbelievable enough as it was.

Duncan held up his hands in a gesture for her to slow down. "Hold there lassie, one thing at a time. I went to talk to our druid, Souyer. He believes himself to be a master druid, but he is far from that," Duncan said with disdain. "This morning, at the dawn of the summer solstice, he made a poorly worded request to the faeries, and it seems yer appearance here is the result."

It was comforting to hear that his story agreed with what Moezell had told her. Some of the pieces were beginning to fit together, but she was far from having a clear picture of the puzzle. She was even more surprised by his apparent acceptance of what to her was an extraordinary experience. "Is it common for druids to make requests of faeries and for people to appear from the future?"

"Nay, lass. I am not aware of this ever happening before. I do my best to stay clear of faeries and druids. I believe neither is to be trusted."

It was amazing to listen to Duncan speak of faeries, magic, and druids as if they were normal parts of everyday life. Before this morning, if she had heard anyone talk of such things, she would have strongly questioned their hold on reality. She had a high regard for the metaphysical and the possibilities of the unknown, but she had never taken her thoughts to the level of such things as wizards, faeries, and time travel. Until today, those things had been outside her realm of experience. Today, her realm of experience had been turned upside down and shaken with a great force until she was bruised to the core of her being. She was moving in unknown territory without a guidebook for reference. However, perhaps she was not without a guide. The appearance of Moezell seemed to indicate some type of assistance would be available to her, if she could only figure out how to access it.

"Now that I'm here, now what? Do you have any ideas on how to proceed? What will become of me? And will I . . ." She took a bracing breath and forced herself to ask the question foremost on her mind, the one she feared the most. "Will I be able to return to my own time?" She stared into his dark brown eyes.

"I'm sorry, lass, I canna say, but I have Souyer working on it."

"The same druid whose mistake brought me here in the first place?" she gasped.

"I know he's not much, but he's all we have for now."

She heard the concern in his voice; it didn't inspire any great confidence in her chances with the druid.

"Can't we ask the faeries to send me back?" Teressa asked.

"'Tis not so easy. The faeries are not easy to commune with, and even then, ye must be very careful how ye deal with them. Yer unexpected appearance here is proof of such."

"But a faerie contacted me," she admitted. "She came to this room while you were out looking for your Souyer."

"Ye talked to a faerie? Are ye sure? What did she say?" It was his turn to pepper her with questions as his eyes bore into hers, his expression changing from one of concern to one of amazement.

"She didn't tell me much more than what you've just learned from your Souyer." Teressa dropped her gaze as she considered her conversation with the faerie. "I think she wanted to comfort me."

"Did she say why ye were brought here?"

"No . . . not really. Only that I should accept my situation as it is for the time being." Teressa shrugged with a lack of conviction. "She also said I can't tell anyone else where I came from; not if I want to return home. And believe me, I want to go home."

There was a long moment of silence while Teressa considered the meaning of the faerie's message and what to do next. The fact Moezell felt it important enough to make an appearance indicated her visit was not expected to be a short one. It certainly didn't bode well for her chances of a speedy return to her time.

Duncan broke the silence, taking charge of the situation. "It looks as though ye will be here for a while. I canna keep ye hidden away in my chamber forever. We need to come up with an explanation of who ye are and where ye come from. And ye canna go about dressed like a man. Ye will need to dress as a woman."

"Dress like a woman?"

"Aye. I've been wondering why ye have chosen to disguise yerself in men's clothes when they easily show ye to be a woman."

Teressa nearly laughed, amused by his suggestion. "This isn't an attempt to disguise myself as a man. This is what women of my time wear."

Duncan looked her over from head to toe. "Things must change a great deal in the future if women must dress as men."

"We do not have to dress as men. It's our choice." She released her laughter, grateful to find some humor in her situation.

"Ye choose to dress as a man?"

Teressa shook her head. "Let's just say a lot has changed when it comes to fashion for men and women." Not wishing to take all afternoon to explain over seven hundred years of fashion evolution, she moved on to the more practical concerns of the moment. "So anyway, what do you suggest I do about my clothes? And what will be my story?"

"For yer clothes, we will need the assistance of my sister, Kayla. She is younger and a wee smaller than you, but I will rely on her to come up with suitable attire. As for yer story, since I found ye on the beach, and many of my clan observed yer arrival, we will need to start with how ye got here," Duncan began.

"We can tell them I was traveling by sea from England, and my boat hit a storm, and I fell overboard, and you found me passed out on the beach," she said, making it up as she went along. Since it was fairly close to the truth, she hoped it would be easier to remember. "I can say I don't remember how I got lost on the beach if anyone tries to press further, which is pretty much the truth."

"We cannot tell people ye were traveling alone. It would be questioned," Duncan reminded her.

"All right, if it makes you feel any better, I was traveling with a group of friends, some companions, and got separated. How's that?" It was obvious she was going to have to make adjustments for their cultural differences.

Duncan nodded in agreement. "We can claim ye are English. It will help account for yer strange manner of speaking. Ye also need to remove yer clothes before my sister sees you. They are not of our time and will be hard to explain."

"Oh, really, and what do you suggest I should do after I take off my clothes?" Teressa asked, rather dismayed at the thought of undressing in front of him.

She saw Duncan's grin before he turned to open the large storage chest where she had recently hidden her backpack. Holding her breath, she wondered if he would find it stashed there. He dug into the chest and pulled out a folded bundle of plaid wool. When he turned to offer her the fabric, she was amazed. It was woven in the same colors and pattern as the scarf she had purchased at the Village Inn.

"What is this?" She reached out to receive the startlingly familiar fabric, once again impressed by the warmth and comfort she felt as she fingered the soft folds of wool.

"'Tis my plaid. Ye can wrap yerself in it while ye await my sister."

"Your plaid. You mean, like the colors of your clan?"

"Aye, they are the colors of Scorrybreac."

She loved the way he said Scorrybreac, with the *r*'s rolling off his tongue.

"It's beautiful. It's exactly like the scarf I was wearing, the one I bought earlier today, in the twenty-first century . . . which is now a future tomorrow, many, many years from now." She tried to shake off her confusion.

"I'm glad ye like it. Our colors are highly honored," Duncan said with pride.

Teressa realized something far bigger than anything she could understand was in control. Everywhere she turned was another reassuring sign she was meant to be here.

"Ye can stash yer clothes along with the pack ye have hidden in the bottom of my chest," he told her.

"You know about my pack?"

"Of course, I noticed it was missing and saw ye had stored it in my chest." It was obvious Duncan did not miss much. "Actually, 'tis quite smart of ye to remove it from sight, along with those manly clothes ye are about to remove. I will tell my sister yer clothes were ruined and had to be discarded. She will not question me." With a parting nod, he left her alone in his chamber to search for his sister.

Once he was gone, Teressa looked down at her clothes and laughed, grateful she could find humor in her situation. She did appear to be dressed in men's clothes. At least it would look that way to a thirteenth-century Scotsman, and she figured she was darn lucky to have been found by this particular Scotsman. When he heard her story, he didn't freak out and call her a witch and threaten to burn her at the stake or anything scary like that. Instead, Duncan was strong, handsome, intelligent, and obviously very much in command of his surroundings. He was also a tad uptight, and her instincts told her he had secrets of his own. Well, who didn't?

She had to give him credit for his ability to deal with what she considered to be a pretty darn unusual—make that freakish—situation and remain remarkably calm and in control. *Him and me both*, she thought, giving herself equal credit. At least she hadn't broken down and cried, although there were a few times when she thought she would. She had so many questions and very few answers. Considering there were faeries and wizards and guardian spirits involved, she supposed anything was possible. Right now, her biggest concern was how she was going to get back home.

Teressa neatly folded her clothes, including her bra and panties, into a pile and then wrapped them up in her overcoat, creating a neat little bundle that she stashed along with her backpack at the bottom of the chest and then covered them up with Duncan's things. She didn't know when, or if, she would have the opportunity to use them again, but she trusted her belongings would be safe here, ready and waiting for her when she needed them.

It was a minor inconvenience to give up the use of her bra and panties, but she was determined to keep her boots and socks. No matter how out of place they looked, she wasn't about to sacrifice her feet to ill-fitting footwear. It would be her one bit of comfort. Besides, since he had called her English—as if that explained away her strangeness—she could very well be English with strange shoes.

She wrapped the plaid around her like an oversized bath towel and began to wonder what would be acceptable fashion for a woman of this time. From what little she knew, she believed women of this era had very few rights. They were governed by the men in their lives, be they husbands, fathers, or even brothers who were clan chiefs, and it was not unusual for a woman to be married off to secure land or create an alliance.

How can I possibly fit into this culture? What twisted reason could the faeries possibly have for kidnapping an independent twenty-first century woman and shoving her seven hundred years into the past? She figured only time would tell, and taking a deep calming breath, she tried to prepare herself for the adventure.

Knowing she was about to meet Duncan's sister made her think of her own family. What would they do when they learned of her disappearance? She had traveled to the remote Isle of Skye and then simply vanished without a trace. Only last night, she had called home and spoken to her brother, Daniel. She had spent the greater part of an hour telling him about her international travels and how much she was enjoying her vacation, wishing he were there. None of her family had any way of knowing what had happened to her. If one of her brothers simply disappeared without a trace, it would break her heart. It was too much to think about for too long, and she added it to the growing list of things for her to worry about later.

Teressa barely registered the knocking sound on the door before it opened. She expected to see Duncan's sister; but instead, she was greeted by one of the most gorgeous men she had ever seen—in any century.

He was the man she had seen out in the training field, the younger version of Duncan, only better. *Damn.* His reddish-brown hair fell in rich, luscious waves down to his broad shoulders, and the sensuous look in his stunning dark green eyes sent blood rushing to her head.

His expressive eyes briefly scanned the chamber before latching on to hers, and judging by the wicked smile spreading across his face, she was acutely aware of the moment he realized she was wearing nothing except the plaid wrapped around her body.

Teressa wasn't sure if it were because she was standing there nearly naked, and he was eyeing her with what could only be described as predatory eyes, or if it were because he was quite possibly the most spectacular specimen of muscular male she had ever seen, but she quickly became aware of several changes in her body. The first was an unmistakable pooling of warmth between her thighs, followed by the need to sit down before her melting legs gave out from beneath her. Her heart rate accelerated to a sprinting pace.

The man must have noticed her sudden case of dizziness. Without a word, he crossed over and caught her to his chest. "Here, lass, take a seat. Ye look a wee bit unsteady."

"Yes, I suppose I am," Teressa managed to say, feeling her legs betray her as she slumped into his arms. With his help, she staggered over to the bench. Gazing up at him, Teressa was aware she probably looked like a nitwit. Unfortunately, she found she was unable to take her eyes off him, much less speak coherently. *They sure don't make them like this anymore.*

"I'm Rory," he said, flashing a disarmingly appealing smile.

For a moment, despite the heat surging through her body, her brain remained locked in frozen slush. His smile was deliciously provocative and thoroughly disarming. Finally, she managed to speak. "I'm . . . I'm Teressa."

His eyes slowly scanned her figure, while her body temperature continued to rise as she felt them bore through the heavy wool fabric. She had no doubt he was mentally removing the plaid and was seriously, if not accurately, imagining her body completely naked.

Rory licked his lips. The subtle movement drew Teressa's eyes to his mouth. *Sexy and kissable* popped into her head.

Before she could explore that thought further, there was another knock on the door, announcing the arrival of Duncan's sister. The door opened slowly, and a face framed by deep red curls peered around the opening.

The girl took in the sight of the two of them, and opened the door wide. "Rory, what the blazes are ye doing here?" she asked.

"I was looking for Duncan. Have ye seen him?" Rory responded with nonchalance.

Teressa had to admire his composure.

"Aye." The younger woman motioned toward the hallway. "He asked me to come tend to the woman he brought in from the beach."

Teressa raised her hand. "That would be me," she said, thankful her breathing and heart rate were returning to normal. Lowering her hand, she touched her neck. The strength of her slowing pulse gave her reassurance. She breathed deeply and exhaled.

"Oh dear Mother of God," Kayla exclaimed as her eyes fastened upon Teressa. "I didn't expect you to be . . ."

"Undressed? Draped in a plaid? Perhaps Duncan told you my clothes were ruined. This seemed better than soggy, ripped clothing," she said, motioning to the plaid. "I was very unpresentable, I can assure you. By the way, I'm Teressa Ellers," she greeted the younger woman, grateful for the interruption. The presence of another woman effectively halted her raging hormones, allowing her body to return to its normal operating mode, at least as much as possible while Roy was still in the room.

"Aye, Duncan told me all about ye, being an Englishwoman and all. I'm his sister, Kayla." She rushed to take Teressa's hands in hers, crouching down in front of her. "How awful to be lost and separated from your family. It must be dreadful," she said.

"I'll be going now, Kayla. I trust ye to take good care of our guest." Rory said. Catching Teressa's eye over Kayla's shoulder, he gave her a slight bow then quietly slipped out of the chamber.

Teressa watched him leave, thankful for his discreet departure. The man was far too distracting. She wondered what had just happened. Of course, his sudden appearance in Duncan's office had been unexpected, but her reaction to him was also beyond anything she had ever felt before. Such an experience was unnerving.

Shaking her head to clear her mind, she turned her attention back to Kayla. "Oh yes, well, I really can't tell you much. One minute, I was enjoying a sea voyage, and the next thing I know, your brother finds me alone on the beach. Lucky me." Teressa shrugged.

She could tell Kayla had come prepared to find a traumatized and distraught victim, but all things considered, Teressa felt remarkably calm. Kayla's reaction also indicated she was not accustomed to strong, adventurous women and probably lived a sheltered life within the walls of Scorrybreac Castle, or the keep, as Duncan had called it. Kayla appeared to be no more than twenty years old, perhaps younger. Her pale green gown enhanced the color of her eyes and her thick red hair bloomed as a mass of curls around her petite face. The young woman's smallish features were a stark contrast to Duncan's strong masculine build.

"Now that ye have been rescued, we must get ye some proper clothes. Come, I'll take ye to my room. I am sure we can find something more proper than Duncan's plaid." The younger woman eyed her with apprehension. "At least, I hope I have something ye may wear," Kayla said, nibbling on her bottom lip.

Teressa could understand her concern. At five foot seven, she was a good three inches taller than Kayla. Sensing Kayla's discomfort, Teressa offered, "Perhaps you'll have something I can alter if needed. I'm pretty good with a needle and thread." She had learned how to sew from her mother and had even been successful at making a few simple outfits of her own, with *simple* being the operative factor.

"Oh, you're a seamstress," declared Kayla. "That can be very useful."

It was apparent Kayla had gotten the wrong impression from Teressa about her sewing abilities, but Teressa let it go for now. She added it to the list of things to worry about later, if she had to.

Teressa followed Kayla to her room. A small fire was burning in the hearth to warm the room against the morning chill, and a smallish bed with ivory bedcovers was tucked against one wall. All of the furniture was small and feminine in design compared to the room they had just left.

Kayla went to her wardrobe and searched its contents; there wasn't much there by modern standards, Teressa observed. She pulled out a long ivory linen shift and a simply gray wool dress.

"These fit quite loose on me, but they should work for ye," Kayla began, then lowered her eyes, as though fearful her comment seemed unkind.

Teressa took no offense. "Okay, let's give it a try." She held the shapeless dress up to her body. It would hang a few inches short of her ankles, but otherwise, it looked acceptable. "I think it might work."

There was a moment of awkward silence as both women stood watching each other. Since Kayla seemed intent on staying to watch over her, Teressa began to remove the plaid from around her shoulders. Kayla blushed when she realized Teressa meant to change right in front of her. She turned away and busied herself with rearranging the few remaining garments in her wardrobe.

Teressa smiled at the back of the younger woman and proceeded to change into the offered garments. As she pulled the shift on over her head, she was relieved to find it fit rather well. The simple cut of the overdress suited her figure, and thankfully, the soft woolen fabric had some give to it as it clung to her body in a flattering but not overly tight manner. It fell several inches short of the floor, with the bottom barely touching the top of her walking boots, which also suited Teressa, since she wasn't accustomed to walking about in full-length dresses. Looking down at the fit, she smoothed the fabric over her body, quite pleased with the overall effect.

When Teressa indicated she had finished changing, Kayla turned to see the results. "It looks . . . ah, like a tight fit. What do ye think?" Kayla looked worried.

"I think this works fine, thank you very much. You've been very kind. It's more than I could ask for."

Visibly relieved, Kayla responded, "Consider it yers. I was beginning to worry it wouldn't be acceptable, and I don't know what my brother would do if I failed."

"Is Duncan such a harsh man that you fear him?" Teressa asked, surprised at Kayla's reaction. She had found Duncan to be rather considerate once she got beyond his commanding facade. Most likely, her years of experience dealing with modern men made it easier for her to be comfortable around the intimidating man.

"Oh, nay, my brother is a kind and fair chief, but I don't want to disappoint him," the younger woman clarified.

"I think you've done quite well. And if it wouldn't be too much more to ask, do you have a shawl I can use? I'm not used to the cold and dampness of this area, and a cover would be a great help. I don't think I should keep using Duncan's plaid."

"Aye, of course, I have the very thing." Kayla turned to pull out a generous shawl in the same Scorrybreac plaid as Duncan's.

As Teressa draped the soft woolen fabric over her shoulders she felt comforted by its warmth.

"Well, if we're finished here, maybe you can give me a tour of your home, if it's not too much to ask." Teressa was anxious to see more of her ancient surroundings.

"It would be my pleasure. And if ye are hungry, we can stop in the great hall for the midday meal," Kayla offered.

Oh good, thirteenth-century food. This should be interesting.

Kayla led Teressa through the central building of the keep, showing her the family living quarters, Duncan's office (Kayla had called it a solar), and the common areas of the keep, including the great hall and the separate kitchens. As they walked through the keep, Teressa noticed Kayla was becoming more comfortable taking on her role as hostess.

When they arrived in the great hall, it was abuzz with activity as the midday meal was being served. A large crowd of guards, warriors, and serfs of the keep were gathered together for their daily meal provided by the chief, keeping the kitchen staff busy.

Teressa's eyes quickly scanned the room looking for Duncan, or maybe Rory, the man she had met in Duncan's room. She found them both sitting at the head table, surrounded by a number of other rough men. Duncan paid her no notice, but Rory briefly locked eyes with her for an intense moment of silent communication then acknowledged her with a nod of his head. Teressa smiled and returned Rory's nod of acknowledgment before he returned his attention to his conversation with one of the other men. She instinctively understood it would be improper for a woman to approach the men, so she let Kayla lead her through the great hall to a table reserved for the women of the keep.

As she took a seat next to Kayla, Teressa resolved to put Rory out of her mind. There was no reason to dwell on the handsome man or on her momentary surge of hormone-driven desire just because her body had overreacted to their unexpected meeting. She assured herself it was nothing more than a normal biological reaction to an exceedingly stressful situation.

She was surprised by the quality of the food brought to their table. For some reason, she had expected much worse. There was a platter of dried meats along with loaves of fresh-baked bread and hunks of cheese. Teressa politely declined the soup, which appeared to be a mixture of fatty meats and overcooked vegetables swimming in a thin broth. While it smelled good enough, it looked far less appealing. She considered how a diet of fats and protein would serve these hardworking people, but for herself, she wanted to stay as close to her normal diet as possible, under the conditions. The food was served family style on large platters, and everyone at the table simply helped themselves as they pleased.

It was obvious that Kayla was the highest ranking woman at the table. She engaged the other women in conversation, telling them about Teressa being lost and Duncan's rescue of her from the beach. Someone new and different like herself could not go unnoticed in such a small community, and the gossip was as severe as any small town she could imagine. Teressa sat politely through the many questions, trying to provide as little information as she could to avoid enlarging any stories already being passed around the Scorrybreac community. Finally, probably frustrated by her lack of cooperation, the ladies moved on to other subjects of local news, and Teressa was able to sit back and observe her surroundings. The sights and sounds, and even the smells, of this historic era fascinated her as she drank in the atmosphere of thirteenth-century culture, feasting on her unique opportunity. It was all pretty amazing, but she'd been to enough renaissance fairs to know this was a great time to visit, but she wouldn't want to live here.

When they had finished eating, Kayla asked Teressa if she would like to view the gardens of the keep. The smattering of coastal clouds and the chill of the morning had been replaced by a bright afternoon sun warming the south-facing gardens of the courtyard. A stroll would allow them to enjoy the sunny afternoon and give Kayla a chance to show off the gardens, which were a source of pride and joy for her mother. It was a lovely haven of peace and comfort, where one could easily spend hours enjoying the earth and its beauty. The garden had an old-fashioned cottage garden feel to it, with patches of flowers and herbs growing in a natural arrangement complementing the landscape. Paths meandered through the plants and flowers to provide access to the various sections of the garden while wooden benches placed among the flowers provided areas of rest and repose.

"These gardens have always been under the care and attention of my mother, Lady Lydia. She designed them and chose all the flowers and herbs planted here," Kayla explained with pride.

"Where is your mother now?"

"She's been away for several months, living with her sister. Aunt Marian has been ill and in need of Mother's healing care."

"You must miss her." Teressa felt a tightness in her chest as she thought of her own mother. Francine was her guiding light—her foundation for love of life, family, and God. The thought of never seeing her again tore at her heart.

"It was hard at first, being without my mother, but I understand my aunt needs her care and attention at this time of her life. I am the youngest of her four children and the only daughter."

"So you have three brothers. I'm guessing Duncan is the oldest, since he's chief of the clan." Teressa was interested to learn more about the MacNicol family.

"Aye, the second oldest is Michael, and Rory, the one ye met in Duncan's solar, is the youngest of the three. Rory's given name is Roderick, but he's been called Rory since he was a bairn. Michael lives with his wife, Shana, and their two boys in the east tower. He's Duncan's captain of the guard and is in charge of the warriors' training. I'm sure ye will meet them all this eve." Kayla's face glowed as she spoke of her family.

Teressa nodded, "Sounds wonderful. I also have three older brothers. I'm sure we have a lot in common." She tried to ignore Kayla's mention of Rory, he was definitely not someone she should be thinking about, but she was touched by Kayla's open display of affection for her mother and all of her family. No matter how cultures changed over the centuries, the love of family wove a continuous thread throughout time.

Teressa was admiring the simple beauty of the gardens when Bonnie, the head servant of the keep, approached Kayla to ask for her assistance.

"I am needed in the kitchens regarding the preparations for the evening meal," Kayla told her. "Will ye mind if I leave ye here in the garden by yerself?"

"I'm sure I'll be just fine," replied Teressa. "It will give me time to sit and relax and enjoy this lovely garden."

She took a seat on the bench with the warmth of the sun at her back and took a minute to appreciate the colorful collection of blooming flowers. A moment later, the reality of her situation threatened to overwhelm her, and she felt the sting of tears filling her eyes. *What the hell have I gotten myself into?*

CHAPTER 5

Teressa blinked away her tears and tried to focus on enjoying her moment of quiet when she heard someone entering the garden. She looked up to see Duncan walking toward her along one of the pathways. He greeted her with formal politeness. "Are ye enjoying yer tour of my keep?"

"Yes, very much, thank you," she answered. "I'm impressed with everything I've seen."

"What has Kayla shown ye?"

"Mostly the common areas, the kitchen, and the great hall. She's been a great tour guide, but she was called away just now as we came to these gardens."

"Aye, I saw her headed to the kitchens with Bonnie. I wanted to check on yer progress. Are ye faring well?"

"Do you always take such a personal interest in your guests?" Teressa asked.

"I consider it my duty to see to the comfort of anyone who has traveled so far to reach my keep. But since ye have been left alone, mayhap I can show ye one of my favorite sights. Would ye be interested in taking a walk with me?"

Teressa nodded and stood to follow him into the fortress courtyard.

Duncan led Teressa to a narrow tower with a staircase built into the outer fortress wall. It was noticeably cooler inside the thick stone walls of the tower, and she felt a mild chill as they entered the arched doorway to climb the circular staircase. When they reemerged in the sunlight, they were standing on the battlement walkway atop the curtain wall. The fortress wall sat high atop the ocean cliffs, overlooking the rugged sea below and the vast ocean spreading out as far as the eye could see. Turning around, she had a commanding view of the fortress grounds, the bailey, and the keep. Teressa immediately understood its appeal. It encompassed everything Duncan held dear in his land.

The view of the keep and the surrounding countryside was as impressive as that of the vast ocean. From this perch high above the bailey, one could freely observe the activity of the people below, smell the fresh scent of the ocean on the breeze, and hear the sounds of song birds competing with the gawking calls of sea gulls. Teressa was struck by the feeling of calm and orderly activity as the workers of the keep went about their daily duties. All was so peaceful, she could almost sense their feelings of contentment.

Looking out beyond the walls of the fortress, she could see the rolling green pastures and the sparse woodlands spread out to meet the rising foothills in the distance. Teressa turned first to face one view and then the other, completely absorbed in the splendor that greeted her senses, accompanied by the scent of the salt air and the sound of crashing waves from the ocean below.

"Oh my goodness," Teressa exclaimed. "This is amazing, truly amazing."

"The wind is strong and cold as it comes from the sea. 'Tis not too cold for ye?" Duncan asked.

"Oh no, I think I could stand here for hours and never tire of this view. The ocean on one side and your family lands on the other, Duncan; it's so grand. I don't know what else to say. Thank you for sharing this with me." Teressa could barely contain her pleasure.

~~~

Duncan felt a surge of pride for his clan and the abundance of their lands. He studied the woman standing before him. She was very different from the women of Skye, certainly more of an irritation, and if he were being honest, more intriguing. But right now, his only concern was to provide her with protection until she could be returned to her time. A woman such as her was a threat to his peace of mind. She had to go.

He had allowed himself to hope for love once before, only to feel bitter disappointment when it was snatched from his grasp. He vividly remembered the day he brought Janet MacDonald to the top of the battlement. She was uncomfortable in his presence and hardly seemed to notice the view, being more concerned about the cold ocean wind and the long drop to the churning ocean below. She had been anxious to return to the warmth of the great hall, where she could return to the company of her mother, Lady Evelyn MacDonald, who had accompanied her daughter to the MacNicol keep. Duncan painfully reminded himself it would truly be a cold day before another MacDonald would be welcomed in the home of a MacNicol.

The MacNicol clan had strived to maintain an uneasy peace with the MacDonalds over the years, but they clashed over basic ideology. The MacNicol clan believed in fairness and cooperation. They weren't a weak clan, but they preferred harmony over battle with their neighbors. They were hardworking farming and fishing people with great love and respect for the land and the sea that supported them. The MacDonald clan was far more aggressive, viewing land as a commodity to add to their wealth. It was a continuous struggle to control the borders between the two clans, and small skirmishes over land and cattle had broken out more often than desired. Duncan's parents had hoped an arranged marriage between him, their eldest son and future chief, and Janet MacDonald, the young daughter of Hugh MacDonald, would bring about a lasting settlement for the two clans, but it never came to pass.

During the summer games and fairs of the island, Duncan had watched Janet grow from a shy, quiet girl to a well-mannered pretty young woman. Duncan had naively allowed himself to believe their marriage could be a union of loving respect, similar to what his parents, Laird Kennon and Lady Lydia, had for each other. He had seen how the strength of their marriage had provided stability for their clan. Lady Lydia had steadfastly demonstrated her support of her husband and in return, she was well loved for her kind and generous spirit.

Duncan had seen how the support of a loving spouse created a stronger foundation for the clan and wanted the same for his life, but his dreams were dashed when Janet demonstrated she was not able to fill such a role. The betrothal was broken, and Janet returned home with her mother, taking her loyalty for the MacDonald clan with her.

He turned to observe the woman next to him. Teressa was not like Janet, she wasn't even of his time. Winds blowing in from the ocean whipped the loose strands of Teressa's hair about her head and shoulders, and she clutched her shawl around her, yet she seemed not to mind the cold.

"Ye're chilled," Duncan insisted. "We should return to the shelter of the keep. The breeze grows stronger during the sunset hours. Our evening meal will be served soon, and Kayla will be disappointed if we are not ready in time. She will want to honor yer visit."

"Oh no, she mustn't go to any trouble. I don't want to create a fuss." Teressa's eyes widened.

"I am not sure what *fuss* ye may create, but ye can be assured, the opportunity to play hostess will be a pleasure for Kayla. In the months since Mother's leaving, Kayla has only recently begun feeling comfortable taking on the duties as mistress of the keep."

"Yes, Kayla told me your mother, Lady Lydia, has left to care for her sister."

"Aye," Duncan nodded gravely. "I expect she shall return soon. 'Tis not in her nature to stay away for too long."

When they reached the entrance to the grand hall, they were greeted by Kayla, who had been looking for them, as Duncan had suspected.

"Duncan, 'tis near time to prepare for the evening meal," his sister informed them.

"I am aware of the hour," Duncan assured his sister. "Teressa, I expect ye will want to refresh before we dine." Before she could answer, he went on to instruct his sister, "Show her to Lydia's guest chamber. She will stay there during her visit. I'm sure Mother would approve." His firmly stated instructions overruled any protest from Kayla.

"As you say," Kayla replied demurely as Duncan made his departure.

~~~

Teressa watched the siblings interact and noticed that Kayla seemed to hesitate for a moment. She seemed unhappy with Duncan's request, and Teressa wondered if there were something she could do to comfort her. "You don't need to make a fuss over me. I'm sure I'll be fine anywhere you choose."

"Duncan is the chief of this keep, and I abide by his choices. 'Tis as he says. Mother would offer the same if she were here. She would not have it any other way." Kayla turned and marched stiffly toward the main staircase with Teressa following close behind.

As they climbed the stairs, Kayla continued to explain. "Mother is always generous to our visitors. She wouldn't want a guest of the MacNicol clan to feel uncomfortable. 'Tis our nature to provide hospitality to all who visit our home. As mistress of the keep in her stead, 'tis my duty to carry on these traditions."

Kayla pointed to one of the closed doors. "Since Father's passing, Duncan has occupied the master's bedchamber. Mother

61

has moved to a smaller chamber with an adjoining sitting room as her personal quarters. 'Tis the sitting room where ye'll be staying. It holds a wee day bed often used by her guests."

The rooms were located next to Duncan's chambers and faced out to the courtyard. As they entered the sitting room, the late afternoon sun streamed in through the one small window, casting a warm golden glow into the room.

Kayla did her utmost to assure Teressa of her welcome and to see to her comforts. She had a chest of Lydia's gowns brought in and reiterated that Teressa should avail herself of whatever she needed. Lydia had left these garments behind, and Teressa couldn't expect to always wear the same gray work dress. Teressa's concerns began to fade as her confidence in Kayla increased.

"As Duncan suggested, ye should relax and refresh before we supper. I will have Bonnie send up fresh water and light the fire. Please make yerself comfortable here. We will dine within the hour," Kayla advised before she left to return to her other duties.

Teressa was left alone to explore the sitting room. Her first impression was that Lady Lydia was a woman of taste and grace. The furnishings were simple, but tasteful, and finely crafted. The small but still ample bed was covered with a thick ivory quilt. Evidence of Lady Lydia's needlework skills was evident in the pillow covers and bed linens adorning the room. It seemed she specialized in floral designs done in soft pastels.

A few personal items and a couple of books lay on a side table. Near the middle of the room, a comfortable armchair sat in the pool of sunlight streaming in through the west-facing window. Teressa could easily imagine Lady Lydia working on her needlework as she enjoyed the warmth of the afternoon sun. Thick woolen tapestries hung on each side of the window as barriers against the chill of the stone walls. Scenes depicting lush gardens gave an impression of a view to the outside world beyond the stone walls of the chamber.

Teressa settled into the sunlit warmth of the armchair. She would be lying to herself if she didn't admit she felt a fair amount of excitement to being swept through time. It was an adventure on a grand scale. But on top of that was a heavy layer of fear whenever she thought about being stuck in this time, away from her family. Her family was her anchor, the heart of her soul, for one very good reason: she knew they always loved her.

She had only been a junior in high school when Sandy, one of her best friends, had attempted suicide. They had just gotten their SAT results, the all-important scores that determined what kind of college you could attend, and in her high school, academic competition was fierce. Eighty-five percent of the graduating class went on to college, many of them Ivy League. When Sandy got her test scores, she knew she was out of the running for the best schools, the only ones her parents expected her to attend. It had sent her over the edge. Seeking an escape from all the pressure, Sandy had called Teressa to let her know she was saying goodbye. Teressa could still hear Sandy's words, the message repeating in her head: "You're so lucky. You have parents who love you. I wish mine did."

Sandy had called her from the shopping mall parking garage, and Teressa could tell she had been drinking. Sandy's cry of desperation had been a sucker punch to her gut. She had gotten her older brother, Daniel, to drive her to the mall; she had been too afraid to have gone there alone. Together, they had been able to find Sandy and talk her down from the fourth story ledge. Sandy had been high on drugs and alcohol, ready to throw herself over the guardrail. When Teressa had peered over the ledge and thought of her friend landing on the hard concrete below, she had almost thrown up, nasty bile rising in her throat.

They had gotten to Sandy before it was too late, and her friend had survived, but they could never give her the one thing she needed and wanted most, the love and acceptance of her family. After that near tragedy, Teressa vowed she would never take her family for granted. She was one of the lucky ones, she was always close to her parents and brothers, and knew their love meant more to her than good grades, her close circle of girlfriends, or even her old boyfriend. She knew the love of a family was strong enough to save a life.

After that incident, Daniel had gone on to become a police officer, and she had pursued a degree in family counseling, specializing in young adult relationships. It had become her calling.

Against her better judgment, her thoughts returned to Rory, the man who had made the unexpected appearance in Duncan's chamber. His effect on her had caught her completely by surprise. Certainly, she was aware of his physical appeal—she wasn't blind—but on an intellectual and pragmatic level, she felt it best to resist thinking about him. Thinking about him too much, especially the thoughts he inspired, was asking for trouble, and she already had enough of that.

Patience and caution, my dear, she reminded herself, *patience and caution.* This adventure had only just begun, and as Moezell had advised, only time would tell.

Teressa's thoughts were interrupted by Bonnie's knock on the door as she arrived with a fresh pitcher of water for the washbasin. Dressed in a simple ivory tunic with a plain brown wool skirt, the elderly servant inspired thoughts of Mother Earth and loving care. She was a round woman, all curves and softness, hardy but not heavyset. The pure merriment in her soft brown eyes fit perfectly with the perpetual smile on her lips. Touches of gray in her chestnut-brown hair were offset by her natural youthful cheeriness.

"'Tis a lovely room," Bonnie offered in her friendly manner as she set down the pitcher. She bent to the task of lighting a fire in the large fireplace. "I for one am glad to see some use of it again. A room as fine as this should not sit idle."

"I see Lady Lydia has an appreciation for nice things," Teressa said, feeling very much at home with Bonnie.

"Aye, she does," Bonnie agreed. "She's a right fine lady, she is. 'Tis Lady Lydia who set the standard of living in this keep for many a years. She raised her children to be fine adults and can be proud of each of them. Duncan is a fine chief for our clan, Michael is a fine captain of our guard, and even our rascal Rory has nothing but a heart of gold where his family is concerned." After she had the fire lit and burning to her liking, Bonnie went to the chest holding Lady Lydia's gowns.

Teressa marveled at Bonnie's running commentary of the MacNicol clan. Leave it to the serving staff to have their opinions of the ruling family. She decided it wouldn't hurt to take advantage of Bonnie's insider knowledge, and hopefully gain an ally along the way. "Rory is the youngest of the brothers, isn't he?" Teressa asked, trying to sound indifferent.

"Aye, and the sharpest of the three, if ye ask me; though, they all be large as trees and as handsome as the day is long. Duncan and Michael are the serious ones. I'm thinking it comes from them being older and such, but 'tis Rory who's got all the charm," she said with true affection, "and laughter," she added, chuckling to herself.

"I look forward to meeting them, if I get the chance," Teressa said, ignoring the fact that she had already met Rory, if only briefly.

"I expect ye will be meeting them at this evening's meal. Michael and his wife, Shana, and Rory, they're all expected for supper." Bonnie began to unpack Lady Lydia's gowns, shaking them out and arranging them on hooks in the wardrobe.

"Does the family always dine together for the evening meal?" Teressa inquired. She hoped they were not making a special occasion for her.

"Aye, miss. On most evenings, the family makes a point to gather for supper. 'Tis one of Lady Lydia's rules to always have her family dine together."

A feeling of anxious anticipation filled Teressa. "If I am to meet the rest of the family, I would like to make a good first impression. Bonnie, do you have time to help me prepare for dinner?"

"It would be my pleasure, lass. When Laird Kennon and Lady Lydia were the head of the MacNicol clan, I had the pleasure of being Lady Lydia's personal chambermaid. I often assisted my lady in dressing for special occasions." Bonnie glowed at the request, obviously excited for the opportunity to revisit her role as personal handmaid. She pulled out a soft buttery-yellow gown from the wardrobe and held it up for Teressa's approval. "How's about this one? I think it will suit ye well."

"Oh no, I don't think I should wear Lady Lydia's clothes." She took a step back with a shake of her head.

"I can assure ye, miss, 'tis what she would want."

"Are you sure?"

"I'm sure," Bonnie stated with a reassuring look.

Teressa was impressed by the selection of the gowns; it reconfirmed Teressa's impression of Lady Lydia as being a woman of good taste. With a nod of approval, Bonnie set about assisting Teressa with her preparations for the evening.

~*~

Duncan made his way to his solar in search of solitude and a stiff drink. A bit of malt whisky would do him good right about now, he figured. *What was I thinking?* Duncan questioned himself. *Or not thinking was more likely. An attractive woman, supposedly from the future, appears on the beach, and suddenly I become charmed, as if I mean to impress her.*

He admitted she was an interesting lass, but even more fascinating were the extraordinary circumstances of her appearance. There had to be a reason why she had been brought to his keep from the future, but until he uncovered the reason, he felt it best to maintain some distance—emotional distance. In the past three years, he'd become quite practiced at maintaining emotional distance.

His reaction to Teressa had provoked memories of Janet MacDonald and their failed engagement. He'd been a moonstruck youth when he first encountered Janet as his betrothed and had willingly imagined a love match as part of the arranged union. Her sweet, youthful beauty and shy, gentle manner had won his affections completely. He could still picture her soft brown hair with its auburn highlights as it framed her delicate face. Large, deep brown eyes dominated her fine features, increasing her appearance of innocence. Duncan had allowed himself to believe she held true affection for him. Janet's gentle touches and quiet conversation had swept him up in youthful desire. But he also remembered the day she left with hardly a backward glance as her mother led her back to the safekeeping of the MacDonald clan. When it had been most important, she had been unable to stand up to her strong-willed mother to declare her loyalty to Duncan and the MacNicol clan.

Reluctantly, he acknowledged the challenge Teressa presented. He found it difficult to believe she had been brought to Skye by the magic of the faeries, and yet his instincts confirmed it to be true. Much as he would like it to be otherwise, he had no other way to explain her strange appearance. Still, he didn't believe many women could be pulled through time and handle it as well as Teressa did. Even so, while she was an attractive woman of notable intelligence, even desirable, Duncan was well aware she wasn't the woman he truly desired.

~~~

Rory gave a hard knock on the heavy wood door and, without waiting for an answer, let himself into his brother's solar.

"I was told I would find ye here. I see ye have found an English lass to keep ye company," Rory said as he took the chair across from his brother.

Duncan raised a questioning eyebrow in response.

"I saw ye earlier in the garden with her." Rory had spied on them from atop the fortress wall. He had also seen Duncan bring her into the keep, draped lifeless in his arms, had seen her face as she scanned the courtyard from Duncan's window, and had caught her watching him as he trained in the bailey. And each time, he had become more and more intrigued. "So tell me about our new visitor. Where is she from? What brings her to our keep?"

"Reasonable questions, 'tis certain, but I have no reasonable answers. I know very little about where she comes from, except 'tis a faraway place, and even less about why she is here."

"Has she told ye nothing?" Rory asked, astonished by the lack of information.

"I believe she has told me all she knows, which is very little. I found her on the beach below the cliffs. She had the unfortunate experience of being tossed overboard while on passage from England, and remembers very little about what happened. The shock of it all, I suppose."

"Will she not be missed? Shouldn't someone be looking for her?" Rory persisted.

"That is to be seen, as she has no family in the area. I have made inquiries at the village, but until we hear something more, there is not much we can do for the moment. I expect time will tell. For now, she is a guest of the MacNicol keep."

Rory liked what he heard. It sounded as though she would be with them for a while. He liked it a lot. There hadn't been a fresh, young female worth pursuing at the keep in months, if not years, and he welcomed the opportunity to sharpen his skills of seduction.

Duncan broke into his thoughts. "How are ye doing with the preparations for our travel to the Isle Faire? Will we be ready to leave by week's end?"

The Isle Faire was a gathering for the clans living on the Isle of Skye when the elders, the chiefs of the clans, met to strengthen their alliances. Rory hardly saw Duncan as an elder, but as chief of the

MacNicol clan, it was his brother's duty to take his rightful place at the gathering. This was only the second such gathering since their father's death, and Duncan's first appearance had been little more than an opportunity for him to observe the other chiefs, as far as Rory could tell.

"No worry, big brother. I have everything well in hand. Michael and I have agreed on which warriors will stay here with Michael to guard the keep and which of the warriors will accompany us to the faire."

Michael, the second oldest of the brothers, was designated to stay at the keep with his wife and family. As captain of the guard, it was his responsibility to keep the fortress well-guarded during the chief's absence. Kayla and Rory would accompany Duncan to the Isle Faire, along with an array of servants, serfs, and warriors. Many of the local villagers would also be attending the faire. It was a festive time for the people of Skye to meet and mingle, to exchange news of distant family members, and an opportunity for them to trade their wares.

"I've also made arrangements for Mother's travel," Rory continued. "She is not expected to return home until near the day of our departure. She was hoping Aunt Marian would be well enough to attend the faire, but since she cannot travel, Mother wishes to stay with her sister as long as possible. Of course, any of these preparations may alter if Mother decides to change her mind." He was quite familiar with his mother's tendency to covertly control the details of her travels.

"Kayla is looking forward to seeing Mother, and I'm sure Michael and Shana would appreciate a few days of her company before she must return to Aunt Marian. But as you say, we will know more once she has arrived."

Duncan and Rory continued to discuss travel arrangements until it was time to move to the great hall for the evening meal. As the family gathered in the great room, each moved to take their place at the large banquet table. As chief of their clan, Duncan sat at the head of the table with Michael on his right and Rory on his left. As usual, Rory positioned himself at the chair to Duncan's left, but he didn't take a seat. Duncan raised a questioning eyebrow in response to the actions of his youngest brother, but before Rory could offer an explanation, he saw Teressa appear at the top of the stairs.

She wore a soft yellow gown that hugged her curves in all the right places. Her long hair had been swept back from her face and braded with ribbon; it hung to the middle of her back. A low, soft whistle escaped Rory's lips.

CHAPTER 6

Teressa stood for a moment at the top of the stairs and made a quick assessment of the MacNicol clan. She couldn't help but notice the three equally large brothers, they seemed to fill the room. While all three were impressively handsome, it was the youngest brother, Rory, who seemed downright godlike in a rough-and-tumble sort of way. She guessed the third man, the one she had not yet met, to be their brother, Michael.

Oh my goodness, they're real Scottish warriors, she thought and hoped her audible gasp wasn't heard by the family gathered below.

She gave herself a moment to gather her wits before she made her way down the staircase and through the great hall to approach the dining table. Despite her nervous anticipation, Teressa was determined to present an appearance of confidence to the members of the MacNicol clan. Smiling sweetly, she stepped into the room.

Kayla advanced to greet Teressa and introduce her to the rest of the family, and Teressa exchanged brief greetings with Shana and Michael. Duncan, she noted, remained seated at the head of the table. It was Rory who moved forward to greet her, guiding her to take the chair at Duncan's left before he sat next to her. Questioning glances were exchanged amongst Duncan, Rory, and Kayla, and she wondered what they were about.

"How nice to finally meet ye, Mistress Ellers," Rory greeted her with enthusiasm, as though for the first time.

Yeah right! Rory's charmingly bold manner immediately made him suspect in Teressa's view. It might seem petty and cliché, but in her experience, exceedingly handsome men were usually skirt chasers, and she doubted much had changed over the centuries. In her opinion, life often did a disservice to men and women of extraordinary good looks by depositing the world at their door.

Appreciating the opportunity to study the man without the distraction of being nearly nude and having blood rush to her head, she noted that Rory appeared to be a younger and apparently more approachable version of Duncan. His dark brown hair was streaked here and there with sun bleached strands and fell in waves to touch his broad shoulders. There was a merry sparkle in his stunning green eyes, strongly hinting at his lively sense of humor, and his smiling, full sensual lips revealed surprisingly straight, white teeth. Her limited observation of the thirteenth century told her that regular dental hygiene was sorely lacking compared to twenty-first-century standards.

Bonnie had been right in her earlier commentary, for while Rory was not quite as tall as his two older brothers, he was in no way lacking in physical stature. He had the same broad muscular chest and arms as his oldest brother, she noticed with heartfelt approval.

After taking her seat, Teressa turned to Duncan with a respectful nod. He presented the perfect image of lord and master of his domain. "Good evening, my lord," she greeted him with a mild hint of sarcasm, wondering if the formal address were politically correct.

He returned her greeting with an equally polite nod. "Good eve, Mistress Ellers. Welcome to our table."

As if on cue, the servants began to bring food to the table, and the meal became the center of attention for everyone. Everyone except Rory, who, Teressa noticed, was making her the center of his attention. Although his behavior wasn't overly obvious, her awareness of him was considerable.

"Mistress Ellers, are ye enjoying yer visit to the MacNicol keep?" Rory began with the usually expected small talk to be exchanged by strangers.

"Yes, thank you. Although I've only just arrived, I am finding it to be most interesting."

"How have ye come to arrive at our fair isle?"

Teressa looked at Duncan for a hint of direction or assistance, but a shift of her eyes in his direction showed him to be engaged in conversation with his brother Michael. If he were aware of Rory's inquiries, he was leaving Teressa on her own to handle his youngest brother.

"It was a boat," she replied honestly, thinking of the ferry that had brought her to the island.

"Do ye have friends or family here?" Rory persisted. If nothing else, the man was good at being persistent.

"No, I was traveling with friends, but my plans were unexpectedly altered when I got tossed overboard." She thought back to Lilly and Zoey, whom she had met briefly in twenty-first century Skye. They could almost qualify as friends.

"Duncan tells me ye have traveled quite some distance to arrive at our Isle of Skye. Are ye from England?" Rory continued his questioning as he spooned up a serving of lamb stew.

"My family's heritage is English, although we no longer live there." Teressa realized Rory was determined to stay on a path of discovery, and she was just as determined to lead him down a primrose path to nowhere. Wanting to direct the spotlight away from herself, she asked him, "Have you lived on Skye all your life?" Even though she was fairly certain she could guess the answer, it was a useful tactic. *If you don't like the direction the conversation is headed, change the direction.*

"I was born here in this keep and have always lived here, except for the years I spent working on a fishing vessel. I've sailed all around these islands. Where were ye born?"

Teressa avoided his direct question and instead focused on the one bit of information he had included in his reply. "You've traveled around Scotland? How grand. I've always wanted to explore the islands. Please tell me more." She stated her inquiry with enough earnest interest to ensure Rory would be unable to deny her request. It was aimed directly at his ego, and it worked.

"My father, Kennon, the MacNicol chief, arranged for me to foster with my uncle. It was his intention to expand my view of the world," Rory began with a hint of pride.

From down the table, Michael interrupted, "I've always thought our father's true motivation was to remove Rory from underfoot for as long as our cousins would tolerate him."

Laughter erupted from the table and soon all of the siblings were engaged in telling anecdotes of family history, many of them centered on Rory's madcap adventures and rebellious nature. True to her initial impression, Rory seemed to take the ribbing all in stride, deflecting the jibes with humor. Teressa listened to their tales and laughed along with them, feeling much more relaxed than when the evening began.

The main course had ended, and they were being served a dessert of sweet cream and berries when an old man in a long pale gray robe and carrying an intricately carved walking stick entered the great hall. He requested a servant to set a place at the table across from Duncan, and to bring him an extra-large serving of the berries and cream. Teressa noted that the old man's appearance brought a tightening to Duncan's jaw, indicating a minor displeasure if not open disapproval of their newly arrived guest.

"Souyer," Duncan greeted the old man with a rather gruff tone. "'Tis unusual for ye to grace us with a visit to our table; although, I suppose I shouldn't be surprised. Ye seem to have a knack for showing up when the sweets are being served." The edge in his voice indicated several levels of meaning between them.

Teressa quickly realized Souyer was the druid responsible for bringing her to this time and place, and her interest went on high alert as she watched the exchange between Duncan and the old man.

"Usually, Bonnie has a serving of the sweets reserved in the kitchen for me to enjoy, along with her very pleasant company. Tonight, I felt I should join ye here in the hall. I wouldn't wish to miss the pleasure of meeting yer new visitor. Surely, ye will do the honors of an introduction," Souyer replied before digging into the large helping of berries placed before him.

Teressa thought she might have heard Duncan's teeth grinding together before he said, "Souyer, this is Mistress Teressa Ellers from England. And, Mistress Ellers, this is our druid, Souyer."

"Master Druid," Souyer interjected, glaring at Duncan.

Teressa was momentarily dumbstruck at how to address a person who had aided the faeries in summoning her back over seven hundred years in time. "Umm, Master Souyer, how nice to meet you."

"I am fairly certain the pleasure is all mine, Mistress Ellers," Souyer said with a snarky grin. "Ye bring a bright star to our dreary daily lives here at the MacNicol keep on the Isle of Skye."

Teressa caught Rory rolling his eyes, and a smile tugged at her lips. It took considerable restraint on her part not to smirk as she silently shared Rory's reaction to Souyer's elaborate greeting. Teressa decided to play along with the old man. "You're most kind, Master Souyer, but I wouldn't think of competing with the stars above. I'm sure they shine bright over the MacNicol keep."

"Aye, the stars do shine bright," Souyer agreed. "Mayhap ye will allow me the pleasure of giving ye a personal viewing from my high tower observatory. A clear night such as this will make for fine viewing."

Teressa shuttered at the thought of being alone with the druid. Though such an opportunity would give her a chance to question the old guy in private about her passage through time, she was leery of being alone with a wizard. "That sounds quite nice, but I'm not sure what plans the MacNicol chief may have for us this evening." Teressa looked pointedly at Duncan, silently demanding his assistance.

Thankfully, this time, Duncan came to her rescue and stated flatly, "If ye wish to see the stars, I shall accompany ye."

For a moment, Souyer directed his hooded gaze at Duncan, but the clan chief pointedly chose to ignore the druid's frosty stare. The old man softened his expression as he turned to address Teressa. "Since 'tis decided by our laird, let us be on our way. The stars await." He scooped up a final spoonful of the berries before rising from the table.

Duncan rose as well and extended his hand to Teressa.

"Allow me," Rory offered then stood, as if to accompany them. Duncan shot him a daunting look and shook his head. Rory looked unhappy, but stayed behind as they left the room.

They must really take this chief thing serious, Teressa thought, as she followed Duncan out of the hall. She hadn't intended to look back, but she heard Rory's laughter sail across the room and felt compelled to look. When she did, their eyes met, and for one brief moment, she had the strongest sense of *déjà vu.* Even though she looked away, she knew he was watching her as she walked out the door.

~*~

The chieftain, the druid, and the time traveler made their way to the top of the high tower and stepped out on the rooftop. Teressa was immediately bedazzled by the brightness of the stars. There were so many, and they appeared much brighter than any she had seen before. These same stars would still hang in the night sky centuries from now, and yet she hadn't been able to experience their true brilliance in her modern age because of the effects of electric lights.

Her enjoyment of the moment was interrupted by Souyer asking, "Mistress Ellers, how fares yer visit to our Isle of Skye? How might it compare to where ye come from?"

"So far, it's been a rather interesting adventure. Like nothing I've ever known before." She kept her face turned skyward, intentionally keeping her answer vague as she anticipated the druid's strategy.

"How is this different?" Souyer persisted.

"Well, for one thing, I live in a big city, and the stars do not shine as brightly as they do here," she replied. She turned to face the druid.

"What could make the stars shine less bright?" The old man sounded intrigued by the concept of such a changed future.

"I'm sure the stars aren't less bright, but there are far more lights in the city. The reflection of all those man-made lights dims the brightness of the stars," she explained.

"Interesting. Where is this city ye speak of?" Souyer asked with a note of irritation.

Teressa looked at Souyer with a contented grin. It was rather fun to string him along, and she wondered for a moment whether she should continue to dance around the druid's inquiries or get right to the heart of the matter. If he had been hoping to trick her into making false revelations, he had failed. Since both the faerie Moezell and Duncan had confirmed he was somehow involved in this situation, she decided to relent and go for the stark facts.

"I live near a city called San Francisco, in California, and until earlier this morning, I was in the twenty-first century. I understand you had something to do with bringing me here, to this time. What can you tell me about *that*?" she shot back at the druid.

Her boldness obviously surprised the old man. He reacted by standing a bit taller as he assessed her. "What makes ye think I had something to do with yer appearance here?" he questioned with forced innocence.

Teressa thought for a moment and then got right to the point. "I was visited by a woman. She was quite lovely; she told me she's a faerie, if you can believe that. She also told me your summer solstice request is the reason for my jaunt through time. Is that right?"

Souyer did not attempt to deny the accusation. Instead, he looked rather amazed. "Ye were visited by a faerie? Did she tell ye her name?"

"She called herself Moezell."

"Moezell!" Souyer exclaimed, taking a step back. "Are ye sure?"

"Of course, I'm sure. Do you think I would make that stuff up?"

From the dim light of the torches flickering nearby, Teressa could see Duncan watching her with a look of approval.

"Moezell is said to be a granddaughter of the Faerie Queen. 'Tis said she is a powerful faerie and quite mischievous when it comes to meddling in the affairs of humans."

"If faeries are so mischievous and meddlesome, why in the world would you go about asking them for favors?"

"Not all faeries are mischievous. Some can be quite nice, sometimes. I didn't expect my request would gain the attention of the queen's granddaughter. These lands are full of lesser fae. How was I to know Moezell would get involved?" Souyer defended his actions.

"Ye were willing to risk yer request would work out the way ye intended?" Duncan interjected.

"I canna see the advantage in focusing on how this has come about. It seems to me we would be better served if we determined what to do now," Souyer said in a manner that was totally self-serving.

Teressa considered his recommendation and had to agree it was the best choice for now. As much as she wanted to continue to berate the druid for his recklessness, she knew it would do no good; done was done. Apparently, Souyer had wanted some kind of knowledge from the future, she had wanted a vacation adventure, and this was the answer the fates had conspired to provide. All she wanted now was to figure out a way to get back home.

"I do not have time for this disturbance," Duncan nearly shouted. "In less than a sennight, we travel to the Isle Faire."

"What's a sennight, and what's the Isle Faire?" Teressa asked.

"A sennight is seven days," Souyer said.

"The Isle Faire is a gathering of the island clans," Duncan provided as a curt explanation.

"A meeting of all the clan chiefs," Souyer added.

"Perhaps I should accompany you to this gathering. It kinda makes sense, you know, the timing and all," Teressa offered without thinking twice. At first, the idea surprised her, but as she thought about it, it seemed reasonable her appearance was somehow tied to this upcoming event. Since she wasn't sure how, or even if, her twenty-first-century relationship coaching skills would be put to use in this time and place, she decided not to offer her services, at least not yet. It was unlikely these thirteenth-century men would see any value in a relationship coach, or even know what one was, but she suspected her skills might prove useful at such a gathering. When the time was right, she would reveal her talents.

"Yer idea has merit." Duncan cupped his chin in his hand, considering her offer. "Agreed," he stated, looking a little leery. He probably didn't want to let her out of his sight. "Ye will travel with Kayla. And we will all agree to keep Teressa's origins secret." He turned his gaze pointedly toward Souyer.

"Moezell said we can't tell anyone," Teressa confirmed.

"I quite agree," Souyer huffed, as if offended by Duncan's insinuation.

"We only need say ye have been separated from your companions while traveling from the south of England. If there are any inquiries into your family or past, I trust ye will deal with such questions," Duncan said.

Teressa nodded, reassured by his confidence in her. She figured she had already demonstrated her ability to deal with Rory, which was a fairly remarkable feat in itself.

Rory was keenly aware of the interactions between Mistress Ellers and his family throughout the evening, and when he saw her leave with Duncan and the druid Souyer under the guise of viewing the stars, his interest continued to grow. His eldest brother would never agree to go anywhere with Souyer if he could avoid it, which meant Teressa was the deciding factor.

He wondered how an attractive, intelligent, and witty woman could show up at their keep without anyone knowing who she was, where she came from, or why she was here. And even more interesting was that Duncan, the chief of their clan, didn't seem concerned. Teressa Ellers created far more questions than answers.

Michael and Shana hadn't shown any undue interest in Teressa, at least no more than they would to any other visitor to their keep. Kayla seemed to know a wee more, but he suspected her knowledge of Teressa was only slightly greater than his, which was very little. It was her connection to Duncan and Souyer that caught his attention.

Her connection to Duncan was reasonable. Besides being his oldest brother and chief of the clan, he was the one who had found her on the beach and brought her to their keep. While it didn't appear Duncan was overly keen on wooing Teressa, at least he hoped that wasn't the case, there was obviously some type of connection between the two of them. Duncan hadn't shown any real interest in another female in years, since his broken betrothal to Janet MacDonald, and for his own sake, Rory hoped there was no reason to believe anything had changed.

Souyer's interest in the lass only added to the mystery surrounding her. The old druid tended to keep to his own company since Kennon died and Duncan became chief of their clan. Not only was it unusual for the druid to show up at their dinner table, his obvious interest in Mistress Ellers was undeniably strange.

These observations alone made Teressa worthy of further investigation, but Rory was well aware of his own interest in the lass. His curiosity had first been piqued when he saw Duncan ride into the bailey with her, and then he had caught her watching him from Duncan's window. Aye, he had caught her interest. Her reaction when he found her nearly disrobed in Duncan's solar was deeply pleasing. Even from a distance she had gained his attention, it was no surprise their brief meeting in Duncan's chamber was nothing less than stimulating. But when she entered the great hall for dinner, his senses went to a whole new level of awareness. She seemed near his age, which suited him quite well. From his experience, mature women were far more interesting than young innocents who hadn't yet learned their way in the world of men. Teressa was comfortable with herself, and it showed in the way she carried herself even as she entered a room full of strangers. She was no shy lass.

There was no denying her appeal, even if the real enticement was yet to be discovered. Granted, much of his interest was due to the unusual circumstances surrounding her arrival, but it didn't hurt that she was someone new and exciting to seduce. Seduction of women came easily to him—sometimes too easily—but Teressa Ellers offered the possibility of a real challenge, one that included a healthy dose of raw physical attraction. Regardless of the reason, learning more about the woman had its appeal.

He'd had enough experience with women to know she was also interested in him. Though she didn't easily give herself away, as a younger lass might, he saw the way she watched him and the attentions she paid him, keeping him in her sights when she thought he wasn't looking. She was a sly one, he'd give her that, and wouldn't be an easy one to bed, but there was little fun in easy. A good challenge was far more enjoyable.

Her unusual circumstances had brought up a whole new set of questions. Where was her family? Where was she from? Since she appeared to be well bred and highly educated, shouldn't her family be worried about her? Being an attractive woman, well past the age of innocence, it seemed reasonable she should be married, and yet no mention of a husband or family had come up during the evening's conversation. In fact, as he thought about it, he realized she had offered very little information about herself and had consistently directed the conversation to stories about him and the MacNicol clan. Aye, she was a sly one.

Rory mulled over the matter while he lingered alone over another tankard of ale in the great hall. His attention was diverted from his speculations when he heard the return of Duncan and Teressa to the upper galley bedchambers. After listening to ensure each had retired to their own chamber, Rory impulsively dashed up the stairs to the guest room assigned to Teressa. He didn't have a well-thought-out plan, but he was certain he could think of some excuse to see her alone, away from the keep.

He crept down the hallway, watching for any signs of his family while keeping one eye trained on Duncan's chamber. Rory knocked softy on Teressa's door and rejoiced when he heard her footsteps on the other side. When she cracked open the door, he raised his finger to his lips to signal her silence, then quietly slipped into her room.

"Rory MacNicol, what are you doing here?" Teressa asked in a whisper, sounding duly surprised.

Aye, what was he doing here? He couldn't very well admit he had come to ask for a late night meeting, alone, in her bedchamber. After a moment of quick thinking, he said, "Ah, I've come to ask ye to go riding with me in the morning . . . so I may show ye the countryside." Hopefully, an early morning ride alone would provide the opportunity he needed to pursue the answers to his many questions.

"Riding? With you? In the morning?" Teressa repeated, as if she misunderstood his meaning.

"Aye, ye do ride, don't ye?"

"Well, yes, of course, I know how to ride." She paused. "You've come here *now* to ask me to go riding?"

"Aye. I hoped we could get an early start, and it seemed best to ask ye now, before ye retire for the night. Aye, an early morning ride before we break fast would be . . ." *Would be what?* He paused, searching for a proper reason. *An opportunity to get ye alone*, he thought, but stopped short of speaking his true intentions.

Before he could think of a reasonable reason, besides the obvious, she asked, "Just how early do you have in mind?"

That was good, surprising, but good. "Would sunrise work for ye? 'Tis a fine time of day, and I am hoping for an early start," he stated again in a hopeful tone.

For a moment, she looked doubtful. "All right, at sunrise," she finally accepted.

"I will send a lad to bring ye to the stables and will have the horses readied. How well do ye ride? I want to choose a suitable mount." Rory felt himself warming to the task. This could prove to be just the type of outing to satisfy his intentions.

"I've ridden most of my life. I grew up on a horse ranch."

"Very well then, I shall have the matter well in hand." *Aye, well in hand indeed*, he thought, as he began to mentally plan the morning's activity. "I'll leave ye now to yer rest and will send for ye in the morning." With a courtly bow, he left her chamber.

~*~

Teressa stared at the closed door for several seconds before releasing her breath. *Oh, my goodness! Riding with Rory. This should be interesting.* A feeling of excitement swelled within her. An invitation to go riding with a thirteenth-century warrior, a brother to the chief of the clan, was nothing less than amazing. She wondered if he qualified as a Scottish prince? Regardless, she was certainly getting more from her summer vacation than she had ever imagined.

When she heard the knock, Teressa had thought it was Duncan at her door with some last bit of advice or encouragement. She wasn't overly surprised when it turned out to be Rory seeking entrance into her room. She'd been aware of his interest all evening and had wondered if he would find a way to approach her. Still, she was a bit surprised at the speed and directness of his chosen contact. Surely, a late night visit to a woman's bedchamber was not considered proper, especially on her first day as their guest. While she had no problem with his impromptu visit, she probably shouldn't have encouraged his behavior.

To be honest, she was somewhat less excited when he had asked her to wake before sunrise. Besides being the longest day of the year, the day had been a taxing one, and she was looking forward to getting a good night's rest. Interestingly, when faced with a choice between sleeping in and going on a ride with Rory, it had been a no-brainer. Rory won out.

Teressa smiled as she considered his request. Rory was itching to get her alone, and she was interested enough to find out why. It was easy enough to guess he wanted to learn more about her; that was to be expected considering she was a stranger to his keep. Even though she had deliberately dodged his questions at dinner, he seemed determined to pursue his investigation. She also considered how time alone with the handsome warrior could be both interesting and adventurous. His physical appeal alone would make the outing enjoyable.

Her first priority was finding a way home as soon as possible, but until the faeries were done with her, she figured she was here to do their bidding. And like it or not, since she was here, she saw no reason why she couldn't have a little fun along the way.

I wonder what women of this time wear to go riding, she thought, looking down at the full-length yellow gown she was wearing. It was unlikely she could wear jeans, which would be her first choice. A smile tugged at her lips as she remembered Duncan's initial reaction; he had believed her to be disguised as a man. She went to the wardrobe to investigate its contents. Hanging on one of the hooks was a long, full skirt of deep burgundy wool with a matching tunic. It would work nicely for sitting a horse.

"Well, well, well, Moezell, my mischievous little faerie, I hope you're pleased by all this." Though she spoke out loud to an empty room, she felt quite certain she heard the slight tinkling sound of a faerie's laughter.

CHAPTER 7

Teressa had just finished lacing up her precious and comfortable hiking boots to go with the riding skirt when a young stable lad came knocking at her door. When they stepped outside, slanting rays of sunlight were beginning to spread over the bailey.

He certainly is prompt, she thought as the boy led her out to the stable yard. Rory was already there, holding the reins of two horses saddled and ready for their early morning ride. One was a rather large breed that looked something like a Clydesdale, which she guessed was Rory's horse, and the other was a chestnut mare for her.

Taking a second to appreciate the view, she gave herself permission to ogle his muscular legs in his tight-fitting breeches and his broad chest peeking out from a loose-fitting shirt.

Rory welcomed her with a relaxed smile, his eyes bright with anticipation. In her opinion, he appeared a bit too perky for such an early morning hour.

"Good morn, Mistress Ellers. I trust ye slept well," he greeted her.

"Oh yes, I slept very well. It was the waking up that gave me trouble," Teressa teased.

"Are ye not accustomed to waking with the sun?" Rory asked.

"I'm very accustomed to waking with the sun." Teressa's alarm clock often woke her before sunrise for her commute into the city. "But I also really enjoy my sleep. So restful and relaxing, don't you think?"

"There is far too much to do in a day to spend it sleeping, and we have been blessed with a beautiful morning for our ride," Rory countered in his perky manner.

"Perhaps I'll have another occasion to argue the merits of spending a lazy morning in bed," Teressa said with a knowing smile. "For now, can you tell me my horse's name?" She approached the mare with slow and steady steps.

"Her name is Sallie, and this is Blazer," he said, patting the rump of his horse. "She's a fine mount with a bit of spirit. I hope I have chosen well."

"I'm sure you have." Teressa moved to the mounting steps, thinking they were unnecessary but convenient, and then graciously accepted Rory's assistance as he lifted her onto the horse. His hands were strong, his arms muscular. *They sure don't make them like this anymore in modern San Francisco.* No offense to the men of modern San Francisco, she amended, but corporate warriors were no match for these sturdy, Scottish warriors.

She swung her leg over the backside of the horse and made sure her skirt was draped properly over her legs. After a few adjustments, pulling the fabric this way and that to get comfortably situated, she was ready. Rory mounted up on Blazer then set them off at an easy gait across the bailey and out the large central gate. Outside the walls of the fortress, the dirt road split in two. One path angled off toward a nearby village, and the other followed the edge of the cliffs rising above the beach below. Rory chose the road along the cliffs, which eventually made its way down to the seaside.

They were blessed with a beautiful but chilly morning. Long shadows still lay across the land as the sun made its way above the horizon, doing little to remove the lingering night chill from the air.

Teressa took a look around and tried to recognize the area where the future town of Portree would be located. Looking down on the sandy beach stretching beneath the cliffs, she mentally retraced the path that had taken her from the twenty-first-century Scorrybreac Village Inn to the thirteenth-century Scorrybreac Castle. Seeing it from this vantage point, it seemed a very short distance to have traveled so far.

"Ye appear to be lost in thought," Rory interrupted her musings, bringing her back to the moment.

"Not truly lost, more like drifting," she offered in a thoughtful manner. "A bit of daydreaming, I suppose. I'm impressed by the magic and beauty of this place."

"Aye, 'tis a magical place. We have a legend that our great-grandmother Sophie appeared on this beach out of the mists of the ocean to meet our great-grandfather Herrick. 'Tis said she came from another time and place to meet her one true love."

"Are you serious?" Teressa was struck by the similarities of the legendary story with her own. Not the part about finding her one true love, of course, but about appearing out of nowhere from another time and place.

"About the legend, aye. If 'tis true, I canna say. That's how legends are. After so many years, they have a life of their own."

"Amazing. Can you tell me more about this legend?" She maneuvered her horse a few paces closer to Rory's as they rode toward the beach so she could hear him better.

"As the story goes, Great-Grandfather Herrick was returning home to Scorrybreac, worn, and wounded from battle, making his way along the coast, when he fell upon the beach to rest his weary bones. As he rested, a beautiful woman appeared out of the mists from off the ocean. She tended to his wounds and restored him to health with loving care. He in turn fell in love with her, and they were married." Rory beamed with pride as he told her the magical tale of his family's legendary history.

"Oh my, how extraordinary," she responded in a hushed tone.

"Aye. We highlanders do enjoy a good legend, and a good romance. Love, 'tis the strongest magic of them all," he said.

"So it seems. I'm impressed." She sat back in the saddle, contemplating the magical tale.

"What impresses me is how well ye manage to tell me very little about yerself."

Teressa looked out over the vast expanse of the ocean to avoid his eyes. "Maybe because my story is not nearly as fascinating as yours," she fibbed.

"I don't believe that to be true. We all have our stories to tell, and I have a feeling I will find yers to be most interesting."

Teressa understood his unspoken challenge; he was testing her. "I might disappoint you," she said as she turned to look at Rory. He was scowling. He knew she was stalling.

Rory turned Blazer to block the path of Sallie, bringing the horses to a halt near the water's edge. "Mistress Ellers, 'tis no surprise I find ye fascinating. Ye are unlike any woman who has passed through our keep. Ye display confidence I don't usually see in women. Ye create more questions than ye answer, and ye seem determined to avoid providing those answers. This all leads me to believe ye are a fascinating woman." He studied her with challenging eyes as he held her gaze.

She knew he had gotten her alone for this very reason. He wasn't going to be put off any longer. His direct approach also impressed her. As a thirteenth-century male, he had a tendency to surprise her.

"It appears you have me cornered, kind sir; however, I have to warn you, you may be disappointed. My family background is remarkably unremarkable."

"Let me be the judge. Please do tell," he prompted her.

Teressa had been mentally preparing for his questions and hoped she could provide enough information to satisfy his curiosity without creating even more questions about her background and where she came from. She intended to stick as close to the truth as possible.

"I grew up on a horse ranch near a small village outside a large city," she began, leaving out the part about the city being San Francisco located in America. "Like your sister, I was raised in a loving family with three very protective older brothers. I enjoyed a happy childhood with relatively few distractions. My father passed away last year, and I now live with my mother and my brother Daniel. Is that boring enough for you?"

"I don't find family boring. Tell me more."

The request sounded sincere. Teressa relaxed a little more and continued. "My parents, Francine and Allen Ellers, had three sons, Brett, Connor, and Daniel. I'm the youngest and only daughter. My mother wanted to break from the alphabet theme and named me after both my grandmothers, Terrie Ellers and Ressa Withers. My eldest brothers, Brett and Connor, are married and have moved away. Now it's just me, my mother, and Daniel."

"Ye still live at home with your family? I expect that means ye are not married."

"Correct. I have been able to avoid that mistake," she stated flatly.

"Ye consider marriage a mistake? 'Tis rather unusual for a woman, especially one as attractive as ye."

His comment was a true reflection of his thirteenth-century mindset. She openly smirked at his chauvinistic thinking, knowing he was merely a product of his culture and time.

"Why do you believe an attractive woman would be any more inclined to marry than someone you find to be less attractive?" she challenged him, warming to the possibility of a debate. It would be interesting to exchange views with this thirteenth-century warrior on the merits of women's relationship choices.

"'Tis not that an attractive woman would be more or less inclined towards marriage. 'Tis that the men of her village would be more inclined to pursue such a match. Can ye honestly tell me no man has found ye worthy of wooing?" he countered with pure male logic.

"Make no mistake, I have been wooed, as you say. I simply chose to avoid marriage." She kept her voice light, refusing to express regret. Jeffery was done and gone, no longer a part of her life.

For a quick moment, the painful memory of her broken engagement stomped across her mind, but she swiftly dismissed the thought. It was in the past, not something to dwell on any longer. Instead, she chose to be pleasantly surprised by the deviation in opinion he employed, focusing on a man's desire to pursue rather than a woman's desire to be pursued.

"The man must have not been up to the task of proper wooing to have missed making a match." Rory said with the type of confidence so easily supplied by the male ego.

"I will allow, the wooing may have been lacking, but mostly we were simply not a good match." A hint of regret slipped into her honest answer.

"What was the man's blunder?" Rory asked. "For certain, he couldn't have found ye lacking." His tone was gentle.

Had he sensed a soft spot in her armor? His gentleness was nearly her undoing. She was unable to conceal the shadow of distress falling across her face as she recalled her experiences with Jeffery, and the disappointment she felt over his withdrawal from her family.

"It was a matter of family. He didn't feel as strongly about family as I do." Reining in her emotions, she stated firmly, "It was simply not a good match."

"Ye say ye feel strongly about family?"

"Yes, I believe family will always be there for you. Right or wrong, good or bad, family is our foundation. My family has always been there for me." It was one of her core values, a firmly held conviction.

"And yet here ye are, traveling alone without the protection of yer family, and ye seem curiously unconcerned. Tell me how that is."

He had a point. Teressa reflected back to when she began planning her vacation. She had taken a number of trips with Jeffery, and as traveling companions, away from home and family, they worked well together. It was the happily ever after that eluded them. For this trip, she had felt the need to reconnect with herself, to seek a new type of adventure, on her own. Self-discovery was the primary reason she had chosen to travel alone to the remote Isle of Skye.

"I'm not a young innocent in need of protection. I understand my travels may seem unconventional to you, and while my family had their concerns, they trust me." Seeing his look of disbelief, she continued, "However, need I remind you, I wasn't alone. I was traveling with friends, until I got separated and lost." Thankfully, she remembered the cover story she had created with Duncan and repeated the fib to soften the impropriety of being a single woman traveling alone in this ancient culture.

"Won't ye be missed? Shouldn't someone be looking for ye?"

"I'm sure they will when they notice I'm missing." She knew her family would come looking for her if she weren't able to return home when expected. Her greatest fear was that they would find a dead end and nothing more. No body to morn or tell its tale of her death. She blinked back her tears, refusing to dwell on such thoughts. Teressa needed to believe Moezell would eventually send her back home.

"I believe Duncan has sent out word regarding my unexpected detour, and to be honest, I'm finding this adventure far more exciting than the travels I had originally planned. I couldn't have imagined the opportunity to spend this beautiful morning riding along this magical seaside. Had my travel plans not been disrupted, I wouldn't be here enjoying your company." A smile of pure delight brightened her face.

"Are ye not worried about being separated from your companions? Are ye not afraid of being lost and alone? And while I'm thinking about it, why is our druid, Souyer, so damned interested in ye?" Agitation streaked across his face as his voice rose with concern.

"Oh, Rory, you are too dear. Yes, of course, I was scared and worried when I realized I was lost, more than you can know. But thanks to Duncan, and you, and your family, I don't feel so lost and scared, or all alone. I'm truly grateful for Duncan's protection. Right now, I'm simply trying to enjoy this adventure. It's the best I can do until arrangements are made for my safe return home." She paused before adding with a knowing grin, "And as for Master Souyer's interest in me, I don't see it as being so very different from yours."

"I very much doubt that." He raised a quizzical brow, looking decidedly unhappy.

"A stranger shows up unexpectedly at your keep, and because he's your druid, he wants to know if it's a bad omen or a mystery to be explored. It seems to me you also want to explore the mystery, am I right?" She held his gaze with wide, steady eyes, a shrewd smile curling her lips.

"Aye, yer mystery does hold its appeal, I will not pretend otherwise."

"Rory, don't be too quick to unravel the mystery. You'll spoil all the fun. I would hate to see your interest fade so soon." Her tone was teasing, but a small part of her recognized her own desire to retain his interest. It was totally inappropriate, considering her circumstances, but she was only being honest with herself.

He leaned forward, as if to put emphasis on his words. "If that is yer concern, I believe ye may be underestimating the nature of my interest."

"Really? Now it's *you* who has *me* intrigued." She laughed lightly in response to his suggestive comment.

Sitting back in his saddle, he offered up one of his charmingly provocative grins before he turned his horse around to head back up the path from which they had come. "The morning grows late, Mistress Ellers. We should return to the keep, or we shall miss our morning meal."

Teressa turned Sallie to fall in step behind Blazer, smiling at Rory. Their ride was going much better than she had expected. Breathing deeply, she took in the crisp ocean air and sighed happily; life was good.

As they approached the rise in the road above the ocean cliffs, Teressa gave a quick kick to Sallie's flank, spurring her horse into a gallop. Rory gave immediate chase. Together they rapidly closed the distance to the fortress gate, arriving in a burst of energy. It was an exhilarating end to their morning ride.

When they reached the stables, Rory dismounted and turned to offer his assistance to Teressa. His hands encircled her waist as he pulled her from her mount, allowing her body to glide along his sturdy frame before bringing her to rest directly in front of him. Her eyes widened at the intimacy of his actions. Her breasts responded by swelling as they rubbed against his chest when he held her close. Lowering his mouth close to her ear, he whispered softly, "Are ye as hungry as I am?"

"Excuse me," she gasped, feeling a quiver snake down her spine. Flustered by his comment and physical proximity, she stumbled, unable to adequately collect her thoughts. Her awareness of his very masculine body was thoroughly distracting, making a rational reply difficult.

"I smell food being served. Are ye not hungry after our ride?" His voice was teasing and provocative.

"Oh yes, breakfast, of course. What else could I have been thinking?" she retorted as her brain finally reemerged from the fog of physical distraction. Her ride with Rory had turned out to be far more interesting than she had anticipated. Apparently, rising with the sun did have its advantages after all.

Kayla spied them as soon as they entered the great hall. "There ye are. I was worried for Mistress Ellers. Where have ye been?" Kayla confronted her brother.

Rory exchanged a speaking glance with Teressa before he answered his sister. "We were out riding," he stated calmly.

"Ye went out riding?" Kayla repeated, looking and sounding indignant.

"Aye, I took Mistress Ellers for an early morning ride to see the seashore at sunrise. It was a rather nice sunrise, wouldn't you agree?" Rory turned to Teressa with a hopeful expression.

"Oh yes, a rather nice sunrise," Teressa mimicked his words, holding her desire to laugh in check.

"Can ye imagine my surprise when I went to Teressa's chambers and she was gone? I wonder how ye were able to sneak her out of the keep so early in the morning." Kayla seemed to feign deep concern, but Teressa began to suspect she was teasing her brother.

"I didn't sneak her out of the keep as ye claim. We made plans last night before she retired, if ye must know. Besides, didn't Gavin tell ye where we were?"

"The stable lad? I wasn't aware he had become yer manservant." Kayla was trying not to smile as her teasing continued, but Teressa could see the upturned curve of her lips.

"Enough. I'm here now to break my fast. I smell Milly's sweetmeats and have no desire to let good food be ignored." Turning to address Teressa, he continued, "Mistress Ellers, thank ye for yer company this morn. I enjoyed the ride and our conversation. Regretfully, I must leave ye with my sister and can only hope ye are in good hands." He gave his sister a meaningful glare.

"Thank you, Sir Rory. It was truly my pleasure," she offered with a note of exaggerated politeness. "And be assured, I believe your sister will take good care of me." Teressa delighted in observing the witty exchange between brother and sister, thinking how much it resembled the interactions in her own family.

Rory left the ladies and made his way over to the serving tables. It looked as though Milly, their cook, had done another grand job of serving up a delicious meal.

Feeling remorse over Kayla's concern for her unexpected disappearance, Teressa turned to offer her apology. "I'm sorry if you were worried over my absence this morning. You should have been told."

"Ye need not worry. Gavin informed me earlier about Rory's plans, but I couldn't pass up an opportunity to tease my brother. 'Tis a wee bit o' fun to catch him in mischief," Kayla assured her.

Teressa saw this as another reminder of the close ties of the MacNicol clan. During breakfast, she provided Kayla with a brief but censored recap of the morning. She relayed how impressed she was with the beauty of the land, but said little about her conversation with Rory, other than his telling of Sophie's legend, which she found fascinating. Kayla confirmed the romantic legend about her great-grandparents, and Sophie's magical love affair with Herrick.

After breakfast, Kayla left her to see to the day's activities with Bonnie and Milly, the head housekeeper and cook. As acting mistress of the keep, there was always something demanding the young woman's attention.

Lingering a moment longer in the great hall, Teressa found herself reviewing the events of the morning and her conversation with Rory. She wondered whether his interest actually went beyond a desire to unravel her mystery, as she suspected. Originally, she had judged him to be a skirt chaser and believed his curiosity was largely due to her being someone new to pursue; that was to be expected. However, his provocative innuendos made her wonder if his interest really did go deeper, and if so, how deep.

She was honest enough to admit she felt a physical attraction to the muscular, handsome warrior, but that's all it was, a normal physical reaction. She refused to believe it was anything more than a superficial connection for either of them. Most likely, she was reading way too much into his comments; they were merely part of his naturally charming and flirtatious personality. He was a skirt chaser and nothing more.

Regaining her perspective, she shook off her imaginative musings, reminding herself she was only a visitor to this time and place. She wasn't here to find the love of her life like their legendary great-grandmother Sophie. Actually, it was probably best if she avoided Rory as much as possible. He presented a temptation far too good to be true, and certainly one doomed to failure.

Besides, she had a fear of falling too hard, too soon, too fast. Such things never lasted. It would be much too easy to fall in love with someone as charming and attractive as Rory, and much too hard to lose him when she left. She'd been down a similar path before, and she had no intention of allowing a repeat performance. She was determined to return home.

Teressa was about to leave the great hall when Duncan approached her. "I see Kayla has left ye alone."

"Yes, she was needed in the kitchens or something like that. You know, mistress of the keep and all."

"I suppose we cannot have ye following her around like a pup to its mother, but I don't have time to keep watch on ye. Can I trust ye to be fine on yer own? Or should I assign ye a guard?"

"I'm a grown woman. I'm sure I can take care of myself," Teressa said, feeling sassy.

"That is not what I mean. If ye are contacted again by one of the fae, I expect ye to let me know. We still have no way of knowing why ye are here or what shall become of ye."

Somewhat shaken, she realized she had underestimated his concern. "I'll be fine. I'll not go far. I was hoping to take another look around your fortress, if that's all right with you."

He nodded firmly. "I advise ye to not leave the fortress alone, for any reason. Ye are under my protection. I won't have ye running off and getting yerself hurt or lost again."

"I think I understand," she said nodding.

"Fine. Then I shall see ye later, for the evening meal." With a parting nod, he turned and walked away.

Feeling properly admonished, and with nothing else to do, she decided she would take a stroll around the bailey and explore more of the ancient fortress. She was fascinated by the opportunity to experience a real thirteenth-century Scottish castle. If she had to be displaced in time, she figured she might as well make the most of it.

Teressa had hardly stepped out the front door of the great hall when Rory intercepted her. "I'm heading back to the bay to do some fishing. Care to join me, keep me company? Ye can mind the horses and hold a drying towel for me." He flashed a lazy grin.

"I was thinking I would explore the castle," she said, trying to stick to her recently set plans. Besides, Duncan had told her not to leave the fortress.

"Nay, come join me. I go to hunt the tide pools for crabs, mussels, and such. Milly makes a very tasty seafood soup if I can gather enough of the little critters. Come, join me, and we can talk of magical legends, and sea sprites."

"Sea sprites? You mean, like mermaids?"

"Aye, mermaids, the lovely women of the sea who lure lonely men to their ocean beds and then cast them out to be lost to the seas." He dramatically pantomimed through his narrative, first reeling in his arms, and then flinging them out wide.

She struggled to repress the smile tugging at her lips, but it escaped anyway; his actions made her laugh. "Really, and have you ever been tempted by such sea sprites?"

"Perhaps, but I would be safe with ye. They wouldn't dare to show themselves for fear of being done in by yer beauty."

His flattery was a blatant attempt to charm her, and unfortunately, it was working.

"Don't you think that's laying it on a little thick, even for you?" He had a way of making her smile better than anyone she had known before. Looking for an excuse to turn him down, she said, "Duncan asked me not to leave the keep. He even offered me a guard."

"Ye will be with me. What better protection could ye need?"

Darn, he's good. She was remiss to find herself seriously considering his request. Only moments earlier, she'd been determined to avoid him, and yet the moment he spoke, the moment he graced her with his provocative smile, her determination melted like fresh butter on a hot summer day. Just being around him gave her a feeling of having melted butter pooling between her thighs. She really needed to take control of her reactions if she had any hope of resisting the man.

"I mean no harm, lass. 'Tis merely a friendly request." He spoke in such a kind, yet suggestive manner, it turned her insides to mush, making it hard to resist.

She paused, hesitant to accept his invitation and yet too tempted to turn him down. What a flimsy fence she was sitting on. If he tugged just a little harder, she feared she would find herself lying in a big ole puddle of lust at his feet.

"Come, spend the day at the bay with me, and I will tell ye my stories. Grand tales from my seafaring days on the high seas. Is it a deal?" His smile deepened, and his eyes sparkled with merriment. It was the last tug she needed to be swayed off her fence.

Teressa rolled her eyes skyward, feeling lost to his charms. "How can I refuse, now that you've aroused my interest?" She flashed him a devious smile to accompany her sly innuendo. Since there was no hope in resisting him, the best she could do was surrender with pleasure.

Before she could change her mind, he reacted quickly. "I will gather everything we need. Leave it all to me. Meet me at the stables as soon as ye are ready."

~*~

"Are ye sure ye don't want to join me in the water?" Rory stood ankle-deep at the tide pool's edge.

"Are you crazy? It's got to be flipping freezing." She held her ground on the dry pebbled beach, well above the grasping reach of the oncoming waves. Even with the sun doing its best to shine through the clouds, there was a cool breeze, and she was sure the brisk temperature of the northern ocean was well beyond her wimpy tolerance.

"'Tis cold, to be sure, but I have lived my life in these waters. They canna frighten me away."

Stripped to the waist, he was wearing only his skintight breeches, and he looked darn good. Suddenly he was hit by a large oncoming wave, and with an athlete's grace, he turned to dive under the water. He resurfaced waist-deep in the receding waves, shaking droplets of sea from his hair.

Teressa caught her breath. Rory was magnificent, rising from the sea like Poseidon, glistening rivulets streaming down from his hair and broad shoulders. *Oh my word*, she thought as she watched the blatant display of male physique, *he's a god, and I'm a goner.*

He reminded her of the surfers back home on the beaches of Southern California. Watching him now, as he rose from the waves, moving effortlessly from rock to tide pool and back again, she laughed easily with outright joy at his grand display of masculine prowess. Apparently, Rory had no need for false modesty. Likewise, she had no qualms about appreciating the physical appeal of a good-looking man. He was certainly a man worth enjoying, and for the moment, life was good.

Rory proved to be serious about his gathering of seafood. In less than an hour, he had filled a large leather bag with dozens of sea creatures.

Teressa had also seriously enjoyed watching him work; his sun bronzed skin and rippling muscles were a joy to behold. She felt very much like a starving woman at a banquet, eating up the hunky eye candy. It was all too cliché, and yet she had no problem taking full advantage of the moment and drinking in the view. It made her wonder how she got so lucky.

When he had gathered enough tide pool crustaceans to satisfy his needs, Rory returned to where Teressa sat waiting. She stood to greet him with the drying cloth and his woolen plaid that she'd been wearing draped over her shoulders. He handed her the leather bag full of sea critters and began drying off. Gingerly, she held the soggy bundle aloft at arm's length. Some of the contents were obviously still alive; she could detect movement coming from inside.

After wrapping the plaid around his waist, Rory dropped his sodden breeches to his feet and stepped out of the wet garment. Breathing deeply while looking off toward the ocean, Teressa smiled silently as she savored the thought of his naked body beneath the plaid. It was a happy thought.

Standing next to her on the pebbled sand, hands on his hips, he turned his face toward the warmth of the afternoon sun and gazed out over the ocean. "The MacNicol clan has lived near these waters for generations. The struggle of man against ocean has made us strong, and also respectful." He stared off into the distant blue of the ocean, watching the never-ending sensuous rise and fall of the waves, seemingly deep in thought. "A man canna live his life near the ocean's edge without respect for the power held within. She can grant her blessing of abundance, as she has today," he gestured toward the undulating leather pouch Teressa held awkwardly away from her body, "or she can wage a war of infinite rage. 'Tis a blessing we are granted, to know such strength and beauty."

He turned to look at Teressa and she felt her heart melting into a pool of mush. Never had she heard a man speak so passionately about his homeland, nor had she expected to hear such eloquence from an ancient warrior. She stared at him with open admiration.

"You amaze me, Rory," she spoke softly. "You simply amaze me."

"'Tis my intent." A lazy, provocative grin emerged on his stunningly handsome face. He relieved her of the leather pouch and headed toward his horse. "Ye have missed yer chance to join me in a swim. I need to get these critters up to Milly while they are still fresh. She'll have my skin if I bring her spoiled seafood."

"It's all for the best," she said as she followed him to the horses. "There's no way I could tolerate such a cold ocean, and besides, I have nothing else to wear."

"Nothing would have worked for me." He flashed her a sly grin, wiggling his brows.

"Rory, you're shameless," she laughed.

"Aye, my lady, 'tis only fair ye should know."

Men, she thought. *Seven hundred years, and they hadn't changed a bit.*

CHAPTER 8

When they returned to the keep, Rory headed off to the kitchens to deliver his catch to Milly, and Teressa retreated to the quiet solitude of the garden. She thought about seeking out Duncan to see if he had learned anything more about how she might return home, or maybe even Souyer, but in her heart, she knew they had nothing new to share. Moezell, it seemed, was in control, not her, nor Duncan, or even Souyer. Spending the day with Rory was all very fun, but knowing she was several hundred years removed from her family was never far from her thoughts. She had tried to take Moezell's advice and just enjoy the moment, but the effort to maintain her sanity while her future was so uncertain was taking its toll.

Tempting as it was to indulge in a good cry, Teressa refused to give in to such despair. Instead, she chose to believe everything would be alright, and that sooner or later, Moezell would send her home. The hard part was to keep believing.

At the evening meal, Milly's seafood stew was every bit as good as Rory had promised, but Teressa found she didn't have much of an appetite. As soon as the meal was over she asked to be excused and went to her room, alone. It helped that Duncan had called Michael and Rory to his office to discuss the upcoming gathering of the clans.

After a good night's sleep, Teressa felt much better. She might not be home, but she was ready to face another day and hope for the best. As she was on her way to the great hall for breakfast, Kayla came to find her.

"I don't wish to pry," Kayla said as she fell in step beside her, "but I noticed ye looked a wee sad last eve. Has Rory done anything to offend thee?"

"No, not at all, he's quite charming," Teressa assured her. "I simply miss my family. I'll be fine. You needn't worry about me." The last thing she wanted was to burden Kayla with her problems. The young woman had enough to handle.

"I'm planning to visit the village after we break our fast and wonder if ye would care to join me?" Kayla offered.

"Sure, if that's what you want," Teressa agreed with as much enthusiasm as she could muster.

"Mayhap this outing will do ye well. We may hear news if anyone has come looking for ye."

"Wouldn't that be wonderful?" Teressa highly doubted anyone would be looking for her, at least not here and now, but perhaps the walk would do her good.

Their first stop was the cottage of Kayla's friend, Fern McLarken. After the two friends exchanged their greetings, Kayla introduced Teressa.

"Mistress Ellers recently became separated from her friends and family. Have ye heard of anyone asking about a lost woman?" Kayla asked.

"Nay, but I've had no visitors this day. My wee one has kept me late in bed." As she spoke, Fern rubbed a hand across her belly.

"Fern was married to Eldon McLarken last summer, and now they are expecting their first bairn," Kayla explained to Teressa. It was still early in her pregnancy, and Fern's belly had only begun to show its burgeoning roundness. "Have ye felt the quickening yet?"

"Nay, but Govina says it may happen any day," Fern told her.

Kayla's excitement over her married friend's condition was quite evident, and Teressa couldn't help but wonder why Kayla had made no mention of suitors. It would seem an attractive young woman of her lineage would be highly sought after. She made a mental note to ask about it if the opportunity became available.

Teressa was already developing a fondness and greater appreciation for the young mistress of Scorrybreac Castle. Running the home of the ruling family of her clan would be a daunting task for any one woman to manage, and yet Kayla demonstrated efficient management skills that would serve any professional woman of the twenty-first century.

She considered how the role of women had improved over the centuries, with women using their innate skills as mothers and housewives to become CEOs of Fortune 500 companies. Even in her time, women were still working hard to create such change and protect their rights in the world. *Many things will change*, she thought, *and many things will always stay the same.*

"Look at us, chattering on like two old women. We've been rude to ignore ye," Kayla spoke to Teressa, bringing her back to the moment.

"No, not at all. I was just letting my mind wander," Teressa assured her.

"Fern needs to visit Govina, our village midwife. Would ye care to join us?" Kayla asked.

"Sure, that'll be great," Teressa agreed. What else did she have to do?

As the three women were approaching the midwife's cottage, they were met by Bonnie, who was on her way through the village. "Good day to ye. Are ye here to visit midwife Govina?"

Kayla barely managed a nod before Bonnie continued speaking, "How grand. I trust all is well with the babe. I'm on me way to me sister's for a wee visit and am wondering if I may borrow Teressa? I know Annie would welcome the additional company.

We have so few visitors to these parts, she wouldn't let me hear the end if I didn't make the plea."

"I'd be delighted," Teressa readily accepted, hoping Kayla wouldn't be offended. Accompanying Bonnie on a visit to her sister had to be more entertaining than a visit to the village midwife. Besides, Teressa had a real affection for the older woman and knew she would enjoy her company.

As they made their way through the village, Teressa was once again impressed by Bonnie's delightful running commentary of everyone they encountered, and used the opportunity to ask Bonnie about Kayla's single status. "Kayla seems happy for her married friend. I imagine she's looking forward to having a family of her own someday," Teressa eased into the conversation, hoping Bonnie would use the nudge to offer up her insider knowledge.

"Aye, I believe 'tis so. Lady Kayla will make a right fine wife and mother someday when the right man comes along," Bonnie proudly endorsed her mistress.

"Wouldn't an attractive young woman like Kayla already have suitors?" Teressa asked.

"Make no mistake, a man or two have shown an interest in Kayla, and no doubt with a desire to woo her into marriage, but a lady of her status, as the only daughter of the MacNicol chief, canna be married to just any man. Her marriage will be based on what's best for the family. 'Tis what's expected of her," Bonnie said in her no-nonsense manner.

"You mean she won't be allowed to choose based on love?"

"A love match? Aye, a smart woman will choose to make a love match with her husband, if he be a good man. She can only hope. But it will be a match of her family's choosing, make no mistake," Bonnie scoffed. "Fern has been graced with the good fortune to marry for love, along with the security provided by a good family. I'm thinking Fern made a good match with Eldon MacLarken. But as the sister to our clan chief, Kayla's fate is not so free."

Teressa knew she shouldn't be surprised; ruling families often protected their clans by creating marriage unions based on political interests. Still, it shocked her modern sensibilities to see how strongly it affected Kayla's choices and the expectations it carried.

"Here, we be at Annie's," Bonnie informed Teressa as they approached the door of a small cottage. "'Tis a welcome visit, to be sure, but there is someone else here I need ye to meet. I couldn't say anything in front of Kayla. 'Tis a secret I must tell ye."

Amazed by Bonnie's ability to keep a secret, considering how freely she shared her thoughts, Teressa began to wonder whom Bonnie would want her to meet in secret, considering how few people even knew of her existence in Scorrybreac.

Barely stopping to knock, Bonnie led them into the one room cottage. Sitting in the room were two older women. They appeared to have been engaged in quiet conversation while they awaited the arrival of their visitors.

"This be my older sister, Annie." Bonnie began to make the introductions, indicating the elder of the two women. Annie was dressed plainly, and Teressa could easily see the family resemblance to Bonnie in the woman's friendly, open face.

Then turning to the second woman, who was finely dressed, Bonnie said, "And this be Lady Lydia of the MacNicol clan. 'Tis proud I am to be presenting her in my own family's home."

Teressa stared at the two women, a bit confused. "Umm, Lady Lydia, how nice to meet you." She hadn't expected to meet the clan matriarch of whom she had heard so much in this humble cottage. The woman looked quite regal, and Teressa found herself feeling rather like a peasant unexpectedly meeting the Queen of England in a roadside pub.

"Mistress Ellers, 'tis my pleasure to meet ye." Lady Lydia's gracious voice resonated with self-confidence. She wore an ivory gown that flattered her mature figure and looked very much like a lady of high birth as she sat with her hands clasped loosely in her lap. "Bonnie was kind enough to assist in arranging our meeting outside the keep. I have much I wish to discuss with ye."

"You have something you wish to discuss with me?" Teressa took a moment to wonder what this was all about as she waited for Lady Lydia to explain further.

"I understand yer surprise. I hope to provide some answers before our discussion is over." Lady Lydia then turned to her hostess. "Annie, ye have been most gracious to provide yer home for my visit."

"My pleasure, my lady," Annie answered. Then, leaning in close toward her mistress, she added, "Are ye sure ye have the right lass? She looks a wee young for the job, if you ask me."

Momentary embarrassment tripped across Lady Lydia's face as she glanced at Teressa. Turning toward Annie, she lowered her voice. "My cousin has assured me she's highly qualified. Please excuse us, I require some private time with Mistress Ellers."

"Of course, my lady," Annie answered with a respectful nod. She motioned to her sister. "Let's be off for a sit outside to enjoy this fine summer day." As the older woman stood from her chair, she reached out to grab Bonnie's arm for support. Together, the sisters headed out to the back of the cottage and closed the door behind them, giving Lady Lydia and Teressa their privacy.

Lady Lydia motioned to Teressa. "Please take a seat. I'm sure ye have many questions. I believe I can help ye, and in return, 'tis my hope ye will help me."

Taking the chair recently vacated by Annie, Teressa was still in awe of this unexpected development. Kayla had told her Lady Lydia was gone somewhere, living with her ill sister. She had expected it to be someplace distant, not the neighboring village. If Lady Lydia were staying this close to home, why didn't she just stay in the keep? Or did Kayla not know where her mother really was? And why was it a secret from Kayla that she was here?

"Okay, you've got my attention. Why do you think you can help me, and how am I to help you?" Teressa asked.

"Let me begin at the beginning," Lady Lydia stated calmly. "Several years ago, my eldest son, Duncan, was betrothed to Janet MacDonald."

Since meeting the brooding MacNicol chief, Teressa had wondered about his romantic history, but so far she had heard nothing.

"Janet is the daughter of Hugh MacDonald, the chief of the MacDonald clan. A few years ago, Janet came with her father and mother, Lady Evelyn, to Scorrybreac with the intention of finalizing the expected betrothal. I believe Duncan may have been in love with Janet. He had been aware of their intended betrothal since his youth and had developed strong feelings for her. During their visit, Duncan pressed Janet for a declaration of her loyalty to the MacNicol clan. He knew one day he would become chief, and he wanted his future wife to disavow her own family in favor of his. Duncan was perhaps naive in some ways. He underestimated the strength of the bond between young Janet and her mother. As much as Janet desired the marriage to Duncan, she couldn't disown her own family. Duncan's pride and expectations were shattered. He sent Janet with her parents back to the MacDonald keep, stating he never wanted to see her at Scorrybreac again. It was quite a disappointment for everyone concerned. Janet's heart was broken. She did as he requested, and they have not seen each other since that time."

"Oh my word, that seems tragic. Why would Duncan do such a thing? Why would he demand that Janet disavow her family?" It seemed stupid, and bullheaded, and so like a man.

"There have been years of discord between the MacNicol and MacDonald clans. It had been hoped the marriage of Duncan and Janet would create a bridge between the two clans and move us closer to peaceful coexistence. Without Janet's pledge of loyalty to the MacNicol clan, Duncan didn't believe it to be possible. He didn't want his house divided. Also, Duncan had grown up watching the loving relationship between my husband, Kennon, and myself and had developed great expectations for a love match of his own. To him, such a match included the undivided loyalty of his wife."

Teressa sat back to digest the story. "That all sounds very interesting, but I still don't see where I fit in."

Lady Lydia paused a moment to collect her words. "When Master Souyer made his summer solstice request, we saw an opening to bring us the resources we need to make some corrections."

Teressa was reminded of her conversation with Moezell, the faerie. *Here we go again with that druid, his solstice request, and the use of* we *all together, again.* "Okay, I'm not sure I want to ask, but who is this *we* you're talking about?"

"Me and the faeries of the Isle of Skye." Lady Lydia spoke with dignified self-assurance, as if it were the most natural thing in the world to talk about faeries.

"You and the faeries of Skye?" Teressa repeated Lady Lydia's words in bewilderment. The mysteries just kept getting bigger.

"Aye. Allow me to explain my connection. I believe ye have been told the legend of my grandmother Sophie," Lady Lydia offered.

"Sophie was your grandmother?" That seemed reasonable enough, since she had already heard the legend of the mysterious Sophie from Rory.

"Aye. Sophie was a full-blooded fae, the youngest sister of the Faerie Queen, Danu. When she fell in love with Herrick, she chose to come to earth to live with her human husband. A most unusual occurrence, I can assure ye," Lady Lydia said with serene confidence.

"Yeah, I'll bet that's most unusual," Teressa interjected, wondering which seemed more unusual, the idea that Lady Lydia believed she had a faerie grandmother or her ability to state such a bizarre idea with such conviction.

Lady Lydia graciously ignored Teressa's expression of amazement and went on. "As Grandmother Sophie stepped through the veil of the mists, she found Grandfather Herrick wounded from his recent battle with the Norse on the isle of Harris. 'Tis said she was so taken with his earthly beauty, she fell in love at first sight. She used her healing power to restore Herrick to health. Grandmother Sophie had the choice to live in the fae world with her sisters or leave to experience life in the human realm. She chose to live in the human realm. And together, my grandparents created a long and happy life. Sophie's eldest daughter was Dianna, my mother. Fae blood is passed from mother to daughter, and my connection to the fae is still quite strong."

"So let me guess. You know Moezell, the faerie who visited me."

"Aye, she is my cousin," Lady Lydia confirmed.

Teressa tried to keep it together as the surprises kept coming. It wasn't easy. "Moezell is your cousin? But I was told she's a granddaughter of the Faerie Queen."

"Correct. Grandmother Sophie's eldest sister, Danu, is the queen of the fae. Moezell's mother is Amanda, Danu's daughter," Lady Lydia explained.

"Let me get this straight. Your great-grandmother was the faerie queen's sister. You're half fae. And Moezell is your cousin!"

"Correct."

"Why am I not surprised?" Teressa responded with sarcasm, throwing up her hands. She didn't mean to be rude, but her natural sense of politeness was overwhelmed by all this new, and downright strange, information.

"As I was explaining," Lady Lydia continued, undeterred, "Souyer made his summer solstice request to the faeries of Skye. Faeries are honor bound to fulfill a solstice request, if properly presented, and for good or bad, Souyer's was properly presented. Moezell, in consideration of my concerns, used Souyer's request as an opportunity to bring ye here from the future. This way, it could appear as if he summoned ye, not me, which, in a manner, he did, except he has very little power over yer situation."

"Why me? Why go so far into the future?" Although Teressa had regained her composure, she still couldn't see the big picture.

"I needed a woman who could fulfill my needs, and she needed to be on Skye during the summer solstice. Ye are an independent woman, ye have developed a career as a matchmaker—Moezell tells me ye call yerself a relationship coach—and ye have similar experiences to both Duncan and Janet," Lady Lydia ticked off the various reasons for choosing Teressa.

"How do I have an experience similar to Duncan's?"

"Ye chose to break an engagement rather than disavow yer family," Lady Lydia stated plainly.

The lights began to turn on as Teressa recalled her broken relationship with Jeffery for very similar reasons.

They had been together as a couple for over two years, and she had truly enjoyed his companionship. They both liked camping, and the great outdoors. She would never forget, nor regret, their time together, but after two years of fun and adventure, she had to accept that Jeffery would always be a playmate and never a partner. Times with him could be full of laughter, but they could also be laced with emotional distance and heartbreaking disappointment.

When it came time to interact with her family, he always pulled back, creating barriers. Teressa realized this as an unacceptable difference in their core values, and as a relationship coach, she was well aware of the importance of core values.

To her, family was a constant you could count on for love and support. The world might let you down, but the one thing she always felt she could rely on was the support of her family.

Jeffery, on the other hand, had left home at eighteen and had hardly looked back.

Emotional scar tissue resurfaced quickly as she thought back to the day of her father's funeral. Jeffery had managed to escort her to the funeral, but had left early from the memorial service. Skipping out early on the Christmas holidays was one thing, but to not be at her side for such an emotionally difficult time was simply unacceptable. Thankfully, her brother Daniel had been there for her.

She had often made excuses for Jeffery's actions, but his lack of support on one of the most stressful days she could imagine was her breaking point. Later, after she recovered her emotional equilibrium, she told Jeffery her family was too important to set aside. She believed the man who wanted to be her husband, her life partner, should also want to be part of her family. It was incomprehensible that he could believe he was competing against them for her affection. Instead of accepting her family and trying to fit in, Jeffery resented them. For Teressa, it was the deal breaker that ended their relationship.

Finally, the pieces were beginning to fit together. She'd been brought here to be a relationship coach for the chief of the MacNicol clan and to draw on their similar experiences to create a bridge of understanding, and hopefully mend past injuries. It seemed rather strange it took Lady Lydia and the faeries seven hundred years to find this perfect fit, but now that she knew why she had been brought here, she felt some relief.

"You've gone to a great deal of trouble to bring me to your time. Now that I'm here, what do you want me to do?" Teressa's relationship skills began to kick into high gear. She could do this;

she was a professional, and she had every intention of doing justice to Lady Lydia's belief in her.

"I knew we could count on ye." Lady Lydia smiled sweetly. "'Tis time for Bonnie to return to the keep. She will tell Kayla ye stayed behind to visit with Annie." As she spoke the words, the two sisters were already walking through the back door into the cottage.

"Lady Lydia, yer visit with Mistress Ellers has gone well, I trust," Annie spoke as she entered the room. "'Tis happy I am to provide my humble home for yer needs."

"'Tis I who must thank ye, dear Annie, and ye, Bonnie, for arranging Teressa's visit here today." Lady Lydia politely thanked the two sisters.

Annie gave her sister a farewell embrace. "I've enjoyed our visit. Ye know well enough what to tell Kayla, am I right?"

"I understand completely, sister. Ye asked Teressa to stay and keep ye company for some time longer. Have no care. I know what to say," Bonnie answered.

Teressa looked from Lady Lydia to the two peasant women and realized some type of unspoken communication was taking place between them.

"Ye won't have any trouble getting back to the keep on yer own, will ye?" Bonnie sought reassurance from Teressa before making her departure.

"I'm sure I'll be fine. The castle's too big to miss."

After Bonnie left to return to Scorrybreac and Annie had settled at the back of the single room cottage with her sewing basket, Lady Lydia directed her attention back to Teressa. "We have much to discuss about yer task. I expect ye still have many more questions."

"You're right. I do. First off, what makes you think Duncan and Janet want to restore their broken relationship?" It occurred to her that even if Jeffery were to suddenly develop an appreciation for her family, she was no longer in love with him. Her love for him was broken and could no longer be fixed. Could such loss of love be felt by either Janet or Duncan?

"I believe Duncan loved Janet, and I feel he still carries a deep desire for success in their relationship. As for Janet, she has not shown an interest in accepting another match. It was her mother, Lady Evelyn, who contacted me with hopes that as matriarchs of our clans, we could come to an agreement on how to mend the broken betrothal. She, of course, loves her daughter and wants her to be happy, but as women, we are limited by certain traditions on how we can affect the workings of our clans."

"Wouldn't your connection to the faeries give you additional powers other women of this time don't have?" Teressa wondered what benefits came with being part fae.

"Even faeries cannot change the free will of a human. A faerie could place an object of desire directly in front of a person, and they would still have free will to choose something different," Lady Lydia informed her.

Teressa understood the matriarch's position well enough. She had seen firsthand how couples very much in love with each other often made bad choices that sabotaged their own happiness.

"Have you considered arranging a meeting to get Duncan and Janet together so they can discuss their past relationship and figure out where it went wrong? How do you know if they still care for each other?" The straightforward approach seemed like the most sensible course of action to Teressa, and the most pragmatic.

"That cannot be done. Neither would agree to such a confrontation, and even if they did, I doubt it would yield positive results. There are too many past hurts to overcome. I believe Janet would be too fearful, and I know Duncan would be too stubborn."

"You can't get them together to work out their past mistakes?" It boggled Teressa's mind.

"I don't recommend such an effort. I don't believe it would work." Lady Lydia was adamant.

"Why not?" There was much she needed to understand if her efforts were to be fruitful.

"'Tis not the way things are done here, in this time. We have very formal rules for the way betrothals are handled."

"How's that working for you?"

"Excuse me?"

"How's that working for you—the not talking thing?"

Lady Lydia looked a bit miffed. "'Tis not. That's why you're here." Her tone was understandably haughty.

"Why do you think my efforts will be any better than yours?" Teressa asked.

"Because grown men rarely listen to their mothers," Lady Lydia admitted. "However, I believe that through yer experience, ye have developed a considerable understanding of how human relationships work, or don't work, as the case may be. I also believe ye are quite capable of presenting solutions that will work. In other words, I have great faith in yer abilities."

Teressa was impressed. Actually, what Lady Lydia said made a lot of sense; it might work. Since she had no attachments to their rules and was not expected to abide by them, that could work in her favor, or it could cause a bigger mess. She would have to tread lightly. Her success was important to all concerned, but because she wasn't guided by their ancient cultural belief system, she figured she could use whatever methods she wanted to get the desired results. This was one job where she had every intention of doing all she could to make it work. Going home would be her reward, the big payoff.

"Thanks for the endorsement." Teressa nodded. "I'm ready and willing to work with you. I only hope you've really considered what's best for Duncan and Janet, and not only your clan's best interest." The relationship coach in Teressa started to take over, and she began to wonder if this were truly best for the two people most deeply concerned. She believed that for relationships to work, they had to be based on love, acceptance, and support. If relationships weren't mutually beneficial, they were doomed to failure.

"I appreciate yer concern. Are ye aware of the upcoming Isle Faire?" Lady Lydia asked.

"Yeah, Duncan told me about it and asked me to attend, along with Souyer."

"This is good, better than I expected. I was going to insist ye join us. Ye will be able to meet Lady Evelyn and Janet at the festival. If after meeting Janet, ye feel ye cannot continue, I will understand, and ye will be allowed to return home to enjoy yer holiday. However, I am certain ye will agree their restored betrothal will benefit them, as well as us all."

"Fair enough," Teressa accepted Lady Lydia's offer. "By the way, you do know that Duncan knows I'm from the future, don't you?"

"Yes, I know all about how he found ye on the beach. Quite an exciting way to transport ye here, wouldn't ye agree? It helps for him to see ye as a mysterious presence. Hopefully, he will think ye're able to provide some benefit to him and his clan. Since he doesn't know why ye're here, I expect he'll be watching ye to learn as much as he can. I'm counting on yer secret to give him greater acceptance of yer opinion."

Teressa was impressed. Lady Lydia seemed to think of everything. Unfortunately, Duncan wasn't the only one who found her to be a mysterious presence, Teressa noted with a mental smirk. She was well aware of Rory's unabashed interest in her.

"I hope Moezell warned ye, if ye wish to return home to yer own time, ye cannot tell anyone else where ye come from. Ye must swear to secrecy and agree to perform this task. Do ye understand?"

Teressa felt an unprofessional desire to squirm as Lady Lydia looked her square in the eyes. Obviously, the half fae matriarch was quite serious in her demands.

"Yes, I understand. Moezell warned me, and besides, I always keep my client's business confidential. I can assure you, I want to go home," Teressa answered, rejecting any possibility of being stuck in the thirteenth century.

"Very well." Lady Lydia's serene smile returned. "Now then, we only have this day before I am expected back at Scorrybreac, and there is much to do. I want ye to plant a seed. Suggest to Duncan that his broken engagement to Janet may have been a mistake. He doesn't appreciate being told what to do, so it must be only a seed. Do ye think ye can manage that?"

"Sure, I already have some ideas." She was eager for their success.

Lady Lydia and Teressa continued to discuss their plans throughout much of the afternoon. Teressa paid close attention as Lady Lydia described her knowledge of Janet and Duncan's previous relationship, as well as her impressions of Janet MacDonald. She described how Janet's youth and inexperience and obvious fear of Duncan had hindered her ability to persuade him that the joining of their families would be far more beneficial than his request for her to disown her own mother and family. Duncan had failed to see how Janet's strong bond to her mother made his request unacceptable. However, Lady Lydia believed in the past three years, Janet had developed a greater understanding of the motivation behind Duncan's request. She had gained an understanding of men and women that would sustain her in the position of wife to the MacNicol chief. Moreover, she was no longer a naive young girl, unschooled in the workings of clan politics. Even Lady Evelyn had realized how much her overprotection of her daughter had contributed to the broken betrothal.

As Teressa listened to everything Lady Lydia had to say, she considered how often people got in the way of their own happiness. Sometimes a person could get so fixated on a desired outcome, they would lose sight of all other alternatives. Duncan had been so focused on getting a declaration of loyalty from his future wife, he lost sight of the benefits the blending of their two families could provide. Her experience in working with her clients proved that plan B often worked as well as, or even better than their original plans. She had developed a strategy to always leave herself open to plan B, even if she didn't know what plan B was until it happened.

When it was time for Teressa to return to the keep, Lady Lydia asked her, "Do ye know how to sew or do needlework?"

"Yes, a little, but not as good as you," Teressa admitted. Learning how to sew was part of growing up on a farm. She had learned how to ride horses, how to bake an apple pie, and how to embroider a tea towel. "I've seen your work. I'm staying in your guest room," she added, thinking Lady Lydia might have something to say about that. Apparently, she didn't.

"That's fine. If asked, Bonnie will tell Kayla yer reason for staying with Annie all afternoon was to help her mend baby clothes being prepared for Fern McLarken."

"That works for me," Teressa agreed. She had noticed Annie busily sewing while she and Lady Lydia talked. As she was preparing to leave, she added, "I look forward to working with you on this project. You seem to have everyone's best interest at heart."

Lady Lydia seemed pleased with Teressa's endorsement of their endeavor. "I'm glad to know ye approve, but we will need more than good intentions if we are to have success. I pray Duncan's heart has not grown too cold."

Teressa could sympathize with Lady Lydia's concerns. She had the impression that Duncan preferred to reside in an emotional cave, creating a polite distance between them. There was a strong possibility Duncan had formed a fortress around his heart that could no longer be breached by good intentions. If that were true, it didn't bode well for her success.

CHAPTER 9

Teressa used her walk back to Scorrybreac to evaluate her situation and everything she had learned from Lady Lydia. When she thought about Moezell using Souyer's request to achieve her desired results, she nearly laughed out loud. He had asked to be given knowledge from the future and *poof*, a twenty-first-century woman shows up on their beach. She had asked for a vacation adventure and *poof*, she travels over seven hundred years back in time to be a relationship coach to the chief of a clan. The whole surreal experience reminded her of the axiom to be careful what you wish for; you just might get it, but not in the way you expect. It was one of the dilemmas of reality; it rarely turned out the way we imagined it to be.

Reminding herself she was summoned here to do a job, she figured the job requirements did not include getting involved with Lady Lydia's youngest son. Also, she was determined to return home when her work here was done. Moezell had promised all would be well, even if it wasn't what she expected. So far, Teressa could agree with the latter.

Her mother and her brothers would go out of their minds with worry if she disappeared on the Isle of Skye and never returned, especially Daniel. Daniel was a police officer, and it wasn't likely he would let her disappearance go unresolved.

She lived and breathed on the thought that once her task was accomplished, she would be sent back to her own time. Until then, it would be better for all them both if she kept Rory at a distance. Teressa wasn't sure she could trust herself to not become involved with the handsome warrior, and she had no intention of allowing an attachment to get in the way of her work or her desire to return home.

With a newfound sense of purpose and an ongoing appreciation for her comfortable hiking boots, she walked up the steep hill to the keep, hoping to find Bonnie. She was walking through the fortress gates when she noticed the MacNicol men surrounded by their guards. From the looks of it, they were training for battle. Duncan, Michael, and Rory, along with several other warriors, were using their swords and other heavy weaponry to pound the snot out of each other. She halted in her tracks, mesmerized by the sight of the warriors engaged in training. It was better than any reality TV show she had ever seen. As much as she disliked fighting, she knew it was important for these ancient warriors to stand ready to defend their people from any possible invaders.

From where she stood, she had a good view of the men as they trained and marveled at their skill of weaponry. While she had no firsthand knowledge of what constituted masterful skills, these men looked darn impressive with their strength and ability to handle a sword. Though enthralled by the artful dance of the one-on-one combat, it was the view of those athletically built men and their blatant display of muscular beauty she enjoyed the most.

When Duncan called for a break in the training to allow for a change of sparring partners, Teressa took it as her cue to leave. She was walking away when she noticed Rory break from the group and rush to catch up with her.

Pulling a shirt over his head, he joined her as she walked through the bailey. "Mistress Ellers, I see we are graced with yer return to our humble keep."

"Hello Rory." Acutely aware of his masculine presence as he walked by her side, she found the musky scent of his sweaty body was rather alluring.

"I can only wonder what pleasures could have demanded yer attentions so long into the afternoon. Kayla returned much earlier without ye. I trust all went well in the village." His inquiry sounded light and nonchalant, but it let her know he had been aware of her absence.

"Well enough. I was visiting with Annie, Bonnie's sister. I'm sure you know her," Teressa replied. His interest was flattering, but she needed to stay focused. Sooner or later she was going home, and it was best not to create any attachments. It would only create problems if she allowed his flirtations to go any further. She admitted she felt drawn to him, and yet the pragmatic side of her resisted her desire to explore their attraction.

Teressa momentarily gave in to a pang of regret. But she immediately steeled herself against such thoughts, reminding herself it was best for everyone, including her, if she maintained her emotional distance.

"Can I expect to see ye at our evening meal?"

"I haven't spoken to Kayla yet, but unless I've been banished to the kitchens with the serving staff, I expect to join you for dinner." Teressa tried to assume a lighthearted attitude to mask her feelings of disappointment. Her situation was her private dilemma.

"I can assure ye, no such banishment will be imposed on ye," he said, sporting a boyish grin.

"Really, and how is that, pray tell?"

"Because I would never allow my dear sister to banish such pleasing company to our kitchens."

"You're too kind." She spoke flippantly, but she couldn't hold back her smile; his flirtations were too much fun.

Rory reached out to grasp her hand, stopping her in her tracks. "'Tis more than simple kindness that prompts my interest, as I am sure ye know."

His gaze was intense; she felt like a deer caught in the headlights, unable to look away. Slowly, he reached out his hand and brushed his fingers across her cheek. The touch of his rough, battle-calloused skin against hers set off a spark of heat. She wanted to lean into his touch, to feel the full force of his hands on her body. Captured by his gaze, her heart pounded in her chest.

If I stand here much longer, he may kiss me, she thought. *I'm sure I look as if I want to be kissed, because I do. I do want him to kiss me.* Her eyes dropped to his lips, sensual and lush and oh so tempting. *NO*, she silently screamed, *this must stop. I cannot allow this to continue.* Her mind whirled with conflicting thoughts and emotions.

Using every ounce of her resolve, she forced herself to step away, removing herself from his touch. "I have to find Bonnie and prepare for dinner. Please, excuse me?" she begged off. Turning from him, she fled into the keep.

~*~

Rory nodded, silently accepting her departure. He let her flee, but he sensed the desire his touch had sparked; he saw it in her eyes. He also sensed her conflicting emotions. It would not bode well to press her further, at least not yet. Smiling broadly, he contemplated ways to slowly and leisurely seduce this mysterious lady, knowing such a seduction would only make the results much more rewarding.

As he watched her hurry into the great hall, he was also aware of a deeper effect she had on him. Sure, he enjoyed her beauty, and their easy banter, but this feeling went beyond those simple pleasures. Rory desired Teressa more than any woman he had met before. She stirred an interest in him that went well beyond the flirtatious games he usually played with women. He was no stranger to the enjoyment provided by the company of a pleasing lass, nor did he lack women to choose from, but Teressa was different, special. Pursuing her was new and exciting, and he liked it.

Still happily contemplating his seduction of Teressa, Rory was about to head back to the lists when he saw Kayla leave the kitchens and head his way. Almost instinctively, he turned to make his getaway when she called out to him.

"Rory, my dear brother, might I have a word with ye?" He could hear Kayla hurrying to catch up with him.

"Kayla, my dear sister," he mimicked her address as he turned to face her. "What can I do for ye?" He'd been wondering when her curiosity would make itself known.

"Mayhap ye can tell me yer intentions with our visitor, Mistress Ellers?" She got right to the point.

"Why, whatever do ye mean?"

"Rory, ye need not play dumb with me. 'Tis easy to see ye have an interest in Teressa. First, ye arrange to sit next to her at our evening meal, and then ye take her out for a ride, and to the bay. Tell me what ye are thinking."

"Are ye annoyed about being displaced at dinner?" he asked, trying to sidestep her questions.

"Nay, of course not, but ye did get my attention with yer little maneuver."

"I should think 'tis reasonable for me to be interested in an attractive visitor. I am a single man."

"'Tis not unusual for women to be interested in ye, but 'tis plain to see ye are taking an active interest in Mistress Ellers."

Kayla was right, and he knew it. His good looks and easy manner often drew the women to him like moths to a flame. Usually, all he had to do was sit back and wait for their flirtations. This time, his interest had spurred him to take action beyond his usual indifference.

"Mayhap, I find Mistress Ellers more interesting than our local ladies. After all, she has come a long way to land at our doorstep."

"Aye, and do ye not find it disturbing we know so little about her?" Kayla made no attempt to hide her dismay. This was unlike his sister, and he wondered what caused her concerns.

"Nay, 'tis what intrigues me most, the mystery of her. Truth be told, I'm not sure what wonders await me, but finding out 'tis half the fun."

"I must caution ye to be careful. Ye don't know who she is or how long she will stay. This may not end well."

"Have no fear, little sister. I think I can handle this on my own." Rory placed his arm around his sister's shoulders in a show of brotherly affection.

"What will ye do when she returns to her family, as ye know she must?" Kayla asked with extraordinary boldness.

"I will deal with that if I have to. Besides, who is to say she must return to her family alone?" He grinned at the possibilities his remark held.

Kayla gave Rory a look of stark apprehension.

"Ye need to trust me on this. I have all well in hand. Ye best hurry off to get ready for supper." Making a shooing motion, he flashed another mischievous grin before heading inside the keep to wash up for the evening meal. He was already looking forward to his next opportunity to woo the mysterious Teressa.

~*~

Teressa stomped down the corridor toward the great hall in search of Bonnie, feeling disturbed and distraught over her encounter with Rory. One minute, she was telling herself not to get involved with him, and the next, she was reacting to the mere touch of his fingers against her cheek, wanting him to kiss her. She felt like a foolish schoolgirl, the kind that usually came to her for coaching.

"This cannot happen," she moaned aloud. "I cannot allow myself to get involved with a man from this time. It's irresponsible and impractical to even think of a relationship with Rory when I know I'm going to leave."

She thought she was alone, when suddenly, Moezell appeared. Stunned, Teressa jumped back a step. The faerie had an unnerving way of showing up unexpectedly.

"How do you know it has no future? How can you know where this attraction will take you?" Moezell asked.

"No," she argued with the faerie. "I don't want to stay here. I want to go home, and I don't want to leave with a broken heart."

"Even if you were of the same time, you of all people know very well there are no guarantees when it comes to the emotions of the human heart."

"But human hearts can be hurt when we lose someone we care for. And I know I can't stay here," she argued, trying to reason with the faerie. She wasn't even sure why she bothered.

"Do you really believe it's better to never love so you will never have to lose? Is that what you want, the illusion of being safe from your feelings?"

"I never said anything about falling in love with Rory, and I'm not afraid of my feelings."

"Then, tell me, what are you afraid of?"

The question weighed heavy on her mind. She paused to consider Moezell's question before answering. "Okay, maybe I am afraid of falling for a man I can't be with," she admitted. "But that seems pretty darn reasonable to me."

"Do you mean be with *now*, or forever? Even faeries have no guarantees when it comes to forever."

Realizing Moezell had an agenda, she asked the faerie, "What do you suggest I do?"

"Your destiny already awaits you. You cannot imagine what fate has in store for you. You can only enjoy today, and leave tomorrow for tomorrow."

Darn, there was that live-in-the-moment thing again. Teressa tried to remain calm. It wasn't working. "No, you're wrong." She pounded a fist against her thigh.

A noise drew her attention, and she turned to see Duncan entering the room. When she looked back, Moezell was gone. Sighing, she welcomed the interruption.

"Mistress Ellers, I've not seen ye around the keep today. Has Kayla kept ye busy down at the village?" Duncan greeted her.

Teressa turned to greet him with a smile, banishing thoughts of conversations with meddlesome faeries. "Kayla took me to meet her friend Fern MacLarken, and Bonnie took me to meet her sister, Annie. We spent the afternoon sewing." After her earlier meeting with Lady Lydia, she knew she needed to establish a friendly relationship with Duncan. It would help her fulfill her assignment.

"It sounds like a fine day full of women's company. I also heard Rory spirited ye away for a ride to the bay yesterday morn." He returned her smile.

"I see not much escapes your notice." *Kind of like your mother,* she mused.

"'Tis a small keep. Secrets are often difficult to maintain." He gave her a knowing look, obviously referring to the secret they shared.

This was good; she could make it work in her favor. Gossip from the village would provide an excuse for how she knew of his broken betrothal to Janet MacDonald. "Duncan, I know it is almost time for the evening meal, but I wonder if I could speak with you later. Would you have time after dinner?"

"Aye, I can make time for ye. What is this about?"

"I'd rather not say anything until we have time to fully discuss the matter." She smiled sweetly. It was time to start planting seeds.

"As ye wish. Ye can join me in my solar where we can speak privately."

"Thanks, Duncan. That'll be perfect. I'll look forward to it. And now, do you know where I can find Bonnie? I'm hoping she'll assist me again." She was becoming quite attached to Bonnie's company.

"If yer appearance these past eves is any indication of her assistance, I will offer she did quite a fine job. I believe ye will find her in the servants' chamber at the back of the great hall."

"It's very nice of you to have noticed. I'll be sure to pass your praise on to Bonnie when I find her." She took note of his veiled compliment and headed off to continue her search.

After finding Bonnie, who agreed to meet her in her chamber, Teressa headed back to her room, thinking about the two men who had recently come into her life. She had learned to trust her instincts when it came to her perception of people's personalities. By closely observing her clients, she often gained valuable insight into their character and usually learned more by reading their body language than by listening to their words. After a few years of practice, she realized key traits had a way of showing up in a person's features.

Duncan's appearance showed his strong capacity for leadership. He carried himself well as the chief of his clan. There was a strong family resemblance between Duncan and Rory, but Duncan's features displayed greater refinement, and he was more conservative in his expression of emotions, whereas Rory's easy nature and witty sense of humor were evident in his smiling eyes and perpetual grin.

Teressa even noticed how strongly their body language indicated their individual personalities. Duncan's stance was stiff and formal while Rory's was so much more relaxed. He was no slouch, but his body language was open and inviting. At least, it certainly felt inviting to her. She acknowledged that any woman who came into his presence would be drawn to him. On the other hand, Duncan could be intimidating, if he so desired, with only a minimum of effort.

While she was aware of Duncan's authority and intelligence, she didn't feel uncomfortable around him. Quite the contrary, their relationship felt fairly friendly, which was probably due to the protective manner with which he had begun their association and the secret they shared. Although it must have been difficult to accept when he discovered she was from another time, he had treated her with respect, not contempt. Another man might have dismissed her as a madwoman, or even a witch. That would have been a bad thing, a very bad thing. Instead, Duncan displayed insight and understanding that served him well as chief of his clan. Most likely he would make a strong and honest ally for the MacDonald clan. It also seemed highly unlikely he would be open to talking about his love life, but by God, she was going to try.

CHAPTER 10

The moment Teressa entered the great hall for the evening meal, Rory felt his senses tingle; she definitely had an effect on him. He couldn't deny, he wanted this woman. His smile deepened at the thought of her in his arms, responding to his caress, giving herself over to the pleasure he knew he could offer her.

Considering his earlier conversation with Kayla, when everyone took their places at the table, Rory sat between Teressa and his sister, thinking it was best to keep the two women separated. Kayla, and it seemed everyone in the great hall, was taking notice of his interest in their visitor.

"I cannot remember the last time I saw Rory falling over himself for a woman," Michael whispered to his wife, grinning with amused satisfaction.

"Why should he? He doesn't have to," Shana said, speaking louder than necessary. "Usually, they're flocking to him." She didn't speak often, which was a good thing, Rory noted, because when she did, her words were often blunt and lacking compassion.

Duncan, on the other hand, was keeping his thoughts to himself.

Rory paid little attention to his family's critiques. He rarely did. Even as a young lad, he had always known Duncan would be chief, and if not Duncan, then Michael. Either way, being the youngest brother had removed any need for him to act responsible or serious.

Right from the cradle, he had developed a preference for a carefree life, cultivating his talents of humor and seduction. The more serious matters of running a keep, he left to his brothers.

"I'm looking forward to seeing Mother tomorrow," Kayla said, as she passed around the bread. "I'm only sorry she couldn't come sooner. 'Tis too soon before we leave for the faire."

"I can hardly believe we will not be attending the Isle Faire this year," Shana complained to Michael.

"Ye know I must stay to guard the keep," Michael reminded his wife with practiced patience. "But as I've said before, there's no need for ye to stay behind. The lads and I will be fine if ye wish to attend with Mother." From the sound of Michael's voice, this was already a well-discussed subject.

"What, and leave ye alone with Tanner and Torrin? I think not," Shana objected. "My bairns are too young to be left without their mother."

"As ye wish. The lads will be staying here with me," Michael said in a tone that indicted the discussion was over.

Rory could feel for his brother. As usual, Shana's comments were more of a show of self-sacrifice than an argument of reason. According to Michael, she actually had a kind heart. Unfortunately, it was not often accompanied by a kind mouth.

"I'm looking forward to meeting Lady Lydia. Do you think she'll want the use of her sitting room?" Teressa questioned Kayla.

Rory thought how he would like nothing more than to have her move into his room, to feel her lush body next to him in his bed, sharing his passion and pleasure. Of course, that wasn't going to happen, but still, he enjoyed the thought. He knew she had her doubts; he had felt her hesitation, but he was willing to give her the time she needed to feel at ease. What mattered most to him was, that in the end, she would be his; of this, he was certain.

"I'm sure Mother will be happy to have ye as her guest, but I would not expect yer stay to be much longer. Are ye not anxious to return to yer family?" Kayla looked pointedly at Rory.

"I've asked Teressa to join us at the Isle Faire," Duncan informed his siblings. "She's new to this land, and I believe she will enjoy the experience."

"Are ye not expected to return home?" Kayla questioned in shock. "Will not yer family be looking for ye?"

"If anyone is looking for her, I will know. I have sent word to the village of her safekeeping with the MacNicol clan. All know of our protection if her companions should return to search for her," Duncan offered in her defense. "Until then, Mistress Ellers is quite safe in our company."

"Duncan is right," Teressa said. "Yes, of course my family will worry when they realize I'm missing, however, for now, Duncan assures me I'm safe. I hope this isn't a problem."

Rory was also a bit surprised at Teressa's lack of concern, but the way he saw it, her refuge in their home worked in his favor.

"Kayla, why are ye so hesitant to offer her our hospitality?" he asked, disturbed by his sister's reaction. He wanted Teressa to feel welcome, to stay as long as possible, but Kayla seemed determined to get rid of the woman, as if she were genuinely distraught over Teressa's presence.

"Ye know I wouldn't refuse our hospitality, but it seems to me, Teressa should be making arrangements to return home, not joining us at a festival. If it were me, I would want to return home as soon as possible," Kayla said, unable to hide her anxiety.

Rory knew his sister would never consider leaving home without her family. Teressa, on the other hand, was handling her situation better than he would have expected. Aye, she had showed moments of fear, and there were times when she tried to hide her emotions, but he could give the lass credit for her show of strength. She was obviously not one to shy away from life's wee worries.

Uncertainties were a part of living, and one either adapted or died trying.

"Kayla, where I come from, it's not unusual for a woman my age to make her own way in the world. I know it's different here. I understand you've enjoyed the shelter of your strong and protective brothers your whole life. My brothers and I also have a strong bond, but they understand I'm capable of taking care of myself. Make no mistake, I want to return home, and I'm sure I will, but for the moment, I feel it's best if I can accept this detour and make the best of an unexpected pleasure."

"The best of an unexpected pleasure?" Kayla repeated Teressa's words, her voice shrill. "How can ye call being separated from yer family an unexpected pleasure?"

Teressa looked as though she were becoming uncomfortable with the situation, and Rory was about to come to her defense when Teressa said, "I believe you misunderstand me. It's the kind comfort of the MacNicol's which I find an unexpected pleasure, not the separation from my family."

She was obviously trying to avoid an argument. Rory could respect that. Kayla voiced valid concerns, but he was impressed by Teressa's display of confidence. He had also questioned Teressa about her family and had voiced some of the same concerns as Kayla. It hadn't occurred to him to consider his sister's point of view; it went a long way toward explaining her reaction earlier in the bailey.

"Mistress Ellers, I will agree, 'tis rare to see someone so accepting of a situation such as yers. And, Kayla, ye are right, ye would never be allowed to travel without yer family. Now, can we talk about something really important, like how much ale the MacLeods will bring to the festival?" He wanted to break the tension between Kayla and Teressa. The conversation had gotten too serious for his liking.

Michael laughed at his younger brother. "Leave it to Rory to prefer drinking over fighting. Ye should be much more concerned about how much ale our brother will drink in the coming days. We may need ye, Kayla, to keep him from making a complete fool of himself."

"I fear 'tis already too late for that," Duncan said, joining in the brotherly banter.

"'Tis only a fool's jest. Yer words canna cut my thick skin." Rory laughed.

More importantly, Teressa laughed too, lightness returning to her eyes.

When the meal ended and the family was moving to take their leave, Rory turned to halt Teressa before she left the great hall. "It would be my pleasure if ye would join me for a walk in the gardens. 'Tis much too early for ye to retire to your chamber, would ye not agree?" He hoped to gain some more valuable time alone with her.

"I'm sorry, I can't. I've asked to speak with Duncan. He's waiting for me." Her gaze was diverted as she watched Duncan head off towards his solar.

This sounded serious. "Should I be worried?" he asked.

"No, don't be silly, it's just a little something I need to discuss with him." She looked distracted, as if anxious to be going.

Rory was frustrated, but not unduly concerned by her request to speak with Duncan. Likely, it had something to do with Kayla's remarks at the evening meal. He damn sure hoped it wasn't something more, like a tryst with his brother, but he brushed that thought aside. He hadn't seen any signs of affection between them, and he had been watching.

Not one to be easily dismissed, he persisted, "Mayhap yer discussion will not take long. I would be happy to wait for ye." He would wait forever for her if it meant she could be his.

Again, she hesitated, as she nibbled on her bottom lip. It was an endearing gesture. He would welcome the opportunity to be the one nibbling on her lips, as well as numerous other parts of her body.

"'Tis merely a walk in the garden." He shrugged, affecting a casual manner. "How fearsome can that be?"

"Okay," she finally agreed, as she picked up her skirts to hurry after Duncan. "If it's not too late."

"I'll be waiting." Rory grinned, filled with confidence and growing expectations.

~*~

Duncan poured a generous quantity of good Scottish whisky into his goblet and relaxed into one of the sturdy leather chairs fronting the hearth in his solar while he waited for Teressa to join him. It hadn't escaped his notice her appearance was rousing memories of Janet and the feelings he once held for the lass. It was only natural a single, attractive woman like Teressa would remind him of his desire to have a wife and a family of his own. There had been a time when he had held high hopes for such a match with Janet, but his hopes had been crushed when she had returned with her mother to her clan. It pained him to admit his feelings of desire for Janet were reemerging from their long, dark slumber, seeking to once again see the light of day.

Shaking himself from memories he had believed to be long buried, he directed his thoughts back to Teressa's request for a private discussion. He wondered what had prompted her to request this meeting. Had she learned something new about why she had been pulled to this time? That seemed unlikely, as she hadn't seemed as happy as he would expect if that were the case.

Her demeanor made him wonder if Rory had done something to provoke her. His youngest brother was obviously drawn to Teressa. Duncan could hardly blame him; she was an attractive woman in so many ways. Were Rory's attentions unwanted or overbearing? His observations of Teressa, and the way she handled unpleasant confrontations, led him to believe she could handle

Rory's attentions on her own. He noticed how firmly she had held her ground against the concerns raised by Kayla. She'd been in their keep only a few days, and already she was causing controversy within his family. She acted far more confidently around men than most women he knew. Considering she came from the future, and had come dressed as a man, perhaps it was her natural way. It made him wonder once again why the fates had brought her to his keep.

He took another swallow of whisky and waited.

~*~

"Thank you for agreeing to see me," Teressa greeted Duncan as she entered the room. She made sure to securely close the door behind her.

He motioned to the chair across from his.

"Ye have something ye wish to discuss with me?" Duncan's expression remained closed as he waited for her to speak first.

She knew it wouldn't be a good idea to jump right into a discussion of his past relationship with Janet. Instead, she planned to begin their conversation with a safer topic, hoping to get a feel for his mood. Rory's attentions would serve her well as a starting point.

"As you know, regardless of how long I'm here, I'm hoping I will eventually return to my own time."

"I spoke to Souyer about that earlier. He tells me he is not yet able to ensure a safe passage for ye. I believe he has tried to contact the faeries, but so far, he has not been successful. I regret I don't have better news for ye," Duncan said.

"I understand." She nodded, looking down. Since she had been informed by Lady Lydia that Souyer had played only a minor part in bringing her to this time, she had very little reason to believe the druid would be the one to send her back home. That magical task was Moezell's responsibility, and Teressa had to trust the faerie to set things right when the time arrived.

She looked up to meet Duncan's eyes before continuing, "I'd guess you've noticed Rory's interest in me."

"Aye, I've noticed. Have his actions been inappropriate?"

"No, not at all. In all fairness, he's been a perfect gentleman. It's just that . . ." She paused, hesitant to reveal too much of herself to Duncan. "I'm afraid his feelings may . . . umm, you know, suffer . . . when I have to leave." She swallowed hard, choking down the lie, knowing it was her fear of loss that scared her.

Duncan laughed. "Ye need have no concerns for Rory. He's a grown man, acting of his own accord. I trust he can handle his feelings and any eventual outcome."

Teressa gave a halfhearted chuckle in reply. "Yeah, I suppose so."

Duncan's expression turned serious. "What about ye, Teressa? How do ye fare? Are ye displeased by his behavior? If ye would like, I can speak to him about withdrawing his attentions."

"No, I don't think that's necessary. It's kind of you to offer, but I need to deal with Rory on my own terms. It's just that I feel bad about deceiving him. I can't tell him where I'm from or how I got here, or when I will leave, only that I have to go back home, and I don't even know when that will be. I feel like I have no control."

By seeking Duncan's advice, Teressa hoped to increase his comfort with her. Hopefully, it would encourage him to open up to her. She certainly appreciated having someone she could talk to. Apparently their shared secret created a stronger bond than she had expected.

"I'm glad ye have come to me with this. I know 'tis necessary to maintain yer secret. We don't want anyone else knowing ye're from the future. 'Tis hard enough for me to believe; I cannot expect the rest of my family to be so understanding. Knowing ye are expected to leave, even if we don't know when, should be enough to satisfy Rory." He spoke like a true chief of his clan. It gave Teressa enough confidence to continue.

"I appreciate you discussing this with me. I feel better knowing I have your support. It can be hard to go it alone. Sometimes relationships can be so complicated." She paused a moment, gathering her thoughts. "I hope I'm not being too forward, but in the village today, I heard of your broken betrothal to Janet MacDonald."

Judging by the immediate stiffening of his body, Teressa knew she had hit a raw nerve. She saw the muscles in his jaw tighten. He was fighting his emotions. It was definitely a sensitive subject for Duncan, and she needed to proceed with caution.

"I am not surprised ye heard of my betrothal; 'tis common knowledge. I am disappointed to hear such private matters are openly discussed." His voice sounded as stiff as his spine.

"I believe the matter was brought to my attention with sincere concern for my welfare, as well as yours."

"I don't understand how my past should be anyone's concern. Surely, no one would mistake my connection to ye to be anything more than the protection I offer as chief of my clan."

"I didn't mean it like that. What I wish to discuss is more personal, something more in the way of shared experiences."

"I don't understand."

"I told you I came to the Isle of Skye after the passing of my father for some private time and to heal. That's all true. What I didn't tell you, because as you mentioned, it was far too private, is that I was also recovering from a broken engagement. From what I've been told, it was for reasons very similar to yours. I was hoping we could share our experiences."

"I see no benefit in the sharing of old wounds." He looked away. His discomfort was apparent, and expected. Most men were uncomfortable talking about their emotions.

This was a risk, she was broaching a painful subject, but she had to persist and hope she could break through his defenses. "I'm going to respectfully disagree. I think sharing helps us heal." She reached out to briefly cover his hand with hers as a gesture of comfort.

"I have no wounds in need of healing." He sat staring at the fire glowing low in the hearth.

He was determined, she would give him that. But so was she.

"Apparently, you're stronger than me. I think I'll always remember that feeling of loss, when I had to accept that Jeffery would never embrace my family. That he didn't love me enough. At least that's how it felt. I know it's affected my view of relationships. I'm far more wary of future disappointments." She paused, watching for his reaction.

Apparently, her words were having their intended effect. Duncan's body language began to soften.

"I think I understand, this thing about memories." Not looking up, he continued to gaze into the fire.

It was time for some support group mentality. I'll show you my pain if you show me yours.

"I met Jeffery when we were still in college. We hit it off right away. He was so much fun, and we were young. Right from the start, I knew he didn't really like my family. It wasn't my family in particular he didn't like; it was families in general. I guess I always expected he would change, but it never happened. Eventually, his refusal to accept my family was too much for me to bear. It was a deal breaker. I felt as though I had to choose between him and my family. I chose my family. I understand something similar between you and Janet MacDonald."

Upon the mention of her name, Duncan abruptly looked up from the fire. "Aye, there was a problem of family loyalty. Janet was too dedicated to her family. She refused to pledge her loyalty to the MacNicol clan."

"Interesting. Actually, Janet's story sounds an awful lot like mine. Both of us are young women with strong family ties. But on the other hand, like you, I wanted Jeffery to declare his acceptance and loyalty to my family. Funny how wanting the same thing can seem so different based on one's point of view."

As she spoke, she began to consider how Jeffery, like Duncan, had wanted her to break away from her family to create a new separate family of their own, and how her loyalty to her "clan" had caused her to break up with him. *Oh my goodness*, she thought, *this really is hitting close to home.*

"I'm sure ye did what ye felt was right. Ye couldn't abandon yer family." Duncan voiced his support.

This was it, the crack she was looking for. Perhaps now he'd be able to see the other side of the fence.

"Yes, and I imagine it was the same for Janet. I heard she was very close with her mother. I can understand how the fear of losing her family was too much for a young woman to bear. It must have weighed heavily on her heart."

"I was offering her the protection of my clan. It should have been enough," Duncan countered. "I had to do what was best for my clan."

"In my time, we say it's the devil you know versus the devil you don't. She'd always had the love and support of her family, but you were asking her to leave that all behind and believe your family would be just as accepting, just as loving. Maybe that was asking too much too soon. Maybe she was just too young," Teressa counseled.

Duncan pounded his fist on the arm of his chair. "I needed Janet to swear her loyalty to me and the MacNicol clan. It was her mother's fault for having too strong of a hold over the lass. It kept her weak. I needed to break the bond of mother and daughter. I needed her loyal to me." There was a great deal of rage and very little remorse in his confession.

Teressa wasn't discouraged. Confession was good for the soul. Releasing his anger was a step he needed to take before he could move on and rebuild a relationship with Janet. Perhaps if she shared her confession with him, she could help him see how Janet must have felt.

"But I could never consider a marriage that didn't include the love and support of my family. How could I? I wanted Jeffery to accept my family as his own. Was that too much to ask?" She put forth to Duncan the same requirement he had made of Janet, seeking his opinion.

"Nay, lass, ye only wanted peace, the true joining of two families." His voice softened with compassion.

"I think you have it right, the true joining of two families. That's what we both wanted, Duncan," she agreed, confirming his viewpoint. "I wonder if Janet felt the same way."

Duncan shot her an uneasy look. "I wouldn't know. When I sent Janet away with her mother, she returned to the MacDonald keep. From what I know, she remains there still."

It was much easier to take a front row seat to peer into other people's lives and tell them how to perfectly manage their relationships, applying the same skill to oneself was much harder. Teressa believed her schooling and training had helped her get through her breakup with Jeffery. He hadn't been the right man for her. And yet, while her coaching skills had helped her end a relationship that had no future, they hadn't been able to shield her from the painful feelings of loss. Teressa realized she'd never been able to fully heal her emotional wounds, or dispel the fear that someone she loved hadn't loved her enough.

"Maybe it's not too late," she murmured, speaking more to herself than to Duncan.

"Not too late for what, lass?" Duncan asked.

"Too late to rebuild our confidence, to try again," she said, looking up.

Duncan's gaze did not meet her eyes. He turned away and remained silent, staring at the low-burning fire.

She wondered if he were remembering his time with Janet and contemplating errors made along the way. Maybe he was thinking about what he could have done differently. Either way, there was nothing more she could do. It was time for her to leave. The seed had been planted as Lady Lydia had suggested. She needed to give him time alone, trusting the seed would do its work.

"Thank you for taking the time to speak with me," she said, rising to leave.

"Ye're welcome," he mumbled without looking up. Barely acknowledging her departure, he took another slow sip of whisky.

He looked weary, his face drawn with sadness and regret. Teressa wanted to reach out to him, to comfort him, but he wouldn't want her pity or her sympathy. Quietly, she slipped out the door, leaving him alone with his thoughts.

After leaving the warmth of Duncan's solar, she walked through the great hall out to the garden in the courtyard. The sun was already low on the horizon, and a smattering of clouds reflected its fading light, painting the sky with crimson, orange, and golden streaks of color. She hadn't planned to rendezvous with Rory, and yet almost without thought, her feet led her right to the garden gate.

Breathing deeply, she took in the cool, clean fragrance of the flowers carried on the evening breeze. As she stepped past the garden gate, she immediately spied Rory peacefully lounging on one of the benches near the entrance. Pausing, she took a moment to drink in the impressive sight. His long legs were stretched out before him, crossed lazily at the ankles, and his arms lay folded across his broad chest. Leaning back against the garden wall with his eyes closed, he appeared to be sleeping. It touched her to think he had dozed off while patiently awaiting her arrival. Sitting there, all relaxed and hunky as he was, he presented quite an appealing image of a handsome warrior in restful repose. A light evening breeze ruffled the chestnut-brown curls framing his finely chiseled face. Smiling wistfully, she wished she had a camera to capture the moment.

Her blatant attraction to him filled her senses, accompanied by a nervous flutter of butterflies. Teressa could actually feel her chest tighten in response to his masculine presence. Try as she might, she couldn't deny the strength of his appeal. She stood there, frozen, mesmerized by the sight of him.

Before she took another step into the garden, Rory broke the silence with his husky Scottish brogue, his eyes still closed. "Do ye like what ye see, lass?"

Feeling her tension melt away, she smiled at his ruse. He'd been well aware of her presence. "*Aye, 'tis* a lovely view of the gardens in the setting sun," she mimicked his brogue.

His eyes cracked open enough to see her face in the twilight. "'Tis only the gardens holding yer attention?" he parried back.

"Lady Lydia has done a fine job of producing a very pleasant creation." Her words could be taken to mean either the gardens or Lady Lydia's son, and she doubted the double meaning of her compliment would be lost on Rory. Nothing was lost on Rory. She took another step into the garden; the fine pebbles lining the path crunched beneath her boots.

"Come sit beside me, Mistress Ellers. I think ye may find the view most pleasant from here." He sat up from his reclined position.

"Really? You find the view from where you sit to be most pleasant?" She turned around, as though she were examining her surroundings. "It would seem that other than me, you're looking at the wall of the keep. Is that what you find most pleasant?"

Rory stood and took three long strides to stand before her. Gazing down at her upturned face, he conceded. "Aye, lass, mayhap the view is best appreciated from here." A provocative grin lit up his face as he brushed a wayward strand of hair from her face.

She beamed back at him. Maybe she was feeling generous after her talk with Duncan, or maybe she found it too hard to resist Rory's flirtations. Either way, she decided it was better to engage Rory as an equal, rather than act like a mealy-mouthed scaredy-cat who ran and hid at the first hint of a challenge. Besides, it wasn't in her nature to be submissive to a man, allowing him to dictate the terms of their encounter. She found Rory's company delightful and stimulating, and if the moment provided stimulation, well then, it certainly made sense to enjoy the moment.

He took her arm to link in his, and they turned to stroll along the garden paths. She allowed herself to enjoy the opportunity his friendly gesture provided by checking out the strong-corded muscles of his arm as her fingers rested lightly on the sleeve of his shirt before lifting her gaze to meet his.

Rory watched her with curious eyes. "Are ye enjoying yer stay here?" he asked.

"Yes, thank you. I enjoyed our ride to the beach, as well as my visit in the village." As she thought about it, she realized her unexpected detour really was quite an interesting adventure, sometimes difficult, but always interesting.

"It pleases me to know ye enjoyed our ride. Tomorrow I will be busy preparing for our journey to the Isle Faire. Everyone will be busy packing," he informed her.

"I'm sure everyone is excited to be going to the festival. I'll help in any way needed," she offered.

"Yer help will be greatly appreciated. Many hands make light work. Kayla will welcome yer assistance." He was being the perfect gentleman, his hand lightly holding hers as it lay nestled in the crook of his arm.

"The sunset is beautiful tonight. Do you have a favorite site for viewing it?" she asked.

"I have often enjoyed viewing the sunset from the battlements. We could go there now. Although your room has one of the best views of the setting sun, since it faces west," he said, his voice heavy with flirtatious innuendo.

"Really! Are you sending me off to my room so soon?" she asked, pretending ignorance to his meaning.

"Only if I am allowed to accompany ye." His dark, sultry look easily conveyed his intentions.

"Don't you think it's a little too early for that?" Consternation crept into her voice. While she wasn't truly surprised by his direct approach, she was a bit miffed at how quickly he tried to seduce her. Apparently, a thirteenth-century warrior wasn't much different from a twenty-first-century businessman. It seemed he was accustomed to easily getting what he sought.

"I can also tell ye my chamber is best for viewing the sunrise." The back of his hand lightly traced a path across her check.

She chuckle nervously. "My goodness, Rory, you are a bold one. What should I do with you?"

"Anything ye would like."

"Wait, you do understand my situation, right?"

"I believe I do."

"I'm only a visitor here. I don't know how long I'll be staying, but sooner or later, I'm going home."

"I expect ye will, eventually. Until then, shouldn't we take advantage of this unexpected pleasure?" He gazed down at her, his sensual smile burning with seduction.

Teressa felt her heart sink. If this was his idea of flirtation, it had gone too far. He was using her own words against her.

Apparently, his interest went no deeper than a momentary tryst in his bed. As far as he was concerned, she was merely a single woman, traveling alone, lost and ripe for picking. She'd have to be a fool if she thought this thirteenth-century warrior were acting from his heart. This wasn't his heart speaking; this was sexual desire. Of course, he was only being a man, and a darn sexy one too. She'd been the foolish one for thinking his attentions were anything more than fleeting seduction.

Knowing she didn't dally in one-night-stands or short-lived affairs, she saw no reason to continue their useless flirtation. Dang, she should never have agreed to this meeting. Teressa felt an overriding urge to return to her room, alone, and she had no one to blame but herself.

"You know, it's getting late. The sun has set, and it's time for me to return to my chamber." All she wanted was a quick and painless exit.

"What's the rush, sweet lass? Are ye afraid of the dark?" There was a note of humor in his voice.

"It's been a long day, and now I'm tired. I want to go to bed, *alone*."

"As ye wish, my sweet. At least allow me to escort ye to yer room."

"That isn't necessary."

"I would prefer."

"Fine, if you insist." Being the reasonable, level-headed person she was, she realized he hadn't actually done anything to deserve her wrath. He was simply being himself, an easygoing, lighthearted, handsome man full of charming seduction—exactly what she needed to avoid. She could kick herself for accepting his invitation and putting them both in this situation. When was she going to learn?

"Have I offended ye in some way?" he asked.

"No, Rory, I'm just tired." She turned away to avoid his gaze. What did he expect her to say? That she was offended because he only wanted to sleep with her? Hardly an appropriate confession to make to a man she barely knew.

At her door, Rory paused, searching her face, as if trying to determine her frame of mind, probably wondering how far she would let him go. He leaned in to narrow the distance between them.

Teressa figured he might try something like this, and she reacted quickly. Turning her head aside, she reached out to hug him as a way to avoid his intended kiss.

Rory's reaction was strong and immediate. He wrapped her in his arms, holding her close to him, caressing her. His chin grazed the top of her head, and one of his hands stroked her long blond hair, letting his fingers flow through the silken strands.

Caught off guard, Teressa was taken aback by his caring tenderness. Surprisingly enough, his embrace didn't feel sexual or seductive. It felt warm and reassuring, and filled with true affection. She pulled back to search his face. His eyes still indicated his physical desire, but she also detected something more, something she couldn't name. She began to question her snap judgment and wondered if his desire actually went beyond sheer lust. There was no way to be sure, and she wasn't taking any chances.

Stepping away, Teressa forced herself to open the chamber door and slipped inside, effectively making her escape. With her back slumped against the door, she took stock of her emotions. It was easy to fall in love with a man like Rory, much too easy, but she had to resist. To do otherwise would only set herself up for inevitable pain.

While she regretted her need to dismiss him so abruptly, she saw no reason to discuss her feelings with him. It was bad enough to feel like a fool in private. Let him go practice his craft of seduction on some other fawning female.

Again, Teressa reminded herself she'd been called here at Lady Lydia's bidding to do a job, to be a relationship coach for Duncan and Janet, not to create a relationship for herself, and certainly not one without any possible future. She always prided herself in being able to keep her emotions on a fairly even keel, and thankfully, she usually recovered quickly from any emotional storms she did encounter, but Rory was a whole new weather pattern.

~*~

Rory took long strides to cross the bailey, heading out to the battlements to check on the guards. Darkness had fallen, and the torches in the watchtowers were lit. As he stood atop the curtain wall, staring out at the blackness of the ocean, he wondered what had just happened with Mistress Ellers.

Teressa was a difficult woman to read. One minute, she breathed hot, as if warmed by his attentions, and the next, she turned cold, closing him off. The evening had begun well enough. They had flirted, and exchanged easy banter. It was a blessing to be granted the beauty of her presence, the warmth of her smile, and the joy of her company.

He wanted this woman, and he had wasted no time in letting her know the full extent of his desires. The thought of her lithe, beautiful body entwined with his, freely sharing his passion and receiving hers in return, made him heavy with desire.

Teressa had willingly joined him in the garden, and she appeared to be enjoying his company, when suddenly he felt her pull away from him. He understood she expected to go home, but there didn't seem to be an urgent need to hurry her departure. As far as he could tell, she seemed to be enjoying her stay at Scorrybreac. She had even called it an unexpected pleasure.

Life came easily to him, including the attentions of beautiful women, but Teressa was proving to be something new. Something, he didn't quite have a name for it, but something had hit him hard the first moment he saw her. He believed she was a woman worth pursuing, and was willing to put in the time and effort to woo her well. The way he figured, given enough time, and if all went well, she wouldn't be traveling home alone, and certainly not to stay. Not if he had his way.

Rory had sensed the change in her demeanor, but he couldn't identify the cause. It was as though something had spooked her and she had needed to flee. He had tried to learn the reason for her sudden apprehension, but she had turned cold, effectively closing him off.

Sensing her reluctance to discuss her sudden mood change, he had been cautious against pressing too hard, too soon. Teressa wasn't like the other women he had known since childhood. This woman had mysteries to reveal, and secrets to unlock; she required a new set of skills in the art of wooing, and he planned to tread cautiously as he learned her ways.

Being a gentleman, as well as a well-disciplined warrior, he had respected her request to return to her room. It had pained him, but he wouldn't allow his desire for her company to conflict with her desire for rest. He preferred to believe she had honestly grown tired rather than think she was actually rejecting his attentions, especially not after the way she had hugged him. Without a doubt, she was a hard woman to understand, but he couldn't believe she would actually reject him.

Tomorrow would be a busy day, but hopefully he'd find time to continue his wooing. He had wanted to kiss her goodnight, to feel the touch of her lips against his, if only for a moment; but when she pulled him close for their embrace, he had nearly lost his mind. The feel of her body as it aligned with his was amazing. Even now, he could still recall the feeling of warmth as it spread throughout his body, his senses fully engaged, his emotions undeniably responding. Rory wanted this woman. And he wanted her to want him.

He wondered if there were a reason he wouldn't be allowed to accompany her to her homeland, to see her returned safely to her clan. Was there something she wasn't telling him? Like a husband or suitor waiting at home for her? Nay, he dismissed the idea; that couldn't be the problem. She had said as much when they rode along the beach. Besides, he hadn't even revealed his intention to accompany her back home. Then it hit him. *That's what's bothering her. She believes I would allow her to simply leave here, alone.*

CHAPTER 11

A misty layer of morning fog kept the air cool, and dimmed the light of the sun behind gray skies. Out in the bailey, Rory stood amidst a flurry of activity, directing the packing of the wagons being used to transport their provisions for the MacNicols' stay at the Isle Faire, while Teressa watched from the window of her room, impressed by his display of management skills.

Confident and in control, as if standing on the bridge of a ship, Rory instructed his crew on their assigned tasks. Occasionally, he conferred with Michael or Duncan on various details, but Teressa could see the responsibility of getting the wagons loaded and ready for the journey fell mostly to Rory. With his easygoing manner, he moved among the workers, issuing orders, directing activity and spurring each one to do his best work. From time to time, one of the workers would shout a humorous comment, creating a jovial atmosphere, but they still continued to work in an efficient manner, striving to please Rory and complete their assigned tasks.

Rory must have felt Teressa watching him; he turned to look up at her window, catching her gaze. He flashed a brilliant smile and nodded in silent salutation. She returned his greeting with a weak smile and a wave of her hand. It was scant food for a hungry man, and yet his smile lingered as he returned to his duties. One of the workers noticed his exchange with Teressa and gave him a playful poke, harassing him with a suggestive smirk. Once again, she found her mind fighting with her emotions, refusing to acknowledge her attraction to a man from the thirteenth century, in a time and place where she didn't belong.

Turning away from the window, Teressa retreated into the chamber. She had spent almost as many hours fighting her emotions as she had sleeping. As hard as her mind tried to command her heart to disregard any feelings for the man, her heart continued to rebel and blatantly defy her objectives.

She was convinced she couldn't stay in the past, and she was absolutely certain Rory couldn't accompany her to the twenty-first century. No matter how she looked at it, one of them would be forced out of their element, a fish out of water. It felt too intolerable to consider.

If she were to stay in this time and place, her disappearance would always be an unsolved mystery to her family, a source of prolonged heartache. If one of her brothers went away and simply disappeared, never to return, it would haunt her for years, always wondering what happened and fearing the worst. Her mother had already lost her husband in the past year, losing her only daughter to the unknown would surly break her dear mother's heart.

While it was temping to wallow in self-pity, for her, that wasn't allowed, it was simply unacceptable. *Sure, I'm feeling doubtful and displaced,* she reasoned. *That's because I am doubtful and displaced. I have a right to feel this way. That doesn't mean I want to go skipping down the yellow brick road looking for the land of Oz, or happily ever after. Even Dorothy knew there's no place like home.*

She had no desire to be displaced in a time without flush toilets, hot showers, shopping centers, and everything else the twenty-first century had to offer. Plus, she was determined to return home to her family. Both Lady Lydia and Moezell had said she would be sent home when her assignment was done, and she clung to that thought with all her might.

Teressa also couldn't conceive of Rory accompanying her back to the twenty-first century. She didn't want him to leave his family any more than she wanted to be away from her own. Even if Lady Lydia and her faerie cousin could accomplish such a thing, she had no reason to believe they would consider such an arrangement, knowing how much family meant to them. Their love and loyalty to family was a quality she truly admired.

Even if he were willing to leave his family, she couldn't just drop-kick him into the twenty-first century, a time so far removed from his own. How could a thirteenth-century warrior possibly survive in modern times without going bat-shit crazy? With fast-moving cars, trains, and planes, and then throw in television, cellphones, the internet and computers; it would all be too much for someone who came from a time before electric lights had even been conceived.

Over and over again, she reminded herself it was best for both of them if she avoided Rory, keeping their contact to a minimum. Being in his presence only encouraged her feelings, and that was courting disaster.

After she finished packing the few garments she was borrowing from Lady Lydia's storage chests, Teressa moved downstairs to assist Kayla and Bonnie with their packing. As she stepped into the great hall, she spied Bonnie laden down with an armful of blankets.

"Here, let me help you with that," Teressa offered as she caught up with the overburdened servant. "I was on my way to help you and Kayla with the packing."

"'Tis a blessing to have another set of hands." Bonnie gratefully passed off some of her load to Teressa. "No matter how many times we do this, and we do this most every year, there is always so much work to be done. Ye would think after so many years, and we have been going to Isle Faire for as long as I can remember, this packing would be easy, but 'tis always a grand bustle of activity. I, for one, am amazed at how well Rory arranges everything, and with such joy. Since he's returned from his seafaring travels, he's been a shining example of responsibility when it comes to this family. Oh, the lad is still a mischievous one, to be sure, but his devotion to family is something to behold." Bonnie said with barely a breath.

Teressa was amused by Bonnie's comments, but her words only cemented her decision to avoid Rory. His love of family, and their love of him, was too valuable to be put at risk.

Bonnie and Teressa joined Kayla in the great hall, where large baskets were being filled with the provisions needed at the faire. As soon as a basket was filled, a worker was there to cart it off to one of the wagons. It impressed Teressa greatly to know this was all being orchestrated by Rory.

~*~

The day passed quickly, and soon the hours had slipped into the late afternoon. Teressa paused to stretch her back before taking a seat near the steps of the keep, staying well out of the way of Rory and the workers. The morning clouds had disbursed enough to allow for patches of blue sky, and she was enjoying the warmth of the afternoon sun as it spread across the front of the keep.

She had just sat down when she noticed Souyer crossing her way from his high tower. Teressa wondered what the old master druid was up to. From what she had seen, he usually kept to himself rather than mingle with the masses. Privately, she acknowledged her conflicting opinions of the old wizard, a combination of amused acceptance of his self-important ways and a slight distrust of the old man, no doubt influenced by the way he interacted with Duncan.

"Mistress Ellers," he called out to her.

"Master Souyer, to what do I owe the pleasure of your company?" Teressa greeted the elderly wizard.

"I'm glad to find a moment to catch ye alone. I want to speak with ye about what brings ye here to Scorrybreac." The old man gingerly took a seat next to Teressa, lowering himself onto the hard, stone bench.

"You mean my jaunt through time?" she whispered, leaning toward the druid to ensure their conversation could not be overheard.

"More specifically, how ye claim to be from the future."

"I am from the future, whether or not you believe me," she whispered harshly.

"Ye have me wrong. I don't doubt yer claim, lass. I only wonder if ye can tell me about yer future time. How well do ye know *our* future?" He shifted on the bench, trying to find a comfortable position.

"Oh!" Teressa sat back and nodded. She had been expecting these inquiries sooner or later. Either his curiosity or his disbelief would have him asking questions like this. If someone told her they were from the future, she'd be doing the same thing. She also believed it wasn't her place to reveal the marvels of the future. What would he think if she told him one day man would travel in space and walk on the moon? It would probably sound too unbelievable to be true. Even everyday things, like being able to travel eighty miles an hour in a motorized vehicle, would seem farfetched. In this century, it took days to traverse eighty miles. And the idea of being able to talk to someone anywhere in the world by a device called a phone would be inconceivable in these ancient times. Tempting as it was to impress him with such glimpses into the future, she didn't believe it was the right thing to do.

"What would you have me tell you? About things that will happen hundreds of years from now? Believe me, I could tell you some pretty amazing things, things you can't even begin to imagine, and you could call me mad, but I've no intentions of disturbing the future. And I don't know enough about your time to be of any use to you. Sorry." She raised her hands in apology.

"Can ye not share even a wee peek into the future of Scorrybreac or Scotland?" he persisted.

"Nope, not going there." She resisted his pleas with a shrug.

"Ye canna blame an old druid for trying. Is there nothing ye can share with a student of knowledge?" he asked, looking hopeful.

She thought about it for a while and decided to throw him a small morsel. "I can tell you most things won't change much for hundreds of years." She considered how the truly advanced changes had happened in the last one hundred years. "And I can tell you people change even less. We still want the same things in the future as you do now; we just have different stories to tell. People remain pretty much the same over the centuries. Greed, power, money, love, none of that goes away. But mostly we want to be loved and appreciated for who we are and what we have to give to each other." Regardless of all the years separating her from this time, Teressa knew one thing remained the same, the desire to be loved. "It's why I want to go home," she added softly.

"About that . . . there's something I need to tell ye," Souyer said. He appeared to be pondering the future of mankind for a moment before proceeding with his confession. "I've given it much thought, and I don't believe I'm able to send ye back home."

"What? Are you saying you *can't* send me back home, or you won't?" A feeling of dread surged through her as he gave voice to her deepest fears.

"I'm saying I don't believe I'll be the one to send ye back. I think that task belongs to Moezell." He looked pretty calm for a man to be delivering such shocking news.

"What makes you think you're not able to send me back?" Teressa asked, starting to feel suspicious. She didn't want to believe his revelation, but her gut instincts told her the master druid wouldn't share this information unless he wanted something in return. Lady Lydia and Moezell had both told her that she was going to be sent back home; although, now that she thought about it, neither of them had said exactly how that was going to happen. She didn't know whom she should trust and wondered what Souyer was up to. Why would he say this to her? Was he trying to scare her into giving up her secrets?

"Ye mentioned ye were visited by Moezell." Souyer gave her a quizzical look.

"Yes, she came to me in Duncan's chamber shortly after I arrived."

"Her visit shows she has a deep personal connection to yer situation. I may not be a very accomplished druid, but I do know a thing or two about faeries. They don't grace mere mortals with their presence, unless they have a very good reason. Many a druid would be thrilled to be so highly honored, but the faeries cannot be so easily commanded. Nay, lass, 'tis only right and fitting I advise ye that yer fate is out of my hands." His confession seemed to carry a heavy dose of humiliation, a bit of overkill on his part.

"You must be underestimating yourself. Wasn't it your request that brought me here? You must have the power to return me to my time." Though he sounded convincing, and a part of Teressa believed him, something didn't fit, something she didn't quite understand.

He had come to her asking questions; maybe this was his way of digging for answers. If so, there wasn't much she could say, even if she wanted to. She had vowed to guard her knowledge of Lady Lydia's involvement in the matter. If he wanted more details, he wouldn't be getting them from her.

"I believe my solstice request may have been the opportunity they used to accomplish their goal, but I am convinced the reason for this madness can only be known by the good faeries. In other words, my dear, ye will need to procure their talents to ensure yer safe return to yer own time."

Teressa searched the old druid's face to determine the true motivation for his revelation. This couldn't have come easy for him.

She figured the idea of being able to move a person through time must have held great appeal for the wizard, even if it were an unexpected result to his request. To acknowledge the power was not truly his had to be a harsh blow to his ego. It made her wonder why he was sharing this information. Keeping it to himself would have gone a long way toward furthering his image as a powerful master druid. The only reason to reveal his lack of power would be in hopes of gaining access to the faeries through her, perhaps in an effort to procure their talents for himself. She wondered if he were testing her to see if she knew more than she was willing to admit. If that were the case, she wasn't about to fall for his ploy.

She reached out her hand to grasp his, giving his aging hand a comforting touch. He looked surprised. "Don't be too hard on yourself. It seems like you had good intentions when you made your request. I'm just an unexpected result. You can't be faulted for creating something that was out of your control. We all like to think we're in control, but really, we're not." Her gaze shifted and traveled out over the horizon as she thought about her efforts to control her reaction to Rory's charms. "Unfortunately, the fates, or faeries, or whatever the case may be, don't feel the same need to accommodate us."

"I am impressed. Ye seem to be taking this quite well, much better than I had expected."

She turned to look the druid square in the face. "I may be young, but there are a few things I've learned in my life. It doesn't help to want what you can't have. I tried it once. It didn't work. Acceptance is much more practical than denial. Should I pretend this isn't happening? What good would that do me? Do you think I haven't thought about this? It's all I think about. But I have to believe that somehow, someway, this will all work out. I have to believe, even if you tell me it's not in your power to help me, I have to believe I'm going home." She trembled with the force of her emotions.

"Aye, lass. 'Tis in yer best interest to believe, but for me, I am not so sure. To claim the power of time travel is a grand boost for my position. To be stripped of such acclaim is hard medicine to swallow." He spoke slowly, as if carefully choosing his words.

"Isn't it a little too soon to throw in the towel? Perhaps you haven't given it enough time, or something new will be revealed when the time is right. Isn't that possible?" She needed an image of hope, and regardless of Souyer's revelation, hope was the lifeboat she clung to.

"Perhaps ye are right. 'Tis too soon to know. I thought it was worse to deceive ye or give ye false hope. But perhaps ye are right; it will all work out as ye say. I cannot help but wonder, when the time comes for ye to leave, what will ye do about Rory?"

The question caught Teressa completely off guard and hit her square in the chest. She hadn't expected the druid to broach such a personal subject, and she had no intentions of revealing anything to him about her feelings for Rory. Keeping her gaze steady and bland, she completely ignored his question.

Instead, choosing to use her own brand of humor, she reached out her hand to pat the old druid's wrinkled cheek. "You know, Souyer, this has really been so enlightening. We must do it again sometime, and soon." With an impish smile, she stood. "But for now, I have to help Kayla finish packing."

Souyer appeared less than pleased by the outcome of their conversation. Grumbling to himself, he pushed off with his staff to stand.

"*Ciao,*" she said, giving him a farewell wave as he turned to retrace his steps back to the high tower. With a satisfied chuckle, Teressa whirled about and started back to the keep. *Being a mystery was kind of fun.*

Teressa was about to step into the great hall when she saw Rory heading her way from across the bailey. Her first impulse was to hurry into the building. She immediately chastised herself for being so childish. Interestingly, and wholly unexpected, her second impulse was to welcome him with open arms. It was getting harder to deny her feelings whenever she saw him. Thankfully, she was able to override both impulses and simply stand her ground. Instead of fleeing into the keep or flying into his arms, she looked directly into his seductive green eyes, breathed deeply, and smiled sweetly.

Just as Rory reached the steps of the keep, a commotion arose at the fortress gate. The noise immediately caught their attention, and they turned to see Lady Lydia ride through the main gate into the bailey on a large gray horse. Rory turned back for a moment, as if to check Teressa's reaction. She smiled and nodded ever so slightly toward Lady Lydia, acknowledging his need to greet his mother. He gave her a wink and a smile before turning to join his family.

The announcement of Lady Lydia's arrival spread quickly, and her offspring appeared instantly from all corners of the keep. Duncan strode out of the wide front doors of the keep with determined dignity to greet his mother. As he helped her down from her horse, Kayla ran to greet her, like an eager child into the waiting arms of her mother. Michael called to one of the servants to fetch his wife and children. Soon the courtyard was filled with the MacNicol clan loudly and warmly greeting their beloved matriarch.

Teressa watched the tender scene for several moments before slipping away into the keep. The family needed an opportunity to enjoy their reunion with Lady Lydia after her long absence. For one quick second, as she was about to step into the keep, Lady Lydia caught Teressa's eye, sending her a knowing glance of greeting, and then just as quickly, she returned her attention to her children and grandchildren as they clustered around her.

Knowing the family gathering would eventually make its way into the great hall, Teressa thought to make use of Duncan's empty solar and settled into one of the expansive leather chairs in front of the hearth for a quiet rest. She looked around the handsomely appointed office, taking in the beauty of the old world décor of the room.

Once again, she was reminded how amazing it was to sit in the office of a thirteenth-century clan chief and meet people who lived hundreds of years before her time. It was amazing to think this could be happening to her, but it must be happening; it felt too real to be anything else. Teressa ran her hands along the leather-covered chair and felt the solid realness of the furniture. She listened to the sounds from the bailey coming through the open windows, and noted how the breeze carried the rich fragrance of the medieval castle, some of it not so good.

Chuckling quietly to herself, she was reminded of those time-travel stories that were always so popular. Of course, no one ever believed them to be real. They were only stories, works of fiction, tall tales not to be believed. But what if, she wondered, what if other people had traveled through time and wrote the stories as a way of recording their experiences? Since they knew no one would believe them, and there was no way to prove their experience, maybe they wrote it all down and called it a story. It would be a viable way of telling their tale without becoming subject to ridicule, knowing all along the unbelievable tale had actually happened to them. A secret revealed in plain sight. There must be hundreds of books and movies about people traveling into the past or to the future, or even to other worlds, and maybe, just maybe, some of those stories were real. If it could happen to her, it must have happened to someone else. She mused on about the tales of time travel, and secrets revealed, until she fell blissfully asleep, weary from the long morning of packing.

~*~

The evening shadows had begun to deepen when Bonnie entered the great hall to light more candles and ask the family if they were ready for the evening meal to be served. Rory leaned over to Kayla, speaking in a low voice. "I haven't seen Teressa since we came into the keep. Do ye know where she is?"

"How could I? I've been with Mother the whole time," Kayla answered in a low, irritated whisper.

Ignoring Kayla's irritation, Rory pressed on, "I should go look for her before supper is served."

"Rory, stay. Ye shouldn't leave the hall. I'll send Bonnie to go find her," Kayla curtly instructed her brother.

"What are ye two whispering about? Is something amiss?" Lady Lydia interrupted their conversation.

Kayla exchanged a frustrated look with her brother. "Rory is asking about a visitor we have here at the keep and is wondering if she will be joining us for dinner," she reluctantly informed her mother.

"We have a visitor? Why was I not told? Who is she?" his mother asked with mild curiosity.

Before Rory or Kayla could answer, Duncan spoke up. "Her name is Teressa Ellers. She was separated from her traveling party and has made an unexpected visit to our keep. I am providing her with the protection of the MacNicol clan until she can safely return to her homeland."

"An unexpected visit . . . That sounds rather interesting. What else can ye tell me?" Lady Lydia asked.

Duncan paused a moment before he answered. "There is not much to tell. She only arrived a few days ago. I've asked her to accompany us to the Isle Faire. I hope ye will enjoy her company," he stated flatly. He had avoided making eye contact with either Rory or Kayla, and for once, Rory was happy he was not the object of their mother's attentions.

"I look forward to meeting her," Lydia stated, then turned her attention back to Michael who had been telling her stories about his sons' recent adventures.

Rory breathed easier when his mother didn't press further for details. The last thing he needed was for Kayla, or anyone else, to start enlightening their mother about his affection for Teressa. It was highly unlikely Mother would approve of his interest in their unknown visitor, especially since it was doubtful her family ties would be of any benefit to the MacNicol clan. The one thing his mother wanted most was to see her sons well wed to women with strong family ties.

Kayla called to Bonnie, instructing her to find Teressa and advise her they were ready for the evening meal to be served. When she turned to press him with a knowing look, Rory knew his instincts had been correct.

~*~

Teressa was curled up in one of Duncan's large leather chairs, sleeping peacefully, when Bonnie gently roused her from her slumber.

"Oh my goodness. I must have fallen asleep. It was all so peaceful." Teressa yawned and stretched as she uncoiled the kinks from dozing in the armchair.

"Never ye mind, lass. Let me remind ye, ye are to meet Lady Lydia again, but as far as the rest of the family know, ye have never met her before. I trust ye will know what to do. Just act natural, as though ye are meeting her for the first time. I'm sure ye will do fine. Here now, let me tidy ye up a bit. Ye are all mussed from sleeping in that chair. Cannot say I blame ye; I would welcome a nap myself if I were not so busy. But off with us now. The family is waiting in the great hall. And don't look nervous, ye will do all right," Bonnie rambled on.

Teressa attempted to pull herself together, smoothing the wrinkles from her dress with limited success and running her fingers through her disheveled hair. A comb would be nice right about now. When her efforts fell short, she allowed Bonnie to fuss with her hair and straighten her dress to prepare her for her presentation to Lady Lydia.

Bonnie grabbed Teressa's hand and pulled her along behind her into the great hall to join the family already gathered there. "Here's our little lass," Bonnie began as they reached the dining tables. "She must have gotten lost and wandered into Duncan's solar, but never ye mind, she was merely enjoying a wee nap, she was. Such a busy morning, it wore the lass out."

Teressa gave Bonnie an appreciative look. The serving woman certainly was a loyal friend.

"Thank ye, Bonnie." Duncan stepped forward to conduct the introductions. "Mother, this is our guest, Teressa Ellers. Mistress Ellers, allow me to introduce my mother, Lady Lydia."

Teressa looked pensive for a moment, speculating on what would be the politically correct way to greet the matriarch of a clan. She wondered if she were expected to curtsey, trying to recall Bonnie's actions at Annie's cottage. Quite sure it wouldn't be correct to shake the woman's hand, she did her best imitation of a curtsey, nodded politely, and smiled. "Lady Lydia, it's my pleasure." One look into the warm, accepting eyes of the older woman put her immediately at ease.

"Mistress Ellers, 'tis my pleasure. I understand this is an unexpected change in yer travels. I hope ye have found our keep to be a comfortable sanctuary during your delay," Lady Lydia warmly greeted Teressa.

"Why, yes, thank you. I was just thinking what an extraordinary experience I'm having. This is such an amazing place," Teressa offered, privately amused by her underlying innuendo.

"Thank ye," Lady Lydia nodded, accepting the compliment. "I should like to hear more about yer travels and where ye are from. Perhaps we can have a quiet moment to speak later this evening, after the meal."

"I would like that," Teressa readily agreed, anxious to report on her progress with Duncan. The man in question, she noticed, eyed her with nervous apprehension.

"Teressa's staying in yer sitting room. It was Duncan's idea. I hope ye don't mind," Kayla offered. Teressa thought the younger woman looked a tad more worried than the announcement warranted.

"Of course. I'm glad to see ye've done yer utmost to make her feel welcome," Lady Lydia said, looking pleased.

Teressa had a childish inclination to make a face at Kayla. *See, your mother likes me*, she thought, but immediately repented her smug immaturity. She knew Kayla was doing her best to deal with what she perceived to be a difficult situation. Sensing the younger woman's discomfort, Teressa regretted she hadn't formed a deeper friendship with her. At this point, she could use all the friends she could get, and realized it was to her disadvantage that she hadn't been able to make a better impression on Kayla. Trying to make amends, she took the seat next to Kayla, who looked every bit as uncomfortable as Teressa felt.

Feeling Rory's scrutinizing stare, she made a supreme effort to avoid looking his way. The man needed no encouragement, and she wasn't sure she could trust her ability to pretend indifference. She was grateful she'd been able to take a catnap. It looked as though she were in for a long and taxing evening.

CHAPTER 12

Teressa had succeeded in avoiding Rory all evening, but apparently that was about to end. While the family still lingered in the great hall after the meal had ended, Rory pulled her aside.

"Come with me. There's another beautiful sunset, and 'tis a fine night for a walk," he said, speaking quietly into her ear.

"How do you know? You've been inside all evening." Her brows rose in a doubtful arc.

"We've a beautiful sunset every night at Scorrybreac," he grinned in reply. Stealthily, he moved her away from the family circle toward the doors of the keep.

"Won't we be missed?" she asked, looking over her shoulder.

"Nay, mother is too busy making sure Duncan has performed well in her absence."

"Oh, how reassuring. For a moment, I thought this was just a ploy to get me alone," she said with a sweet-and-sour smile.

"There may be some truth to that," he allowed.

With obstinate determination, he moved them out into the bailey. He placed his hand at the small of her back, resting upon the gentle swell of her hips. As they walked, she felt his hand tense ever so slightly in a possessive hold.

"I leave at first light with the supply wagons for the festival," he informed her as they walked toward the fortress wall. "'Tis my duty to leave ahead of the family to make ready our camp at the faire. I expect ye will leave later with Duncan and the family."

"You mean we won't be traveling together?" Teressa surprised herself with the earnestness of the impulsive question. Hard as she tried to contain her thoughts, words, and emotions, they still had a way of slipping past her defenses.

Rory's grin grew wide. "Nay, lass, it wouldn't be right. Ye must travel with my mother and sister, but ye will be well guarded by Duncan and his men."

"Of course, how silly of me. I don't know what I was thinking." She tried to recover her composure, wondering where he was taking her as they walked across the bailey.

"Nay, not silly at all. I would wish to keep ye safe by my side, but travel with the wagons is slow and tiresome. Ye will have greater comfort with the family."

She noticed his hand was still resting on the small of her back, and wrong as it was, she liked it.

They reached an outer stone staircase leading to the top of the battlements running along the curtain wall. He grasped her hand and led her up the steps to the top of the battlement. She was greeted with yet another glorious view of the village and the distant shoreline. Twilight was settling upon the land as the sun dipped low on the horizon.

"This place is so beautiful," she whispered with a loving sigh, riveted by the sight before her. She felt she would never tire of looking at the rugged and beautiful landscape.

Even as she took in the grandeur before her, she knew Rory kept his eyes on her.

The view of the countryside, with its rough and rolling hills falling away to the seashore held her interest for a long moment before she felt a need to fill the silence. She turned to him and asked, "Tell me about the Isle Faire. What is it all about?"

"The faire is a gathering of the people of Skye, the MacLeods, the MacDonalds, and the MacNicols. During the faire, the clans meet to feast, drink, and exchange news. I've always thought of the chiefs' gathering as more of a chest pounding, but then, I'm not the chief, and never expect to be."

"What do you mean by 'chest pounding'?" Teressa chuckled at his comment.

"Each chief does his best to appear strong and commanding, to ensure he has everyone's approval and the acceptance of his clan. 'Tis a way of protecting the power and image of their people. The clans of this isle have not always kept an easy peace, and these gatherings are an effort to keep us on friendly terms."

"Has there been a lot of fighting on this island?" she asked, remembering the military training she had observed.

"In the past, there have been fierce uprisings. It requires an ongoing effort to maintain a balance of power and ensure the protection of each clan. Chiefs often seek to expand their lands, and in return, each clan must protect what is theirs. Land is for the taking, and home must be defended."

Teressa considered the violent feudal hostilities recorded throughout history and was grateful Scotland had eventually evolved to experience long-term peace. "Thankfully, my country hasn't seen an invasion within our borders for many generations. Instead, we send soldiers out to other countries to do battle." Realizing she had offered a thin window of insight into her background, she caught herself and moved on to change the subject. "But you mentioned feasting and drinking at this gathering. Tell me about that."

"Aye, the gathering is a time of feasting and drinking, lots of drinking. The MacLeods are known for their fine ale." There was a provocative gleam in his merry eyes.

"It sounds as though you're looking forward to the drinking part," she chided him.

"A tankard of good ale never hurt a soul, and it has been my experience it does a lot more good than harm. It makes all the women look good to the men, and the men look a lot better to the women. We're all winners," he jested.

"Do women do much drinking at this faire?"

"Some do, most don't, and them that do, don't do enough." Rory laughed at his own joke. He was definitely incorrigible.

"Okay, what else can I expect?" she asked, warming to the subject.

"There will be peddlers there with their wares for sale and games of chance. 'Tis a grand time to part with yer coin."

The faire sounded like a good old-fashioned neighborhood party, only on a much larger scale. The town she lived in when she was younger had held an annual festival in the park, and everyone in her neighborhood attended. The result was a peaceful, friendly place to live.

"Your description sounds grand. I think I'll enjoy myself."

"I'm sure of it, lass. I will personally see to yer enjoyment." Rory flashed his provocative grin. It was hard to misunderstand the intention behind his comment.

Teressa shook her head and rolled her eyes, laughing at his flirtatious remark. "Yeah, I'm sure you will, or go down trying," she teased in return. She felt her guard slipping further away and briefly wondered where it was going.

"Ye tease much, for a woman," he remarked.

"You're a fine one to talk."

"I enjoy yer show of spirit, yer sparring abilities. It shows ye to be a woman of strength."

Had she detected a touch of pride in his voice? This was unexpected. A skirt chaser usually looked for easy pickings, not competent sparring partners. "You surprise me, Rory."

"Ye don't back down or let me intimidate ye. Yer confidence pleases me."

"So I please you, do I?" she probed with an impish smile.

"Aye, lass, greatly," he replied, pulling her close.

Almost instinctually, her arms wrapped around him. Dang, he felt good. It wasn't her intent to encourage him, but it was so darn easy, as if she couldn't stop herself, or resist the pull he exerted upon her.

His hands moved swiftly but gently to cup her face while he lowered his head to touch his lips against hers.

Teressa wasn't prepared for his actions or the sparks igniting her body. With the first gentle touch of his lips, her body responded in a quest for more, more of the warmth swelling within her. He felt her response and deepened his kiss, covering her lips with his warm, spicy mouth, slipping his tongue between her lips ever so gently in a smooth velvety stroke. His kiss progressed from slow and tender to deeply passionate, touching the very core of her being. It was passion fueling passion, creating a reaction far greater than the sum of its parts.

Her body grew liquid and limp as it pressed against his, not only for support, but to increase the physical connection of his embrace. She wrapped her arms tighter around him, seeking an anchor, as her hands moved over the hard muscles of his back, discovering the extent of his strength and the impressive shape of his muscular body. In response, his hands caressed her with an unexpected display of loving tenderness.

Holy crapola, this was grand; this was glorious; this was fireworks worthy of the fourth of July. Was there music in the air? The kiss seemed to go on and on. It spread from her lips to her belly to her toes and every space in between, straight into her soul.

She always believed a woman would know if a man would be her lover with the very first kiss. Physical attraction was all well and good, but the first kiss was the tipping point that sealed the deal, an either make it or break it moment. She believed the first kiss would tell her all she needed to know, and here was Rory, gifting her with the most soul-stirring kiss she had ever known. Never before had she felt her very soul melt and meld with another, nor had she experienced a kiss so pure and intense in its passion. It sparked a blaze that would slowly but surely burn its way to her heart.

It took some effort for her to finally pull back from their embrace. When she did, her eyes remained locked with his, hoping to read his emotions.

"Rory, did you . . . did you feel something . . . I mean, what the blaze just happened?" she stammered breathlessly, her voice barely above a whisper.

"Our first kiss," he replied, sounding rather pleased. "Our first of many, I believe."

"Surely you've kissed other women," she ventured.

"Aye, lass. I will not lie," he confirmed.

"I too have been kissed before, but I have never felt . . ." She hesitated, searching for the right words.

"This way before?" he offered simply.

"Yes. No. Rory, I don't understand. What was that?" She felt confused, struggling to understand the depth of her feelings, swimming in a sea of uncharted emotions.

"'Tis obvious. Ye have never been kissed by a man who wants ye as much as I do, and I've never wanted a woman as much as I want ye." She had to give him credit, true to his nature, he had a way of stating his feelings plain and simple.

"Are you serious?"

"I speak my truth. Would ye deny what ye just felt? Admit it, ye felt it too." His eyes remained locked on hers, waiting for her response.

I cannot do this, I cannot feel this way. The words screamed in her head, but the fearful cries were gently silenced by the calm, clear voice of her heart. *Don't deny what you feel.*

"Yes, I felt it," she confessed.

His face lit up with a smile of unrestrained satisfaction that reached deep into his dark green eyes. She felt his need, his desire. Rory wanted her. He pulled her back into his arms, cradling her, comforting her.

Teressa leaned into his embrace, wanting him to hold her. She didn't want to think, much less speak of the day when this would all end, when she would leave his world to return to her own. *Now,* she reminded herself. *I will only think of now. And right now, all I can think about is how he makes me feel.* Feelings so strong, they overruled all reason and rational thought.

"Can you kiss me again, Rory?" she asked, hoping, wondering if she would feel the passion again.

He laughed lightly. "Aye, lass, I will kiss ye again, and again, until you grow weak with my kisses."

With each kiss the sparks flew, the passion flowed, and she was lost.

They stood there together for quite some time, locked in their lovers' embrace. Rory held her wrapped in his arms, his hand cradling her head as it rested against his shoulder. She breathed in his uniquely sensual scent as it mingled with the salt air wafting off the ocean, and a peaceful comfort enveloped them as twilight gave way to darkness of night.

With a sudden jerk, Teressa pulled back, stepping out of his arms. "Oh my goodness, it's getting late. Lady Lydia wanted to meet with me."

"Must ye go?"

"Rory, she's your mother. It's probably not a good idea to keep her waiting."

Rory nodded in understanding. "I'm sure ye are right." Grudgingly, he led her back to the great hall.

~*~

After bidding him goodnight with one final kiss, Teressa made her way to Lady Lydia's bedchamber. Taking a moment to smooth her gown and tidy her hair, she hoped she could conceal her feelings for Rory, which now churned perilously close to the surface. She took another moment to compose her thoughts before softly knocking on the door. Lady Lydia bid her enter.

"I was beginning to think ye may have forgotten," Lady Lydia said as she gestured for Teressa to take a seat.

"I'm sorry, my lady, I was distracted and lost track of time," Teressa shrugged, wishing she had a better excuse. "It can happen, you know."

Lady Lydia waved off her excuse and got right to the point. "Did ye have an opportunity to speak with Duncan?"

Teressa released her breath in a sigh. "Yes, I'm pleased to report. I planted a seed, as we discussed." Grateful to step into the comfort of her professional role as relationship coach, Teressa proceeded to give Lady Lydia a full report of the conversation she had with Duncan regarding Janet MacDonald. "When I left, he appeared to be deep in thought about our conversation. Now we must watch to see if the seed has taken root."

"Agreed. I believe we will learn much by watching his reaction when he sees Janet at the Isle Faire. She has not attended for the past few years," Lady Lydia informed her.

"Why not? I got the impression the Isle Faire is kinda like the party of the year."

"The broken betrothal caused tension and discord between our clans. Janet was not comfortable being in Duncan's presence, and her father, Hugh MacDonald, holds deep resentments over his daughter's dismissal by Duncan. Kennon, my husband, was also disappointed over his son's actions, but he chose to accept Duncan's choices. Kennon was able to do much to calm the waters of discord with the MacDonalds, but the tensions have remained, buried close to the surface and ready to reemerge if not properly addressed. Now that Duncan is chief, he must assume his rightful responsibilities."

More pieces of the puzzle began to fit into place. The elder MacNicol chief had been able to soften the blow of the broken betrothal by his oldest son, but now that Duncan had assumed the position of chief, his past errors could easily return to upset the peace of the island clans. Lady Lydia's quest to see her son united with Janet MacDonald went well beyond the simple desire to play matchmaker. The peaceful relationship of her clan with their neighbors was at stake.

"Have you spoken to Duncan about this need to marry Janet out of duty to his clan? Certainly, a love match would be preferred, but a marriage of duty must carry some weight for Duncan." Teressa questioned the lack of success to secure the necessary union.

"I have, but it did little good. Duncan's heart needed time to heal, and he needed time to learn what being chief of his clan really entails. Without love and acceptance, the marriage would have been doomed to a painful existence. I've seen the results of such unions. They are not pretty to observe," Lady Lydia explained.

"Very sensible," Teressa remarked. She continued to be impressed by Lady Lydia's keen insight.

"Shortly after Kennon's death, I left to visit my sister. Marian lives with her husband, a MacLeod, on the far side of the isle. Her health has not always been robust, and it provided me with an excuse to depart the keep. In my absence, Duncan has taken on the role of chief on his own. It has been a time of learning for my son, and I believe he has benefited greatly from the experience."

Teressa was impressed by how hard Lady Lydia worked at running her family's affairs from behind the scenes. In this age, it was probably the only way a woman was allowed to execute her influence.

"You seem to have this so well planned," Teressa said. "I'm impressed. But still, I have to wonder. Why me? Why suck me back in time? I know Duncan and I share a similar history—of course, that's helpful—but you seem quite capable of handling this without me. Why did you need to bring me here from seven hundred years in the future?" She continued to question her part in the endeavor. It seemed Lady Lydia had gone to great lengths to accomplish her task.

"I needed a woman such as ye to test Duncan's emotions. He has shown no interest in developing another love match with anyone since Janet. Along with yer other qualities, I needed a woman who could test his affections, a woman of intelligence, someone who would appeal to Duncan. It was a risk I needed to take to ensure he still holds affection for Janet." Lady Lydia said, calmly explaining the motives behind her risky strategy.

The compliment was not lost on Teressa, and Lady Lydia's approval rating ratcheted up a notch in her mind. Not only was Lady Lydia a woman of strategic intellect, she was also proving to be a high-stakes gambler, willing to draw on supernatural resources to accomplish her goals.

"And while ye appear to have impressed him greatly as an equal, from what I see, he has not developed a romantic attachment to ye. Am I correct?" Lady Lydia turned her watchful eyes on Teressa.

"Yes, you're correct," Teressa confirmed, thinking back to when Duncan had discovered her on the beach. It was possible he had shown some interest in her at the beginning, aside from her being a freaking enigma, but if that were true, he had refused to pursue his interest. She considered how easily they might have developed a romantic attachment if he had been so inclined. After all, he was the rescuing hero to her damsel in distress. But he hadn't appealed to her, not like that, not the way Rory did. Duncan could be intimidating and somewhat daunting, but she accepted his gruff ways, and instead of romance, they had developed an alliance as equals. She had to appreciate Lady Lydia's daring.

"Then all is well, as I had hoped." Lady Lydia smiled with satisfaction.

It occurred to Teressa that there was one factor in this whole situation Lady Lydia might not have expected. Her thoughts returned to Rory and her developing relationship with the woman's youngest son.

"I was just thinking, you are planning to send me back home after this project is over, aren't you? I mean, back to my own time?" Teressa needed to confirm her plans for the future.

"Of course, my dear. We would be remiss if we did't return ye to yer own time and place. Why do ye ask?"

"Just checking. That's what I expected. I just wanted to be sure."

Though it was what she wanted to hear, Teressa's heart waffled between soaring with delight over her feelings for Rory and plunging with despair over her feelings for Rory. No matter how she viewed the situation, nothing had changed from her previous assessment. She would be leaving, and Rory would be staying. There was no future for them together in his time or hers.

CHAPTER 13

Early the next morning, Teressa awoke to the sounds of horses being hitched to wagons in the bailey below. She jumped out of bed and rushed to the window in time to see Rory preparing to lead the caravan of wagons out through the fortress gate to begin the journey from Scorrybreac to the Isle Faire. The chill of the night still hung in the air, with the sun barely breaking over the horizon as the wagons prepared to set out on their slow trek to the faire. He must have been awake and preparing for the departure long before the sunrise.

Teressa pulled a blanket from the foot of the bed and wrapped it around her for protection from the cold morning air. Returning to the window, she settled in to watch the action below. Rory looked strikingly handsome in an ivory shirt that brought out the sun-bronzed glow of his skin. A length of the MacNicol plaid was draped over one shoulder and wrapped around his waist, secured by a thick leather belt.

He made a final inspection of the wagons ready for departure before mounting his horse, and then turned for one last look toward the window of her room. She rewarded him with a lazy smile as she ran a hand through her hair, realizing her tousled tresses revealed she had just risen from her bed.

Rory raised his hand in a farewell salute to Teressa and completed the movement with a wave to order the wagons forward, appearing strong and self-assured as he took control of the servants under his command. The warrior's training was evident in him. He could have been leading a brigade of soldiers off to war instead of a caravan of wagons heading off to make camp at a faire; however, the peaceful caravan was far more appealing to Teressa's modern sense of nonviolent diplomacy.

Teressa washed and changed into a burgundy wool skirt with a long ivory tunic before heading down to the bailey. Soon the second wave of travelers were gathered and ready to leave the keep. Duncan, who was also wearing the MacNicol plaid, accompanied the remaining family members to the faire, along with a score of select guards. Kayla and Teressa had joined Lady Lydia in her coach, which was hardly more than a covered wagon and provided little comfort, even with the supply of cushions and blankets used to pad their seats. Souyer, Teressa noticed, also accompanied the MacNicol clan, traveling in his own little donkey cart.

It was late in the evening when they finally arrived at the designated faire grounds. The earlier departure of the supply wagons had given the servants enough time to set up the tents that would house the various family members. Teressa would be joining Lady Lydia and Kayla in their tent. After the wagons had been unloaded, they would double as sleeping quarters for the servants. Travel to the Isle Faire was an annual tradition that had developed into a well-worn routine.

Bone weary and hungry by the time they reached the faire, Teressa insisted Lady Lydia and Kayla leave her on her own while they went to greet old friends.

After securing a cold meat and cheese sandwich with Bonnie's assistance, Teressa opted to stretch her cramped and aching muscles by taking a walk through the camp to have a look around. The grounds were abuzz with activity. Servants and villagers from the attending clans were busy erecting the last few tents and stalls that would comprise the Isle Faire. Brightly colored flags representing the various clans or the peddlers in attendance waved in the breeze from atop the standing tents, creating a festive feeling. Many of the peddlers were still busy working to set up their markets to showcase their wares. Several apprentices were at work near the cook wagons, washing vegetables and preparing preserved meats for the upcoming meal. Temporary horse corrals had been constructed to contain the large number of horses used to transport people and supplies. It reminded her of the Renaissance fairs she had attended back home, only far more ancient, and certainly far more authentic.

Meandering aimlessly through the camp, she drank in the historical experience. Just as she rounded the pathway leading through the peddlers market, she came upon Rory.

He advanced toward her in long, angry strides. "Teressa, where have ye been? I've been looking everywhere." He sounded a bit angry, as if she had done something wrong, or maybe he was just overly concerned.

"I've been exploring. I've never been to an Isle Faire before, and I wanted to look around," she explained.

"'Tis not a good idea. This may be a friendly gathering, but a woman such as ye should not be wandering alone." He reached out to take hold of her arm, but she jerked away.

"Really! Just what kind of woman do you think I am? I'm quite capable of taking care of myself." Her stomach tightened as she felt a sudden need to defend her actions.

"Look around. Ye're a woman, wandering alone, without protection. There are men here who would gladly take advantage of one such as ye," he scolded her.

Teressa gawked at him. He was actually scolding her, as if she were an errant child. She looked about, considering his point of view. Dozens of men were working and milling about the area. Any one of them could have approached her with dubious intentions, but they hadn't. Perhaps his concerns were justified; perhaps they weren't. Either way, she wasn't ready to admit defeat. She didn't like being scolded, and she didn't like being seen as a harlot, which was how his words made her feel.

"You make it sound like I've done something wrong, when all I wanted was to have a look around." She lifted her chin in defiance.

"If a man thinks ye are without protection, he will consider ye fair game. Only a brazen, woman would wander alone," he informed her through gritted teeth.

"I thought I had the protection of the MacNicol clan," she snapped back, the urge to defend herself growing stronger.

"'Tis not the MacNicol clan that lays claim to ye. 'Tis me. And I say ye are not to wander alone." He stepped closer to emphasize his statement, his face mere inches from hers.

"What do you mean, you lay claim to me?" She met his stare with indignation. He was going a tad too far in his assumptions.

"Surely, ye have not forgotten last night." His voice rumbled with fury. She noticed how his brogue seemed to be deepening along with his anger.

"Of course, I haven't forgotten last night, but where I come from, a few kisses don't make one *claimed*," she sassed back.

"I'm aware ye are not from here, but ye are here now, and ye belong to me."

"Who says?" She couldn't believe he was serious. Surely he didn't believe he could own her like some prized horse.

"I do." He grabbed her hand and started to walk back toward their tents.

Teressa considered pulling away from his grasp, but she knew she was no match for his strength. Rather than cause a scene so soon after their arrival, she allowed herself to be led by Rory back to their camp. Along the way, she experienced an unsettling mixture of amusement and irritation at the absurd scene being played out. Here she was, a twenty-first-century woman being *claimed* by a thirteenth-century warrior. She had to admit it had a certain primitive appeal. It was an old-fashioned recipe of strong male testosterone mixed with ancient cultural attitudes and heavily laden with a dose of possessiveness and desire. What more could a modern woman ask for?

Respect, she thought. First and foremost, along with his desire, she wanted his respect.

By the time they reached Rory's tent, his fury over the situation had increased, along with her irritation. When he pulled her into his tent, it was her turn to take action. She flashed him an overly bright fake smile, and did something he wasn't expecting. Grabbing him around his waist, she pulled him into a passionate kiss. She would show him exactly what a woman like her was capable of.

Rory's response was fast and furious. She felt his unleashed anger in the heat of the kiss as he held her close.

Teressa in turn unleashed her vengeance, darting her tongue across his mouth and suckling his bottom lip. She lowered her hands from his waist to run them along the back of his muscular thighs. *What great legs he has*, she thought. And then in a final display of wanton boldness, she grabbed his ass. *Nice, tight buns too.*

Rory stiffened abruptly, pulled back from the kiss, and stared at her with a startled expression. There was a long, disquieting pause before he spoke. "What is this about, lass?" he questioned.

"I wanted to show you just what kind of *woman* I can be," she said, her voice laced with defiance. Her kiss had been hot and furious, filled with heated emotions with little of the passion they had previously shared.

"What kind of woman is that?" he challenged. His harsh glare bore down on her.

"I told you, I'm not an innocent child. I'm a grown woman. I can take care of myself. Do you think you can handle me?" she challenged him, no longer smiling, no longer amused.

Standing strong, she rallied the full force of her womanly power. Teressa was taking a chance, but she needed to lay it on the line. Did he really want to know the truth about her, or was he only interested in some ideal image he had created? She was an experienced woman, not a naive schoolgirl—and certainly not innocent. It was better to know sooner rather than later whether he intended to walk away from her once he learned the truth.

"Ye speak nonsense."

"When Duncan found me, I wasn't separated from my traveling companions. I was traveling alone. Alone, do you hear me? Without the protection of a man." Her anger continued to grow, fueled by her fearful apprehension of how she would be perceived by his ancient standards. Would he judge her harshly for not being young and innocent, the kind of woman so highly valued by the men of these medieval times? Would he think her a witch, or even worse, if he knew she had traveled through time?

"I don't believe you." He was shocked, as she expected.

"You said you were laying claim to me, right? Then you darn well better know what you're getting. I'll ask again. Do you think you can handle me?" She knew she was forcing his hand, but something inside her had snapped, releasing a fountain of unsettled emotions surging out of control.

He stared at the wild woman she had become. "Of course, I can handle ye. I can handle any woman."

"I'm not just any woman," she stated flatly, the emotion draining from her voice. She turned on her heel and departed the tent.

Teressa hurried over to the women's tent and threw herself onto her pallet, hot tears burning her eyes. She had enough of this adventure, and was tired of being nothing more than a pawn for Lady Lydia and the freaking faeries. Enough of these strategies and strange ways of ancient clans. She didn't belong here. She wanted to go home, back to a time when men didn't lay claim to their women, and her independent ways wouldn't be a black mark against her. She wanted to come and go as she pleased and speak her mind without condemnation. She wanted to be herself again in a world that made sense.

But most of all, she didn't want to risk falling in love.

She stared at the corner seams of the tent, fixated on the meticulously fine stitching done by hand, not machine. "Send me home," she cried out to the empty space. "I don't belong here. Send me home."

Her plea was met with silence.

~*~

Exasperated and confused over what had just happened, Rory sat heavily on a nearby chest and stared mutely at the empty space where Teressa had just stood. He was tempted to go after her and show her who was in control, but the warrior in him knew this was one battle he wouldn't win by sheer force. It was best probably to give her time and space until he could rally his forces and determine the next course of action.

He spent a good deal of time sitting like that in his tent, mulling over what had happened with Teressa. Everything had seemed to be going so well, and then all hell had broken loose. One day she was sharing the passion of their kisses, telling him she wanted him, and then suddenly, she had turned into an angry wench when he tried to protect her. She should be honored to have his protection. A woman should expect nothing less from the man who would claim her as his own. His fear for her safety may have turned into unrestrained anger over her foolish actions, but she was far too beautiful, and he felt far too possessive to simply accept her lapse in judgment.

What could she have been thinking to walk through the camp alone without a female companion? His only concern had been for her welfare. How could she have been so reckless to wander alone as a stranger in a strange place? Did she not know the danger? He wondered what had happened to upset her. It couldn't have been anything he had done.

This business of wooing Teressa was still new to him, and she was proving to be more of a mystery than he had expected.

Oh, but that kiss. Such fury. Such passion. Only a woman of strong emotions could have delivered a kiss with such fervor. *Imagine if she were to come to me with desire instead of anger. That would be a thrill to enjoy.* He could still feel the imprint of how she had boldly grabbed his arse. The woman would be a wild ride in bed, and given half a chance, he had every intention of experiencing it for himself. He didn't care where she came from, or what her life had been before. She was his now. If he were to have his way, she would be his now and forever.

His mind and body reacted with a single thought as he recalled their embrace. She had felt so good, so right cradled against him. Just the thought of holding her in a naked embrace was enough to arouse him, raising a fever in his blood.

The best way he knew to quell the aching need in his loins was to fill his belly with ale, and the MacLeods were known for brewing the best ale on the island. Rory laid the matter of Teressa to rest for the moment and went in search of some good drinking buddies. Strong ale and friendly male companions could go a long way towards dulling the distractions of feminine whims.

Later that night, much later, after a heavy dose of drinking, Rory was helped by Duncan to his bed. Sadly, Rory didn't share in Duncan's laughter over his drunkenness; he knew in the morning his head would surely be aching.

~*~

Teressa was curled up in a cocoon of self-pity and depression when Lady Lydia entered their tent. The MacNicol matriarch didn't seem to take notice of Teressa's emotional state, or if she did, she made no mention of it. Apparently, Lady Lydia had other things on her mind.

"Get up. Ye must come with me. 'Tis time for ye to meet Janet," Lady Lydia stated.

"Now? Do we have to do this now?" After her run-in with Rory, Teressa was in no mood to be acting as a matchmaker for anyone.

"Aye, now. Janet's waiting. We've not much time."

Reluctantly, Teressa pulled herself up from her cot and followed Lady Lydia to one of the larger tents. Lady Lydia introduced her to the two women seated inside. "Mistress Ellers, this is Lady Evelyn and her daughter, Lady Janet."

Teressa pulled in a breath. Janet was lovely. For some reason, she had been expecting a rather homely or mousy woman, someone who wouldn't appeal to Duncan. Instead, she saw before her an exquisite beauty to whom men would flock. Wearing a simple, yet graceful golden gown, Janet sat with a relaxed, but regal posture. Masses of auburn-brown curls framed her heart-shaped face, and her large brown eyes held specks of gold. Her refined nose sat above her equally elegant mouth. She reminded Teressa of Olivia Newton-John from the movie *Grease*, a regular Sandra Dee, except with a Scottish mane.

"Well, Lady Janet, it's a pleasure to finally meet you." Teressa greeted her. As a natural reflex, she offered her hand for a handshake, then quickly drew it back to her side, remembering who she was dealing with.

"Thank ye, Mistress Ellers, the pleasure is mine," Janet spoke softly, her eyes not meeting Teressa's.

"Lady Lydia tells me you're interested in renewing your relationship with Duncan. Is that right?" Teressa jumped right into business. She was still feeling edgy from her encounter with Rory and felt no need to break the ice with small talk as she usually would with a new client.

Janet's eyes flew to her mother. Lady Evelyn nodded, as though giving her permission to proceed. "'Tis correct, Mistress Ellers."

"Okay then, let's start with your side of the story. Tell me what happened three years ago."

Lady Lydia began to speak for Janet, but Teressa stopped her. "From her." Teressa glared at Lady Lydia. "I want to hear it from Janet."

Using her kindest coaching voice, she asked again. "In your own words, Lady Janet, tell me what happened with you and Duncan."

Looking down, Janet fiddled with the lacings of her wrap. Teressa was about to repeat her question when Janet took a deep breath and began to speak. "I've known Duncan nearly all my life. From the time I was small, I would see him at the gatherings. We were betrothed when I was six and ten years old. He's near twelve years my senior. When mother took me to the MacNicol keep to discuss our betrothal, I was awed by his age and years of experience. I wasn't ready to become his wife." Janet paused, her eyes still downcast. It was a good start.

"What's changed since then?" Teressa asked.

"For a time, after Duncan sent me away, I was relieved, almost happy, to be sent back to my family. But then the pain settled in. Living in my family's keep, I'd never known rejection or disapproval until my broken betrothal with Duncan. It was harsh, but it also made me stronger. I started watching my mother interact with my father, something I hadn't taken much notice of in my younger days." Janet paused again.

Teressa accepted Janet's trepidation. It was typical for her clients to collect their thoughts before continuing. Usually, they needed prompting. "Please, tell me more."

"These past three years have given me time to mend and, I believe, mature. I'm nearing twenty, and I've gained a better understanding of what it means to be a good wife. My mother doesn't always agree with my father, but she always stays true by his side, as his partner. Mother told me 'tis men who make war, 'tis women who must keep the peace."

Teressa nodded, "I'm impressed."

Janet looked up, for the first time, meeting Teressa's eyes. She rushed on, as if inspired. "Three years ago, I thought Duncan's request for unfailing loyalty to his clan seemed too harsh and overbearing; now it seems perfectly reasonable, even to be expected. I believe I'm ready to be a loyal wife to the chief of the MacNicol clan, if he'll still have me." There was another pause before Janet continued. "My only fear is . . ."

"Don't stop now," Teressa encouraged her.

Janet tried again. "I've always been a bit shy, and my fear is that Duncan is so handsome, and well . . ."

From the corner of her eye Teressa could see that Lady Lydia was about to speak again. She held up her hand, halting Lydia's words. "Let her finish."

"Big," Janet finished her thought.

"Big! Does he intimidate you?" Teressa asked. Janet was shy, reserved, and overly protected by her family; it was easy to believe she'd be intimidated by Duncan. Lady Janet was no match for his domineering personality. Teressa had her work cut out for her.

"Intimidate me?" Janet repeated, not understanding.

"Make you feel small and insecure? You said you were shy."

"Sometimes he scares me." Janet looked down again.

That was one of the things Teressa was going to have to work on.

"Why is that?" Teressa ducked her head, trying to catch Janet's eyes. "Has he ever been mean to you?"

Janet's eyes snapped up to meet Teressa's. "Oh, nay, Mistress Ellers. He's always been a perfect gentleman."

It was good to see she was defending him.

"'Tis just that . . . if we were married . . ." Janet looked at Teressa pointedly, unable or unwilling to say more.

"Yes, if you were married . . ." Teressa rolled her hand through the air, prompting Janet to continue.

"He's big," Janet said again, as if that explained it all. "And if we were married . . ."

"Oh!" Teressa finally got it. Apparently, adolescent girls of the thirteenth century whispered tales about men and the pain of intercourse much like young girls would seven hundred years in the future. She did her best to hold back her chuckle. "You don't have to be afraid because he's a big man."

"I don't?" A mixture of relief and disbelief crossed Janet's face.

"No, you don't." Teressa looked at the two older women sitting with them in the tent. "Maybe it would be better if I could have some time alone with Lady Janet," she said.

"I'm her mother. I want to hear what ye have to say," Lady Evelyn said, leaning forward on the edge of her seat. Lady Lydia remained quiet for once.

Teressa wasn't about to have the sex talk with two women old enough to be her mother. "Give us a few minutes. Please. You can wait outside." She figured they would be hanging close by, hoping to catch every word. That was okay with her as long as they kept quiet and out of sight.

Lady Lydia seemed reluctant to move. Teressa stared her down until she finally stood to leave, taking Lady Evelyn along with her.

When they were gone, Teressa turned her attention to Janet. "Okay, let me explain a few things."

Twenty minutes later, she had gone over enough of the basics to assure Janet her wedding night would be wonderful, if she wanted it to be. Maybe not completely painless, she didn't want to deceive the girl, but she assured her it could be grand if she let Duncan know how she felt. Maybe it was only wishful thinking on

Teressa's part, but she had the feeling Duncan would be a loving and considerate husband if given the proper chance.

Teressa called the two ladies back inside. She could tell they had been listening. Lady Evelyn was flushed, looking girlishly excited.

"So, what's next on our agenda?" Teressa asked.

"Duncan is meeting with Tormod MacLeod at his tents, which makes me think it would be fitting for us to pay a call to Tormod's wife. It would give us an excuse to walk through the MacLeods' camp. Wouldn't ye agree, Lady Evelyn?" Lady Lydia advised.

"Certainly, Lady Lydia, by all means. We should pay our respects to Lady Jenna. And, Janet, you must walk with us." Lady Evelyn smiled broadly at Lady Lydia's suggestion.

Janet nodded her agreement.

"I'll go with you," Teressa said. She needed to be there to ensure they didn't ruin the effort.

"Now, my dear, you understand the men may be engaged in important discussions, and we cannot expect them to acknowledge us womenfolk. We cannot speak to them directly. They must be the ones to address us. Do ye understand?" Lady Lydia's remarks were directed to Janet, but Teressa had the feeling she was included in the instructions.

Janet nodded. "I understand."

Teressa rolled her eyes. How archaic.

Hopefully, this walk-by would be an important step toward learning Duncan's state of mind. Hopefully, Duncan would show his interest, or lack thereof, and Teressa would be closely observing his reactions, looking for the silent language that spoke loudly when one took the time to listen.

As a show of support to Lady Janet, Teressa walked beside the younger woman, linking Janet's arm in hers. They walked a couple of steps behind Lady Lydia and Lady Evelyn on their way through the camp to Lady Jenna's tent, making certain their route took them past the men assembled in the MacLeods' camp. Many of the men had gathered there to share tankards of ale and exchange rowdy stories. It was the end of a long travel day and time to relax. The sun was nearing the horizon, and many of the fire grates had already been lit.

As they approached the MacLeods' camp, an elderly man took center stage, eager to entertain the men with his animated style of storytelling. However, Duncan's attention seemed immediately drawn to their presence. His eyes locked on their small group, and he kept them in his sight as they made their way toward the gathering of men. Teressa watched every nuance of emotion from Duncan, searching for clues. He stood his ground, but she noted how his eyes followed their progress. When his mother and her companions reached the circle of light from the blazers, Duncan was the first to acknowledge their passing.

Giving a shallow bow, he greeted them. "Good eve to ye, ladies, Mother."

"Good eve to ye, Duncan. 'Tis a pleasure to see ye again, Tormod," Lady Lydia spoke for their group as they paused to exchange pleasantries.

Janet stood with her head bent downward, her eyes glued to the ground.

"Look up," Teressa hissed under her breath.

Janet flinched. Startled, she looked up at Teressa.

"Not at me, at Duncan." Teressa kept her voice low.

Janet's eyes widened with apprehension.

"Look at him. He won't bite." Teressa grabbed Janet's hand to reassure the young woman. She could see the immense effort it took for Janet to comply with her instructions. Janet turned her eyes toward the men, focusing on Duncan. "Hold his gaze. I'm here. You're safe." Teressa kept her instructions short and pointed. She needed Janet to perform outside her normal comfort zone. It was the only way this was going to work. If she were allowed to slip back to her mousy ways, she would get no respect from Duncan.

Duncan was watching them in stoic silence. Was it anger or irritation flashing in his eyes? Good, let him be irritated. His emotional response was an indication of interest. Disinterest would have been worse. Teressa rather enjoyed seeing Duncan's ire. Suddenly, his expression softened. Teressa looked to see what had caused the noticeable change.

~~~

It required great effort to push past her long held reserves, but Janet turned to gaze directly at Duncan from beneath her long lashes, allowing the slightest hint of a smile to brush her lips. Her heart fluttered anxiously in her chest as she waited, watching for his reaction.

"Lady Janet, 'tis a pleasure to see ye return to the faire," Duncan said, singling her out for a greeting. "Ye have denied us yer presence for too long."

Janet could barely speak, her delight at his acknowledgment was so overwhelming. "Ye are too kind to notice," she replied with a slight curtsy. Her heart swelled with hope for the possibilities carried in his greeting. He had said he was pleased to see her. It could mean so much.

Duncan looked as though he were about to say something more when Tormod spoke up. "Lady Lydia, Lady Evelyn, what brings ye our way?"

"We've come to visit your lovely wife. Is she receiving?" Lady Lydia answered for them.

"Aye, she'll be pleased to see ye. She's in her tent, the next one down," the MacLeod chief said. He looked anxious to return to his story, and really, there was no reason why they should linger.

"Then we'll be on our way," Lady Evelyn said, acknowledging his dismissal.

The exchange of greetings was over in a moment, and the ladies continued on their way. As soon as they had moved beyond the circle of men and out of their sight, Janet's mother rushed to hug her, barely able to maintain her composure. "He greeted ye, daughter. Did ye see that, Lydia? He greeted her!" Lady Evelyn was beside herself with zeal.

"Aye, Lady Evelyn, I noticed. 'Tis encouraging," Lady Lydia replied, the barest hint of a smile revealing her approval.

Janet accepted her mother's enthusiastic embrace with equanimity. A shy smile was the only outward indication of her extreme inner happiness while her heart skipped with nervous joy. Seeing Duncan again elicited some of her old pain and fears, but rising high above those dark thoughts was a soaring desire for a second chance. A second chance to prove her loyalty and truly be the wife he deserved gave her cause to hope.

Just before they reached Lady Jenna's tent, Lady Lydia paused for a moment. "Lady Evelyn, I recommend we not say overly much when we see Jenna. I shouldn't like to see undue speculation spread throughout the faire."

Janet understood. Lady Lydia was admonishing her mother against discussing what had happened when they saw Duncan and the other men. It would be a significant setback if stories began circulating around the campgrounds. If such rumors reached Duncan, it would certainly undermine all their efforts. Janet looked to her mother.

It took a long second for Lady Evelyn to grasp Lady Lydia's meaning, but soon her face brightened in understanding. "Quite right, Lady Lydia. And ye too, Janet. We shouldn't engage in gossip. It may give the wrong impression." It pleased Janet to see her mother doing her best to contain her enthusiasm. Hopefully her mother's expectations, as well as her own, would be well met.

As they were about to enter Lady Jenna's tent, Janet turned spoke softly to the woman by her side. "Thank ye, Mistress Ellers. I couldn't have done it without ye."

"Glad to be of service," Teressa replied.

CHAPTER 14

Teressa lay quietly awake on her pallet in the early predawn hours, formulating plans to resolve her dilemma with Rory. Mornings were always her best time for problem solving.

It hardly lessened her pain to realize, as a relationship coach, she was no more immune to relationship problems than a doctor was immune to getting sick. And much like a doctor, she was finding it harder to properly diagnose and treat herself than she would like to believe.

She didn't feel good about the way she had reacted to Rory, and her first thought was to stay confined to her tent until Moezell and Lady Lydia agreed to send her home. Unfortunately, she also realized it was an unrealistic course of action.

It took a good deal of self-evaluation, but eventually she understood her anger at Rory wasn't about him being overly protective. That event had only served as an excuse to explode the conflicting emotions swirling around in her head and heart. Who could blame her? Her situation was bound to cause even the most levelheaded woman stress. She was trying to deal with the unbelievable experience of being swept back in time, complicated by several hundred years of cultural differences, and added to all that were her growing feelings for a man she couldn't be with. It was enough to make anyone run for the hills.

If, or when, she had an opportunity to speak with Rory, she would need to apologize. It wasn't going to be pretty, but she needed to explain her outburst, at least as well as possibly without saying too much.

Teressa needed to make him understand they didn't have a chance of staying together. As soon as her job was done, she planned to return home, and she had never led him to believe otherwise. He must not fully grasp that concept, or he wouldn't still be pursuing her. Once she got him to see the harsh truth, she was sure he would go back to turning his considerable charms on someone else. There must be plenty of women at an event like this willing to fall at his feet; all he needed to do was show them a little interest. He certainly didn't need her misery.

While her moaning, groaning, and self-evaluation made her feel better, it wasn't enough to make her want to get out of bed. During the night, she had cried her heart out, cleansed her soul, and determined to carry on as best she could. She would seal her soul against the emotions she had developed for Rory and bide her time until Lady Lydia released her from her spell. If possible, she planned to spend the day hidden away in the tent, avoiding all contact with everyone. The cure would be painful, but she would survive.

While Lady Lydia and Kayla dressed to go to breakfast, Teressa remained curled up on her bed, pretending to sleep. When the matriarch had finished dressing, she sent Kayla out to break her fast alone.

"Teressa, I know ye're awake. Do ye plan to lie there all day?" Lady Lydia asked, sounding very much like a mother admonishing a wayward child.

"Yes, as a matter of fact, I do," Teressa replied from under the covers, sounding very much like that wayward child.

"Are you going to tell me what happened to put ye in this mood?" Lady Lydia persisted.

"No," Teressa answered abruptly from beneath the covers.

"Self-pity is not attractive. Ye need to get dressed and break yer fast. Ye have to eat," Lady Lydia said.

"I don't plan on leaving this tent. I'll ask Bonnie to bring me something."

"'Tis not acceptable. I will not allow Bonnie or anyone else to bring ye food."

Teressa took a moment to consider her options before she responded to Lydia's statement. Her last meal had been the dried-meat and cheese sandwich she had eaten early yesterday evening, and she was getting pretty hungry. She wondered how long she could go without eating. It was worth a bluff.

"Fine. Have it your way. I'll fast," she pouted.

Lady Lydia softened her voice. "Nay, ye will not, Teressa. Ye're going to get out of bed, wash yer face, and tell me what happened."

Teressa was silent.

"I'm not leaving until ye do." Lady Lydia was adamant.

Peeking out from under her covers, she could see that Lady Lydia had taken a seat on her cot, determined to wait her out.

Teressa continued to lie unmoving for a long moment, considering her options. It was obvious Lady Lydia wasn't going to let her lie there all day and pout. And sooner or later, she needed to get something to eat. She might as well deal with it now. Teressa slowly rolled over and sat up on her pallet.

"Tell me about it, lass. Mayhap, I can help."

"Send me home, Lydia. You don't need me anymore. You can handle this, and I don't belong here. Send me home," she pleaded, holding back her tears.

"Ye agreed to stay until the match is made between Duncan and Janet," Lady Lydia reminded her.

"I didn't agree to anything. I didn't ask for any of this," Teressa protested.

"Ye asked for an adventure, and ye accepted the job, if ye will recall."

"I've changed my mind. This isn't my idea of a grand adventure, to be snatched out of my own time, surrounded by circumstances out of my control. I don't want to be here." Teressa knew she was whining, and she didn't like the sound of her voice, but the release felt good.

"'Tis a bit late to make such a choice. Ye're already here. Since ye are dependent on me to send ye back to yer time, and since I'm still determined to have ye help bring Duncan and Janet together, it benefits ye to get up and put yerself together."

Teressa thought about continuing the fight, but she knew Lady Lydia was right. She didn't say anything. Instead, she brushed her hair from her eyes, crawled out of bed, and began to wash and dress.

Lady Lydia sat quietly waiting for Teressa to finish her preparations. "Are ye ready to tell me what happened to hurt ye so?" Lady Lydia asked again, compassion creeping into the hard edge of her voice.

"No, Lydia. I appreciate your concern, but this is something I need to work out on my own." Teressa's voice was soft, but sure. It was the second time she had addressed Lydia as an equal, dropping her title of lady. For Teressa, it indicated a new status in their relationship.

Lady Lydia nodded her acceptance. "Please know I am here if ye need me."

"Yeah, right. I'll be sure to let you know." Teressa managed a weak, accommodating smile.

~*~

The pain Rory felt the next morning exceeded even Duncan's expectations. The MacLeods had reached a personal best in producing some of the finest and strongest ale at the faire. It had been far too easy for Rory to drink far too much. Luckily, he'd been able to crawl out of bed long enough to relieve himself of the contents of his stomach before returning to the comfort of his pallet. It was nearly high noon before he emerged from his tent in an acceptable condition to face the day.

The chiefs of the clans and their close council of advisors were scheduled to spend the day together to discuss the issues of the isle. They heard complaints of disputes, and if all went well, together they ruled on settlements. Duncan probably would have appreciated the counsel of his brother Michael. Instead, he was accompanied by Souyer, his master druid, Willard Hardy, his master-at-arms, and Rory, who was currently out of commission.

Rory had dragged his sad and sore self to the meeting long after it had started. His head still ached, his stomach had no desire for food, and his mouth felt as though he had licked the hair of a wet dog. Fighting all that, he gathered his wits about him as best he could and made his much delayed entrance to the chiefs' meeting tent. It wasn't a pretty sight for his sore eyes. Duncan shook his head in disgust. Rory just shrugged his shoulders.

"Rising a bit late, I see," Duncan admonished his brother in a hushed tone.

Rory saw the unmistakable hint of a smirk behind Duncan's stern facade as he took a seat next to his oldest brother.

"'Tis the best I could do. After last night, ye should be grateful I made it here at all. Have I missed much?" Rory whispered in reply. He was doing his best to sit upright, considering the pain in his head.

"Not as much as ye would like. Hugh MacDonald has been on a tirade. I don't think he's done yet." Duncan returned his attention to the elderly chief, who stood to speak again.

As Rory listened, Hugh MacDonald dropped several pointed comments about broken promises and the need for assurance that any agreements made by the chiefs would be honored. He blustered on about the reliability of chiefs to take care of the families in their clans. Rory suspected the accusations were directed at his brother, but thankfully, Duncan refused to take the bait and abstained from responding to the elder chief. He sat stone-faced and stoic in the face of the MacDonald's onslaught.

Hugh refrained from mentioning Duncan's broken betrothal directly, but he danced close enough to the subject to leave no doubt. Even Rory knew it was considered a breach of protocol for the MacDonald to discuss their private history at this public gathering. Besides, this was old news, the event had taken place while Duncan's father was the chief of the MacNicol clan. Everyone here knew Kennon MacNicol and Hugh MacDonald had come to an understanding regarding the broken betrothal and Lady Janet's return to her family home. All things considered, Rory would have thought the matter was settled and no longer open for discussion. But then again, what did he know? He wasn't a clan chieftain.

Through lidded eyes, Rory took advantage of the moment to sit back and watch his brother's reaction as the old chief rambled on and on. From the looks of things, Duncan was betting everyone would grow tired of MacDonald's posturing, seeing it as nothing more than spoiled bluster by a self-righteous old man. By refusing to respond to Hugh MacDonald, Duncan risked appearing weak and intimidated by the elder chief, but the longer Duncan held his stoic silence against Hugh's tirade, the more the mood of the meeting turned in his favor. It was a bit of a gamble to hope Hugh would overplay his hand, but in the final analysis, Rory believed his brother's wager paid off handsomely. Hugh continued to lose the support of his peers as his bluster wore on, and their respect for Duncan increased as the MacNicol chief's demeanor remained decidedly calm. Rory felt a growing admiration for his brother.

In the end, it was Tormod, the MacLeod, who put an end to the useless discussion, stating firmly, "Hugh, I believe ye have made yer point, many times over. We are all good and honorable men here, ready to stand by the agreements reached here today. Each of us has sworn our allegiance. Unless you can prove a man untrustworthy, his word will be accepted and honored."

Hugh scanned the faces of the men at the gathering. Many of them, including Rory, had already lost interest in the subject. Several nodded their acceptance, probably hoping to put an end to his long-winded speech while still according him the respect his position required.

~*~

It took some effort, but Teressa was able to shake off the gloom of her dark mood well enough to convince Lady Lydia she wouldn't crawl back into bed. She accompanied Lady Lydia to breakfast and put on her best happy face. It must have worked. When Lady Evelyn showed up asking to speak with Lady Lydia, she hardly hesitated before she left Teressa on her own, apparently trusting that her overreacting matchmaker was back in control.

Teressa took advantage of the time to wander off on her own, again. Only this time, she planned to stay close to the women's section of the camp to avoid another encounter with Rory. Even though she had resolved to clear the air and tell him once and for all he had to stop pursuing her, she still wasn't ready to face him and actually put her thoughts into action.

Looking for a place to rest in private, Teressa headed off toward a clump of shade trees. She stopped short when she found the place already occupied by another, only to have her disappointment fade when she saw that it was Lady Janet sitting quietly on a cushion, working on a piece of hand embroidery. When she heard Teressa approach, she looked up.

"Good day, Mistress Ellers," Lady Janet greeted her with a smile.

"Good day to you also. Would you mind if I joined you?"

"Please, stay. I would be happy to share my retreat with ye."

Teressa sat down beside Janet. "Thanks. That's a rather unusual piece you're working on," she commented, referring to Janet's embroidery. It depicted a faerie-tale castle by the sea.

"Needle work keeps my hands busy while my mind wanders. I was wondering how ye met Lady Lydia. Are ye a friend of Kayla's?" Janet asked.

"No, I'm more of a lost traveler who happened to show up at the keep. Actually, you could say I'm a friend of Duncan's. He was the one who found me and offered me the protection of his clan," Teressa informed her.

Looking confused, Janet lowered her eyes to her lap. "A friend of Duncan's? Have ye been under his protection for long?" Picking up the embroidery piece, she nervously worked a few more stitches.

"No, only a few days, but I'm learning a lot can happen in only a few days." Teressa smiled discreetly, thinking of the progress she was making with Duncan and Janet. She was also acutely aware of her emotional rollercoaster ride with Rory.

Janet tried to keep her eyes on her work, but was unable to conceal her interest.

"I've learned a lot about Duncan and your broken betrothal. In fact, I heard he's free to choose another woman as his wife." She waited for Janet's reaction, testing her resolve. Teressa wanted to be sure dear sweet Lady Janet was ready to make some serious changes to move her relationship forward.

Janet lifted her chin in pride. "That's correct. I have no claim to the MacNicol chief." Again, she stabbed the fabric with her needle.

"Exactly. He's been free to choose another, but he hasn't," Teressa pointed out with a knowing grin.

"I don't understand. Ye just said ye have gained his protection." Her hands stopped in mid stitch.

"His protection, not his affection," Teressa clarified.

Janet eyed her with uncertainty.

"Last night, you told me you love Duncan."

"Aye."

"And you want to marry him, right?" Teressa was tired of beating around the bush. These people moved too slowly.

"Aye, Mistress Ellers, I do." Janet nodded.

"Then, by God, you will," Teressa stated. "Even if I have to hog-tie you two together and drag you to a judge, or a priest, or a druid, or whoever performs your weddings. You're getting married, and I'm going home."

Janet was obviously taken aback by Teressa's bold statement. She sat in silence for a long moment before she spoke.

"I do love Duncan MacNicol. I always have. I was a naive young woman three years ago. I was afraid," Janet stated with increased confidence. There was a slight hesitation before she added, "I want to be a good wife, his wife, but I fear it may be too late for second chances."

Teressa's smile widened. "Don't be so sure. I think he still holds feelings for you. We've talked about you."

"Ye talked about me!"

"Yes, as friends," Teressa assured her. "It just so happens we share similar experiences. I've also experienced a broken engagement because of family issues." Teressa could see that she had Janet's interest now, and after last night, she knew she had gained the young woman's confidence. "I was once engaged to marry a man, but he couldn't accept my family. It came to a point where I had to make the choice to be with Jeffery and lose contact with my family, or chose my family and break off my engagement with Jeffery. I chose my family."

"Ye chose yer family over yer beloved?"

"That's just it. A man who claimed he loved me but couldn't accept my family didn't seem to be the right *beloved*. You see, like Duncan, I wanted a spouse, a partner who wanted to be part of my family, not separate. But like you, I couldn't accept giving up my family for the sake of a husband. Do you see my point here?" Teressa hoped she was making sense to a woman separated from her by several hundred years of cultural evolution.

"To be honest, not really. I don't see how yer experience can help me mend my relationship with Duncan. We may have similar experiences, but excuse me for pointing out, Mistress Ellers, ye are still single, and I'm no closer to reuniting with the MacNicol chief." The poor girl looked lost. It was understandable.

"When I talked to Duncan, not only was I able to see his point of view, which supported his choices, but I was also able to express your point of view, which helped him understand your choices. I believe it gave him something to think about."

"Does Lady Lydia know about yer discussions with Duncan?" Janet asked.

"Yes, as you know, she supports you in this quest. And now, after meeting you, so do I. I want to help set things right between you and Duncan." Teressa was finding it harder to convince Janet of her good intentions than she had expected.

"Why? You hardly know me," Janet questioned softly, still perplexed.

"No, but I have come to know Duncan, and I believe he still cares for you. You tell me you still care for him. And let's just say this is what I do." Teressa put up her hands in a gesture of openness.

"Are ye a matchmaker?" Janet's eyes lit up with hope.

"No, not really. Okay, yes, let's say that I am." Teressa decided it was the best explanation she could offer. There wasn't a better way she could explain the job of a relationship coach to a thirteenth-century woman. And then she saw it, a look in Janet's eyes that let Teressa know she was gaining her trust. It was restrained trust, but it was there.

"What do ye recommend? I cannot very well approach Duncan. He must send for me. I was dismissed by him, sent home."

"I know, according to your rules, you can't approach him, but I can. I can check things out and see if he's interested in meeting with you." Teressa was pleased with both her role as matchmaker and the friendly relationship she'd been able to establish with Duncan.

"Oh, nay, Mistress Ellers, that would be too bold. What if ye offend him?" Janet seemed shocked by the very idea, but behind her reasonable concerns, Teressa detected a note of hopeful optimism.

"You can call me Teressa, and I think Duncan accepts my unconventional ways. Even if he is offended, he'll be mad at me, not you." Teressa felt fairly confident in her ability to persuade Duncan to at least meet with Janet.

"Ye would risk his wrath? Ye would do this for me?" Her interest was growing.

"Trust me. I don't think it's going to be a problem. I've done this kind of thing before. So, tell me, are you seriously ready to do this?" It was important for Teressa to have Janet's full acceptance of the plan, or it risked failure.

Janet paused for a moment, considering the idea. "Aye. I trust you," she confirmed.

"Great. We'll get started right away." Teressa was thrilled. With Janet fully on board, her scheme had a much better chance of working.

"Mistress . . . er, Teressa, I do have one other question, if ye don't mind." A puzzled look had crossed Janet's face.

"Sure, what's bothering you?" Teressa asked, wanting to address any last lingering fears Janet might have. She needed the woman's complete buy-in.

"Please excuse my bold remark, but I've noticed ye have an unusual way of speaking, one I've never heard before." She admitted her curiosity with a note of embarrassment.

"Oh yes, I know. I'm English, from the south of England," Teressa offered, remembering Duncan's earlier explanation.

"Oh, I see." Janet nodded, visibly relieved.

~*~

After Teressa had worked out her plan to arrange for a private meeting between Janet and Duncan, she went in search of the MacNicol chief. Straightaway, she headed off for the cook wagons, knowing the clan servants were usually a good source of information. Besides being in the know regarding their chiefs and ladies, as a rule, they were typically eager to assist anyone who took the time to show them some respect. She wasn't disappointed when they pointed her in the direction of the chiefs' tent. They also told her the chiefs' meeting was expected to break soon, as it was nearly time for supper. She hurried to the tent to wait for Duncan to emerge.

Souyer, the master druid, was one of the first to exit the large meeting tent. Seeing Teressa standing near the entrance, he approached her. "Good day to ye, Mistress Ellers. What brings ye to the chiefs' tent?" he asked.

"Good day to you too, Master Souyer. I'm here to find the MacNicol chief," she responded with innocent politeness.

"Ye seek an audience with Duncan?" He sounded suspicious.

"Yes. I've urgent business with him," she said with a note of arrogance. She had made too much progress to let the snoopy old druid stand in her way.

"How interesting. Please, do tell."

She looked each way over her shoulders, as if checking for eavesdroppers, and leaned in toward the old druid. "I can tell you one thing," she whispered in a tone of conspiracy.

"Aye." He drew out the single word, leaning in closer.

"I can tell you it's none of your business." She stared up at the old man with an impish grin.

The old druid pulled back in disgust and dismissed her with a wave of his hand. "Harrumph, ye canna blame an old wizard for trying," he muttered as he turned to walk away. "I tell ye, druids get no respect anymore."

Teressa smiled at his retreating back, barely containing her chuckles.

Her attention was drawn away from the druid when Duncan, Rory, and several other men began to exit the meeting tent. Teressa hurried to approach Duncan, dropping into a deep curtsy. "Chief MacNicol, forgive my interruption, but I have an urgent message for you, my lord." She hoped to present an image of utmost respect for her friend, thinking it would make him look good in front of the other men. If nothing else, it was sure to gain his attention.

It worked. If Duncan were taken aback by her show of extreme formality, he apparently decided to play along. "An urgent message, ye say. That does sound important." He eyed her with skepticism.

"Come, my lord. I need a moment alone with you, in private." She reached out to grab his hand for emphasis in an unguarded display of familiarity.

"It appears the MacNicol chief has a new fancy," someone in the crowd of men joked.

Standing next to Duncan, Rory watched Teressa's actions in silence, his expression dreadfully neutral. Teressa caught his gaze, pleading with her eyes for him to accept her actions. The slightest tip of his head indicated his agreement.

Duncan, playing along with her ploy, made his leave and allowed Teressa to practically pull him through the campgrounds. When they had moved beyond the hearing of his fellow clansmen, he reined her in, bringing her to an abrupt stop.

"Enough now, Teressa. I demand ye tell me what this is all about. That was quite a show ye put on back there."

"Duncan, I'm sorry for the pretense. You know I don't know your ways, and I do tend to do things a little differently, but I need to speak with you. You have to agree, it worked. Don't deny it, you're intrigued?"

"Now? It couldn't wait until I returned to my tent?" he asked incredulously.

"The way I see it, the sooner the better. I'm on a mission here," she replied with a sly smile and a significant note of purpose in her voice.

"What the hell are ye talking about?" Fury blazed in his eyes.

Her smile faded. She might have gained his interest, but she was losing his patience.

Boldly, Teressa wasted no words in broaching her subject. "Remember how I talked to you about your broken betrothal to Janet MacDonald?"

He nodded. "Aye."

She could see his impatience was held in check by a rapidly thinning strand of politeness.

"What I need to ask, and I know it's very personal, but do you still care for Janet?" Teressa held her breath in anticipation of his answer. So much was riding on his response. Did he still care for Janet as she believed? And if so, would he admit to his feelings for her?

"Why would ye ask me such a question? This is of no concern to you," he pushed back. He started to walk away.

"Oh no you don't. You can't just plow through me and run away." Teressa's voice was loud and sharp.

"I don't run away. This is none of yer business." His voice was equally loud and sharp as he continued to walk away.

Teressa hurried after him. "Then face your fears and meet with Janet. What's it going to hurt? Your pride? I think you're stronger than that. So you spend a few minutes with Janet, no more than an hour. It'll give you two a chance to talk, maybe even give you closure."

"Closure?" he snapped. "What in hades does that mean?" He stopped walking.

"A feeling of completeness. That you've done all you can, or need to do. So you know you've done the right thing."

"I am confident I did the right thing. My duty is to my clan. I don't need *closure*." Duncan glared at her.

Teressa glared back. "You know how important it is for the MacNicols to have an alliance with the MacDonalds. But no, your big old ego is in the way. You pretend this is all about clan loyalty, but it's really because she didn't pledge her undying love to you. She's ready to give you that pledge, and you won't even give her a chance."

Duncan looked as though he were fit to be tied. He was waging a war of wills, and it was with himself. Teressa thought she detected a crack in his armor and figured she needed to take advantage of it.

"You can refuse to meet with Janet—a harmless little meeting—or you can let go of your pride for a few minutes and hear what she has to say. Your pride will still be there if you need it later. All I'm asking is that you set it aside for a while."

He was still glaring at her, but she could see he was considering her suggestion.

"Come on, Duncan. Open your heart. Take a chance. I believe it's a risk worth taking." Her voice was soft and soothing as she coached him along.

"I'll agree to meet with her, but I'll not make any promises."

"Look, I care about you, as a friend of course, but as your friend, I want to see you happy. Instead, I see something's missing from your life." She hoped she sounded more confident than she felt.

"Ye think that's Janet?" He crossed his arms over his chest, looking prepared to challenge her theory.

"Yes, Duncan, I do. I'm willing to be wrong, and I'm sure you'll tell me if I am, but I think you miss the love of a good woman by your side. Not just any woman, I think you want the woman to be Lady Janet. You give a great performance of being the strong, silent type, but I see a place in your heart that longs to be filled. Now, tell me if I'm wrong, or tell me if you still have feelings for Janet," she challenged him in return, crossing her arms under her breasts.

"Maybe I do, but it's been too long," he finally admitted, letting his guard down.

"Good. That's all I need to know. Let me handle the rest." Grabbing his hand again, she led him toward the copse where Janet sat waiting. She hoped she had gained his confidence, along with his interest. This needed to work, because right now, she didn't have a plan B.

"There are not many men who would stand up to me as well as ye do," he informed her as he allowed her to lead him though the camp.

"Yeah, well you may have noticed, I'm not like many men," she shot back at him, looking over her shoulder.

"Aye, I've noticed," he said, grinning and looking a lot less fierce. It was an improvement.

When they neared the grove of trees, she stopped short a few yards away and turned to Duncan. "Okay, Duncan, just go talk to her. Tell her how you feel. You can do this."

"Are ye not coming?" he asked.

"Nope, you're on your own now. Janet waits for *you*. Make me proud." She smiled up at him, joy and genuine care shining in her eyes.

He hesitated. "Does she know?"

"Yes, of course she knows. We've talked. Now, go for it." Teressa reached up to kiss Duncan lightly on his cheek, sending him off with her best wishes. She watched for a moment longer as Duncan closed the distance between him and Janet. When she saw how he greeted her, she knew her plan had worked. She turned back toward the camp with a smile of satisfaction. He had done her proud. Filled with the happiness of a job well done, she decided it was time to deal with her other problem.

~*~

Duncan's heart began racing at the sight of Janet waiting serenely under the trees. *For me,* he thought. *She waits for me. After all this time, she still waits for me.*

Janet had been sitting, but as he approached, she stood. Shoulders back, head held high, she looked him in the eyes. She looked serene, almost regal in the way she held herself. He was taken in by the sight of her.

In the space of a moment, his feelings for Janet ignited from the smoldering embers banked in the confines of his heart to a flash of heated desire. His feelings of disappointment over misplaced loyalties dissipated, replaced by his far more enduring feelings of love and affection for the woman he wanted by his side. He crossed over to the grove of trees where Janet stood waiting.

Janet greeted Duncan with a polite curtsy, but he felt no need for a formal greeting. Taking her in his arms, he pulled Janet into a loving embrace. He had waited too long for this moment. He was determined to make the most of it.

CHAPTER 15

Rory stood outside the chiefs' tent, watching Teressa depart with Duncan. He waited a few minutes while he thought it over, and even though he knew from experience it was a bad idea, he decided to discreetly follow them. His curiosity had gotten the better of him. He had just caught up with them as they approached the grove of trees.

She seemed intent on seeking a private, and perhaps intimate, moment alone with Duncan. From the looks of it, Teressa's affections weren't with him, but with his brother. It seemed impossible. He didn't want to believe, and yet it explained so much: her constant efforts to avoid him, her relaxed confidence around Duncan, and most of all, her severe reaction when he claimed she was his.

Claimed she was his. The words repeated in his head. Never had she asked for his protection, nor had she agreed to be claimed. Hadn't she told him, more than once, she was under Duncan's protection. It dawned on him that a woman as strongly independent as Teressa wouldn't take kindly to being claimed against her will.

Still, he needed to be sure. His heart found it hard to accept what his eyes were seeing. He moved closer and watched.

Rory couldn't hear their conversation, but from his hiding place he could see Teressa speaking with Duncan. She seemed so happy, so pleased with his brother. He wanted to believe there was a perfectly reasonable explanation for their private little conversation, but that seemed highly unlikely. Teressa wouldn't have gone to such efforts to get Duncan alone if it wasn't something important and very personal. The scene before him went a long way towards explaining her anger with him. It also explained the look she had given him earlier, beseeching him to understand.

And then, as if to confirm his worst suspicions, she gave Duncan a kiss that spoke of comfortable familiarity. *Heart be damned!* There was no denying what his eyes had seen. Duncan hadn't forced himself on her; she had given her affection freely. She belonged to Duncan; he'd been a fool to claim he was her protector. Aye, he understood. Once again, he was reminded that Duncan was the chief. Duncan ruled the clan. Duncan set the rules. And as always, Duncan took first prize.

Teressa had chosen Duncan, and there was nothing he could do. Rory turned away to give the lovers their privacy, unwilling to see more.

As he headed back to his tent, he heard Teressa call his name. She sounded surprised, as though she knew she had been caught. Rory kept on walking.

"Rory, stop," she yelled again.

He didn't look back.

"Roderick MacNicol, stop, I say. Can you not hear me?"

Glancing over his shoulder, he saw she was running after him. He stopped and waited, wondering what she could possibly have to say that he would want to hear.

~~~

"Rory, I was just coming to find you," Teressa said breathlessly as she caught up with him. Seeing him so soon after leaving Duncan meant he must have followed her, but that was fine with her. It gave her a chance to make amends, and this was as good a time as any. She was happy to see Duncan reunited with his true love, and it carried over in her desire to set things right with Rory. Teressa knew Duncan and Janet's journey might not always be smooth sailing, but at least she had gotten them in the same boat.

"What do ye want?" Rory asked with a hateful glare.

Teressa had been about to reach out and touch his arm but drew back her hand. "I wanted to talk to you."

"Why? Do ye wish to tell me now about you and Duncan?" His voice was mean, even spiteful.

"What are you talking about?"

"I know what I saw. I'd be a horse's arse to listen to you."

Teressa set her hands on her hips. "Oh really, and what did you see?"

"I'm not blind, lass. I saw you kiss Duncan." Rory waved off in the direction of the trees.

"I was showing him my gratitude, you ninny, because he agreed to meet with Janet."

"Janet?"

"Yes, Lady Janet MacDonald. You remember her, Duncan's betrothed."

Teressa glanced over her shoulder and motioned in the direction of Duncan and Janet to watch the lovers retreat into their private world as they slipped deeper into the shadows of the trees. She knew they had much to discuss and a lot of lost time to recover.

"Were ye playing matchmaker?"

"Not really matchmaker. Their match was already made. I merely acted as a facilitator to move things along. Cut to the chase, so to speak," she answered.

"Is someone being chased?" he asked. His eyes softened and a lazy grin teased at his lips.

"Good question. Maybe you can tell me. Should I be surprised to find you so conveniently located?" Though she tried, she couldn't contain the smile she felt brighten her face. It wasn't in her to stay sad or mad; anger, sadness and regret required too much work. She preferred to be happy, and her gloom often dissipated as quickly as it flared. Her satisfaction from a job well done went a long way toward restoring her naturally pleasant attitude.

"Should I be surprised to find ye wandering alone, again?" There was a hint of a grin upon his lips. My, how she liked those lips.

"I wasn't wandering alone. I was taking Duncan to Janet, which I'm sure you know, since I suspect you were following me."

"Didn't you just say ye were coming to find me?" he replied languidly. "Here I am, at yer service. What may I do for ye, milady?" He gave a courtly bow, his grin rascally as ever.

She was relieved to see how easily they slipped back into their comfortable banter. It helped to ease her anxiety.

"It's more like what I need to do for you." Her voice took on a soft but serious tone. "I want to apologize for my outburst yesterday. It was unwarranted and unjustified. Can you forgive me?"

Teressa saw surprise in Rory's eyes. "I will happily forgive ye, my sweet, if ye tell me what made you so mad."

"That's just it. You didn't do anything to deserve my outburst. You were only looking out for my wellbeing. I realize that now. It's just that I've been so distraught over everything that's happened to me: getting lost, being here away from my family, meeting you. It's all been a little overwhelming." She gave him a weary half smile, knowing she needed to set things right.

"Ye are distraught about meeting me?" he asked, looking wounded.

"Not distraught, afraid. Afraid I'd fall in love only to lose you." Dang, that was unexpected, certainly not what she had planned to say. She had intended to remind him she would be leaving soon, but instead she'd been honest and put her feelings on the line. It looked as if her moment of truth had arrived; there was no turning back. *I can't lose something if I never had it to begin with*, she told herself. What could be worse than not knowing? Imaginations tended to create powerful illusions, justified or not. If he rejected her now, at least she would know how he really felt and could move on.

"Are ye saying ye care for me, lass?" His voice was light, but his eyes were dark and intense, focused solely on hers, not allowing her to look away.

"Yes, Rory, I care for you." *God help me, I care for you.* And that was the problem. She had allowed herself to care too much. When her job was done, she would be going home, alone.

"Then ye canna lose me, lass. Haven't ye noticed? I'm not so easy to get rid of." He tucked a wayward strand of hair behind her ear and smiled his infectious grin, as though all were right in the world.

"I'll be going home soon." Teressa lowered her eyes to the ground. She couldn't watch his reaction.

"Aye." He cupped his palm under her chin, forcing her to look up. "I've been hoping I'll be the one to take ye there."

"If only you could. But you can't go with me. Where I come from is too far away. Your family would never allow it." She tried to hide her pain, but was clearly failing.

"Nonsense. If ye can make the journey, certainly I can too. Don't they allow Scotsmen in yer homeland?" He was jesting with her, trying to lighten her dark mood.

"I'm sorry, but I don't see how you can. You wouldn't fit in. It's too big, and busy, and strange, and different, and your family needs you here. If you went home with me, you could never return, and I can't take you away from your family. They love you too much." Teressa was on the verge of tears but she held them in check. She had stated her concerns as plainly as she could without saying where she really came from, without breaking her vow to Moezell and Lady Lydia; although, she doubted he would believe her if she did tell him everything. The only reason Duncan believed her was because he had seen her arrive and had seen the contents of her backpack.

"Is that what's been bothering you? That I wouldn't want to leave my family?" He seemed relieved.

She nodded. "Even if you want to leave, it would never be allowed. It's too much to ask."

He embraced her, laughing with delight. "Sometimes ye simply need to believe in magic."

"Magic!" She pulled back to search his face, wondering what he was thinking. How much did he know?

"Aye, my sweet, 'tis magic that makes all things possible. My life is full of magic; 'tis everywhere. All ye need is to believe. I've learned when all else fails, believe in magic and something mysterious happens; things always work out."

She stared at him, dumbstruck. His confidence was amazing.

But as she thought about what he said, she realized it was eerie, if not downright ironic, how easily she had accepted magic as the power that had brought her back in time and how strongly she believed magic would send her back home. If magic could do all that, she reasoned, couldn't it also fix this problem? Even if she didn't know how, it was certainly worth a try.

Suddenly, she understood. It was all based on believing. Moezell's words finally hit their mark. Teressa had spent so much time and effort worrying about what could or couldn't happen, she'd wasted precious time she could have spent enjoying the experience and the adventure. Enjoy the moment, Moezell had told her. Rory had calmed her fears by telling her to believe in magic, and everything had changed, dramatically. Instead of worrying about how it couldn't work, she could choose to believe it would work. Thoughts were powerful things. Change the way you look at something and everything changes. Beliefs had the power to move mountains of fear.

"I believe in you, Rory," she said, her voice soft and low, overcome with emotions and thoughts whirling in her head. "If nothing else, I believe in you."

"That's all ye need," he assured her. He pulled her close, cradling her head against his chest.

Oh my God, she thought, *this man is too wonderful. He makes it all seem so easy. Loving him is so easy.* She hugged him tightly, drawing on his strength. Come what may, she knew she didn't have to face it alone. She had his support. It was grand, far too grand to deny any longer.

"Now that that's all settled, what would ye like to do?" Rory tipped his head to check her reaction. "Are ye hungry? I haven't eaten anything since yesterday."

"I believe I smelled roasted chicken over at the cook wagons. I'd really like to have dinner with you, kind of like a date," she happily requested with a bright smile.

He looked at her oddly, not quite understanding. "Ye want to have dates for dinner?"

"No, dinner alone with you," she laughed. "Where I come from, we call it a date. Would that be all right?" The idea was exciting. She rather liked the idea of having a dinner date with this wonderfully handsome warrior.

"Aye, my sweet. I'll make arrangements with Bonnie. Anything else ye might like?"

"How about some wine? Can we have wine instead of ale with our dinner? And candles, of course." Her hands rested on his chest.

"Aye, my sweet. Ye can have anything ye want."

~*~

Rory had made sure their dinner *date*, as she had called it, would be a truly magical affair. Teressa had gone to change into the yellow gown she had borrowed from his mother while Rory had arranged with Bonnie to have a meal fit for a chief brought to his tent. They had roasted chicken and potatoes, creamy pumpkin soup, and fresh baked bread. There was a sampling of cheese, and for dessert, a fruit-filled pastry. Rory had even found a peddler in the marketplace selling quality wine. He was quite pleased when Teressa praised him for all he had done.

She fed him hunks of chicken, and he licked her fingers. They told stories of their families, talked of favorite things, and they laughed, immersed in the joy of their romantic evening. When the meal was done, and Teressa had drunk her fill of wine, they relaxed against the cushions, and he held her close.

Rory couldn't take his eyes off her, thinking how lovely she looked in the soft glow of the setting sun. Muted rays played on her pale blond hair, bringing out the golden highlights to brighten her already lovely face. *My stars, she's beautiful when she's happy. She absolutely glows.* Something indescribable about her attracted him like no other woman. He doubted he would never tire of looking at her. Smiling with pleasure, he looked forward to the morning when she would be lying beside him as they woke together to greet a new dawn. Rory turned her brilliantly smiling face toward him and kissed her softly. She seemed to melt in his arms, giving him all her sweet desire, holding nothing back, and in this moment of time, he felt all was right with the world.

Exceptionally pleased with how well the evening was progressing, Rory had that comfortable feeling of having known her all his life even though they had just met. He could tell the wine muddled her mind, but before their hugs and kisses had progressed too far, and before he had even asked, she spoke up to make her views perfectly clear.

"I want you to know, so there aren't any misunderstandings, I'm having a great time and everything, but we're not going to have sex tonight."

Rory nearly choked. "Pardon me?"

"That's right, no sex, not tonight. A woman has her rights, you know."

Blast, but this woman was bold, and unexpected, and amazingly desirable. "Mayhap I missed something, lass, but I don't recall asking." *At least not yet*, he thought.

"Oh, I know, I'm supposed to wait until you properly woo me and sweep me off my feet so I'll melt into a pool of lustful desire at your feet . . ."

The idea sounded great to Rory.

". . . but I think it's best if I let you know, I don't put out on the first date." She looked entirely serious.

Would she never cease to amaze him? Never before had he heard a woman speak so boldly. He stared at her for a long moment, taking it all in before he threw his head back and laughed. "Am I to believe ye'll tell me when the time is right?" he asked when he finally stopped laughing.

"Yeah, I'll let you know," she said smiling, apparently pleased with her proclamation.

"Is this something women do where ye come from?" he questioned, still perplexed by her outspoken behavior.

"Actually, no, not as often as they should, but I highly recommend it. Avoids a lot of miscommunication and hurt feelings if we're up front about it. Don't you agree?" She looked completely earnest.

"I really couldn't say. I've never had a woman turn me away," he boasted with a smirking grin.

"Oh really!"

"Nay."

"Well, it just goes to show you there's a first time for everything." She settled back into his arms, satisfied she had made her position clear.

Perhaps not tonight, he consoled himself. *But soon.* Soon she would be his, and he would experience the fullness of her passion. He would show her all the pleasures passion could provide. He would give, and she would receive, and it would be grand.

Rory had breached her physical defenses and gently touched her heart. Silently, he vowed, he would continue to woo her. Soon, his soul claimed, soon she would be his, this woman of strange words and strange ways. She was the woman who would hold his interest and ignite his passion for all the years to come. Aye, their time would come soon enough, and then he would never let her go. Teressa would be his until the end of time.

CHAPTER 16

Teressa stretched and yawned like a contented cat, waking the next morning in a very different mood from the previous day. She felt bright, filled with love and light. Though she hardly remembered leaving the wonderfully warm embrace of Rory's arms to walk the short distance back to her tent, she dearly remembered the love she felt as he held her in his arms. She had felt safe and secure.

She had just finished dressing for the day in a simple plum-colored wool skirt with a pale gray tunic when Bonnie rushed into the tent, searching for her.

"The MacNicol chief seeks ye, lass, and I think 'tis important. Not that he looks upset or anything. In fact, I think he looks quite happy. Ye are looking right cheerful yerself this morn. A might better than yesterday, I would say. Ye must have slept well." Bonnie's running commentary continued, accompanied by cushion fluffing and bed straightening as she went about cleaning and tidying the tent, restoring order to an already rather tidy space. "But ye must hurry. Duncan is waiting for ye over by the trees. He said ye would know where to go."

Teressa quickly finished tying her boots then hurried from the tent. "This should be interesting," she muttered under her breath.

~*~

Duncan had to smile when he recalled how cunningly Teressa had maneuvered his meeting with Lady Janet. The woman had crossed all lines of proper behavior to accomplish her goal, and yet she had succeeded where others had failed. She had dared to discuss his romantic past with him on personal levels that went well beyond acceptable standards. He learned from Janet that Teressa had entered into the same type of conversation with her, a virtual stranger. Teressa had risked creating a spectacle when she had dragged him away from the chiefs' tent to arrange his meeting with Janet, alone, away from prying eyes. The secrecy had given them the time and privacy he and Janet needed to set things right. All in all, Teressa had managed to set the stage for a reunion with a high probability of success by stripping away any roadblocks, physical or emotional, that could have been erected by either party. This woman from a far distant time had proven to be a fierce and determined matchmaker.

By acting in such a forthright manner, she had been willing to risk his wrath to see him reunited with Janet. Much like a master matchmaker, she had easily read his unspoken desire for his long-lost love. While his mother had managed to maneuver a simple walk-by to catch his interest, Teressa had personally dragged him to where Janet was waiting.

Their private time alone had allotted them the opportunity they needed to discuss their past choices and rekindle their shared affections. Duncan had moved quickly to ascertain Janet's feelings regarding their broken betrothal. Following Teressa's instructions, they had both let down their guard, and in the end, they acknowledged their feelings had remained true over the years. Thanks to Teressa's counsel, Duncan believed he and Janet were much better prepared to enter into marriage as both lovers and partners. Janet would be the loving partner of his dreams.

In her own unconventional manner, Teressa had proven to be a true friend; he could ask for none better. She had shown up on his beach and somehow managed to ingrain herself into his confidence merely by being her honest and authentic self. He wanted her to be the first to hear the news that he intended to marry Janet MacDonald and take her home as his bride.

He shouldn't have been surprised when Teressa greeted him with an affectionate hug. She looked as happy as he felt.

"Good morning, Duncan. Such a pleasure, don't you think? Anything new and exciting?" she asked him with a sly grin.

Duncan warmly received her friendly embrace, an experience he would have been far less comfortable with only days before. Was it truly possible this whirlwind of unconventional ideas had been in his company for no more than a week? How had she managed to change his attitude in such a short time? This visitor from the future was definitely having an effect on his life, and he could see it was for the better. To be able to embrace a woman with open and friendly affection, and expect nothing more, wasn't something he had allowed himself to experience before.

"Funny ye should ask, after yer little shenanigans yesterday." He tried to look grim, crossing his arms over his chest, but either she was too happy to fall for it or she saw right through his pretense.

"I'm guessing my little shenanigans may have had their desired effect. Or have you called me here to tell me I was wrong to give you and Janet some time alone together? By the way, be careful how you answer. I saw how you greeted her," Teressa happily replied.

"Ye cannot deny ye took great risks with yer brash actions." He glared at her.

She had the good sense to look remiss.

"But I will not deny yer efforts have worked. I have asked Janet to be my bride," he brightly informed her. "If all goes well, I plan for her to return to Scorrybreac as my wife."

"Oh, Duncan." She hugged him again. This woman was full of hugs. "I'm so happy for you. I want everyone to be happy in love.

But tell me, what do you mean, if all goes well? Could there be problems?" She searched his face.

"There is the hurdle of getting approval from her father. 'Tis well known he didn't take the broken betrothal well, and I fear he still holds a grudge." Duncan rolled his shoulders to relieve the tension in his muscles.

"Do you have a plan on how to approach him?"

"I plan to announce my intentions to marry Lady Janet today at the final gathering and request his blessing, man-to-man. He may have his reservations, but I wouldn't expect him to refuse his daughter's happiness."

Teressa tapped a finger to her chin. "Actually, I think it's very likely he would refuse," she said, surprising him with her contrary opinion. "From what Rory told me about yesterday's meeting, I can easily see Hugh MacDonald using your request as an opportunity to publicly disgrace you. Besides, it'll be so much better if you can make it look as though it's in his best interest to have you marry his daughter." The gleam in her eyes told him she had a plan. He could almost see the wheels of her mind whirling away with ideas.

"I'm hesitant to ask, but what do ye suggest?" Duncan wasn't ready to abandon his plan to directly deal with the elder chief, but he was interested to hear what Teressa had to say. She had already demonstrated her unique ability to see past a person's facade.

"Is there a way for you to have someone else bring up Janet or the broken betrothal at the meeting?" she asked.

"'Tis very unlikely. 'Tis old news. Even MacDonald didn't address the matter directly."

"That's just it. He danced around the subject, but you know it still rubs him the wrong way. He couldn't mention it because it would have been seen as petty or bad manners, am I right?"

"Aye. And no one else would think to mention such past events," he assured her.

"What about a cantankerous old druid like Souyer? Couldn't he be persuaded to mention the subject with the right coaching? Like from a relationship coach?"

Duncan didn't exactly catch her meaning. "Perhaps, with the right coaching, as you say." He was reticent to admit he was gaining interest in her plan. "But then what?"

"I'll talk to Souyer and get him to bring up Janet, or the broken betrothal, something that will give the MacDonald chief an opportunity to publicly address the past injury. You can offer to make amends by asking him to require the marriage be performed here and now. Then the matter can be settled once and for all. Since you would be agreeing to honor the past betrothal, it would be to his benefit to accept, or else risk losing face. What do you think?" Her face was lit up with a sly grin of conspiracy.

Duncan was warming to her plan. He could see it offered a couple of benefits. It did have a higher chance of being successful, even if he did prefer a more direct approach, and it would go a long way towards easing the tensions between him and his future father-in-law. If the elder chief were allowed to believe he had the upper hand, he was more likely to be accepting of the marriage in the long run. Once Duncan had swallowed his pride, he reluctantly accepted that securing an alliance with the MacDonalds was as important as securing a love match. Still, it tasted of crow.

Duncan nodded in agreement. "It might work, if ye're able to convince Souyer to play his part."

"I'm sure of it. I have a feeling about this." Her eyes were glazed over, as though she were deep in thought.

Watching her think on Souyer's role, he couldn't help but bring up another matter that had been plaguing his thoughts. "Lass, I think ye should know, I don't believe Souyer knows how to send ye back to yer time. He doesn't know how ye got here, other than ye were the answer to his summer solstice request, and it may well be another year before he can send ye back. I wish I had better news, but I thought ye should know."

"Yes, Duncan, I know. Souyer told me as much. Since it was the faeries who brought me here, I'll trust the faeries will send me home, when the time is right. Until then, all I can do is believe in their magic and, hopefully, their good intentions. I have to believe everything will be all right," she softly assured him, resting her hand on his forearm as if to comfort him.

He searched her expression for signs of distress, thinking she was the one who should need comforting. "I'm impressed, ye don't seem worried."

"Oh, believe me, I've done my fair share of worrying." She dismissed the idea with a wave of her hand. "But I've come to realize worrying doesn't make anything better; in fact, it usually makes things a whole lot worse. Since I can't change the way things are . . ." her words trailed off with a shrug.

"What if it doesn't work out the way ye hope?" Duncan couldn't shake off his concern so easily.

Another shrug of her shoulders was her immediate response. "Honestly, I don't know, since I'm not the one in control. Either it will work, or it won't. Besides, there's always plan B." She calmly smiled, but there was sadness in her eyes.

"What's plan B?" He had to ask.

"Usually, I don't know until it happens, but there's always a plan B. Speaking of plans," she said, perking up again, "let me go talk to Souyer before your next meeting. Where do you think I can find him?"

"Knowing Souyer, I expect him to be at the serving tables, having his morning meal. Should I go with ye?"

"No. Let me talk to him alone. Trust me, Duncan, it will all work out fine." With one last comforting pat on his forearm, she headed off to the serving tables.

~*~

The serving tables were located next to the cramped and overworked camp kitchen. The area had been set up by the collection of servants in charge of supplying the never-ending flow of meals needed to feed such a large gathering. The shared space provided for better efficiencies and allowed the cooks to pool their resources. As a result, the food at the faire was usually hot and plentiful, and sometimes quite tasty, as the cooks openly engaged in friendly competition.

Teressa quickly spotted Souyer sitting off by himself at one of the large benches. She helped herself to some warm apple oatcakes covered in a heavy fruit sauce before taking a seat next to Souyer.

"To what do I owe this pleasure, Mistress Ellers?" Souyer greeted her with suspicion. His wooden plate was laden with meat sausage, chunks of potatoes, and eggs scrambled together in a heaping pile. It didn't exactly appeal to Teressa.

"Good morning, Master Souyer. Such a lovely morning, don't you think?" Her early morning cheerfulness was lost on the old wizard as he barely looked up from his meal.

"I think ye are up to something, as usual," he said around a mouthful of food. It wasn't a pleasant sight, but Teressa made the necessary effort not to look away or turn up her nose.

"You're right, as usual. I know I owe you an apology for yesterday. I was having a little fun, but I meant no disrespect. Can you forgive my rudeness?"

"Only if you tell me what mischief ye were about that required Duncan's immediate attention," he negotiated, not succumbing to her attempt to lightly dismiss the event.

"Actually, I'm glad you asked. Did you know Duncan and Janet MacDonald were once betrothed and that Duncan broke the betrothal and sent her home with her mother?" She spoke as though it were some scandalous piece of gossip.

"Aye, of course I know. Everyone knows that." Souyer displayed his disinterest by returning his attention to his plate of food.

"Okay, did you know Janet MacDonald is here at the festival with her family? Apparently, she hasn't been here for three years since their broken betrothal," she persisted, acting as if she were sharing another juicy piece of information.

"Try telling me something I don't know." He gave her a smug grin as if he held the upper hand.

"Well, then I guess you also know the MacDonald chief all but called Duncan out about his broken betrothal yesterday at the gathering?" She pouted, hoping to appear done in by his superior knowledge.

"Of course, I was there. But how do ye know about that? Does it have anything to do with ye charging in to see Duncan as soon as the meeting was over?" Souyer took another spoonful of eggs and sausage. He seemed to be enjoying Teressa's attempt at intrigue almost as much as he was enjoying his meal.

"I didn't know what happened at the meeting until later, but I wanted to warn Duncan about Janet being at the faire." She was laying out her strategy, bit by bit, to gain Souyer's participation in her plan.

"I'm sure Duncan was already aware of Janet's presence. Yer grand attempt to warn him was surely not needed."

"It wasn't only to warn him that she's here." Again, she took on the air of grand conspirator, eyeing their surroundings. "I think she might try to compromise Duncan so he'll have to marry her. You know what I mean, don't you?" She stared at Souyer with an intense expression of concern, as if this horrible idea deeply offended her.

"Bah. Lady Janet would never try to force herself on Duncan. And even if she did, Duncan would never allow such a thing. He's quite capable of fending for himself." Souyer dismissed her, as though her womanly concerns were overly dramatic.

"Yeah, that's pretty much what Duncan said." She paused, letting her shoulders slump, as if she were done in by the master druid's superior insight. After a moment of thoughtful hesitation, she continued, as though inspired by a new thought. "What if Hugh MacDonald tries to force the issue at the meeting today? Didn't you say he almost did that yesterday?" She wasn't about to allow the matter to rest.

"He came close, but as a clan chief and elder, it would appear petty to bring up a grudge over his daughter's past hurt. She's not the first woman to experience a broken betrothal."

Her strategy was getting tricky. She wanted Souyer to believe it was his idea to play the part of a concerned advisor to Duncan.

"I guess you're right, Souyer, I don't know enough about your ways. Where I come from, fathers often force young men to marry their daughters. We call it a marriage trap. I was just thinking if someone in a position of power could force the MacDonald chief's hand on the issue, he wouldn't be able to trap Duncan unaware. Then Duncan would have a chance to be done with the old man's threats once and for all. But I'm sure you know better than me." She took a bite of her breakfast. "Have you tried these apple cakes? They sure are good."

Teressa turned her focus to savoring the fresh baked biscuits, appearing to put the matter to rest, all the while watching Souyer's face for any telling signs her words had made an impression. Though she hoped to avoid asking the druid for an outright favor, if she had to, she would use his botched solstice request as her bargaining chip. She held it in reserve as plan B.

It seemed she had gotten his attention. Souyer stopped eating and was definitely considering her words. He eyed her with interest. "Ye are right; ye don't understand our ways. I doubt ye know the proper way to handle such a delicate discussion as an arranged marriage in the company of men. Women tend to get far too emotional over such matters."

He was trying to entice her into revealing her thoughts, and she wasn't about to disappoint the old druid. He had taken her bait, and now she merely needed to keep him on the hook.

"Too emotional! Me!" she exclaimed, as though she were offended, but hiding a smile inside. "I'm sure I could find a way to bring up the matter without looking like a fool. I'd just have to . . . well, I would have to give it some thought," she said feigning insecurity at this dare.

"Aye, so it seems," he said in a tone of disbelief. And he was smirking. The old druid was smirking.

"Okay. From what you tell me, it would be wrong to bring up the issue directly, am I correct?"

"Aye, lass, ye're learning." He sat back, still smirking, waiting for her to go on.

"So, if a person of respect, maybe someone like Rory . . ."

Souyer solemnly shook his head.

"No, you're right, that wouldn't work. Okay, maybe someone . . . like you; if you commented to Hugh MacDonald about his daughter's return to the faire, with the right amount of innuendo, the elderly MacDonald would have an opening to address the slight against his daughter. He could either continue his tirade, which would be seen as petty and not in his best interests, or let it go in a public acknowledgment of putting it to rest, which would be in Duncan's best interest. Does that sound right, or am I giving too much credit to the MacDonald to act appropriately?" She earnestly looked to the druid, like a student would to a respected teacher, hoping for a good evaluation of her presentation.

"Yer idea has merit, but ye are correct. It would take a very skilled negotiator to complete the task with the proper finesse."

"Then it's a good thing I won't be allowed anywhere near the meeting. I'm sure I would blow it completely, knowing me." She laughed at her own shortcomings.

"Aye, lass, ye wear yer emotions too much on our face. Ye are far too easy to read." He stared at her with a bland expression.

She could read him like a clock.

"Do you really think so?" she responded with a haughty look, as if to dispute his observation, knowing very well she was falling far short of the mark.

The druid held his grim poker face while Teressa made a halfhearted attempt to mimic him before she lowered her guard once again.

"Okay, I'll admit, I could learn a lot from you. Maybe I should become your student." She knew there was no greater compliment for the master druid.

"Aye, perhaps ye should. 'Tis an idea to be considered. But for now, I have an important meeting to attend." Wiping the crumbs of his meal from his face, he left her sitting alone at the table, supremely happy.

Everything was going so well. *So far, so good,* she thought.

CHAPTER 17

Duncan walked into the meeting tent provided for the chiefs and evaluated the situation. Men were taking their places or gathering in small groups to converse. The space was comprised of three seating areas grouped around the center of the tent, one for each clan represented at the faire. Hugh MacDonald stood near the middle of the tent, taking center stage. When Duncan saw Souyer enter the tent and approach the MacDonald chief, he positioned himself close enough to overhear their conversation without being directly within their circle.

"Good day Hugh," Souyer greeted the MacDonald chief. "That was quite a speech ye delivered yesterday. I would say ye made yer views well known."

Duncan evaluated the druid's greeting. To his ears, it sounded like empty flattery to impress the haughty chief, even though Souyer's comment conveyed neither approval nor disapproval.

For a short moment, Hugh appeared to be taken aback, undoubtedly surprised to be receiving any acknowledgment from Scorrybreac's druid. Souyer rarely spoke to anyone. Fortunately, it was often better that way.

"I'm encouraged to see such wisdom from a venerable representative of Scorrybreac," Hugh replied. The tenor of his voice made it clear he wanted Duncan to hear.

Souyer nodded, accepting MacDonald's grudging compliment. "'Tis a pleasure to see Lady Janet at the faire this year. I trust young Janet has been well these past years, during her absence."

It was Duncan's turn to be surprised. He hadn't expected Souyer to bring up the subject of Lady Janet so quickly or so purposefully. The old druid made it sound as if his comment to the rival chief were the most natural thing to be expected, which was hardly true. It was no more natural than if a wild bird of prey had flown into the tent and landed on Souyer's shoulder, and certainly no less unsettling.

Souyer darted a look at Duncan, mayhap to catch his reaction. Duncan refrained from actually acknowledging the conversation taking place only steps from where he stood. Instead, he merely tilted his head in their direction as though he were interested in what was being said.

"'Tis thoughtful of ye to notice. Wouldn't it be grand if all of Scorrybreac displayed such respect?" Duncan didn't have to strain to listen. The MacDonald chief had nearly shouted his response.

It was time for Duncan to react. He turned towards the MacDonald chief, as though he couldn't allow the slight to go unnoticed. "I assure ye, Lady Janet is well respected by all the MacNicol clan. She honors us all with her presence."

By now, several of the other men in attendance were beginning to take notice of the exchange. Souyer's eyes darted between the two men as he stepped away, taking a position of detached observation.

"I'm impressed ye would state such high regard for my daughter after so many years of neglect for her welfare. As I recall, yer regard was quite different three years ago."

Teressa had been right again. Hugh MacDonald had wasted no time seizing the opportunity to dredge up the past.

Duncan had learned from Janet that Hugh had never approved of his daughter's rejection by the young heir of the MacNicol clan. At the time, the MacDonald had accepted Kennon MacNicol's settlement for the broken betrothal, and had greatly enriched his sheep herd in the process, but apparently even such compensation couldn't soothe the MacDonald's wounded ego where his daughter was concerned. Hugh had been incredulous when Janet told him it was her choice to return home with her mother. He had accused her of being too young to know her own mind, and blamed her for being unprepared to take on the role of wife to seal their alliance. It had taken months for his rift with Janet to heal.

Duncan swallowed another bite of crow. "'Tis true, the past years have been a time of deep reflection, but I have always held a high regard for Lady Janet," Duncan assured the MacDonald, keeping his emotions firmly in check.

"Yer high regard, as ye claim, apparently wasn't high enough for ye to take her as yer wife. 'Tis yer loss, *laddie*, for she is truly a well-respected woman of my clan. Ye will find none better. Nay, Duncan, ye are the loser now." Hugh grinned angrily, his face turned a searing red.

Duncan breathed deeply, his expression rock solid. To those watching, he hoped it appeared as if he were striving to contain his anger. He stepped forward.

"Hugh MacDonald, ye have a beautiful and worthy daughter. I would be honored and pleased to take her as my wife." Duncan addressed the elder chief with respect.

There was a gasping cough from someone in the gathering.

Tormord MacLeod stepped forward, joining their circle. "'Tis time ye came to yer senses, MacNicol."

The MacLeod chief was an unexpected ally, but Duncan would accept all the support he could garner.

MacDonald stared at them in disbelief, and then blinked as he digested Duncan's declaration of acceptance for his daughter.

Visibly struggling to regain his composure, he spat back at the younger man, "Aye, 'tis easy for ye to say such now. What assurance do I have when ye return to yer fortress by the sea?"

A twisted smile reached Duncan's lips. "We shall perform the marriage here, at this gathering of clans, to ensure 'tis done with yer approval."

All present heard the exchange. His words hung heavy in the air.

Hugh MacDonald paused, as though considering Duncan's statement of acceptance. "Well done, MacNicol." His stare bore down on Duncan. "'Tis past time for ye to honor yer past agreements. It may bode well for yer clan." Not surprising, Hugh's statement was delivered with a heavy dose of arrogance.

Stone-faced, Duncan remained silent, allowing the old man's bluster to pass. The moment was too perfect, just as Teressa had predicted.

Hugh turned to his master-at-arms. "Have my wife and my daughter brought here. Lady Janet will be allowed to choose."

Turning to Duncan, he stated in no uncertain terms, "Ye understand, MacNicol, I will grant her the right of refusal." Then lowering his voice, he added, "Mayhap ye should be worried."

It was highly unusual and rarely allowed for a woman to be permitted to accept or refuse a marriage proposal. Duncan realized this might be the MacDonald's way of getting one last swipe at him. He nodded curtly. Indeed, he would welcome her public declaration. If Janet's acknowledgement of love had been no more than a ruse to achieve her father's vengeance and humiliate him, so be it. He would turn his back on the MacDonald clan once and for all and walk away. But in his heart, he knew, the love she had pledged was real.

Duncan watched as Janet entered the tent with Lady Evelyn. He wondered if she had told her mother about their meeting and his desire to marry her. He had asked her to wait until he had a chance to address the matter with her father, and she had assured him she would, claiming her loyalty was now with him. He wondered if she had kept her word, if he could depend on her support as his wife.

~~~

Janet took her place next to her mother and father, unsure why they had been called, since it was highly unusual to allow women at the chiefs' proceedings. She hadn't told her mother of her meeting with Duncan and their desire to marry. Duncan had assured her he wanted to address the matter of their marriage with her father first, and she had willingly agreed as a show of her loyalty to him. She wanted him to know he could depend on her support as his wife.

Nervous butterflies fluttered about in Janet's core as her gaze darted between her father and Duncan. Both men wore stern expressions, but in Duncan's eyes, she saw his love and felt his strength. The butterflies eased off from their furious assault on her nerves. The women curtsied low in respect to the elders then waited to be addressed.

Her father spoke to those assembled in a loud, demanding voice. "All of ye gathered here know the history of our two clans." He motioned towards Duncan. "The young MacNicol chief has informed us, after all these years, he is now prepared to take my own dear daughter, Lady Janet, as his wife." Hugh paused to let his words take effect.

Janet's eyes grew wide as she bit her bottom lip, struggling to contain her joy. Her every nerve tingled with happiness.

"What say ye, Lady Janet? Do ye accept this proposal of marriage from the MacNicol chief?" His voice softened as he spoke to her.

It took all of her manners as a well-bred woman, well informed regarding public etiquette, to maintain her composure and refrain from flying into her father's arms. Looking to Duncan for one last glance of reassurance, she replied with a soft, clear voice, "Aye, Father, I do."

Lady Evelyn reached out to hold Janet's hand, overcome with happiness for her daughter, while her father seemed momentarily bewildered at her response. He quickly recovered and once more displayed a righteous countenance.

"Then it shall be done. Ye shall be wed this day." Hugh began his final declaration of acceptance, but Lady Evelyn quickly stepped forward to touch her husband's arm.

"Tomorrow," she said softly.

"What?" Hugh stared down at his wife.

"Tomorrow. The wedding shall be tomorrow. We need proper time to prepare." Her mother's voice was low, but firm, as she confidently returned her husband's glare.

With a nod, he accepted. "Let it be known that tomorrow," his eyes darted meaningfully towards his wife, "Duncan MacNicol will take my daughter, Lady Janet MacDonald, as his wedded wife."

Lady Evelyn smiled sweetly.

Janet dropped her reserve and rushed to hug her father. "Thank you, Father, thank you. Thank you so much for making this happen. I'm so happy." Her embrace released a floodgate of emotion between father and daughter.

"I had no idea, child." His burly arms held her longer, tighter, and more loving than she could ever remember before.

~*~

The rest of the day and into the night, the camp was a flurry of activity in preparation for the upcoming wedding that would unite the two clans. Lady Lydia, Kayla, and Teressa joined Lady Evelyn to assist in preparing Janet's best gown for the ceremony.

Over at the serving kitchen, the cooks gathered their remaining provisions to prepare the wedding feast. Teressa had heard them complain it was exceedingly difficult to prepare an adequate feast on the last day of the fair, grumbling about not having access to their pantries and wine cellars, but Bonnie had assured her, in the end, they would rise to the challenge and create a delectable feast fit for the wedding of a chief to his lady. As a whole, they seemed proud to present their best effort to ensure a delicious feast for the important occasion.

Coming upon Teressa as she was making her way back to the ladies' tents from an errand, Souyer couldn't seem to resist gloating over her failed plan. "It appears yer little scheme didn't work out quite the way ye expected. Duncan is set to marry Janet MacDonald tomorrow."

"I know. Isn't it wonderful? I couldn't be more pleased," Teressa gushed.

"Ye're pleased?" he scoffed. "Ye surprise me. I thought ye were against their marriage. I had begun to believe ye wanted the MacNicol chief for yerself."

It touched her to think the druid might have played his part as a favor to her. "I know it may have seemed that way, but all I really want is to see Duncan happy. All that matters is that the clans will be united by two people who love and respect each other. There are no losers here. Everyone feels like a winner, and you helped to make it happen. I would think you'd be happy."

"Unlike ye, lass, I have no attachment to the outcome. It matters little to me whom Duncan marries. If he is truly happy, as ye believe, then I am pleased with the results. As far as I'm concerned, he couldn't have done it without me."

"Are you trying to tell me you have no romance in your old bones?" she teased the old druid.

"My bones have all the romance they need," he informed her. "But what about ye? Have ye found what ye are looking for?"

Her mirth immediately faded. "What makes you think I'm looking for something?" His question took her by surprise.

"A woman doesn't travel halfway around the world and over seven hundred years in time and not be looking for something. Mayhap when ye find what ye're looking for, ye'll let me know."

Souyer appeared quite satisfied with his surprisingly astute observation. With a look of smug authority, he headed off toward his tent.

Watching him shuffle off, Teressa stood there for some time, considering his words. *Why did I come to Scorrybreac,* she wondered? *Was it for something more than a summer vacation adventure?* With or without the unexpected time travel, she had to admit she had made a rather long journey to arrive alone at Scorrybreac. What had she really hoped to find? Souyer's question tugged at her brain, begging to be considered.

Still lost in thought, she turned to continue on to Lady Evelyn's tent and bumped right into Rory.

"My goodness," she sputtered into his wonderfully broad chest before taking a step back. "I thought you'd be off drinking with Duncan."

"I'd rather have another *date* while everyone is busy getting ready for tomorrow's celebration. They'll never miss us. Besides, I would much rather have time alone with ye than drinking time with Duncan, much as I do enjoy MacLeods' ale." He flashed a heart-stopping provocative grin.

Teressa smiled in return. How could she not? He always made her smile. It was pure splendor to imagine what life would be like with this fiercely handsome and humorous man.

"Oh Rory, I happen to be one of the busy ones," she said, sorry to disappoint him. "I agreed to help Lady Lydia and Lady Evelyn prepare Janet's gown for tomorrow. I was just returning from the peddler's market with some ribbons." She held up the basket in her hand.

"Will they require yer service all night long?" he asked, putting emphasis on the last three words.

"Well, maybe not all night. Janet and I agree it's best to keep the gown simple. Perhaps, if all goes well, I can slip away after a few hours. That'll give you time to attend Duncan's bachelor party. As his brother, you really should make an appearance, don't you think?" She liked the idea of meeting up with Rory after their duties were fulfilled.

"Mayhap, ye are right. As his brother, I have a duty to see him drink more than his fair share of MacLeods' ale. 'Tis a sight I haven't yet had the pleasure to experience. This celebration has been a long time coming." Rory laughed as he considered the idea.

"Try not to drink more than your fair share. I wouldn't want you to fall asleep on me," she warned.

"My sweet, it would be my pleasure to fall asleep on ye, under ye, or next to ye, as long as ye were sharing my bed and had exhausted me beyond all use." He pulled her close, running his hand up and down her back, inducing a tingling up her spine.

"My goodness, Rory, how you turn a girl's head." She made a motion to fan herself, as if she were overheated by his words, which was very close to the truth. The idea of sharing his bed sounded very appealing, but Teressa wasn't ready to admit that to Rory, at least not yet. "We must behave ourselves. This evening is for your brother and his bride-to-be."

"Are ye always so practical?" He bent his head to nuzzle her neck.

"Usually, but not always." She sighed, feeling herself succumbing to his seductions. *Darn the man.* He made it difficult to be practical, or to even think. Doing her best to pull her head out of the clouds, she reminded him of her duties. "Your mother's expecting me to return with these ribbons. Should I risk disappointing her?"

"Hmm," he considered. "Probably not. Promise ye will find time for me later before I let ye go."

"I promise I'll try. I'll do my best," she assured him.

"I've yet to see how good yer best can be. I shall look forward to seeing ye later," he persisted.

"Yes. Now scoot. I've got to get back to Lady Evelyn's tent." She pushed against his formidable chest, sending him on his way.

Reluctantly, they parted, Teressa returning to a tent full of women and Rory headed off to help Duncan make the most of his last night as a single man.

~*~

Janet was pleasantly pleased by the ideas Teressa suggested for turning her simple gown into an image of beauty. Besides the benefit of several hundred years of fashion design, Teressa had a better-than-average talent for sewing to assist in the gown's transformation. They reshaped the neckline to dip respectably low across Janet's breasts. It clung to her delicate shoulders, exposing her elegant neck and just enough cleavage to entice. The sage-green gown fitted snugly around Janet's torso then fanned out from a dropped waist, draping softly over her hips before falling gracefully to skim the tops of her slippers. Kayla wove a circlet of flowers with bright colored ribbons that would flow down Janet's back.

Lady Evelyn carried on a steady stream of chatter while Lady Lydia and Teressa made the necessary alterations to Janet's gown. "This is better than I could have hoped for," she said as she combed and braided Janet's thick brown hair. When removed tomorrow, the braids would leave behind soft waves. "To have the wedding performed here at the faire truly makes it a grand occasion."

Kayla looked up from circlet of flowers she was weaving with ribbons. "I still don't understand how Duncan and Lady Janet were able to make amends and repair their relationship. It happened all so fast. When we left Scorrybreac, I would never have thought . . ."

"Duncan would want to marry me," Lady Janet interjected.

"Exactly. I mean, it's only been a few days," Kayla said, appearing slightly befuddled.

"I owe it all to Teressa. She talked with Duncan and arranged for us to meet, privately. I couldn't have done it without her help," Janet said, looking kindly at Teressa.

"Hold stead," Lady Evelyn said as she tied off the braid with a ribbon. "I still don't know how she managed to talk ye into meeting the man alone, and why wasn't I informed?"

"Mother, there wasn't time." Janet reached back to run her hand down the braid to check her mother's work.

"I had no idea Teressa was a matchmaker. Why didn't someone tell me? How did ye know Duncan was still interested in marrying Janet?" Kayla continued with her questions. Teressa understood her confusion. The young woman had never been informed of Lady Lydia's intentions, or her scheme to use Teressa to do her bidding.

"It was simple, I asked him," Teressa said.

"And he told ye?" Kayla asked, incredulous. "He never tells us anything."

"I guess that's my skill," Teressa offered vaguely, wanting to say as little as possible. She glanced over at Lady Lydia. Not surprisingly, the major manipulator remained quiet, offering no assistance.

"I cannot thank ye enough," Janet said once again.

"I'm sure you two lovers would have managed a reunion on your own, if given the chance," Teressa assured her. Privately, she was pleased she'd been able to facilitate a faster resolution.

"I'm not so sure. It was like magic," Janet said shaking her head.

"Well, yes, love is the strongest magic of them all," Teressa said, remembering Rory's words.

It was later than Teressa had expected when Janet put the dress on for one last fitting, to ensure everything was perfect for the wedding, and twirled happily in her lovely new gown. In her enthusiasm, she reached out to grasp Teressa's hands in hers.

"Oh, Teressa, I know I shall be happy as Duncan's wife. And I shall be doubly blessed to have ye as my friend at the MacNicol keep."

Teressa's heart lurched in her chest. Janet's happiness was a reminder that her job here was done; she would be returning home soon.

"I have great confidence in your future happiness," Teressa said. She took a quick look at Lady Lydia before she turned back to Janet with a forced smile. "I'm sorry to say, I don't expect to stay at Scorrybreac much longer. I imagine I'll be returning home soon." She kept her voice light, hoping to hide her true feelings.

Fearful thoughts of losing Rory tugged at her consciousness. Somewhere in the back of her mind, the fear she would leave and never see him again lived in a small dark space where worries reside. She tried to ignore them as best she could, but it wasn't easy. He had asked her to believe in magic, the magic of love, and she was determined to not give up on him or on her newfound faith.

Janet was stunned by Teressa's announcement. "But I thought . . . Kayla told me Rory has been courting ye."

There was no reason to deny the gossip. Teressa wasn't surprised to know the affections she and Rory shared had not gone unnoticed. It was like living in a very small town where everyone knew everyone else's business. The only difference here was that very few people knew the whole truth of her rather extraordinary circumstances.

"Rory and I are quite fond of each other. Kayla's not wrong. But I have family waiting for me back home. I'm expected to return," she said, glancing pointedly at Lady Lydia.

"Certainly, there is no need to discuss such things tonight." Lady Lydia said, stepping forward to speak. "I trust all will be well in due time. Janet, dear, I'm sure ye're excited for tomorrow, but tonight ye need yer rest. Lady Evelyn, we should leave ye now to retire."

Lady Lydia began packing up the collection of sewing supplies. When Teressa moved to assist in the cleanup, Lydia reached out to stay her hand. "Ye look a little tired," she said. "Ye should go on ahead. We can finish here without you. Ye've already been most helpful."

The meaning in Lydia's words didn't go unnoticed by Teressa, and she accepted the kindness of the gesture with a nod. Giving Janet a quick hug of friendly affection and her best wishes, Teressa slipped out from the tent into the cool, refreshing chill of the night air. It was late, and she was sorely tempted to forgo her meeting with Rory in favor of once again retreating into the solitude of her tent. But she had given him her word, and in all honesty, being comforted by Rory seemed a whole lot better than returning to her bed alone.

CHAPTER 18

Picking her way by the light of the campfires, Teressa made her way to Rory's tent and was disappointed to find he had not yet returned from celebrating with Duncan. She felt weary and a bit worn out from the day's activities and decided to rest a bit before Rory returned. Wanting to make herself comfortable, she removed her hiking boots and stepped out of the long woolen skirt, leaving only the knee-length tunic as a nightshirt. She placed her boots next to Rory's storage chest and draped her skirt over the top before settling in under the blankets on his bed of cushions.

With a wedding in the works, Teressa wasn't surprised her thoughts should turn to romance, passion, and shared commitments. As she lay there in his tent, on Rory's bed, she finally admitted to herself what she had known all along: she wanted to be with him. But she wanted a lifetime of love and laughter, not merely a moment of pleasure. If there was anything they could do to make that happen, she was willing to try. She sighed, thinking how wonderful it would be to release herself to their passion.

As painful as it was, she also considered this might very well be their one and only night to be together. She didn't want to risk missing the opportunity. *There are no guarantees in this world,* she told herself. *I might not be allowed a lifetime of love with him, but God help me, in this moment of here and now, I'm going to open myself to all the love this one night can bring.*

Pulling his blanket over her for warmth, she breathed in his lingering scent in the soft handwoven wool. The strain of the long day washed over her, and she closed her eyes.

~*~

When Rory arrived back at his tent, he was pleasantly surprised and totally pleased to find Teressa asleep on his pallet. Her long lashes rested on her cheek, and a wisp of a smile curved her lips. She looked peaceful indeed, but two warring thoughts immediately raced through his brain. The first was to wake her so he could seduce her into making love with him; his desire for her grew heavy as he watched her in splendid slumber. The second was to let her sleep and take his place next to her, settling for the simple pleasure of holding her warm body next to his.

Alas, she looked so serene; he couldn't bear to disturb her dreams. Besides, hadn't she warned him she didn't easily give in to seduction? She had been wise to do so, because right now, seduction was very tempting. It took great effort, but he opted to lie down on the pallet beside her, his hands laced behind his head as he stared up at the roof of his tent.

Soon, he consoled himself once again, as he had so many times before. Soon he would experience their passion. *It better be soon*, he thought. *There's only so much waiting one man can take.*

Rory was itching to get his hands on her lovely body, run his fingers through her hair, and kiss her passionate lips. He felt he had made great progress in his wooing of her and was anxiously anticipating the moment when he would feel the sweet heat of her complete surrender.

He gazed at her intently, thinking how much he wanted to touch her. He wanted to touch her skin, to cradle her face in his hand, and run his fingers through her soft, long hair. He wanted to feel the hollow at the small of her back as it gave way to the gentle curve of her hips and feel the plump heaviness of her breasts. Now, in this moment, he wanted to touch her. He was also painfully aware how much he wanted that touch to lead to another and another, and in the end, he knew nothing short of complete exploration of all her physical pleasures would satisfy him. But for now, all he wanted was to touch her. Reaching out his hand, he slowly, softly, brushed his fingers across her cheek.

Rolling to his side, he slipped under the covers beside her and cradled her body to fit against his. It didn't take long for him to discover her bare legs. *Dear Father in heaven*, he thought as his rough, weathered hand slid along the long, sensuous span of her bare leg. *What in the name of all that is holy has she done with her skirt?* He popped his head up to look about the tent. In the dim glow of moonlight, he spied her skirt draped carefully across his wooden chest and her boots placed neatly nearby.

How very practical of her, he mused. *Practical, but not very sensible.* Thanks to her efficiencies in reduced sleeping apparel, it would take more effort to adhere to his plan of letting her slumber undisturbed than he could manage. He considered himself to be a strong-willed, self-disciplined man regarding his duty to honor his woman, but this abundance of exposed flesh was too much for even the strongest of warriors.

A passing thought that he wouldn't have found this abundance of exposed flesh had he not chosen to slip uninvited beneath the covers was quickly dismissed as impractical. How could he have resisted?

Heated blood surged through his veins, pumping up his manhood. He found he was quite willing to engage in a little exploration of her naked body when presented with such a treasured opportunity.

Lying beside her, he reached his hand down to begin his exploration at her softly curved calves, intending to slowly work his way up to her thighs and beyond. With sweet anticipation, he considered what his exploration would uncover. He took note of how shapely and muscular her calves felt. They were an indication of a well-toned body, all the more tempting to explore. Slowly, he lingered over each inch of her uncharted flesh, savoring the exquisite moments of expectation for the treasure he was uncovering. His hand continued to map the length of her leg, reaching the slight bend of her knee as she lay curled on her side, then following the natural curve of her leg, he continued his discovery along her sinewy thighs. He imagined her as a powerhouse of passion with those strong legs wrapped around his waist.

As any good explorer, he carefully considered his path of investigation. Should he seek the silky softness of her inner thigh, or opt for the feel of the rounded curve of her backside? Wanting to draw out the pleasure of the moment, he chose the curve of her backside. As the flat of his palm reached around to enjoy the sweet curve of her buttocks, he felt her stir. He stopped mid grope and froze for a moment as he considered whether he should move his hand to a more suitable location, like outside the covers.

Before his blood-depleted mind was able to decide, she rolled over onto her back, putting him for a quick moment in the interesting position of having his hand poised directly above her most private terrain. Burning with the heat of temptation, he quickly drew back his hand to his side as she stretched and uncoiled from her sleeping position. He watched her, rather fascinated by the process of her waking. Her eyes held his interest most keenly. They went from drowsy slits to wide open, and even wider still as she became fully aware of his presence.

"Rory, what are you doing here?" she blurted as she sat up in bed, clutching the covers.

"Actually, since this is my bed, I could ask ye the same question." He grinned, enjoying her state of confusion.

"Oh yes, but I thought you would wake me," she exclaimed, rubbing the sleep from her eyes.

"Apparently, I have." He grinned provocatively.

"I mean, before you crawled into bed."

"What would have been the fun in that? This has been far more fascinating," he teased. He hoped her hesitation to leave his bed, coupled with her lack of demand for his departure, was a positive sign.

Settling back down, she gazed at him intensely as she brought her hands up to touch his bare chest, and his muscles grew taut beneath her slender fingers. He shuddered ever so slightly as her fingers wove their own path of discovery across his broad shoulders. Her eyes roamed freely over his body, as if drinking in the sight of his exposed chest and stomach. It was her turn to smile lazily as she became the explorer, discovering the fine mat of hair gracing his upper torso, and laying a pathway toward his manhood. He knew his state of arousal couldn't go unnoticed as she eyed the region below the boundaries of his breeches.

"I was thinking, before you arrived . . ." she began in a husky whisper, her eyes latching on to his.

"Aye?" He worked to hold his voice steady, daring to hope, as her fingers snaked a slow circular path down his stomach.

She took a deep breath. "I was thinking I have made a decision."

"Go on," he encouraged her, his eyes never leaving hers, waiting for her to speak.

"I'm thinking . . . I want you. I know this is rather brazen, but I want you."

Rory's reaction was swift and decisive. He crushed her to him, his hands moving to hold the length of her body against his. He wanted to devour her, to wrap himself around her and never let her go. He felt the force of his passion bursting through his veins, rushing to feed every cell of his body. He claimed her mouth in a fiercely possessive kiss, releasing his passion in the very touch of her lips. He savored the sweet taste of her lips, her mouth. She was his, and only his.

As he pulled back to remove his breeches in quick fashion, a voice from the corner of his mind reminded him to go slow. Proper loving required a long, slow arousal of sensations. He would take his time making love to her, not rush into hasty and hurried relief. Gently removing her tunic, he rendered them both naked. There was a quick intake of his breath as he marveled at the beauty of her well-toned body. She was even more beautiful than he had imagined, and he believed he had a very vivid imagination.

"Allow me to show ye the fine art of making love," he whispered, leaning down to touch his lips against her neck.

"Oh, my goodness," she gasped. Her fingers slid down to the taut muscles of his abdomen, absorbing the feel of his skin and the heat radiating from his body.

He kissed her again, softly at first, teasing her senses into heightened awareness. His hands moved slowly and methodically along the length of her, learning every curve of her shapely body. Determined to resume his earlier exploration of her, he moved his hands along her long slender legs and up across her abdomen. He reached to grasp the fullness of her breasts, kissing and suckling on the rosy nipples until her body strained for release from the sensual torture.

"Rory," she called out his name. "Please, Rory."

"Good lord, woman, ye are a sight to behold," he breathed, his voice low and ardent.

She snaked her arms around his back and bound him to her with a steely grip. "I need you," she declared as she arched toward him. "My God, Rory, how I want you."

"My sweet Teressa," Rory moaned, marveling at her unreserved reaction. She was everything he wanted in a woman, everything he wanted in his life. He held her close, her need an equal match to his own.

He touched her most intimate place, her womanhood, savoring the wet readiness he encountered as he sought her sensual arousal.

When he could wait no longer, when he felt her body crying out for him, he moved to position himself between her thighs. He paused one precious moment longer in sweet anticipation before he sank himself deep inside her and felt her muscles clench around him. The oneness of their bodies joined together in sacred passion surged through him, and he wanted to shout to the world the words screaming in his head. *I love this woman.*

She pulled her legs up to wrap around his waist, fully welcoming and embracing his body with her own. Never before had he experienced such a soulful connection as their two bodies strived to become one in an intimate lovers' embrace.

He began to move within her, slowly at first, gaining momentum to create a rhythmic thrust and pull that stirred her senses. She matched his rhythm, moving in sync, building a mounting force of pleasure. Together they created soul-soaring bliss that continued to build until their bodies reached the peak of sensual delight. Teressa led the way in a burst of pleasure, taking them both soaring to a brilliant, passionate explosion.

Satiated by their intense release of pleasure and pent-up passions, Rory collapsed beside her. It was a long moment before either was able to speak as they worked to slow their labored breath. Rolling to his side, Rory pulled Teressa to face him. He kissed her again, and again.

She searched his eyes, locked in a visual embrace. "I've never . . .," she whispered with a ragged breath. "I've never felt like this before. I can't even describe what I've just experienced."

Holding her close, he declared, "I claim ye, woman. Ye canna deny me now. I claim ye now and forever as my own."

"Yes, Rory, you have me. Now and forever, I shall always love you." Her eyes filled with bittersweet tears of joy.

"Aye," he said. "I shall love ye forever." He gazed at her with awe as he pledged his eternal love.

~*~

Early the next morning, before the first rays of sunlight sneaked above the horizon, Rory and Teressa awoke to prepare for the day's activities. Teressa smiled brilliantly, deeply comforted by Rory's words of love, and the assurance she heard in his voice. She had no idea what tomorrow would bring, but for this one bright shining moment in time, she was supremely happy. As she lay in his arms, somewhere deep inside she knew he would always love her. Somehow, he would always be with her. They had succumbed to the alchemy of intimacy, the magic of love. They were forever changed.

Knowing her absence would not go unnoticed by her tent mates, in the predawn darkness Teressa kissed Rory goodbye, hurried back to the tent she shared with Lady Lydia and Kayla, and quietly slipped beneath the covers of her bed.

Upon waking, Kayla seemed to be eyeing her with guarded suspicion, but neither Lydia nor her daughter made any comments about her absence. If they were aware of her overnight sleeping arrangements, they either chose to accept her improper behavior or preferred to ignore the matter, as if it didn't exist. Either way, she was grateful.

After grabbing a quick breakfast, Teressa joined Kayla at Janet's tent to assist the young bride in dressing for the ceremony. Teressa sensed Kayla was quietly brooding and probably feeling profoundly uncomfortable about her suspicions regarding Teressa's late night activities. Privately, Teressa preferred not to discuss the matter with Rory's sister, so she willingly acquiesced to Kayla's need for emotional distance. There was no need to force the young woman into a discussion she found uncomfortable or distasteful. Actually, Teressa was grateful she wasn't being asked to explain herself. She lived by a different set of rules than was acceptable to Kayla, and she wanted very much to respect the younger woman's comfort zone.

When they finished, Janet looked like a picture-perfect image of a princess bride. The sage-green gown looked even lovelier in the light of day. The halo of flowers she wore highlighted the soft waves of her lush auburn hair as the ribbons fluttered gently in the late morning breeze. Serene joy settled over Janet's delicate features as they left her tent and made their way to the meadow where she would marry the man she would love for the rest of her life.

Duncan was already there, looking noble and handsome as he anticipated the arrival of his bride wearing the plaid of his clan. Rory stood by his brother's side, appearing equally handsome to Teressa's eyes. He also wore the MacNicol plaid. Teressa remembered her scarf in the same distinctive plaid stashed with her other belongings in Duncan's trunk. For one bright moment, she allowed herself to imagine the possible grandeur of being part of this proud and noble clan. With sad acceptance, she reminded herself of her obligation to return to her own family and her own time. She was a misplaced traveler, out of time and out of place.

Souyer, Scorrybreac's master druid, presided over the public blessing of the marriage as the MacDonald chief gave the hand of his daughter to her new husband, Duncan MacNicol. Publicly, they declared their commitment to honor the union. Officially, the union was completed when Hugh and Duncan put their signatures to the marriage contract.

During the signing of the wedding contract, Teressa overheard Hugh make a pointed comment to Duncan. "I'll be expecting ye to take good care of her. If I hear my daughter is unhappy, I'll be unhappy. Do ye understand my meaning?" Even as he clasped his large hand across Duncan's shoulder, there was no mistaking the underlying threat being issued by the MacDonald chief.

"In this we can agree," Duncan assured him. "Janet's happiness is my priority now, and shall be forevermore."

The wedding feast began soon after the marriage ceremony and lasted well into the dark of night with torch lights burning. All in attendance to the faire joined in the wedding feast to celebrate the joyful union of the MacNicol Chief and Lady Janet MacDonald.

Later, as the feast wore on into the evening, Duncan and his new bride sought out Teressa as she stood with Rory, thoroughly enjoying the party. Her face was flushed with joy as she tapped her feet and gently swayed to the music being played by an assembly of diverse musicians.

"I don't believe I have properly thanked ye for the role ye played in bringing us back together," Duncan greeted her, looking very much like a happy married man.

"It was my pleasure, Duncan. I'm happy to see you happy. I wish you both a long and loving life together." Teressa raised her goblet of wine in a toast.

"To a long and loving life," Rory agreed as the foursome clinked their cups together to seal the toast.

"My only regret is that I wasted three years we could have spent together." Lady Janet was speaking to Teressa, but her eyes never left Duncan.

"Don't think of them as wasted years; think of them as lessons learned," Teressa counseled, offering up a bit of relationship advice. "It was time you both needed to become who you are, instead of who you thought you should be. Think how much more you now value each other. Consider it a learning experience that will make you stronger in your marriage."

"These are wise words ye speak," Duncan said. "Am I to understand ye are an established matchmaker?"

"You could say that," Teressa agreed with a bob of her head. She had come to accept the thirteenth-century description for her relationship coaching skills.

"Why didn't ye tell me when ye first arrived?" Duncan asked.

"You didn't ask," she shrugged. "It didn't seem to occur to you that I came equipped with talents beyond my sewing skills.

Besides, it wouldn't have been as much fun putting you two together if you knew what I was about." She offered up a sly smile.

"I suppose ye are right," Duncan said, looking less than convinced.

"I don't believe I would've had the courage to meet ye on my own without Teressa's help," Lady Janet told her husband.

"I doubt Duncan would've been as amenable to such a meeting without Teressa's influence," Rory offered.

"You're together now; that's all that matters," Teressa said to Duncan and his bride.

Lady Evelyn approached the group and asked for another moment of time with her daughter. The following day would be busy with each clan preparing to return to their homes, and she requested a moment to discuss final details of their departure with Janet. It was probably the third or fourth private moment she had requested, but Duncan reluctantly released his bride to her mother.

After watching her walk away, Duncan drank the last of the ale from the mug he was holding. "Rory, my fine brother, can ye do me the honor of refilling my tankard?" He held the empty cup out for his brother.

"Certainly, my chief." Rory bowed low in jest to his brother's request. Turning to Teressa, he asked, "While I am at this all important task for my brother, can I get anything for ye, my sweet?"

"No, I'm fine. Thanks for asking," Teressa declined.

Disregarding the watchful eyes of his brother, Rory gave Teressa a lingering kiss before heading off toward the barrels of ale.

Having maneuvered a moment alone with her, Duncan turned to address Teressa. "Janet tells me ye expect to return home soon. How can that be?"

"As far as I know, Moezell plans to send me home, eventually. I don't expect to stay here much longer." She had agreed to keep Lady Lydia's involvement in her time-travel adventure a secret, and in keeping with her professional ethics, she continued to honor their agreement.

"Does Rory know?" he asked.

"That I plan to return home? Yes. How I got here, or where I came from? No." She felt it best not to mention Rory's offer to journey home with her since she had no idea if such a thing were even possible. Silently she prayed there was a way they could stay together.

"Have ye considered staying?"

"Many times, but I have a family who has no idea where I am. Try to imagine Kayla leaving on a trip and never returning. How would you feel if you never knew what happened to her?" she asked.

"It would be too much to bear." He shook his head, and his eyes filled with compassion, as if the full weight of her predicament had become abundantly clear.

"A lifetime of not knowing . . . I couldn't do that to them. It was never my intention when I started my trip that I wouldn't return."

It would be painful to leave this magical place and time, but the decision was out of her hands, and perhaps that was best. As much as she wanted to stay to be with Rory, she knew she was honor-bound to return to her life and her family, where she belonged.

"What about Rory? I'm sorry, but ye understand, I must ask." There was no mistaking his brotherly concern for them both.

"I don't know. I'm sorry, I don't have an answer." She could only offer a sad smile with a shake of her head. Rory had asked her to believe in the magic of love, and she desperately clung to that belief. "This is out of my control, but I appreciate your concern."

"Yer short visit here has been deeply felt. I appreciate yer friendship." Unexpectedly, Duncan stepped forward to give her a brief hug, and Teressa warmly welcomed his show of affection. "I believe I have learned from the best," he added with a brotherly grin.

Rory returned with two full tankards of ale and handed one to Duncan. "A toast to my fine brother. To a long and lusty wedding night. May it be only one of many." He lifted his mug to clank against Duncan's, and the two brothers drank deeply.

"Speaking of long, lusty nights . . ." Rory turned to Teressa with a look that could only mean one thing.

"Rory!" Teressa tried to sound affronted, but her smile gave her away. She felt little need to censure her love for Rory. They had become lovers, and she would not attempt to hide that reality from Duncan or anyone else. Let them judge her if they wished, but she had no need for anyone's approval. Her time with Rory was too uncertain.

"I will leave you two to your vices. I have pleasures of my own to pursue." There was no hint of judgment from Duncan. He gave a farewell salute and headed off to find his bride.

A short while later, Rory and Teressa slipped away to his tent. Again, their night of loving passion went beyond anything Teressa had ever known before, and yet it was everything she had ever hoped a loving relationship would be. It wasn't just the physical pleasure of their intimate loving that amazed her. There seemed to be an intense, soulful connection between them that went beyond the physical experience. The passion in Rory's kisses, the tenderness in his embrace, the oneness in their physical joining, all went above and beyond being simple lovers. As Rory drew her into his arms, Teressa believed this was exactly where she was meant to be. She refused to question how or why.

Later, as she fell asleep in the comfort of his arms, she profoundly wished this could last forever. *Maybe someday, maybe somehow*, a voice whispered in her head.

CHAPTER 19

Rory had been awake for the better part of an hour watching Teressa sleep. Gazing at her while she lay peacefully beside him, he sent a silent prayer of thanks to all the powers of heaven and earth for bringing this amazing woman into his life. He could think of no greater blessing than to spend the rest of his days enjoying the magic of their love. She'd proven to be a far greater lover than he had ever imagined. Her release of passion was pure and unrestrained.

Now wasn't the time—he didn't want to overshadow his brother's wedding—but as soon as they returned to Scorrybreac, he would declare his intentions to marry Teressa and formally seal their union. She had shared his bed, and soon she would share his name. If she still insisted on traveling back to see her family, he would insist they journey together as husband and wife.

When she finally began to stir from her slumber, he greeted her with yet another tender kiss. "Good morning, my sweet." He brushed wayward strands of hair from her face.

She returned his affections, cradling his face in her hands as they kissed.

Sitting up, he reached for a small carved box he had earlier retrieved from his storage chest. "I have something for ye." He opened the wooden box to reveal a finely carved silver brooch nestled in a hunk of velvet fabric. "This is the badge of my clan. I want ye to have it. Wear it always, and it will keep ye safe." She sat up, and he handed her the box.

"It's too beautiful. I don't know what to say." Her eyes glazed with tears of joy as her fingers gently traced the fine carving of the MacNicol shield.

"Will ye accept it as a symbol of my love?" He felt as though his heart would burst from his chest, it was so full of love.

"Yes Rory, I will. I'll keep it with me always," she promised clutching it to her chest.

He felt complete. She was pledged to him now. All that was left was the public ceremony to seal their union forever.

~*~

Teressa strolled through the camp, basking in the early morning sun, somewhat sad to think this was the last day of the faire. Earlier, when she and Rory had emerged from his tent, the servants and the workers had already begun the arduous task of disassembling their camp and packing the wagons, which would take them the better part of the day to complete. Most of the family members would depart long before noon, leaving Rory to oversee the servants and the final packing.

As to be expected, it was later than usual when Duncan made his appearance. It was even later when Janet appeared and joined Teressa in grabbing a last minute bite at the serving tables. The kitchen stations were already being broken down to be loaded on the wagons for the trip home.

It was nearing midmorning when the MacNicol women gathered around Lady Lydia's coach for the trip back to Scorrybreac. Rory pulled Teressa aside for one last passionate embrace before he released her to the protection of his family. Conflicting emotions tore at her heart. She wanted to stay with Rory, and yet, she knew she needed to return home. Adding to all that, her willpower was near breaking with the struggle not to tell Rory everything about who she was and where she was from.

Teressa didn't want his embrace to end, but end it did, and she hurriedly climbed into Lydia's coach before she dissolved into a puddle of tears.

Duncan and his guards were to accompany the women back to the keep, along with Souyer and his donkey cart. It would take several hours to reach Scorrybreac, and Duncan was anxious to get started. Since it was Rory's duty to oversee the caravan of workers, he would not be expected back at the keep until much later in the day.

During their journey to Scorrybreac, most of the talk in the women's coach centered around Janet's marriage and plans for her to take over the responsibility of being mistress of Scorrybreac. Kayla seemed more than ready to relinquish her short-lived duties, taking the opportunity to inform Janet about every aspect of running the keep. Her happiness at having Janet for a sister-in-law was evident.

Teressa was grateful for the distraction occupying her fellow travelers; it allowed her to be alone with her thoughts. Lady Lydia hadn't said anything to Teressa regarding her return to her own time, but as they approached the MacNicol fortress, Teressa became acutely aware her time was growing short.

Adding to Teressa's gloom, their day of travel was marred by heavy storm clouds rolling in from the northern seas, darkening the afternoon skies. The Isle Faire had been blessed with days of pleasant summer weather, but balmy skies were changing quickly to brooding heavens. Duncan ordered the small troupe of travelers to quicken their pace in hopes of reaching the keep before the storm broke.

They almost reached their goal.

The fortress had barely come into sight when the dark clouds released a downpour of torrential rains. Duncan sent one of the guards ahead to alert Michael of their pending arrival, with instructions to have fires lit in the hearths and blankets prepared to warm them after the harsh cold of the storm.

~*~

After enjoying the luxury of a lukewarm bath, the first she had experienced in days, Teressa changed into a long white night shift, preparing for the warmth and comfort of a good night's sleep. She was sitting alone in the guest chamber drying her hair near the fire when Lady Lydia knocked on the adjoining door. Teressa bid her enter.

"The storm is quite heavy. I think ye should know we don't expect Rory and the caravan to return tonight. They will have to make camp and ride out the storm as best they can. 'Tis too dangerous to travel in this weather," Lady Lydia informed Teressa, taking a seat near the hearth.

"I was afraid of that. Do you think they will be all right?" Teressa stopped brushing her hair and dropped her hands to her lap.

"Rory has experience with storms such as this. I trust he's capable of handling the situation. His first concern will be to ensure the safety of those under his command." Lydia said, displaying complete confidence in her son.

Teressa turned her gaze back to the fire. She was well aware of the next question that needed to be discussed, but it was difficult to broach the subject. Finally, taking a deep breath, she looked at Lady Lydia and asked, "How much more time do I have?"

"Tomorrow. Ye will be sent back in the morning, as when ye arrived," Lady Lydia said, without a hint of regret.

"What! So soon?" Teressa was taken aback by Lydia's abrupt announcement. "Will Rory be back by then?"

"'Tis not expected. I believe 'tis better this way."

"How can you say that? I won't even have a chance to say goodbye." Teressa couldn't hold back the tear spilling from her eye. She wiped it away with the back of her hand. How could Lydia be so cruel after everything Teressa had done for her? It seemed so unreasonable, so unfair, even though she had known this was inevitable.

"Do ye really believe saying goodbye will make it easier?" Lady Lydia asked with frank skepticism.

Teressa dropped her gaze to the floor. "No, nothing will make this easier." She paused a moment before looking back at Lady Lydia. "Somehow this doesn't seem fair, being brought here without my consent, falling in love, and now having to leave. I feel as though I don't have any say in the matter."

Lady Lydia seemed prepared to take a firm stand on her decision. "Ye were not brought here to fall in love with my youngest son," she admonished Teressa.

Teressa's anger surge, fueled by the pain in her heart. "What if it had been Duncan? You said you brought me here to test his affections. What if he had fallen in love with me?"

"It wouldn't have mattered. If he had shown an interest in ye, I would have simply sent ye back sooner to get ye out of the way. Duncan and Janet needed to marry. The two clans must be united to preserve our peaceful relations. Old wrongs needed to be made right. I loved my husband, but Kennon should never have allowed Duncan to break the betrothal. He was too soft on him. As the eldest son, he has duties to perform and responsibilities to consider. The peace of our clan is more important than a love match."

"Wasn't that why you brought me here in the first place, to ensure a love match? If you just wanted them to marry, couldn't you have forced the issue?"

"Kennon believed in time Duncan would accept his duty to marry Janet, and I didn't wish to undermine my husband. When he died, Duncan became chief, and I couldn't undermine my son. Ye have no idea. Women in this time have very little authority in the ways of men. Our actions and influence must all take place from behind the scenes. Allowing Duncan to consider his marriage to

Janet as a love match was the best way to ensure he would fulfill his duties and, in so doing, ensure peaceful relations between the two clans. I couldn't risk failure."

"You had me fooled. For some reason, I thought you cared." Teressa knew her comment was cruel and inappropriate, but she couldn't help herself. She was hurting, and she needed to strike back.

"I care more than ye can know. If the resentments between Hugh MacDonald and Duncan had been allowed to fester, it could have created a senseless fight. Both our clans would have suffered. I could not allow that to happen. I give birth to three healthy, strong sons, heirs to the chief of the MacNicol clan. 'Tis incumbent upon Duncan to protect his clan and forge strong alliances. I am a loving mother, and I want to see Duncan happy, but I am also the matriarch of my clan. I need to ensure peace for my family and the people of Scorrybreac. Men make war, women make peace. I had to make peace in the only way I know. If it required a matchmaker from the future, then so be it."

"What about Rory? He'll think I abandoned him."

"It cannot be helped."

Her answer provoked Teressa's fury. "You may not know this, but he wants to go home with me. What do you think about that?" Even as she spoke the words, she knew how foolish they sounded. He had no way of knowing what going home with her entailed.

"Does he know where ye come from? Where home is for ye? Or that ye come from the future?" Lady Lydia asked, the first hint of fear gracing her face.

"No, I never told him," Teressa admitted, looking down. She had kept her vow to Moezell and Lady Lydia, afraid that if she broke it she would never go home. That fear was enough to prevent her from discussing her origins with anyone, even Rory. But she had other reasons for remaining silent. Giving voice to her fears would have made them too real. It wasn't a burden she was willing to dump on Rory. Perhaps it was foolish to want to protect him, but it had seemed like the right thing to do.

"'Tis for the best," Lady Lydia said, visibly relieved. "He couldn't travel to yer time, even if he wanted. Besides knowing nothing of your world, without the enchantment, he couldn't even understand yer language."

Teressa had forgotten about the enchantment that allowed them to understand each other. Lady Lydia was right, Rory would truly be out of place in the twenty-first century. Hard as it was for her to admit, Lady Lydia was justified in wanting to protect her clan, even if it meant using Teressa as a pawn. She couldn't resent the matriarch's desire to create peace for her people, nor would she hold ill feelings against the woman. It would only serve to poison her heart. Her anger began to drain away, replaced by a sad acceptance.

"Did you know your son believes in magic? He said everything would be all right. But he doesn't know it was magic that brought us together, and magic that will keep us apart." Teressa shook her head, unable to say more. Rory had asked her to believe, but like it or not, there was nothing that could change the way things were. She had to return home, and Rory had to stay.

"Yer belongings will be brought to ye. Tomorrow morning, ye must dress in the clothes ye wore when ye arrived. Take only what belongings to ye. Moezell will escort ye back to the beach where ye were found." Lady Lydia rose to leave. She stopped when she reached the door and turned to say one last thing. "This may seem unfair to ye now, but I believe ye will leave here with far more than when ye arrived." She closed the door behind her, leaving Teressa alone with her thoughts.

In spite of Lady Lydia's instructions, Teressa planned to take Rory's brooch back with her. He had given it to her, asking her to keep it with her always as a pledge of his love. It was one promise she planned to keep. Along with her love for Rory, she would take his gift home with her.

CHAPTER 20

The passing of the storm left behind a glorious sunrise. When Moezell appeared in her room the next morning, Teressa was dressed and ready to return home. She left a note for Duncan, telling him to watch over Rory and give him her love. There were no farewells to anyone in the keep. No one could know she was leaving or where she was going.

In silence, Moezell and Teressa walked from the keep, across the courtyard, and out through the large stone gates of the fortress walls. They passed unnoticed, as if they were invisible; no one looked their way. In silence, Moezell led her down to the beach below the castle, and together they slowly walked back along the sand toward the place where Teressa had once before been picked up by raging winds to travel through time.

Looking down, Teressa noticed Moezell left no prints in the sand. "You really are a faerie, aren't you?"

"Some call us faeries, some call us angels. We are spirits who guide and protect our humans," Moezell explained.

"I can't believe this is happening, not to me. Faeries and time travel weren't what I had in mind when I came to Skye," Teressa said, hitching the straps of her backpack higher on her shoulders. Tucked deep within was Rory's brooch, his gift to her.

"Believing in something is a very powerful thing. You may be surprised to learn what believing can do," Moezell answered in her usual mysterious way.

Teressa gave her a blank stare. "Rory asked me to believe in the magic of love, and I do, but it doesn't seem to be keeping us together." She dug her hands deeper into the pockets of her long green overcoat.

"Perhaps it will in ways you cannot yet understand," Moezell offered. "This is merely a moment in time, a wrinkle in your destiny."

"Yeah, welcome to my destiny—a shitty life of heartache and misery." Teressa's shoulders dropped as she slowed her pace. She felt no need to hurry.

"Do you really believe I would bring you so far and leave you with so little?"

Teressa barely registered the faerie's comment as she stopped in her tracks. "What's that noise?" she asked, listening. Off in the distance was the sound of a horse galloping across the land.

Before she could see him, she knew it was Rory, racing to be with her. She glanced at Moezell, wondering if Rory knew she was about to be swept from his life. Moezell's face was a perfect picture of pure innocence as she gave a nearly undetectable shrug of her delicate shoulders. Teressa wasn't fooled for a second. She knew in a heartbeat Moezell had alerted Rory of her impending departure.

A moment later, Rory appeared on the bluff astride Blazer, looking windblown and more magnificent than ever. The sight of him took her breath away. The instant he reached the bluff, his eyes homed in on Teressa standing on the beach below. Rory turned Blazer onto the path leading to the sand, the same path they had taken together only days earlier.

When he reached the beach, Teressa took off running toward him as fast as her long legs could carry her.

"No, wait. You must wait for him to come to you," Moezell cautioned.

The faerie's words were lost to Teressa; she was too determined to reach Rory. All she could see was the man she loved, and she raced to be with him.

The moment her foot touched down at the precise point of her arrival, she was engulfed by a hot, fierce wind. It sprang up around her without warning, as though she had run headlong into a dense cushion of swirling air that held her trapped in its grip. It happened so fast she couldn't see it coming, or halt her running. In the blink of an eye, she was swept up in the windstorm.

"R-o-r-y" she screamed his name. The sound was drawn out for an eon as she was thrown forward, hurtling through time. Once again, she was swept up in the blackness of the storm. The swirling tempest gripped her body, shaking her like a child's rattle, and scattered her thoughts. As she felt the air being sucked from her lungs, she thought, *this is going to hurt*. Then all went black as she fell to the hard-packed sand with a thud.

~~~

Rory leaped from his horse as right before his eyes Teressa was swept up in a sudden raging windstorm.

"Teressa," he shouted, running to her. But when he reached for her, she was no longer there. Suspended in a moment of disbelief, he dropped to his knees, reaching out to touch the last meager sign of her presence, her footprint in the sand. It was only a fleeting impression, soon to be washed away with the tide, but it was proof she had been there. Sorrow and rage tore through his body.

Suddenly, he felt a presence beside him, and was bewildered by the wave of calm that reached out to soothe his raging soul. He looked up to see an ethereal being standing before him on the beach. Surly, she must be a faerie, for no ordinary woman could be so pale and beautiful, or give off such an aura of loving peace. She had long silver-white hair and sparkling ice-blue eyes. Her gown, a liquid silver blue, flowed around her body like water, and she was surrounded by a dazzling white light.

His day, nay, his life was becoming stranger and stranger by the moment. He had awakened that morning with a terrible sense of foreboding and had raced to return to Scorrybreac only to watch as Teressa disappeared right before his eyes. Now a being he believed to be a faerie had appeared before him, and for the first time in his life, Rory feared he was losing his mind. He wasn't sure whether he should speak to the apparition and acknowledge her presence, or close his eyes and hope she wasn't real. Choosing the latter, he closed his eyes for a long moment, breathed deeply, and struggled to gather his wits. When he looked again, she was still there.

"Who are ye? What are ye? What happened to Teressa?" He spoke softly, overwhelmed by her presence.

"I am Moezell. I'm a faerie, and I am here to offer you hope." Her words came to him tenderly, like a whisper in the breeze.

"Are ye real?" he asked, his mind still questioning what his eyes beheld.

Moezell smiled. "Yes, I'm very real, however, I'm not of your world. I come from the unseen world that lies behind the veil. I am here for you."

Rory watched in awe as the faerie knelt before him in one fluid motion. Resting lightly on the sand, she gazed lovingly into his eyes. He felt a blanket of warmth surround him.

"Teressa had to return home, to her own time," Moezell began to explain.

"Her own time?"

"She comes from the far distant future."

"I don't believe ye. What have ye done with her?" He stood and stepped away from the faerie.

Moezell also stood. "I've sent her home. It is where she belongs."

"No. She belongs with me." Rory was tempted to grab the woman and shake some sense out of her, but was smart enough to know it wasn't nice to mess with faeries. Controlling his anger, he clenched his fists at his sides.

"Where she goes, you cannot follow."

"I don't believe ye. I swear I will find her. I'll cross time and space if I have to, but I swear to ye, I will find her."

The faerie smiled. "A sure sign your destiny awaits you. Do you believe all things are possible?"

Without hesitation, he answered, "I do."

"Continue to believe, and you shall be with her again someday."

"Will she return?" He reached for the thread of hope the faerie offered.

"Actually, it is you who may return to her, if your soul desires."

Rory gave her a blank stare. *What on earth does that mean*? The faerie's words were too mysterious for him to fully understand, but there was one thing he did know: there was nothing he wanted more than to be with Teressa. "Tell me what I must do, where I must go."

"It is important you live life well, for you take it all with you, and you bring it all back. Live well, dear Roderick. This is of the utmost importance. Believe in magic, and it will serve you well." The faerie reached out to touch his cheek. Her fingers were as soft as a feather sliding across his skin. She stepped away, and then she was gone, vanished as easily as she had first appeared.

He stood staring into empty space. *What shall I do now? I've built my dreams around a life with Teressa, and now she's gone. How can I possibly live well?*

It was too much to consider.

Retracing his steps, he mounted Blazer, and turned his horse to return to his men and the caravan awaiting his command. He had duties to fulfill and a family who needed him.

On his journey back to the caravan, he relived the past several days over and over, searching for clues to the mystery of Teressa. She had told him she came from a faraway place, far removed from the Isle of Skye. She called it busy and strange. He realized she had been trying to warn him, but he hadn't listened. He had only heard or seen what appealed to him. She had tried to avoid him, tried to avoid their mutual attraction, because she knew what he couldn't accept. She knew she would be returning to her own time and he wouldn't be allowed to follow.

Moezell had said they could be together again someday if he so desired. Nay, he recalled more clearly, she said, ". . . if your soul desires." Those had been her words, and he knew, deep in his soul, he would do whatever it took to find her. Up until then he had lived the easy life, always taking the path of least resistance. That was all going to change. He knew he could no longer rest until he found a way to be with her once more. It was a mystery, far beyond his understanding, but somehow he knew, he had to believe, someday they would be together again. But in this moment, there was only loss and sorrow, and duties to fulfill.

CHAPTER 21

Teressa awoke to find herself on the beach in exactly the same place she had been when her adventure began. Looking about, she saw her footprints in the sand coming from the Village Inn, but there were no footprints coming from the direction of Scorrybreac keep. The once glorious castle was now only ruins sitting high upon the cliffs. She had returned to the moment when she had left. No one would ever suspect, much less believe she had traveled through time.

Perhaps she hadn't. Still reeling from all she'd been through, she began to question if any of it had been real. Had she really traveled through time, or was it all a vivid hallucination brought on by her fall? In her fractured mind, she knew one thing for sure: her feelings were real. The love she felt for Rory was real, and so was the pain of her broken heart as it shattered into a hundred aching pieces. For several minutes, she sat on the sand and wept.

When the tears had finally drained from her eyes, she stood and looked toward the ruins of Scorrybreac. *Tomorrow*, she thought. *Perhaps tomorrow I will visit the ruins, but not today. I've not the strength.* Turning her back on the fortress, she retraced her steps back to the Village Inn to seek out the comfort it could provide.

Back in her room, she shed her clothes, dropping everything on the floor, and took a long hot bath. As she relaxed in the soothing water, she began to recount the days and nights she had spent in the past, and she knew what she had to do. She left the cooling tub

273

and pulled out her journal, the one she had left sitting on the bedside table, and began to write. She wrote, and wrote, and wrote, pouring her heart and soul onto the blank pages, filling the book with her memories in hope of purging her pain.

When she had finished, she crawled back into the warm, soft bed she had left earlier that morning. If it were earlier that morning, or several days ago, she couldn't be sure. Feeling as though she had the worst case of jet lag ever imagined, she needed time alone to rest, and to heal. Some things needed to be experienced alone. Among them was the misery of a lost soulmate.

Teressa had met the man of her dreams, and that was where he would forever live, safe in her dreams and in her heart. She would never regret loving Rory; from him, she had gained a far greater understanding of true love. He had taught her the rewards of releasing her fears, and in return, she had experienced true passion. Perhaps someday she would make peace with her memories, knowing Rory was better off living his life with his clan in his time.

He's where he belongs, she reasoned, *which is seven hundred years in the past*. Painful as it was to accept, somehow, someway, she knew she had to carry on. *This is the way it has to be*, she told herself with pragmatic determination. Now was not the time to question what the future would bring; now was a time to be alone, and heal. Burying her head beneath the covers, she gave in to the deep, dark void of dreamless sleep, where she could escape from the pain and loss she had so strongly feared. Seeking only to escape, she turned off her mind, and slept.

The following morning, after sleeping off her emotional hangover, Teressa finally dragged herself out of bed, determined to face the new day alone. Wallowing in self-pity accomplished nothing. Hearing a soft thump against the door of her room, she opened it to find the international edition of an American newspaper. The banner carried the date, June 22, reconfirming she had slept through the year's longest day of sunlight, and darkest day of her life.

After dressing in blue jeans, a light yellow sweater, and her treasured hiking boots, she pulled on her long green overcoat and slung her backpack over her shoulder. As she reached for the door, she spied the green-and-violet plaid wool scarf she had purchased from the Village Inn gift shop lying atop her rumpled bed. With quaking hands, she wrapped it around her neck and left the room, determined to reach the ruins of Scorrybreac Castle. This time, she decided to forgo the scenic route along the beach, opting instead to call for a cab to take her to the fortress ruins.

~*~

It was the day after Sawyer's annual summer solstice party held at the High Tower pub, and Robert MacNicol was feeling the effects of one too many beers from the MacLeods' private brewery. He attacked his headache with some aspirin and a large glass of tomato juice before heading out for the beckoning aroma of fresh brewed coffee at the Village Inn.

"You're looking pretty fine this morning, considering your condition when you left Sawyer's last night," Zoey greeted him as he entered the shop. "You've cleaned up real good."

"It's my day off. I always look good when I'm not working." Robert grinned in spite of his still-fading hangover.

"Yeah, don't I know it? Want your usual?" she asked, reaching for a fresh pot of coffee.

"Aye." He nodded, taking a seat on one of the counter stools. "Hey, do you know what happened to the lass who was in here yesterday? I didn't see her at Sawyer's."

Zoey's eyes widened. "Why? You interested?"

"It's just that, I'd swear I've seen her before." He wondered if he looked as lame as he felt.

"Yeah, right. Nice try. Lilly says she's never been to Skye before, and you've never left the isle."

"Lilly was at Sawyer's. I thought maybe she'd bring her along." Robert shrugged, trying to look nonchalant.

"She came back to the inn no more than an hour after she left. Looked like something the cat dragged in, poor thing. She went right to her room, and no one's seen her since. Ask Lilly," Zoey said, motioning over Robert's shoulder.

"Ye talking about Ms. Ellers?" Lilly asked. She had just walked over from the gift store.

Zoey nodded.

"I just saw her leaving the inn. She caught a cab," Lilly said.

"Is she leaving?" Robert asked, his voice rising.

"She didn't check out, if that's what you mean. She's booked to stay one more night."

One more day, one more night, then she would be gone. Robert had the strongest feeling he needed to find her before that happened. "Do you know where she's going?"

The girls exchanged glances and giggled. He didn't care, nor did he have time to be subtle.

"Don't know. It looked like she was headed for the Scorrybreac ruins." Lilly shrugged.

"Great. I'll catch you later." Robert rushed out to his jeep, running through the lobby of the inn and across the gravel-covered drive. He jerked the door open, jumped in, and started the engine, barely taking the time to buckle his seat belt. Quickly shifting through the gears, he pulled out of the parking lot and then sped down the main road, his tires spitting pellets of stone.

There were only a few cars on the road, and it was easy to spot the taxi. He had almost caught up with them when the cabbie pulled into the parking lot for Scorrybreac Castle. Robert parked his jeep and rushed to catch up with Teressa. He reached her just before she entered the castle ruins.

"Teressa, you've come back."

She stopped and turned to look at him. "What do you mean?"

"Didn't you come here yesterday?"

"No, not really. I didn't make it." She seemed confused, as if lost.

"Well, you're here now. Do you mind if I join you? I'll show you around. I know this place as though I've lived here before."

"Yes . . . I'm sure you do," she said.

~~~

Teressa stared at the man standing before her in amazement, the Scottish ship's captain she'd met at the inn only yesterday. How could it be true? It wasn't possible; and yet, there he was. Why hadn't she seen it before? Robert was the spitting image of a modern-day Rory.

A wave of bewilderment washed over her. Her stomach clenched and twisted as competing emotions rolled through her body. She felt delighted, lightheaded, dazed, and confused all at once. It took every mental resource she could muster to keep from babbling incoherently about time travel and thirteenth-century warriors. Instead, she focused on putting one foot in front of the other as she allowed Robert to lead her through the ancient stone entrance.

Unable to take her eyes off Robert, Teressa felt a gusty breeze, and energy swirled in the air the moment they walked under the portcullis and through the castle gates. It felt as though they were surrounded by an invisible, yet all-powerful force—like magic.

True to his word, he started showing her around the fortress. Everything looked so familiar and yet so different. She could see remnants of the original fortress and keep, but much had changed over the centuries.

"This was the training field. It used to be bigger. Over there were the barracks. They're gone now. They were built of wood. And the stables, they burned down once a long time ago, but they were rebuilt," Robert said as he began describing the castle.

"How do you know all that?" Teressa asked.

"It's just something I know." Robert shrugged, but he was watching her, perhaps checking her reaction. He was probably disappointed. She was in too much of a daze to react, trying to figure it all out.

They continued walking, and Robert continued with his tour. "Here's the original keep. It's been added onto over the years, but I can still see the way it looked."

Teressa gave him a questioning look.

"The way it must have looked. The way I pictured it as a kid," he said.

She looked back at the keep, remembering. "There used to be a garden on the south side, but it's gone now."

"Yeah. How did you know?"

She shrugged. "It's just something I know," she said, repeating his words. How could she say it was because she had been there before, when the garden was still new? How could she tell him she believed she had traveled through time and he was a seven-hundred-year-old warrior she had fallen in love with? How could she explain she had met him in the past and not sound crazy?

"Would you like to go into the keep?" Robert asked. "The old part is closed off, but we can see the newer section."

"No, that doesn't interest me." She sighed. It was sad to see the once-magnificent keep brought to ruin.

"I understand," he said, and she believed he did.

As they wandered about the grounds, she remembered it all, the way it had been. Teressa refused to believe it had only been a vivid hallucination. She was certain she had been here before, in the past, over seven hundred years ago. But who would believe her? Then she recalled Moezell's words. "Believing in something is a powerful thing. You'll be surprised to learn what believing can do." Kind of like how Robert would no doubt turn and run if he believed she were crazy.

Circling the courtyard, they reached the place where Rory had led her up the outer stone staircase to reach the top of the curtain wall. There, upon the fortress walkway, was where she had experienced their first kiss. That first moment of wonder-filled passion when she knew there was something very special about Rory, something beyond his good looks and charming ways. It was the moment she had begun to fall in love with him.

"The best view is from up there, on the battlement," Robert said, pointing.

She looked to where he was pointing. It was the same place Rory had taken her to show her the sunset. "Yes, the view would be marvelous from there." A bud of excitement began growing inside her.

"Here, let me show you." He reached for her hand as though they were intimate old friends.

Rather than shy away, she held on. Together, they climbed the outer stairs to the top of the battlement. These were the same stone steps her boots had trod so many centuries ago—only yesterday.

When they reached the curtain wall, Robert stepped to the edge and breathed deep. "'Tis grand, is it not? This meeting of land and sea." His brogue had grown thick. "The struggle of man against ocean is one of the things that make us strong, and also respectful. A man canna live his life near the water's edge without respect for her power. She can grant her blessings, or she can wage war of infinite rage. 'Tis a blessing to know such beauty and strength." Robert turned to her, looking windblown and magnificent.

"Rory." Her voice was barely audible. "You really are Rory."

"Umm, no, my name's Robert. Don't you remember? We met before, in the coffee shop at the Village Inn."

"Yes, I remember." She smiled sadly, staring into his deep green eyes, remembering the way they sparkled when he smiled.

"I know this sounds like a line, but I think I've met you before. I mean, like a long time ago. I can't remember when, but you feel so familiar." His smile had turned serious. This was important to him.

Her mind flashed to the day she met Robert and then to that first evening with Rory, when she had been overcome with a sense of *déjà vu*. "I do remember." She grew excited. "Yes, now I remember."

"You do? You remember me?" He seemed more than pleased, he was thrilled.

Suddenly she thought of Rory's gift to her. It didn't make any sense, but she had to try. "Let me show you something." Renewed hope poured through her. Fishing through her backpack, she prayed it was still there, that she had been able to carry it back through time. Greatly relieved, she pulled out the finely carved wooden box.

She opened the box and showed him the ancient silver brooch, holding it in her hand. "Do you recognize this?"

He eyed the object. "Where did you get it?"

"It was a gift. Please, take a closer look. Does it look familiar?"

~~~

He reached out to take the silver brooch and examine it as she requested. The moment his hand touched the ancient metal, a shot of heat raced up his arm and into his chest, spreading quickly through his body. Visions of a distant past flashed through his brain. Hard and fast, they hit him with vivid force. These weren't just visions, they were memories. Memories of another life in another time flooded his senses. He could smell the air, filled with the scent of animals and men working. He could taste the food, hardy but bland. He remembered the feel of a sword in his hand and the sound of men training for battle. These weren't just random images, they were memories—his memories from a life lived long ago.

As he looked at the castle and the surrounding countryside, he saw everything in a whole new light. This had been his home, the place where he slept and ate and lived his life. In the flicker of a moment, he remembered he had been here, on this battlement, with this woman, once before. In the space of an eternal moment, he was filled with the memories of their time together, and all the love they shared.

Now, as he looked at Teressa standing before him, he knew why she felt so familiar. He had known her before. She was his love, his life, his soulmate.

Robert reached out, searching for balance, overcome with emotions held in his soul from a life in the distant past. It was almost too much for his rational mind to believe, but he did believe. He remembered he had chosen to believe. He stared deeply into the eyes of the woman standing before him, and he remembered. "Teressa, it's you. You've come back to me."

"Rory, it's you that's come back to me." Tears of joy streamed down her face. "But how can it be . . . how can it be you?"

"I chose to return," he said. "To be born in this life, in this time, to be with you." He reached out to wipe the tears from her cheeks. "It's the magic," he whispered, his modern mind amazed by the magical experience of love transcending time.

"The magic?" she questioned, her eyes locked with his.

"Aye. Remember, I asked you to believe in the magic of this place?" He watched as her emotions—confusion, joy, and wonderment—played across her beautifully expressive face.

"Yes, and I said I would. I said I believed in you."

"Believing is a powerful thing. Didn't Moezell tell you?" He stared at her intently.

"You know Moezell?"

"She's the one who put my memories in the brooch. She said I would return to you if my soul desired. It was the touchstone I needed to remember my previous life. And now I do. I remember it all."

"All of it?" she asked.

"Aye, all of it," he said with a mischievous grin. "I never intended for you to go home alone . . . without me. When we returned to the keep, I was going to pursue you in a proper fashion. This time, I hope to set things right."

Actually, he remembered that he had intended to marry her, but he didn't want to scare her away; they had only just met. In this life, as Robert, he had not yet had the pleasure of even dating the lass. He was very much aware that getting to know Teressa, this Teressa, not merely a memory from a life lived long ago, was what appealed to him now. He felt as if he were about to embark on the grandest adventure of his life, the discovery of his soulmate.

Previously, as Rory, he had fallen in love with a mysterious stranger. Now he hoped they would be free to develop a deeper, more meaningful relationship, one firmly rooted in the present.

"Wooing." Teressa laughed. "As I recall, you called it wooing."

"Aye, wooing. Now that we've both made it safely back to Scorrybreac, Teressa Ellers, I plan on wooing you, if that's all right with you." Robert anxiously awaited her answer. He had no idea how long it had been for her since their time together, and he prayed she still held the same feelings for him.

"Oh, my goodness, Rory. Of course, you can woo me. I would hope for nothing less. Or should I call you Robert?"

"You can call me anything you want." He pulled her into his arms, wanting to feel her closeness once again.

His heart soared. The divine magic Rory so deeply believed in had found a way to bring them together. Looking down at the beauty of her upturned face, he kissed her. It was the same soul-stirring kiss they had first shared on this very castle wall over seven hundred years ago. He kissed her slowly and thoroughly, a tender, romantic, and deeply passionate kiss that once again touched her to her core.

~*~

Three weeks later, Robert MacNicol walked through the rooms of his house, switching off lights as he made a final inspection of his home. His bags were packed and sitting by the front door in preparation for his early morning departure. He would not be back for at least a month, possibly much longer, depending on the outcome of his upcoming travels.

After finishing with his inspection and feeling satisfied that all was in order, Robert entered his bedroom and stripped off his clothes. Secure and peaceful in anticipation of the morning's journey, he lay awake in his bed for a moment longer, recalling a memory from a life lived long ago. In another life, he had made a vow to himself that he would marry Teressa Ellers and accompany her back home to her family.

In this life, there had been a change of plans.

He had chosen not to marry her, at least not yet. Not until *after* he accompanied her to her home to meet her family.

After their reunion at Scorrybreac Castle, Teressa had arranged to delay her return to San Francisco. In the past few weeks, she had met his family, and they all loved her. He had shown her the Isle of Skye, which she loved, and they had made love; oh, how they had made love. In their loving, he felt the full strength of their passion, a passion created by the intimate joining of two souls bound in a spiritual connection that transcended time.

As he turned to gaze at the woman lying next to him, he marveled at the blessings life had provided them both. She had traveled across oceans and time to meet him, and he had been granted a new life to be reunited with her. Tomorrow morning he would accompany her back to her homeland, a journey he had anticipated once before in another life. In that life, he had always believed in the magic of love as Moezell had advised. He had lived and died believing, never giving up. Deep in his soul, he had believed. And now he would create a new life with the woman of his dreams, his soulmate, the one for whom he had returned in time.

Love, 'tis the strongest magic of them all.
—Rory MacNicol

Dear Reader,

I hope you've enjoyed traveling through time and love with Teressa and Rory (a.k.a. Robert) as much as I have. The question I'm asked most often is *what happened to Rory after Teressa left*? It's sad to think he lived his life without her.

Rest assured this question doesn't go unanswered. I also wanted to know what happened to Rory, so I wrote the sequel, *A Time to Belong*, in which Teressa's brother, Daniel, is swept back in time to meet Rory and discover his fate. And much like his sister, he learns that love knows no time.

Keep reading for a preview of the next book in the MacNicol Clan series, *A Time to Belong*.

A Time To Belong

While on vacation on the Isle of Skye, **Daniel Ellers** is swept back to thirteenth century Scotland for one hell of a kick-ass, time-travel adventure. He quickly realizes the depth of his dilemma when he learns his fate is controlled by the whim of a particularly meddlesome fairy. The uncertainty surrounding his future creates a significant kink in his desire to pursue Kayla, the beautiful young woman who found him stranded in the past. Adding to his problems are Kayla's three big brothers who stand ready, willing, and able to kick butt to protect their innocent sister.

Kayla MacNicol is tired of her family's smothering ways. The last straw is her mother's attempt to arrange her betrothal to a man she doesn't love. She's ready to break free from her family's overly protective rule; all she needs is a little encouragement and some well-deserved support. Her initial reaction to Daniel is one of resentment and rejection. She sees him as an outlander, not fit to spend one night in Scorrybreac keep. But when repeated exposure to his charming seduction sparks her untapped passion she begins to question her harsh assessment.

As Kayla begins to wonder if Daniel could possibly be the man of her dreams, Daniel is forced to take control of his destiny and fight for the woman he loves.

A modern urban cowboy, swept back to 13th century Scotland, is forced take control of his destiny and fight for the woman he loves.

Chapter 1

Daniel had heard all he wanted to hear, it was time to leave. Besides, he'd heard it all before in the rumor mill, this grandiose announcement only made it official. He just wished the damn meeting would end so he could get the hell out of there.

This made it final, a done deal. The votes were in; the docs were signed. They were dropping the mounted patrol from Golden Gate Park, another casualty of the city's budget cuts. The last team of horses would be pulled from the streets at the end of the month, and he'd be in a patrol car full-time. The way management spun it, he should be grateful he still had a job, even if it wasn't the job he wanted.

As soon as he and his colleagues were dismissed from the briefing room, he headed for the door to the parking garage. He didn't feel like hanging around at a local bar to commiserate with his fellow patrol officers. Right now, his only thought was to put some distance between him and police headquarters before he said or did something he might regret later. Maybe it was time to leave San Francisco behind for a while and rethink his life.

Sunlight from the exceptionally clear spring day was quickly giving way to streetlights and city glow as Daniel maneuvered his fire-engine-red Ford Mustang onto the Bay Bridge and headed out toward the Oakland hills. On the other side was Over Yonder, the place he called home, a large four-bedroom, semi-rural ranch house sitting on twelve acres tucked into the rolling hills of Diablo Valley. It was the house he'd grown up in along with his two elder brothers and younger sister. The years had slipped by, his siblings had moved away, his parents had passed on, and Daniel had become a thirty-one-year-old, single man living alone in a family home that no longer fit.

Rather than going straight home to the empty ranch, he decided to call his sister, Teressa, to see if she were up for a little company; he needed a dose of family right about now. After stopping to get gas, he hit his sister's number on the speed dial of his cell phone. Thankfully, it was still holding a charge.

"Hey, sis, what's up?" Daniel greeted Teressa when she answered.

"Hi, Daniel. Rory and I were just going to pick up Chinese and watch a movie. What are you up to?" Teressa was the only one who called her husband Rory instead of Robert. Daniel never asked why, and they didn't say.

"I just left work and was thinking I might stop by, if you don't mind. I'm near the Bay Bridge."

"You're close. Come on over and join us. No use spending Friday night alone."

"You sure? I don't want to rain on your parade," he hedged, hoping she would call his bluff. This was one night he didn't want to go home to an empty house, but he didn't exactly like the idea of being a third wheel either.

"Don't worry. Rory and I get plenty of alone time. Even newlyweds like to relax with family sometimes. Come on over."

He paused only for a moment. After all, it was what he wanted, to be with family. "Okay, you talked me into it. Is there anything I can bring?"

"You can pick up something to drink, unless you're happy with tea or water. Is Chinese okay with you?"

"Yeah, I'm good as long as you include some hot and sour soup. I'll pick up a six-pack, okay?"

"Rory will be glad to hear you're bringing the good beer. See you soon." Teressa clicked off her phone.

Looking forward to a hot meal and familiar company, Daniel smiled as he pulled onto the freeway and headed north toward Berkeley.

~*~

The remains of dinner covered the kitchen table, and the plan to watch a movie was forgotten. Once Daniel started talking about his problems at work, he couldn't stop until his frustrations were well vented. Teressa, being a certified relationship coach at San Francisco University, was eager to listen and lend her advice.

"When I signed up for the police academy, the only thing I wanted to do was mounted patrol. Maybe I had some romantic notion of being an urban cowboy, dispensing justice from the back of a horse, but the idea of being stuck in a patrol car doesn't exactly appeal to me."

"I know you, Daniel. I can't see you sitting in a car all day," Teressa agreed.

"Then there's the paperwork. With all these budget cuts, we have more paperwork than ever. The internal auditors are constantly breathing down our necks, making sure we dot our *i*'s and cross our *t*'s. It's eff'ing ridiculous, and I'm getting tired of it all."

"Why don't you take a break? Give yourself time to figure out what you want to do next," Teressa advised.

"That might be a good idea. I've got a ton of vacation stored up. I didn't want to take any time off until I knew what was going to happen to my unit. I figured as long as I could go to work and sit on a horse, I would."

"You know, Rory and I are going back to Scotland in June. Why don't you come with us? We're leaving right after they shut down your unit. It'll be a perfect time for you to get away."

"Scotland? That's a bit of a trip. I was thinking someplace close, like Yosemite."

"Oh, come on. You've been to Yosemite a dozen times. You need something bigger. This could be a life-changing decision. Besides, you've never even been out of the country. It's time for you to see the world."

"You and Robert are going to be gone for at least two weeks. I can't be gone from the ranch that long."

"Sure you can. I've got a plan."

Sure she did. His sister always had a plan.

"Rory's cousins, Jack and Jenny, are looking for a place to stay. They're moving here from Oregon. There's plenty of room at the ranch, and they can watch the place while you're gone. It wouldn't have to be forever, just until they find a place of their own."

Daniel looked over at his brother-in-law to confirm.

"Works for me," Robert said with a shrug. "You'd be doing us both a favor. I'd like to help them out, but our place is too small."

"You know I'd like to help, but I need to think about it." He hadn't considered taking on housemates, but it sounded like a good idea, especially if they were anything like Robert. In the short time he'd known Teressa's husband, they had become like brothers.

"Come on, what's not to like? Jenny and Jack need a place to stay, and you can use the extra help. It's a win-win situation," Teressa continued her campaign.

"I'm surprised you're already planning to go back to Skye," Daniel said. A year ago his sister had taken a trip to Scotland and had returned home with Robert as her new fiancé. At one o'clock in the afternoon on New Year's Day, Robert MacNicol and Teressa Ellers had become husband and wife. His sister had claimed there wasn't a better way to start the New Year.

"Rory still has a home and a business over there. He needs to check on his fishing boats. What if I told you there's a great horse ranch on the island not far from Rory's cottage?"

Daniel appreciated his sister's efforts to sell him on the idea of a Scottish vacation, but he wouldn't put deception beyond her as a means to get her way. He figured she was using his love of horses as leverage to get him to say yes, and he had to admit it was working. Or maybe he was just looking for a good excuse. Daniel looked to his brother-in-law for confirmation. "Would she lie to me just to get me to go?"

"Aye, she would, but no, she's not," Robert confirmed with a grin as he relaxed in his chair, his Scottish brogue as strong as ever. Apparently, he enjoyed watching his wife banter with her sibling.

Not missing a beat, Teressa continued on, "It won't cost you much, only the price of the plane ticket. You'll be able to stay at Rory's house."

"Our house," Robert interrupted.

She smiled brightly at her husband. "Our house," she corrected. "We'll show you around, or you can go off on your own as much as you want. What do you think?"

"That you're not going to let up until I say yes."

"See, I knew you were a smart man. I'll book you a ticket on our flight right now before you can change your mind. If I leave it up to you, it'll never get done." She jumped up and grabbed her laptop.

She was right. The Internet wasn't his thing, along with most other technologies of the twenty-first century. He had to admit, the ease and convenience of a cell phone was worth the venture into modern technology, but he couldn't see the appeal of video games, social-media, or the Internet. To him, they were just a time suck. And forget about e-mail, texting, IM, or all the other ways technology was trying to speed up people's lives. He was perfectly happy living life in the slow lane. Well, maybe not perfectly happy, but certainly better off. Heck, his car had windows that rolled down with a crank handle, not the push of an electric button.

Unfortunately, his lack of techno savvy was also a significant deterrent to any real success in the world of women and dating. More often than not, the women he met wanted the immediate gratification of being able to contact him electronically, but tech wasn't his style. Most of the time, he didn't even have his cell phone on unless he wanted to make a call, and it could be days before he listened to his voice messages. His cell phone battery had a tendency to die faster than he could remember to plug it in to be recharged. Though his family and closest friends had learned to accept his anti-technology quirk, the rest of the world seemed much less forgiving.

"Okay, all set." Teressa looked up from her laptop, satisfied with her effort. "We leave on the eighteenth of June. We'll be in Skye in time for the summer solstice."

"What's so special about the summer solstice?" Daniel asked.

"It's the anniversary of the day we met," she said, exchanging a sly glance with Robert. They were grinning like two kids sharing a secret, and Daniel knew well enough when to leave secrets alone.

~*~

A few weeks later, Daniel found himself on a plane sitting next to his sister and brother-in-law, questioning his choices as they headed toward the Atlantic coast on their way to Glasgow. It wasn't as though he didn't like to see new places. He had traveled up and down the West Coast with his dad visiting horse shows, and had been to Canada and Mexico, but this was the first time he'd be leaving the North American continent. Honestly, he found the prospect of a long transatlantic flight to be a bit unnerving. Knowing they would be spending the next few hours flying over miles of ocean before they reached land again was not in his comfort zone, he wondered how he had let his conniving little sister talk him into this adventure.

Dinner had been served, and the cabin lights were dimmed to encourage the passengers to sleep or rest quietly. Daniel figured it made the long hours of the flight a lot easier on the passengers and flight attendants, but it hardly helped to quell his anxiety. He was uncomfortably aware of his seatmates as he tried not to fidget, but hell, a body wasn't meant to sit still in one place for so long, and it was his bad luck to have ended up with the window seat.

Robert and Teressa were already sleeping, curled up under their airline-issued blankets. Apparently, they were okay with the long overnight trip, but Daniel was finding it much harder to settle in. The journey was long, and the large plane was nearly full for the nonstop flight. He was grateful Teressa and Robert had used their frequent-flyer miles to upgrade to roomier seats, but the space was still cramped for his six-foot-three-inch frame. And instead of being a soothing white noise, the hum of the engines created an annoying vibrating buzz in his ears.

He wanted to get up and stretch his legs, but he didn't want to disturb Teressa and Robert, so he sat and stared out the small oval window into the reflective blackness of the nighttime sky, regretting his misfortune of getting stuck with the inside seat. When they were boarding, he had agreed to let Robert take the aisle seat, always being the nice guy, and as he knew, nice guys always finished last. He glanced again at Teressa, his younger sister, happily married to the man of her dreams, and knew he was definitely finishing last. He was the last unmarried sibling and the last one still at home.

Daniel sat in the dim light cast by the overhead reading lamp, wondering what he could do to get some sleep, or at least relax enough to forget he was thirty thousand feet above endless ocean. Maybe not exactly endless ocean, but close enough.

He searched the seat back pocket in front of him and flipped through the airline's in-flight magazine. It was beyond boring and of no use for his insomnia. Looking over at the seat back pocket in front of Teressa, he noticed her travel journal poking halfway out. She'd been writing in it earlier. When he had asked her about the journal, she had explained she had started the travel journal during her first trip to the Isle of Skye. With each succeeding trip, she planned to add to the journal, creating a memoir of her travels to Scotland.

Daniel didn't usually go snooping into his sister's personal stuff, but since she hadn't seemed particularly secretive when she had told him about her journal, he figured she wouldn't mind. Hopefully, it would tell him about the places they planned to visit, and perhaps provide a little insight into his sister's opinions on their intended destination. With hardly a second thought, he reached for his sister's journal, flipped it open, and started reading.

A few hours later, and several disbelieving glances at the two people sleeping next to him, he wasn't sure if he had read a credible account of an incredible journey, or if his sister was a fantastic storyteller. She'd written about faeries, wizards, and time travel, and the kicker of it all was her belief that Robert, a.k.a. Rory, was the reincarnation of a thirteenth-century warrior and her soulmate. What the hell was she thinking?

Although it had kept him enthralled for the past few hours, allowing him to completely forget his insomnia and discomfort with the overseas flight, it was darn near impossible to believe her fantastic tale. He wondered if Robert was aware of his wife's vivid imagination.

Daniel didn't know what to think of his sister's story except that it was simply unbelievable. Interesting, but unbelievable. He'd give her credit on one count: she and Robert seemed made for each other. Whether it was because they were soulmates across time or just lucky in love, he couldn't say, but they certainly seemed to belong together.

With a final shake of his head, Daniel tucked Teressa's journal back into the seat pocket in front of her and switched off his overhead light. It was time to close his eyes and rest even if he couldn't sleep. As he reached to close the shade of the little oval window next to him, he paused a moment and gazed out into the early morning sky.

The glow of the rising sun rushing to meet the eastward-flying plane was just beginning to leak above the horizon. A lone star still shone bright in his limited view of the vast endless sky. It occurred to him that this single star, shining alone in the vastness of space, had spent eons shining its light out into the cosmos, always existing exactly where it was meant to be. In a moment of honest confession, he softly whispered, "I wish I knew where I belong."

He dropped the shade, closed his eyes, and laid his head back to relax. A soft breeze danced across his forehead. Just before he unexpectedly fell into a deep and peaceful sleep, he heard a woman's voice softly whisper, "A wish expressed, a favor bestowed."

Tricia Linden, author of timeless romance with a touch of magic.

An International Banker by trade, and a romance writer by desire.

In this lifetime, Tricia has lived in five states, on two islands, and on a farm. She's currently living with her soulmate in Northern California. Her love of travel has taken her across the U.S. and to several countries around the world. Besides her love of reading and writing romance, she has a great fondness for Pink Flamingos. Over the years, she has gathered a rather large collection of the fun pink birds.

Website: https://tricia-linden.com/

Facebook: https://www.facebook.com/TriciaLindenAuthor/

Tweeter: @TriciaLinden69

Email: Tricia.Linden@ymail.com

www.ingramcontent.com/pod-product-compliance
Lightning Source LLC
Chambersburg PA
CBHW020343180626
46812CB00001B/326